Half-Hearts

By

KEALOHILANI

Artwork by Steven Squire and Kealohilani

Markados Whovern Books

An Imprint of Jellinek & Murray Publishing

Honolulu Hawai'i

Markados Whovern Books
An Imprint of Jellinek & Murray Publishing
Honolulu, Hawai'i
Visit The Half-Hearts Trilogy Website at www.HalfHearts.com

First Paperback Edition: May 2014

Summary: Lani Johnson is a twenty-one-year-old college senior from California. Yanked out of her world and its relative safety, she is swept into Vranah's final war for Alamea. As she discovers that everyone has extraordinary gifts, and as she works to develop her own, she has no idea what is at stake or what could be the key to saving both Alamea and Earth— or whether it is all simply an elaborate dream world that her broken heart constructed in order to distract her from her own reality.

Library of Congress Control Number: 2013958203

ISBN: 0990977099
ISBN-13: 978-0990977094

Alamea World Map

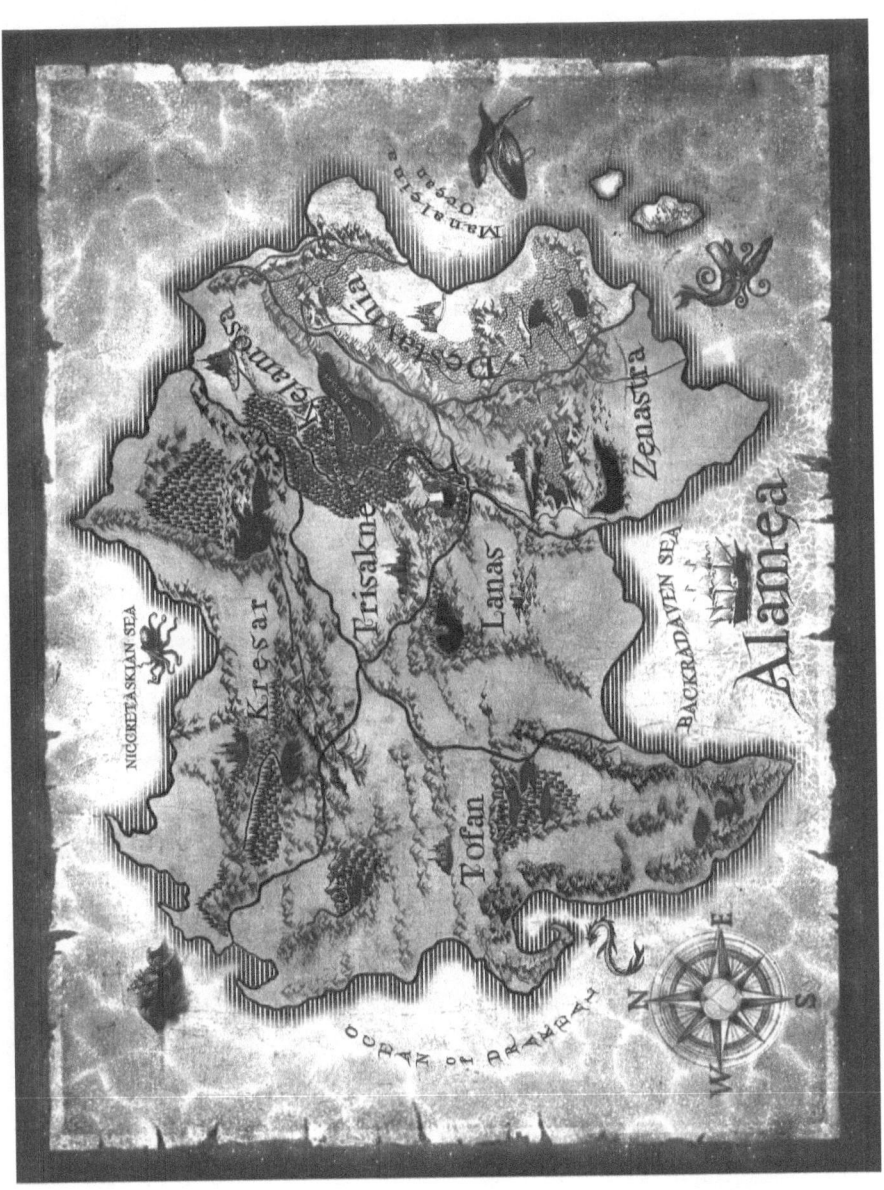

DEDICATION

This book is dedicated to Jared Kealoha Ulapatasi Manase Fotu, the first real-life Half-Heart to inspire this series as well as the character of Jharate— and the first man to ever tell me that my work should be published.

WHAT PEOPLE ARE SAYING ABOUT HALF-HEARTS

...a wondrous world of magic and imagination. Half-Hearts is right up there with The Hobbit, Chronicles of Narnia, Wizard of Oz, and Harry Potter! ~ Lisa Linsky, voting member of the Grammys

The female Tolkien. ~ Mark Kubr, stunt man and actor from the Iron Man movies, about authoress, Kealohilani

In this literary masterpiece of 582 pages and [Heaven] only knows how many words - four of them jumped out at me: "magically prepared" & "gastronomic nirvana." These two pairs sum up the whole succinctly. I literally was transported to another world [and] I am now having severe Alamea withdrawals. Never in my life have I eagerly anticipated Books two and three of any series which such ferocity. ~ Veronica Grey, popular TV guest and critically acclaimed author.

For those of us who grew up with Harry Potter, our next adventure awaits! ~ Shaun Laqeretabua, composer

Too many movies nowadays try to show the ugly and the dirty "reality" of our world and our daily lives. What I love about Half-Hearts is that it inspires you to dream again. ~ Khotan, actor and international soap star sensation

I could not put it down. As I read it, it took me on an adventure... I went through a broad range of emotions; exhilaration, anxiety, grief (I wept), anger, fear, the whole gamut and even felt/ experienced the joy & serenity of true love and its confusions and mysteries when challenged! ~ Sakura Thompson Williams, Film Development Consultant

It certainly is a magical world that could have the success of Harry Potter or Twilight... I knew that it would be good but I didn't know that it would be THIS good. The characters are fantastic! ~ Tiffany Hofstetter, actress

Book One of the Half Hearts Trilogy is an epic tale of love and loss, good and evil, and the fight for justice, woven together beautifully by Kealohilani... Half-Hearts will leave you touched, tearful, hopeful, and shocked, making you desperately wish the next novel was in your hands so you could find out what happens next to the characters you have become so involved with throughout book one. ~ Amanda Meredith, author and blogger

Been hooked from the very beginning. The whole time I'm reading I can't help but wonder, what if this is true? It's flat out an amazing read! ~ Joseph Faifili, filmmaker

So awesome! I loved every bit of it. I felt all the emotions... It was written so well. And [the] vision and imagination is incredible! I believe this book will help so many [people because] it's very inspiring! ~ Jay Mataele, professional dancer

CONTENTS

CONTENTS

CONTENTS

PRELUDE TO AN ONSLAUGHT

The entire world is crashing down around the human race and yet no one is aware of it. Although, perhaps it would be more correct to say that no one on Earth is aware. Even now, as you read these pages, there are things happening around you that you accept as normal, as a sign of the times, or simply as the reality of the world in which we now live. You, like everyone else on Earth, have no idea that you have lost every ounce of control and that, at any second, your very life could be prematurely ended by an unseen force and that your death would raise no more suspicion than any other death on Earth ever does. It would simply appear to be the way that life is— the way this world is.

But there have always been two worlds that have existed parallel to one another: Earth, which prizes increasing the power of man through science and technology, and Alamea, which embraces their world of magic, wonder, and mystery. Many fantasy authors on Earth have written about Alamea's world, but oddly enough they don't actually believe in its existence. They too fall victim to the common Earth ideology that knowledge must precede belief, when in reality belief has always been the beginning of any true knowledge.

The two worlds were once highly connected to each other. The portals were constantly open and the inhabitants traveled and traded through them freely. However, there came a time when the ancient Egyptians and the ancient Alameans decided that their respective worlds threatened each other's way of life. Working together, they put into place magical barriers, which closed the portals, so that both societies could live and thrive independently. The Egyptians erased all history and knowledge of Alamea so that future generations would not try to link the two worlds together again. With all written records of Alamea gone, the concept of magic on Earth eventually became myth.

With the separation in place, Earth gained astonishing knowledge in science, while Alamea perfected the art of magic and their grasp of the intangible. Each planet, with approximately the same size, landmass, and population, prospered and their populations greatly increased. But the shields were abruptly destroyed in the early nineteen-sixties, and since that time the two planets have been magically linked together once more. A domino effect has now gained momentum and is making that link stronger than ever. Now, for every person who dies in the world of Alamea, the equivalent of that person dies on Earth— sending rapidly increasing numbers of good people on Earth to their graves long before their time. And it is only going to accelerate.

The Evil One executed this re-linking as a strategy to conquer and rule both worlds. Repercussions were first felt on Earth when conflict broke out in Vietnam. Many tried in vain to explain why the United States went to war there. The unseen truth was that simultaneously the first major battles were being fought in Alamea for control over its seven kingdoms. This is what had truly triggered hundreds of thousands of soldiers on Earth to go off to a war that few understood or supported.

On Alamea, the war against this powerful being has been waged for decades. Millions of Alameans have been brutally murdered as they resisted subjugation and fought to defend their countries, their homes, and their families. As this evil gained momentum in its conquest of Alamea, genocide erupted nearly worldwide on Earth. Cambodia, Rwanda, and The Sudan were plagued by unspeakable acts of violence and torture while millions of people were ruthlessly slaughtered. Horrors that had seemingly ended with the close of World War II now became so commonplace around the globe that they rarely made the evening news.

Inexplicable deaths continued to haunt Earth in the years that followed. Many extraordinary leaders in Alamea who could have turned the tide of the war were mercilessly assassinated. Earth felt the first shockwaves of these events with the arbitrary losses of its own great leaders, including John F. Kennedy, Martin Luther King Jr., Robert F. Kennedy, Anwar Sadat, and Benazir Bhutto, prompting endless conspiracy theories for crimes that were never solved. These were all people who, were they given more time on Earth, could have affected sweeping change that would have bolstered worldwide hope, ethics, and ideals. The opposite was also true. Alameans were sometimes able to achieve a great victory and kill a key leader from the forces of evil. Consequently, people like Saddam Hussein were then found and eventually killed.

However, the balance is still tipped against good. Most of the casualties in Alamea are normal everyday people. So people on Earth continue to wonder why the drunk driver walks away without so much as a scratch, but the mother of five and her newborn baby in the back seat of the car he crashed into aren't so lucky. They question why beloved figures such as Princess Diana, John Lennon, Elvis Presley, Michael Jackson, and Whitney Houston have all mysteriously died long before their time. The answer is simply that their destinies were interlocked with the deaths of their equivalents in Alamea.

Recently the tide of evil has been rising so quickly in Alamea that wars, genocide, assassinations, and mysterious deaths on Earth have not been enough to counterbalance it. In order to keep up with the staggering death toll on their planet, the magical link with our world has been escalating the rate of natural disasters that assault Earth. A European heat wave, Hurricane Katrina, tsunamis in Indonesia and Western Samoa, volcanic eruptions in Columbia and Mexico, earthquakes in Turkey, Haiti, Chile, and Japan, gigantic floods in Pakistan and Thailand, Typhoon Haiyan in the Philippines, and almost innumerable similar events are no coincidence.

There are seven kingdoms in Alamea on one supercontinent, also called Alamea, much like Pangaea on ancient Earth. Of those seven, five have already fallen. Destavnia is one of the last two lands left at liberty to fight against the encroaching darkness, but soon it will fight alone. Its last ally, the Kingdom of Trisakne, has been surrounded for years. Exhausted from waging war on all sides, the military lines of Trisakne will soon be breached and the kingdom will be overrun. The moment the Evil One completes his conquest of Alamea, Earth's destiny will no longer be its own.

Although he has many names, "Vranah" is the name the people of Alamea have given to the evil force. Literally translated it means "The Great Evil." Vranah existed long before either world came to be. He has no physical body and therefore can take countless forms. However, Vranah typically takes the form of a human man. The illusion is so convincing that the only way to shatter it is to touch him— if one dared. He can travel between the two worlds of Earth and Alamea at will, but has had very different agendas in each.

On Earth he has convinced mankind that he does not exist, that he is a fable, a spectral devil conjured to keep children in line with threats of eternal damnation, a comical figure who cavorts on the left shoulders of people stuck in dilemmas— even a sports mascot. He has been content to wreak havoc in the shadows. Until Alamea's fate is sealed, Earth will remain blissfully unaware of his true nature and even less aware of the impending onslaught.

On Alamea, however, he has an unmistakable presence. There is no doubt as to his reality. There are no intellectual debates as to his existence. And he is certainly no joke. He is the quintessential threat looming over their daily lives. With the imminent fall of Trisakne, Vranah has now set his sights on Destavnia. It is the last kingdom he needs in order to secure his conquest of both worlds.

Destavnia has always had the greatest concentration of good. When the surrounding kingdoms fell, survivors who could make it to Destavnia joined its forces and hoped that one day they could return to reclaim their own lands. Thus the majority of the moral, courageous and upstanding people of Alamea now reside there. It is impossible to imagine what the sudden and complete annihilation of the over two billion very good people in Destavnia would do to Earth as their equivalents perished with them. The human race would likely live on, but what a wretched and loathsome race would be left!

But there is a ray of hope. One of the primal legends of Alamea promises that, "If two of the Half-Hearts are completed, The Great Evil may be defeated forever."

There are only twenty-four Half-Hearts born in Alamea in each and every generation—twelve women of remarkable virtue, character, and beauty, and twelve men with great strength, valor, and honor. Each has a phenomenally strong and relentless drive to seek his or her other half. These men and women have full hearts, but they have a magical Half-Heart inside of their normal one— one that no medical scanner can ever detect. If one could see it, one would discover a very distinct shape, much like an interlocking puzzle piece. In fact, that special shape would only match another Half-Heart of the opposite sex. The only way for any Half-Heart to be completed is for two of them to find, fall in love with, and marry each other in a special place magically prepared for such a union. Although love is already the strongest force in the Universe, a Half-Heart completion creates a bond that is unalterably sealed and inexplicably powerful.

However, with billions of people on the planet of Alamea, it is an extraordinary challenge for one Half-Heart to even meet another. Moreover, the only one who knows the identities of the Half-Hearts is Vranah himself. Since Vranah was there from the beginning of time, he has known every Half-Heart the Universe selected from before they were even born. For millennia he has watched and laughed as generation after generation has failed to produce two Half-Hearts who even came close to falling in love, much less marrying. If two ever did manage to find each other, he cast powerful spells of apathy, contempt, jealousy, or other destructive emotions to drive a wedge between them, easily destroying any chance of a union.

As the war continues, Destavnia will fight, along with the surviving rebel factions that trickle in from the Kingdoms of Zenastra, Kelamosa, and soon Trisakne. Tragically, the other Kingdoms of Lanas, Tofan, and Kresar have been taken over for too long. The minds of their people have assimilated the evil that surrounds them, their spirits have been crushed, and their hearts broken. Many now feel that the rescue promised by the legend was never true, or they have forgotten it altogether.

As complete annihilation draws near, it is clear that this generation is humanity's last hope before Destavnia falls and the worlds of Alamea and Earth become the property of the master of all wickedness forever. Given the fact that Vranah knows the true name of every Half-Heart who could oppose him, even most of those who still believe in the Half-Heart prophecy have lost hope. After the re-linking opened the magic portals, hundreds of children on Alamea were whisked through to Earth as an eleventh-hour measure to save their lives from Vranah's massive attacks against the kingdoms. Their names were changed to mask them from Vranah and they have lived their lives in complete ignorance of the turmoil that exists in their former world and of the potential destiny of Alamean children.

Despite the daring, the defiant, and the desperate efforts of millions of Alameans, the fate of billions and billions of people in both worlds now rests in the hands of the twenty-four Half-Hearts.

Half-Hearts

TWO DOWN

A man and a woman run through the dense and darkening forest, dodging branches and leaping over rocks and roots as they race for safety. The cold wind whips at their faces, stinging their eyes as they continue to barrel forward, struggling to stay together. The man hears a stifled cry behind him and stops dead in his tracks. He whirls to see the woman as she falls to her knees, a few yards behind him. Rushing to her side, he catches her before her face can hit the ground.

"Sarana!"

"I will survive this but you must act quickly, Khanye. There is no time!"

Khanye now sees the deadly arrow buried deep in her right shoulder and cringes at the thought of what he must do. He gently lays her on her left side and instantly grasps the shaft of the arrow.

"Brace yourself, my love."

Sarana takes a deep breath and waits. She hears him break the fletching off the arrow and closes her eyes, flinching a little. She grimaces as Khanye shoves the shaft through the back of her right shoulder and out the other side. Birds flee from the tops of the dark trees like a fluttering black explosion as her tortured scream echoes through the shadowy woods. Khanye pulls the rest of the arrow out and tosses it into the forest, then quickly tears off a piece of his shirt and bandages her shoulder tightly.

"I will carry you."

"No, it is faster if I run. I can do it."

"But you are injured!"

"Khanye! There is no time."

Khanye sighs, carefully helps her up, and they return to their frenzied dash. They do not get far before Sarana blanches and falters in her steps.

"Are you all right, my love?"

"Yes— I'm—"

Sarana collapses and Khanye struggles to catch her and slow her descent to the forest floor as he drops to his knees and pulls her into his bronze muscular arms.

"Leave me! You can still save yourself. I am growing weak far too rapidly. I will not survive much longer no matter what you do. Go!"

"I will not leave you!"

"You must!"

"No! We live or die together!"

Khanye picks up Sarana to run with her in his arms. He scans the deep forest purposefully, knowing that they are mere seconds from the underground hideaway where they will be safe for the night. But before he can take even one step forward, the two of them are surrounded by twenty soldiers, clad in shiny armor that reflects the remnants of the setting sun through the thick black trees, weapons drawn and holding ready. The Captain of the Guard steps forward until his face is nearly touching

Khanye. He meets Khanye's seething glare with a cold and determined stare.

"Turn around, and take her back to the castle."

Khanye stays where he is with his jaw clenched and his eyes locked on the captain's soulless orbs.

"Move now, or you both die here!"

The Captain of the Guard takes a step back and folds his arms. Khanye's eyes move back to Sarana's and he sighs heavily as he slowly turns around. Walking back in the direction he had just been running from, he keeps his head held high and his eyes fixed on some far-off point in the distance— holding Sarana close to his heart.

"Faster!" the Captain of the Guard demands, shoving Khanye so hard in the back that he nearly falls.

Khanye regains his balance and takes a deep breath as his muscles tense and his eyes close for a split second. He straightens back up and marches forward faster, at the speed demanded of him, remaining silent as the soldiers take turns prodding him roughly in the back to make him keep pace.

As Khanye sees the castle appear from behind the thick trees, he shudders. He can barely recognize his childhood home. For *centuries* this very castle stood as a symbol of freedom, justice, and peace... but now the sparkling white stone walls have turned grey and ashen, as if covered in soot. The grand spires, which once caught the glory of the sun and gleamed under the light of the moon, look like evil creatures conspiring beneath the artificially darkened sky. Khanye glares at the vast magically-summoned clouds as they encircle the two topmost turrets of his home, striking the ground constantly with hundreds of lightning bolts. He feels his stomach turn over as he thinks of the increased power that this access to energy will give to any dark spell Vranah may use. He lowers his head and fixes his eyes on the ground in front of him. *It was better that my home should have been destroyed!*

Vranah's fleshless, boneless, fingers are clenched into tight fists as he storms about on the green marble floor of the large rectangular throne room, beneath a cathedral ceiling more than fifty feet above. The shape Vranah has chosen to take on now is his most common form. He appears to be a man in his mid-forties— a tall menacing figure with sharp features and rugged good looks. His eyes are cold and dark like deep empty wells. His short sable-colored hair is greying ever so slightly at the temples, as are his neatly trimmed beard and mustache. His pseudo-skin is white, with a slight tan, and is so convincing that no one looking at him would ever know he is only a spirit.

He walks tall as he glides forcefully about the room, with his simulated clothes flawlessly mimicking the rippling motion of tangible fabric as he moves. His shirt looks as if it is made of a shimmering grey silk, embroidered with silver thread. It has no buttons and the neckline opens to the center of his sternum. The long, wide sleeves fall to his wrists. Black pants disappear into black leather boots. A sleeveless tunic-style black satin robe rests on his shoulders and flows nearly to the floor in the front, and trails two feet behind him in the back. Intertwining serpents, which line the outer edges of the robe in emerald embroidery, appear to glint whenever light "touches" them. A silver serpent ring with blood red eyes adorns his right index finger.

Vranah treads over to a wide, hundred-foot-long deep-plush royal purple carpet that leads from the large bronze double doors to five short stairs going up to a raised platform, bearing two golden thrones with Tyrian purple upholstery. Long matching velvet curtains hang behind the two thrones. The lighting is dim, coming only from the torches, which are spaced at even intervals on the walls from the front of the room all the way to the back. The once brilliantly illuminated giant chandeliers are left dark, hanging above like giant spiders. Once ascended to the platform, Vranah paces back and forth in front of the thrones, glaring at everything his eyes fall upon. His servants shrink back from before him and scamper like frightened mice into the shadows, in order to escape his notice, whenever they are caught in his gaze— all except one.

A solitary servant stands in the center of the great throne room on the long carpet, with his shoulders back, eyes forward, feet spread a small distance apart, and his hands held in place together behind his back. He is a tall, thin man with ivory skin and unnaturally-black, long, smooth, straight hair that falls to his waist. He is in his early thirties and has intense brown eyes, so dark that they often seem entirely black. His nose is straight and his lips are full. He is clean-shaven and remarkably attractive, but, like his master, the handsome physical features cannot hide what lies within. He is dressed head to toe in black, including a black cape, black leather gloves, and tall black leather boots, so that only his face is uncovered— but even his face has thin lines of black outlining his eyes, making an even starker contrast between them and the white of his skin.

Vranah suddenly spins around, fury in his eyes, and walks down the steps, directly toward the man on the long carpet, with a controlled but unmistakably menacing tone.

"How could you let this happen? You have failed me for the last time, Drakne!"

Drakne does not answer the question, but remains still—staring forward as if Vranah is not there, even as Vranah comes face to face with him. Without taking his eyes off of Drakne, Vranah raises his voice and his words hiss forth as if he is exhaling fire.

"LEAVE US!"

Silently relieved to be excused from their master's presence, the other servants scurry out into the darkness. Vranah intensifies the murderous glare in his dark eyes.

Drakne ceases his emotionless stare and lowers his gaze and his head slightly— but his lip twitches with annoyance as he bows apologetically to his master. He keeps his head bowed and proceeds to speak in the perfect pretense of outward deference and humility.

"My lord, we have captured them. They are now yours to deal with as you see fit. No damage or loss has been sustained by Your Excellency, nor will there ever be under my command."

"Lucky for you, you did capture them. But you let them get too close first! Go and bring the prisoners before me now and do not fail me again. Your powers may be second only to mine, but remember, they are still *second* to mine. I do not have to put up with your failures! Do not forget what happened to my last apprentice."

"Your Grace is surely generous, my lord," Drakne says, gritting his teeth.

"Dismissed."

"As you command."

Drakne turns to exit the room purposefully with his black cape billowing behind him over the purple carpet. He snaps his fingers and the two great doors of the throne room throw themselves open for him to walk through and abruptly shut once he has passed the threshold. He passes several soldiers who are guarding the entrance.

"Two of you, come with me, now," Drakne orders without glancing at them.

Two of the henchmen spring into action and jog to catch up as Drakne continues to stride down the halls of the castle, looking intently forward. Isolating himself from everyone around him, he plunges farther and farther down into the depths of the castle until he reaches the dungeons. He does not look at the prisoners as he passes them in their crowded cells, nearly bursting at the seams. Nor does he hear the cries of the unfortunate men, women, and even small children who are strapped to torture devices, which never had a place in this castle before Vranah came, as they are beaten in clear view of their fellow dissenters, who await with terror— their turn.

Only one torch burns in the entryway to the rows of cells that Drakne now reaches. The light is so dim that it almost makes one trapped here pray for darkness, for this feeble light is more painful than none at all. It is quieter here and the air is colder. The silence that has fallen has an eerie palpable quality broken only by the echoing footsteps of Drakne and his two henchmen. Drakne stalks through the gloom until he reaches the last cell.

"Guards, retrieve the Prince of Trisakne and his bride-to-be and follow me!"

His order is obeyed as quickly as it is spoken.

Back in his purloined throne room, Vranah turns and smiles as he sees Drakne return with his henchmen behind him, dragging the two prisoners up the long violet carpet. The soldiers throw them into a freshly drawn circle on the cold marble floor. The two guards bow to Drakne and Vranah and then turn, exiting the room as quickly as possible. Drakne, without so much as a glance at the unfortunate captives, mutters some enchanted words. An energy field rises around the man and woman, trapping them inside a bubble with visible blue current running throughout it, enveloping them like some monstrous electric jellyfish. The menacing current crackles like bees swarming through a bonfire.

The two prisoners are both in their early twenties. Khanye is tall, strong, smooth-faced, and strikingly handsome. His dark features complement his skin, which is the color of toffee. Kneeling on the ground, he holds his wounded love gently in his strong arms. He looks at her warm brown eyes, her ruby lips, her porcelain skin, and her perfect face as he strokes her long dark hair, trying to commit every last detail to his memory. He smiles at her, but his tortured expression and tear-brimmed eyes show that he knows the truth. Sarana turns ghostly pale and struggles to look up at her fiancé.

Khanye swallows hard as he continues to hold her close. He had felt sure that she would survive— until she had faltered in her steps back in the forest. In that sickening instant, he had realized that the arrow must have been laced with a deadly and slow-acting poison. It has been mere hours since she was struck, and Sarana's condition has become increasingly grave.

Khanye's mind races through the many moments they have shared together. He remembers riding down from his castle home, through the verdant and flower-filled valley, that very first day— not expecting anything but to attend to a minor matter of business for his father in the small town of Kellinsi. He could still envision Sarana's gentle smile and the way the wind swept through her glossy raven hair and wrapped it around her waist as she helped an elderly woman through the cobblestone streets. Time had slowed in the instant where her eyes had locked with his and his heart began to beat so fast that he was barely able to return her smile before she passed him. He knew then and there that she was the only girl for him.

The anxious feeling in his stomach, which he had felt that very first day, had continued throughout the weeks that followed, as he made every excuse to remain in Kellinsi, while struggling to devise a plausible reason to speak with her. His heart did a cartwheel the first time he held her soft hand in his, and fire had burned in his soul during their first kiss under a blossoming cherry tree. The thought of how his heart had never beaten so frantically as when he approached Sarana's father to ask for her hand in marriage, and his jubilance when her father had given his blessing, almost makes him forget where he is.

As he looks into her eyes now, he still sees the unborn children who should have been theirs. This could not all be ending now— not like this. Why was their future being so ruthlessly stolen from their grasp? Khanye shakes his head and shoves the facts far from his mind. She is not lost to him yet.

"You are going to be well again, my love... You must hold on... We *will* find a way to save you..."

Khanye's pleas become more and more inaudible and his sobs interrupt his expression of hope as he chokes on his words. He knows he is wrong, but cannot bring himself to admit it even in his mind. Tears flowing, Sarana does her best to smile at Khanye as she speaks despite the pain.

"I love you, Khanye... I always have... and I always will... I love you."

CHAPTER ONE

"I love you, Sarana."

With one final longing look at each other she closes her eyes and the last breath leaves her body.

"Sarana?"

Khanye looks at her intently through the magnification of the tears in his eyes. She remains motionless— no sign of breath, and the warmth seems to be slowly draining from her body beneath his touch. Khanye forces his eyes shut and an anguished cry of sorrow escapes his very soul. He desperately clutches her lifeless body close to him one last time, kissing her forehead and crying aloud once more. He gently places her on the ground, looking forlornly at the way her hair flows around her and makes her look as if she is only a sleeping angel. His gaze drifts from her face to a spot on the floor.

Khanye's eyes narrow as he stands up inside the electric cage. His expression hardens, his tears dry, and every muscle in his body tenses as he reels to face his captor, who has begun to laugh.

"VRANAH! YOU SON OF A MISBEGOTTEN DEMON! YOU VILE V—"

"Hold your tongue, Khanye! You forget to whom you speak! Besides, there is no need to make this personal. You are merely part of a larger plan that you, in your insignificant mortal state, fail to comprehend."

"I forget nothing, Vranah! I know exactly who you are and your plan will never work! My brother will come for me!"

"You are wrong on both counts. My plan will work, and your brother will not get the chance to rescue you— unless he intends to come for your dead body."

"Killing a hostage would be foolish. You would lose the opportunity for ransom."

"My dear boy, although I must admit that I admire your bravery and insolence, I must also wonder if it truly is bravery or simply extreme folly. But it does not matter. And in case you are wondering, swearing allegiance to me has worked for others in the past, but I am afraid *you* cannot have that option."

"I would never join you under any circumstance, Vranah!"

Khanye spits toward Vranah in repulsion at the very thought, but the spittle hits the electric field and crackles into non-existence. Vranah's eyes light up with amusement and he half-smiles before continuing his speech.

"Oh, I can think of one… but as I informed you, it does not matter." Vranah pauses to scan Khanye's face. "I can see that you are wondering why I have done this to you— singled you out, along with your late fiancée, rather than targeting the would-be-heir to the kingdom. Very well, since you will soon be dead, allow me to enlighten you."

Vranah comes even closer to Khanye until they are face to face through the force field and looks into his eyes with a cruel smile and a bone-chilling voice.

"You, my dear boy, and that girl there, are both Half-Hearts."

Once again, Vranah pauses, watching Khanye carefully and savoring every reaction. Khanye's mouth falls open slightly, his muscles lose their tension, and his lowered eyes say the rest— shock, horror, and depression. Vranah smiles widely and works to suppress a chuckle as he speaks again.

"Although it may be more correct to say that you *were* Half-Hearts, as you will be joining her momentarily."

Khanye's eyes glaze over and his breathing becomes shallow, sometimes pausing altogether. The world spins slowly around him as his mind tries hopelessly to account for this pivotal information. He had not even entirely believed in the legend about the Half-Hearts to begin with— and never would have guessed that he, himself, was one. And even more astonishing, that somehow, so was the woman he had fallen in love with. The heavy weight of the knowledge that their union would have had the power to stop this terrible war crashes upon him. His eyes drift to his lifeless love and he stares on, unable to make a sound. His insides turn to ice and he feels as though death has already seized him. Khanye falls to his knees by Sarana's side and strokes her hair unconsciously.

"My brother will avenge us," he whispers.

Vranah grins and this time makes no attempt to stifle the laugh that comes.

"Although I hope he attempts it, for it would bring him to me so conveniently, I do not believe he will even have the chance to plan a retaliatory strike, let alone carry it out, as I will be sending my men to retrieve him presently."

Khanye's eyes fly open wide as he jumps up in alarm.

"Why? You have me! Leave him alone!"

"Ah, how quaint, the bonds of brotherhood. You quite amuse me. Pity you have to die. You see the problem with that is, although you posed the immediate threat— with your wedding, what, a week away? Your brother still poses a great threat to me. Apparently, your family was *twice* blessed… for he is a Half-Heart as well! It may only be a matter of time before he runs into another— and time is the one thing I intend to see he never gets. He does not know of course. He is quite as in the dark about his situation as you were until a few moments ago. But he will meet the same end— although it may be more painful than yours if you do not cooperate. However, if you tell me where he is, I might give you the luxury of an instant and painless death by the power of my word, and perchance my generosity could also extend to him. Now— where is your brother?"

Khanye folds his arms, clenches his jaw, and remains silent.

"Very well, Khanye— have it your way."

Vranah moves his hand parallel to the cage, and an energy bolt strikes Khanye. He groans, but remains standing and still. Vranah lifts his arm up and gestures sharply, as if hurling invisible objects at the cage, and two more energy bolts strike Khanye, causing his body to flinch and jolt, but still he holds his ground, glaring back at Vranah. Vranah repeats the motion toward the cage again, and again, and again. Each time, energy bolts hit Khanye, and each time they weaken him a little more. Khanye falls to his hands and knees and is no longer able to suppress his groans and screams as each excruciating strike hits its mark. Khanye finally cries out in anger.

"Even if I knew I would never tell you!"

Vranah ceases the torture for a moment and looks carefully at Khanye.

"I think what you mean by that is that you do not know where your brother is and therefore cannot tell me."

Breathing hard, Khanye's arms and legs shake, threatening to collapse at any second. One arm fatigues and Khanye nearly falls to the ground sideways. Khanye forces his head up to glare at Vranah. Sweat pours down his face and his eyes struggle to retain focus.

"Very well! Any last words?"

Khanye looks down and speaks quietly to himself, "Heaven help my brother . . . If you can hear me Jharate, by any power in this world, dear brother stay away!"

CHAPTER ONE

The cage's coursing current slowly diverts its power directly into Khanye in a deadly constant stream. He screams in agony, anger, and fear for his brother one last time before finally falling dead on the ground next to Sarana as the force field disappears.

On the border of the former great Kingdoms of Trisakne and Kelamosa, hidden deep in the Forest of Kar, Jharate's eyes fly open as he wakes up in a cold sweat with a silent scream of terror.

Drakne had been standing against a wall in the shadows while his master worked on Khanye, waiting to be called upon. He quickly stood at attention as his master turned around to speak.

"Spread the news that Khanye is still alive and that we are holding him captive. Make sure it is the talk of every underground rebellion by sunset!"

"I understand, my lord."

Drakne walked forward slowly, each footstep echoing in the silence of the room, until he stood beside Vranah. Drakne lowered his gaze until it fell upon Khanye's dead body for the first time.

"Shall I create a double?"

"Yes! Perfect!"

Drakne could hear the admiration in his master's tone and felt immense gratification as he began to murmur ancient and powerful words of darkness, with his eyes fixed on Khanye.

Drakne felt a second rush of pride swelling within him as he worked because he did not perform spells in the classic sense— for spells often require an instrument, such as a staff, a wand, a potion, or an orb. Long gone were the days when he needed any such assistance for magic. Those forms of magic were nothing compared to the power of certain words, which he now had full command of. He suppressed a smile as he realized he was more Vranah's equal than perhaps his master would like to admit.

As Drakne finished muttering, an identical replica of Khanye materialized and stood in front of the dead lovers. Drakne felt immensely proud of the fact that *his* copy would be able to speak, walk, even remember everything exactly as if it were Khanye, and his physical appearance would fool anyone who beheld him. However, the copy would pose no threat to Vranah, as it was not a Half-Heart, but merely a soulless shell.

The double looked down at the bodies of the two unfortunate lovers who could have saved both worlds, had their destiny not been interrupted, but showed no emotion. Drakne circled around the duplicate, inspecting it from head to toe with a smile on his face and a malevolent gleam in his eye. Drakne turned sharply to his master with a mocking obsequious bow.

"He is complete, my lord."

"Good work, Drakne. You have learned much under my guidance."

"What would you have me do with the bodies, Master?"

"No ordinary disposal will do. After all, these are two of the famed Half-Hearts! Go to the topmost turret of this castle at the east end. There, you will find I have prepared a room. Within that room lie twenty-four empty glass coffins. You will find two with their names engraved in gold. Take them there, restore them, and seal the coffins with a preservation spell so that their bodies will never decay."

Drakne stared at his master without emotion as if awaiting further instruction.

"The reason, Drakne, that I am giving them such an honor, is not for their sake but for mine. When at last all twenty-four coffins are filled, and mark my words they *will* be filled, they shall stand as an everlasting testament of my triumph and power— a trophy room if you will."

"Of course, my lord."

Drakne's eyes lit up at the thought of the trophy room. He turned and faced the ill-fated lovers, and moved his palms upward in a fluid motion, commanding the air to bring them forth. The lifeless bodies floated five feet above the ground as Drakne indicated the direction they should go with a simple wave of his hand. He turned to face his master and bowed before walking back down the long purple carpet and exiting the throne room.

Drakne headed for the turret and looked at the Half-Hearts floating in front of him as he walked. A slight smile of satisfaction came over his face as he realized what he had done. No mortal had ever captured or killed two Half-Hearts like this before. In fact, even Vranah himself had never done so, simply because until now he had been content to distract them from each other and ruin their lives with simple spells. Drakne smiled again, congratulating himself as he thought of how he would be remembered through the ages as the only mortal to ever bring down a Half-Heart.

Drakne frowned as a much less comforting thought crossed his mind. No Half-Hearts in the history of their world had ever gotten that close before! They had been just days away from gaining the power to defeat Vranah. No wonder his master was no longer content to leave any Half-Heart alive. But what had changed? Had they gotten stronger? Was some other force helping them to find each other? No. Not possible. Drakne and Vranah were the most powerful forces in all of Alamea. He shook his head to help divert his thoughts back to his triumph and the triumph of his master. They had begun to hunt the Half-Hearts now and they would be no match against the powers of evil. *Besides,* he thought, *the Half-Hearts do not even know who they are.* They would not stand a chance.

With these last thoughts, he reached the top of the long and winding staircase that led to the eastern turret. A giant mahogany door decorated with a glimmering gold tree stood closed in front of him. Surrounding the tree were three distinct celestial symbols, also forged in gold— one of the sun, one of the moon, and one of a solitary star. The gold doorknob was very ornate with a curious design in the center of it made of inlaid mother of pearl. It was a heart with a smaller upside-down heart inside of it. Below the doorknob, the keyhole had a faint impression of an upside down heart around it as well. Drakne examined the mark on the doorknob and recognized it immediately. He could not help but laugh. *How ironic*, he thought to himself as he waved the door open.

He stepped into the room, ushering the corpses before him. One of Drakne's eyebrows rose. He could not help but admire the beauty of the chamber. It shone as if it were made of diamonds and a brilliant glowing white light surrounded everything in it. Even though it was nighttime outside, the room looked as bright as if it were noonday. Some of this light came from a gigantic crystal chandelier that hung from the center of the high domed ceiling, but the whole interior seemed to glow on its own as well. The twelve sides of the room made the space feel almost circular. An elegant white marble column stood at each junction of the walls. Gold branches and leaves spiraled up the columns to Corinthian capitals, where the mysterious heart shaped design stood proudly as a symbol of hope and virtue.

Between every two pillars, were glorious, tall, etched-glass windows, trimmed with sheer-white drapery with golden ties. One of these magnificent arched windows was set into each of the walls, which flooded the room with sunlight during the day. The walls themselves were made of seamless floor-to-ceiling mirrors. They reflected all of the light and elegance in the room, mimicking the great expanse of eternity.

This chamber had been left untouched by the evil that had overtaken the castle. However, it now contained twenty-four coffins— two in front of each window. Drakne guessed from the aura of the room that it must have taken a great effort to get them in. He noticed that each coffin had been made from the same materials as the surroundings and figured they must have been charmed with the same good magic that had been used to create the room itself.

Drakne was correct. A great deal of good magic had been required in order for the room to accept the coffins in the first place. Even more magic had been required to *keep* them in the room. Vranah had forced a good person to construct and charm the coffins with good enchantments. The man he had summoned to do this work was an exceptionally skilled carpenter, named Dustrahn, from one of the outlying villages. His father's side of the family had served the Trisaknen royalty for generations whenever new thrones or other unique items were needed. On his mother's side, they were known for their knowledge in healing and good magic. These coffins were proof that he had inherited both skills. Although Dustrahn hated the idea of working for Vranah, he dearly loved his wife and eight children and did not wish for his outward rebellion to create a fatherless family. So he did his best and worked quickly in order to return safely home. Vranah had smiled at the nearly perfect results of his new secret project and felt that Dustrahn deserved a great reward. Therefore, Dustrahn's death had been instantaneous.

Drakne took a closer look at the coffins. He observed the same raised pattern of gold branches and leaves wrapped around each coffin, with the heart-in-heart seal on the center of the top of each lid. Again, he smiled at the irony. The crystal clear glass of the lids also had the same delicate branches and leaves pattern etched around the edges. White marble pedestals supported the coffins and were draped in the same sheer white material as the curtains.

The longer Drakne spent here, the more uncomfortable he became. This space had such intensely good magic coursing throughout it that it could not be removed by any evil, and it almost felt as if it were somehow burning the skin on his face. A sudden desire to flee overtook him, but at the same time he found the room captivating. He finally noticed that the two coffins he had been searching for were the closest to the entrance on the left side. He had passed them on his way in. There was a gold plaque in front of each coffin, and the full names of Khanye and Sarana were magically engraving themselves before his very eyes.

Drakne motioned to the lids of the two coffins until they hovered three feet above the cases. With his other hand, he motioned the two bodies inside. The lids lowered gently until they sank into place. Drakne whispered the magic words for preservation and the bodies transformed as if they and their clothes had been cleaned and repaired. No marks defaced their bodies any longer. They were perfectly and permanently restored.

Drakne took a final look at the faces of the fallen Half-Hearts, unsure of what he expected to see. His eyes widened. Their faces had changed! It was a deeper change, beyond that of the obvious repairs— one that greatly disturbed him. Their final looks of anguish had been replaced by peaceful and serene expressions, as if they had died during a wonderful dream.

Troubling thoughts raced through his mind. What if they had found each other in the next life? That could explain why their faces had changed— but how? Would that affect his master's plans here? The idea was more than a little unnerving. He finally caught hold of a thought that comforted him. No, they must marry while still in their physical bodies or the foretold magic could have no effect on the physical realm. They could be happy together now, but that would not affect this world. Yes, that was it. But one thing bothered him still. They were happy.

Drakne frowned as he looked at them. He could not stand for people to be happy in any way. He made a promise to himself at that moment that he would not only endeavor to kill all of the Half-Hearts before they could marry, but that he would also ensure that when they died, they would not die in love with each other as these two had. No. They would die alone and in misery, with no comfort to take with them into the next life. Contention, despair, neglect, suspicion, forgetfulness, infidelity— any and every possible form of self-centeredness would mar their lives before they ever left this world, alone and bitter.

He exited the room quickly and slammed the great door behind him with an echoing thud and one final thought— *Two down, twenty-two to go.*

LOOSE ENDS

"End of chapter one," Lani said aloud as she typed the last words of her book's first chapter on her computer.

Lani smiled. She felt a warm sensation spreading through her heart. It seemed as if it had been so long since she had felt like smiling that she had nearly forgotten this delightful fuzzy feeling. In truth, it hadn't been as long as it seemed, and as it came back it felt right and familiar, like reuniting with a life-long friend. If this was how it felt to finish one chapter, she was sure finishing the novel would complete her emotional healing. She had just been through *another* horrible breakup. She thought she would have been used to this by now. Lani had always had terrible luck with guys. But this time things were different— this time she was sure that her bad luck had cost her the love of her life.

A soft glowing light came from a lamp on a nightstand next to a window seat filled with cushions, nestled in a large bay window. On the other side of the window seat was an identical nightstand and lamp. Two matching pearl-white wrought iron twin beds stood, next to the nightstands, one of which Lani was currently sitting on with her MacBook Pro balanced carefully on her lap. Elegantly designed in a purple and white color scheme, Lani's bedroom had Victorian-style furniture neatly and symmetrically arranged around the room— including two cherry wood dressers, two matching bookcases, and two golden-framed mirrors, which hung on the wall opposite the foot of each of the beds. Between the mirrors was a large closet with white louver doors.

On the wall on Lani's side of the room, hung a valedictorian medal from high school, several academic awards from UCSD, and a couple of fencing medals— however they were all very understated in their display. Most prominent were the pictures of her friends and family— and her books. The bookshelves were filled with the works of Jane Austen, Charlotte Bronte, Agatha Christie, and a large volume of the complete works of William Shakespeare. Mary Shelley's *Frankenstein*, Bram Stoker's *Dracula*, at least three translations of Gaston Leroux's *The Phantom of the Opera*, and many other classics also had a home in her overcrowded bookcase. There were very few modern books in her collection: some of them were personal growth books and business books including some of her favorites written by Tony Robbins and Robert Kiyosaki, but most of them were fiction— chief among them being the entire set of the Harry Potter series and The Chronicles of Narnia.

On the bottom shelf of her bookcase, was a large, light-blue, suede-covered box with a matching lid. At *that* box, she rarely looked. She knew what was in it and she didn't like being reminded. Inside it lay the remnants of her shattered heart: three engagement rings, two dried corsages from Junior and Senior Prom, a few sentimental pieces of jewelry, love letters, and a stack of photos of fading, nearly forgotten memories— all from boyfriends long since gone. The box caught her eye for a moment, but she looked away. It wasn't time yet… or was it?

Lani's gaze moved to a picture of her and her latest boyfriend, Josiah Harding, which still stood framed on her nightstand. They were both wearing jeans but she wore a black short-sleeved shirt and he wore a nice white T-shirt. Josiah was giving her a piggyback ride in the picture, which was taken from his waist up. Her arms were around his neck and they were both beaming with so much happiness that it could have been an engagement photo. She sighed as she realized she still hadn't taken it down.

Lani set her computer aside and picked up the frame, staring at it intently. She studied his deep brown eyes, his brown skin, his white smile, and his shoulder-length, somewhat curly, bleached-blonde hair, which made him look like the surfer he was. He reminded her of a six-foot-three Tongan version of the Versace model, Tuki Brando. She had always thought Josiah looked better with black hair, his natural color— but she thought he was handsome no matter what he did because of her deep love for who he was inside. And that smile! Oh, how she missed that!

Actually, she missed *him*. She missed how Josiah would talk to her for hours when he wouldn't talk to anyone else for more than a minute. She missed the sweet and inexplicable innocence that exuded from him, she missed the way his honesty was matched only by his intellect, making it easy to put faith in any advice he gave, and she missed the way he had encouraged her to reach for the stars rather than competing with her, trying to slow her down, or trying to change or control her. It was all so irreplaceable! There had always been such an extraordinary feeling of peace and bliss whenever they were together. He was her shelter from the storm of life.

Lani shook her head to pull herself out of the downward dwelling cycle, but she still couldn't take her eyes off of the picture. She knew it belonged in that tiny box of shattered promises, broken dreams, and lost hopes— but this boyfriend had been different from all the others. He had accepted all of the love she had to give and, in the beginning, he had returned it all. She remembered how, when Josiah had sat down to read her English 315 paper on *The Phantom of the Opera,* he had smiled at her and said, "This is really good, Lani. You should really think about getting it published." His genuine support and the tone of his voice had given her strength to believe that maybe one day that kind of thing would be possible for her.

And that wasn't an isolated incident. He was always telling her how smart she was— always building her up. Josiah hadn't cheated on her, he hadn't emotionally or verbally abused her, and he hadn't even tried to "put her in her place" or to "leave her for her own good." He hadn't done any of the horrible things the other guys had done, so how could she relegate him to that box?

Lani jumped from her musing state as her younger brother Taylor walked into the room. She had been so lost in thought that she hadn't even noticed that he had entered. In her surprise, the picture frame slipped from her hand to the carpeted floor with a quiet thud and the now-empty hand flew to her heart.

"You scared me!" Lani squealed.

"Sorry," Taylor laughed, "I knocked."

Lani sighed in relief as her heartbeat slowly returned to normal. Taylor cringed as he saw the picture of Lani and Josiah where it had fallen, face up, on the floor.

"You're not still hung up on that jerk, are you?"

"Don't call him a jerk, please. We were perfect for each other."

"Like how? Seriously!"

"Well, since you ask, we could do anything together," Lani sighed, picking up the picture and replacing it on the nightstand. Seeing the look on Taylor's face, she continued, "I'll give you an example of what I mean. We had the most magical date one day. It was nothing special or planned— it just happened. We went to the beach and played all day— laughing and tickling each other while racing on the sand. Josiah kept chasing me back into the water where we splashed and laughed even more."

Taylor couldn't help but smile a little as he saw his sister's face light up in the recollection, but he shook his head slightly and his smile was quickly replaced by an incredulous look and then a frown as he remembered what Josiah had ended up doing in the end.

"After the sun went down, we came back here and he greeted Mom and Dad respectfully and sweetly, like he always did, and then he and I sat on the couch to watch football. After the game, Josiah channel surfed until he happened to find a historical program about Julius Caesar. He asked me what I knew about him. I answered honestly that I didn't know that much about Caesar, other than what had been written about him in Shakespeare's tragedy. Do you know how most guys get when I even *mention* Shakespeare?"

"I can imagine," Taylor answered with an impish smile, knowing how he would react if a girl started prattling on about Shakespeare.

Lani smiled at his tone, "My point exactly. But you know what Josiah did?"

"Wouldn't be asking you if I did," Taylor teased.

"He asked me if he could see the play! He actually cared about what I was interested in! He wanted to share it with me. I ran for my copy and the two of us sat side-by-side as I read it aloud to him for over an hour. He told me later that it was the first time that he had ever understood it because I brought it to life for him. He loved it so much that he wanted to see it and so we ordered the DVD of the old 1953 version online."

"*Okaaay.* So he liked Shakespeare. So do a lot of really preppy elitist snobs at your college. But you don't like *them.*"

"Josiah wasn't like that! He was interested in it and saw it in a new light because *I* was passionate about it. That night when he went to go home, he said goodbye to me in the most romantic way, mimicking Shakespeare's language! He brought things to life for me too. He loved football like nothing else. I had never hated it, but I was never really into it before either. But with him, I could watch it for hours on end. I'd go with him all the time to his nephew's games at his old high school where he used to play."

"Yeah, I'd like a girl that would watch football with me too!"

"I know you would," Lani laughed. "But that wasn't the point— I liked *who I was* with him. And he liked who he was with me. Whenever we were together, we were the best versions of ourselves. And we could be happy just doing nothing but studying together for hours. Sometimes he would just sing to me for no reason. Everything was so easy. We could just flow from one thing to another with no difficulty. We were the perfect match..."

Lani's eyes lost their sparkle as they stared at the photograph without really seeing it. Taylor noticed. His eyes also fell on the picture and his hand slowly clenched into a fist. *Hasn't Lani suffered long enough?* Taylor thought, before speaking again, "Well you broke up with him for a reason, Lani. I may not know everything, but I saw enough to know he wasn't treating you right! I should've kicked his sorry—"

"Taylor! Watch your language."

"You're giving him too many excuses, Sis! Stop blaming yourself! You treated him like a flippin' king and saw only the good in him, but he started taking you for granted right after he finally got up the nerve to ask you to be his girlfriend! And, you totally gave him like a billion chances to change before you dumped him."

"That's true… But then I found out I was his first girlfriend! How was I supposed to know that? He's five years older than me for cryin' out loud! I thought he didn't love me as more than a really good friend, but it turns out he was just scared and didn't know how to tell me how he felt. I found out from his brother later that Josiah was going to ask me to marry him! I ruined everything!"

"So what if you did the breaking up?! Come on, Lani! You tried to get back with him like a million times over the last eight months and all he ever kept saying was, 'It's over,' again, and again, even though you guys never cheated on each other or anything big and so it would have been easy to fix things."

"Yes it would have been… very easy, but…"

"But nothing! *Everyone* saw that you two should get back together and he was just stubborn. Lame! He should have gotten over it and come back after you like a man! *AND*, he was stupid enough to go get a new girlfriend when he was obviously still in love with you!"

"But that's just because I made the mistake of telling him neither of us had been able to move on since our break up. The *next day* he held this girl's hand right in front of me. She knew it too. She kept playing it up and moving her hands all around his chest and shoulders just to show that he was hers now and not mine!"

"So he's a jerk, and she's a witch. Sounds like a perfect match to me!"

"*Please* stop calling him that! I've given up, okay? You don't need to talk me into it. I'm not going to go after a taken man even if he was mine first!"

"You never go after any man, Lani, and you shouldn't start now. You deserve to have a guy come after *you*, just like you always have. What you *do* need to do is to get out there so that someone new *can* find you, Sis. You should stop coming straight home the minute class is over, and you should stay out there in the real world where the real men are. Even the library would be better than your room."

"I know… I'm just afraid I'll never find my guy. I mean I've had three failed engagements already and how many ex-boyfriends? And Josiah was the best one I ever dated. It's hard to replace the love of your life, you know. I'm not sure if I'll ever find anyone as good as him again."

"I'm sorry… But that's the stupidest thing I've ever heard!"

"Thanks for that…"

Taylor grabbed her gently by the shoulders and spoke in a very firm but loving voice.

"No, hear me out, 'cuz I'm only gonna say this once. You are a beautiful, smart, funny girl who deserves better than Josiah! And the right guy is out there and he'll find you someday when you least expect it."

"Thanks."

Lani reached behind her to pull a pillow off of her bed and smacked him playfully in the head with it. Taylor smiled widely. It was a little out of character for Taylor to be so complimentary to her. He wasn't rude or anything, but she didn't know until now that he had such a high opinion of her. It felt really good, but a little too serious to be comfortable.

"You're right! I just need to push forward with my life. I'm good at that, at least."

"You do that! And let's start with this."

Taylor picked up the picture of Josiah and backed away from his sister slowly.

"What are you doing, Taylor?"

Lani tried to reach for the picture, but she missed as Taylor pulled it farther away from her and held it high in the air.

"See this? Little blue box time."

"How do you know about that?" Lani's eyes narrowed suspiciously.

"Please! I'm your little brother. It's my job to know these things. Look here... we're taking the picture to its new home... We're getting closer now... Almost there..."

Lani hugged her pillow and bit her lip tensely as she watched Taylor approach the little suede box on her bottom shelf.

"And we're opening the lid now... Here it goes... Bye-bye... And now it's gone! Feel better yet, Sis?"

"I think I'll plead the Fifth."

Lani laughed nervously. She appreciated what her brother was trying to do but...

"Well it's a start. Now you keep that in there. It's for your own good."

Taylor walked back over and sat on the edge of the bed next to Lani.

"Thanks."

"Anytime, Sis, anytime! And my offer still stands to beat him up!"

"Taylor!"

"Well I *can*!"

Taylor and Lani laughed happily. Taylor's phone began to play *I'm Yours* by Jason Mraz. He pulled it out of his pocket but did not answer— looking uncertainly from Lani to his phone and back again. Lani smiled.

"Go talk to Michelle."

"You sure?"

"Yes! One of us should be happy in love," Lani said with a cheerful but insistent tone, as she whacked him with the pillow once more for good measure.

"Thanks!" Taylor said, giving Lani a great big hug as she laughed. "You're the best sister in the world!"

"You're just saying that because Jenna's gone."

"I'm closer to you though."

"Hurry up and answer it before she goes to voicemail, Tay-Tay!"

"Okay, okay! – Hey babe! What's up?"

Taylor left the room to continue his conversation with his girlfriend in private. Lani smiled, jumped out of bed, walked over to the box, and pulled out the picture of Josiah, closing the lid on the past once again. She hugged Josiah's picture close as she flopped back down on her bed. Taylor had given her hope that maybe someday there would be another Josiah in her life… maybe. That boy! Why did Josiah have to be so adorable? Could she really meet another like him? Until that unfathomable day came, her writing would keep her busy.

Work was always the way she distracted herself from heartache— and it was a good thing too. Her past boyfriends always had the most unbelievable timing! Almost all of her break-ups had taken place without even the slightest warning, during midterms or finals weeks at school— forcing her to finish projects and exams, sometimes as she struggled to even see the test paper through a veil of tears. Through sheer will power, and what could only be described as a series of minor miracles, even in those stressful times, she still managed to get good grades.

But writing this novel meant more to Lani than just maintaining a GPA— her writing gave her soul a place where it belonged, where it was understood, and where it could thrive in the perfect escape from reality. In her little writing universe, she could control everything and her creative dreams could be realized. She would often lose herself so completely in her novel that she would actually forget she was even on Earth— an unparalleled therapy for a gut-wrenching break-up. Lani placed the picture back on the nightstand, grabbed her MacBook Pro and settled in with her back against her pillows on her twin bed to read over the chapter she had just finished.

Her family lived on Corte Verano Avenue in Oceanside, California in a typical Southern California home in the suburbs: a three-bedroom, two-and-a-half bath stucco house with all the standard features and of course the customary red-tile roof. Lani was twenty-one years old now, and she had lived in this house for as long as she could remember with her family, the Johnsons. Mr. Johnson was a respected and beloved professor of finance at UCSD. Mrs. Johnson had been an advertising executive but believed in being a stay-at-home mother in order to give her children the best possible environment. Early on in their marriage, Mr. and Mrs. Johnson had been told by numerous doctors that they would never be able to have children, even though Mrs. Johnson had been barely twenty years old when they married, and so they had decided to adopt.

Lani had never cared about finding her biological parents— probably because she was so happy with her family that she figured it didn't really matter. Not that she had never wondered about them, but it had just never become a priority. The Johnsons had gotten her when she was a baby and were the only parents she had ever known. Lani was actually the second child, whom they had adopted, and was only two years younger than her sister Jenna. Four years after Lani's adoption, Taylor had been a great surprise and a miracle to Lani's parents as their first and only biological child.

But looking through the family photos that hung on the walls throughout the house, you would never have known that two of the children had not been born into the family. The three siblings had a natural blend of looks between them, but even more balanced was the wall space and mantle space that was dedicated to each child. There were photos of Taylor's soccer triumphs and surfing competitions next to photos of Lani's fencing meets and graduation, which were next to photos of Jenna holding her viola before and sometimes after various important concerts— and most recently, pictures of the entire family at Jenna's wedding.

Lani looked up from her computer and gazed pensively across the room. Jenna's empty bookshelf, the perfectly-made untouched bed, and the lack of any objects on top of her dresser was a stark reminder that she was gone. *Has it really been over a year since Jenna married Jonathon and moved to New York?* Lani asked herself, as she recalled the day that Jenna's dream guy had come home to meet the family.

It seemed like it was only yesterday. Lani had known the first moment she saw the tall, curly-dark-haired, half-Italian, half-Irish, young professor, who had just been hired to teach at Columbia University in the coming fall, that he was going to be a member of their family. Two weeks later when Jenna came home with Jonathon once again, displaying the rock on her left finger, Lani had giggled as her theory was confirmed and joined the other women in the family in screaming for joy. Taylor rolled his eyes while their father narrowed his, folding his arms and glaring at Jonathon until Jenna ran up to him and kissed the reluctant future father-in-law on the cheek.

A pang of loss tugged at Lani's heart as she continued to stare at the vacant side of the room. Since they were children, it had always been Jenna who knew everything about Lani and had kept all her secrets. Dealing with the changes Jenna's wedding brought to their sisterly bond would have been hard enough if Jenna had remained in the same state. But, due to the added distance, even phone calls were hard because the time difference made it difficult to find a time when they could both talk, despite their absolute commitment to keep their relationship strong. Lani's face changed from sad to determined as she once again set her laptop aside and picked up her cell phone.

"Hi, you've reached Jonathon and Jenna Mason," Jenna's voice sweetly declared. "We're not available right now, but if you leave us your name, number, and a brief message, we'll get back to you as soon as possible. Have a wonderful day!"

The beep of the answering machine informed Lani that it was time for her to say something.

"Oh, hi… Hey Jenna, it's Lani… your sister."

Lani cringed and smacked herself on the forehead. This was already sounding stupid. Of course Jenna knew who she was!

"Anyways," Lani said trying to regain any semblance of composure, "I was just calling to say… I really miss you Jenna… Wait, I probably shouldn't tell you that… um… Things are great here… Taylor's great… How are you?"

Lani glanced at her bedroom clock and her eyes went wide with panic.

"Oh no! I'm so sorry! I didn't realize how late it was in New York! I hope I didn't wake you up! Oh, I'm so sorry! Oh my goodness! I feel like such an idiot now! Sorry again, call me back when you g-"

"*You have reached the maximum recording length for a message,*" the cold mechanical answering machine voice interrupted. "Goodbye."

"Great!" Lani blurted out to the open air.

She threw her head back onto her pillow and closed her eyes, wondering if she shouldn't have called. Not only did she still miss her sister, but now on top of that she sounded like a complete loser on tape! What she wouldn't give for a magical power to go erase that stupid message before Jenna could hear it. Lani wondered what it was that made her brain shut off whenever she heard the diabolical beep of her arch nemesis, the answering machine.

Running frantically through empty winding cobblestone streets, a slender young woman with long golden hair raced toward a charming and well-kept thatched-roofed lodge. A small, simply-carved wooden sign swinging in the breeze over the double doors read *Hapri's Creek Inn*. Many of the shops and peddlers' carts that she rushed past in the pleasant town square had been left so abruptly, that the merchants' wares were still laid out expectantly. Every door and window was shut up tight, and only the creaking of the inn's little sign gave any hint that the town had not been frozen in time.

The woman darted beneath the sign and burst through the doors of the tavern. The large room was dim, despite the late afternoon sunlight, which came through the panes of the distorted hand blown glass windows and filtered in over the scores of empty chairs and tables— illuminating the small particles of dust, which floated through the air and swirled chaotically as the woman entered. As her eyes adjusted, she saw the shadowy figure of a large sturdy man seated in a chair at the end of one of the far tables and hurried over to him, stumbling over one of the chairs that had fallen over in everyone's haste to leave. The man looked up at her slowly with deep concern etched into his chiseled face as he waited for her to speak.

"He is coming! He has discovered our plans!"

"I feared as much when Rayel came in here to warn everyone to run home and hide. I had hoped that perhaps it was just one of his routine visits, but I think even before you came I knew better. I still do not understand how he could have found us out. The only people who knew of our plans were myself, you, and…"

"Kezick," the two gasped in unison.

Zareth pounded his fist on the table.

"He must have told someone!"

"What can we do?"

Tesara's eyes darted wildly about the abandoned room while she waited for Zareth to answer her. He stared off into the distance and remained silent. Suddenly, a crashing sound louder than a roaring cannon thundered through the town and shook the very ground beneath them. Zareth and Tesara braced themselves until the ground settled again. A man's magnified voice followed this boom and reverberated with a sickening magically enhanced echo as he made a very formal announcement.

"People of Kellinsi, there are those in this town who have committed crimes against your rightful lord and master."

"How dare he call *him* the rightful master of this land?!"

Zareth spat angrily, and the voice continued.

"Because of the crimes of those few, it is my duty to inform you that the price will be paid by *all*."

"No! We cannot allow this!"

Zareth nodded and the two of them burst out into the town square and fell to their knees at the feet of a tall man, dressed entirely in black. Tesara was the first to beg.

"No! Please! We are to blame!"

"We acted alone! Do what you will to us, but do not harm our people!"

"That is not up to Drakne to decide," stated a malicious voice.

Vranah emerged from behind his right-hand man as though he were Drakne's shadow. Zareth and Tesara quickly bowed their heads even lower before him.

"Please, Your Excellency. They are innocent. Kill us and us alone!"

"Silence woman! This town has long caused me too much trouble. It started decades ago with the birth of your former queen. This day has been coming long before you two ever interfered. Your actions only proved what I already knew. Kellinsi must not stand!"

"Let the women and children leave at least!"

"No, Zareth. It was a child who grew into a woman to become queen. You two were children who grew into traitors who tried to overthrow me. Women and children are just as dangerous as men. You will all perish."

"No, please!" Zareth and Tesara called in unison.

"Silence!"

Vranah struck them both with an electric current from his hand. Tesara cried out in pain, and Zareth pulled her closer to him, placing his massive arms around her protectively.

"Master, what are your orders?" Drakne inquired.

"You are to leave the boundaries of this town immediately. Wait for me there. I will not be long."

"As you wish, Master. I shall await you at Mersi Crossing."

Drakne bowed and turned, never glancing back as he swept rapidly through the cobblestone streets, until he vanished from sight. Once Vranah was sure that Drakne was far enough away, he turned to look down on Zareth and Tesara once more.

"Because your treachery has brought this upon your village, I think it is only fitting that you should be the last to die so that you may hear the screams of every last living soul... as they burn to death."

"No! Don't hurt them! It was our fault!" Tesara screamed wildly. "It was us, not them! Please!"

"You have us! Kill us and us alone!" Zareth begged.

Vranah was deaf to their continued pleas as he casually moved his hand to surround Zareth and Tesara in a force field to protect them until he was ready for them to die. He took a few steps back from them, turned his face to the sky and raised his arms straight up, muttering ancient words to himself as he lowered his arms down until they came once again to his side. A gigantic energy field materialized like an enormous bubble enclosing the entire town and the outlying farms.

Vranah whispered again and the sound of every door and window shutter in the village locking echoed through the square with sickening clacks, clanks, and thuds. The beginnings of panic filled the air where only silence had existed moments earlier, as the hidden townspeople came to the horrifying realization that they were trapped inside their own homes.

Vranah stretched his arms forward with a sweeping motion and watched as flames began to appear at the base of every building. The shrieks and cries of every man, woman, and child in the town began to ascend, loudly filling the air faster than the smoke from the fire. Vranah pointed randomly at rooftops, which exploded into flames that rapidly jumped from one structure to the next. Zareth and Tesara screamed in agony, eyes wild with shock and terror.

The black smoke filled the gargantuan dome so quickly that visibility was soon entirely gone. The force field allowed oxygen in to continue the fire, but let none of the smoke out. Those who did not burn to death fast enough were asphyxiated. The sounds slowly began to diminish as the unfortunate villagers died until all that was left was the roar of giant flames and the groaning of the buildings as they crumbled and gave way. Finally came silence that saturated the once happy town with thick noiseless nothingness that contrasted eerily with the screams that had filled it only moments before.

Zareth and Tesara had frozen inside their protective bubble. Their eyes were glazed over, stinging but unable to blink— staring out at the black smoke around them, but no longer seeing. Zareth still had his arms around Tesara, and the two were unconsciously rocking back and forth together. Tesara hummed a nursery rhyme she had learned in her childhood, eyes still unseeing, while Zareth held her closer with a single tear rolling down his cheek.

"To think it was all because of you."

Still catatonic, they stared vacantly beyond the smoke around them. Vranah's comment, malevolent grin, and fiendish laughter went unnoticed as Vranah released the shield that protected them. He, however, listened raptly to the chokes and sputters of Zareth and Tesara as they coughed to death in the black vapor. As they fell silent, Vranah deactivated the outer shield and allowed the fresh invigorating winds from the nearby mountains to blow the smoke away into the crystal blue sky.

Vranah staggered back a little and a worried expression crossed his face. He paused, focusing intently on remaining still and appearing tangible. Vranah turned and slowly worked his way through the smoldering piles of rubble and ash until he came to a small bridge that spanned a small creek. Beyond the bridge stood Drakne, waiting near a black globe-shaped carriage made of interlocking iron swirls with bejeweled iron snakes intertwined throughout. Despite a strained effort on Vranah's part to appear normal, Vranah staggered again as he approached.

"Are you well, my lord?"

"Yes, you fool! Take me to the castle now!"

Vranah staggered once more as Drakne opened the door to let Vranah inside the carriage that had been conjured specifically for him. Drakne worked to conceal any look of disapproval from his face. The power his master had just used was far too much to be handled by a non-corporeal being and it would be a very long time before Vranah would be able to manage full use of his abilities again. Drakne thought Vranah should know better than anyone else that a body is a receptacle of power that contains and amplifies energy and that without this containment, it was much more difficult to control that energy because power and magic naturally pass through a spirit, much like water through a sieve! Using that much power without a body was nothing but pure folly! But Drakne also knew better than to point this out to Vranah.

Still, the fact remained that the whole town did not need to be destroyed. The two traitors had come forward, and their public, non-magical execution would have sufficed as a warning to the rest. Drakne felt that his master had let his personal feelings cloud his judgment and had consequently worn himself out so greatly that it would take an inordinate amount of time to heal. This would mean much more work for Drakne.

Drakne climbed into the carriage and slammed the door behind him.

"To the castle!" Drakne demanded.

The driver cracked the reigns, the horses whinnied, and carriage sped off down the dirt road leading away from Kellinsi. As the carriage jostled back and forth, Drakne kept his gaze fixed away from his master, and looked out the carriage window so that he would not have to work as hard to hide the scowl on his face or the irritation in his eyes. Not once did he look back at the burned crater that just moments ago had been a charming town.

"No. Please! Stop! You can't do that! You can't! Help! Help! Somebody help! Anyone!"

"Lani, wake up!" Taylor said, shaking his sister.

"HELP! Someone please help them! Please!"

"Lani you're alright! You're safe! Everyone is safe! Wake up!"

Lani screamed one last time before sitting bolt upright in her bed. She was breathing exceptionally hard and was covered in a cold sweat.

"Taylor?"

Lani tried to focus through the dark of her bedroom. Her little brother had turned on her lamp, but it seemed remarkably dim at the moment. Taylor was sitting on her bed in his long black-and-blue plaid pajama pants and a white T-Shirt with a worried expression on his face. His haphazard hair and the dazed look in his eyes made it clear that he had been startled out of a dead sleep.

"You're alright, Lani. You were just having a bad dream. I could hear you screaming from my room. Are you okay?"

The images of her dream flashed through her mind again— the sights, the sounds, even the smells rushed at her all at once.

"Oh Taylor!" Lani cried out as she threw her arms around him. "It was so real! It was awful! Vranah murdered an entire town. He killed them *all!* The men, the women, *and the children!*"

Taylor responded by sweetly shushing her and stroking her hair. Lani sighed and started to relax as she finally let go of him.

"It was just a dream, Sis. Go back to sleep. It's three o'clock in the morning."

"Okay. Thank you, Tay-Tay."

"What are brothers for?"

Lani gave him a great big hug and then lay back down, pulling her covers over her shoulders and snuggling into them. Taylor pulled the cord on the lamp, and left her room. Lani sighed comfortably and quickly fell back to sleep.

REALITY CHECK

Morning came, and Lani moved downstairs to the couch in the living room, with her computer on her lap. The bright light of day poured in through the sliding glass door, which led to the backyard, and reflected off the few tiny areas of the low glass table in front of the couch that were still barely visible beneath the myriad papers and photos scattered around her senior year high school yearbook. Lani alternated between searching through the nostalgic chaos before her and sifting through emails detailing the plans that she and the rest of the former senior class presidency were making for their five-year reunion. It was almost a year away but there was just so much to do! They had to find a venue, a band, a DJ, a caterer, create the invitations, track everyone's current mailing address down, buy and design epic decorations, and make sure it was a night that no one would forget!

As Lani had been the secretary their senior year, she was acting as the secretary now— which was oddly more work than ever. The former class president was deluging Lani with email after email of itemized instructions, including cc's on *every* conversation she was having with the other two members of their presidency. Lani felt like she was drowning under a mass of digital messages. It seemed as if she would just barely finish reading one when three more would appear! And they weren't all easy tasks either. The one she was currently in the process of completing was going through the yearbook and trying to find everyone from their class on Facebook to invite them into a group for their reunion. As she pored through the various photo-filled pages, the friendship page that she and her friends had designed and paid for fell open.

Lani smiled as she saw the staggered individual pictures of herself, two boys, and two other girls spaced out evenly across the two-page spread. The last square on the far right held a picture of a ferret wearing pink bunny ears that were tied on with a bow under its chin, to make the layout even. She laughed as she saw six white question marks printed above the ferret where the name should be. She was curious as to how many people had actually seen that photo and wondered about it. The ferret hadn't belonged to any of them— it had just been a random picture that Lani had found on the Internet and couldn't resist putting it in the extra space.

She looked back to the left-hand page. First was her picture with her name written below it. A pair of sunglasses rested on top of her head, her back was against a wall with her arms folded, and she was smiling directly at the camera. Her long light brown hair was in a braid that fell to her waist. She couldn't help but notice how short it was in comparison to the present— her hair had almost doubled in length and now whenever she let it down all the way, it fell to her knees.

However, she had stayed close to the same size ever since ninth grade— five-foot-five and slender, or as she liked to call it, "travel size for your convenience." Other things that had not changed included her crystal blue eyes, and her full lips. It was funny, considering the fact that the Johnsons were not her biological parents, but her lips had always borne a striking resemblance to her dad's lips when he was young. He had always hated it as a child because they were super full and ruby red, and that was not fun for a boy. But Lani had been more than happy with them, and although it was genetically impossible, she had always joked that she had gotten her lips from her dad.

She looked at her picture with a scrutinizing eye. Her eyes were lit up with happiness and looking forward to the future, and her smile was free and easy. Lani remembered how that had felt. There was hope in her heart that she was on her way to becoming that carefree again. But she couldn't help but laugh a little.

"You had no idea what was coming, did you?"

Lani smacked her palm against her forehead and burst into a fit of giggles. Why was she talking to her seventeen-year-old self? She couldn't hear her and it was good thing too! Knowing her future all at once would have been way too stressful and might have even stopped it altogether. She knew that everyone went through heartache, and so she was no one special in that respect, but she also knew that if she had been told about everything she was going to go through ahead of time, she would have been tempted to run away more than once— and although the pain had not been fun, she would not trade even one of her experiences for an easier romantic journey. She had learned so much by living through them and had been able to help so many other people by being able to relate to their personal dramas in ways that even the greatest sympathy could never have done otherwise.

Lani regarded the picture next to hers. This one was of a tall boy with dark skin, who reminded Lani of a cross between a young Tiger Woods and a young Will Smith, staring intently at the camera like a model from GQ. Lani giggled at the seriousness of his expression. It was funny how such a colossal goof-off could only look serious when he was goofing off even more. She loved it when he "vogued" for the camera! He knew exactly how to use his captivating deep brown eyes rimmed with lashes that were so full and thick that many a girl in their high school had been horribly jealous of them. Lani herself had often wished she could trade him eyelashes and had told him that it didn't seem quite fair that a boy had been born with them— especially since he didn't even like them. Above this picture was his name, *Justin Michael Iremia,* written in the same white font as everyone else's caption, so that all their names stood out nicely against the tardis-blue background of the two pages.

"Justin, you've been gone too long! When are you getting back, already?"

As Justin could not answer, Lani directed her focus to the picture next to his. An alluring short Asian girl with thick, long, curly hair that fell to her waist was lying on the grass with her arms folded and her chin resting on her dainty hands. The girl looked directly into the camera and her mischievous grin and knowing look made one want to ask what her secret was. Written below this picture was *Kara Marie Shiro.* Lani looked up at a gilt-framed pencil drawing that Kara had made for her as a Christmas present in their senior year after the two of them had watched the 2004 version of *The Phantom of the Opera* together over and over again. It was a collage of images from that film and depicted The Phantom standing behind Christine, who was looking in the mirror. Lani wondered where Kara was now. It was strange to think that she had almost completely lost touch with someone she had been so close to in high school. Come to think of it, she hadn't even seen her since the summer after they all graduated.

Lani blinked and glanced back down to the first picture on the right-hand page and smiled freely.

"You never change, do you? I love that!"

Above this picture was written *Raoul Kimura Evans*. His short frame, handsome face and fair skin, set off by dark features, hinted at the possibility of some Asian genetics. His root-beer-colored eyes sparkled, even though his closed smile hid his teeth completely. This picture looked the same as the ones he had been sending to Lani from Indonesia over the past two years. He had just gotten back recently, was still only five-foot-four, and his face hadn't aged a day.

Finally, in-between the picture of Raoul and the unknown ferret, was a picture of the last girl. She had a heart-shaped face, stunning green eyes, and a glowing smile with the cutest dimples. Her hair fell past her shoulders, and it seemed as if a breeze had conveniently arranged some of it across her face to assist in creating the perfect glamour shot. Below this picture was written *Kendra Michelle Sanchez*. Lani didn't have to wonder what Kendra had been up to all these years. Kendra had been the only one who hadn't left for longer than a few months at a time since graduation. The two of them had done nearly everything together, including comforting each other through their various breakups throughout the early college years.

Underneath the staggered row of pictures in large white letters was the caption, *BEST FRIENDS FOREVER!!!* Lani's eyes lit up as she looked at the dozens of smaller photos below these words. It was as if hundreds of good memories lived on in this frozen 2-D realm. There was the time her friends had come early to help her fill up over one thousand water balloons for their senior opening social on the beach. Lani could still remember the numb feeling in her slightly swollen fingers from tying off each balloon. In the picture, the three girls were smiling widely and lying carefully on top of the full balloons, which were piled high and held together by a tarp— each girl visibly hoping that the balloons would not pop beneath them all while they took the picture.

In another photo, Lani's friends were helping her demonstrate proper fencing moves for the club she had started their junior year. Lani suddenly realized how much she missed that sport. She hadn't picked up a blade for anything other than goofing off with Raoul and Justin while making home videos since that photo had been taken. There just never seemed to be a trained person around to spar with when she had time to do so. *Oh well.* Perhaps after she finished her bachelor's degree there would be time to revive her rusty skills. As she continued to peruse the two pages, she recalled the happy feelings depicted in the numerous pictures of the whole group together at football games, at Justin's band concerts, at Raoul and Kendra's choir events, at Kara's art shows, at various formal and casual dances, and during holiday celebrations for nearly every holiday they could find an excuse to celebrate, as well as many other miscellaneous occasions.

Lani now came to some of her favorite random photos. First was the picture of Kara holding out a sheer piece of black material behind her, with her arms outstretched as if it were a cape. Lani had taken that picture at a sleepover when Kara had grabbed the material and abruptly held it up, before spontaneously declaring, "Look! I'm a bat!" Those words became a running joke for the entire year. Next was a picture of Raoul wearing a serious expression with a trench coat flaring around him as the photo caught him in the middle of a Matrix move.

Another classic was the photo of Raoul now sporting a flat expression, with sleepy eyes and an index card that he had taped to his forehead, which read "BORED" in big block letters. However, he looked very alive in the next photo, which was of their homework bonfire in the backyard at the end of their junior year, as he and the other four friends danced around the fire and threw a good portion of the year's work into the flames. The boys contributed more to the small inferno than the girls, who had insisted on keeping some of their favorite assignments.

Then there were the pictures of Lani and Justin together at both Junior Prom and Senior Prom, dressed to the nines and looking happier than ever. Lani's eyes held a tinge of pain as she viewed those photos, but she blinked it away and looked at the next photos with a wide smile. Looking back at all these memories made her so glad that she had made the decision to skip the sixth grade! Otherwise all her wonderful friends, who had made high school such an absolute *dream*, would have been a full year above her— and she might never have met them.

Eventually, Lani turned the page and got back to her email inbox to resume the business of cross-referencing the senior class list with the yearbook. She noticed a new message from one of her college friends, Jessica. It had been a few weeks since she and Jessica had been able to see each other, and she was excited to hear from her. She opened the email with a smile on her face, which quickly disappeared as she realized it hadn't been meant for her at all.

Like, oh my gosh! Lani gets everything she wants. Everything! She graduated from high school as a flippin' valedictorian! And she's got a full ride scholarship, when the rest of us actually have to work for our education. She thinks she's sooo perfect!

Lani's eyes widened. *How could Jessica think that?* Her finger hovered over the delete button. This hadn't been meant for her after all, and if this was how it was starting, how would it end? Lani wanted to look away but found herself unable to do so. She sighed as she lost the battle with herself and scrolled down to see more of the message. Tears welled up in her eyes as she continued to read.

Lani has all the guys drop at her feet all the time when the rest of us can't even get a guy to hit on us! She thinks she's soooo beautiful. You don't know what I have to put up with! And the worst thing is that she ACTS like she's NOT stuck up. She tells me she thinks I'm prettier than she is and whenever anyone tells her she's smart she's always like, "I just work hard, that's all." It makes me sick! She's such a liar! Anyway, it's so not fair, Melanie! Lani gets everything that she wants so easily! I don't even know why I'm friends with her!

Lani laughed in disbelief as the welled up tears spilled over their banks and fell, streaming down her face. *Why did Jessica write all of this?*

CHAPTER THREE

I'm planning a trip to Palm Springs the same day she graduates so I don't have to sit in the audience and pretend to be happy for her and risk throwing up on the person in front of me! Lol.

Lani wiped her tears away and sighed as more tears continued to fall. Out of the corner of her eye, Lani saw a large picture of her and Josiah that had somehow fallen in with her high school memories as she had grabbed everything she needed for the reunion project. She clutched it and hugged it close as she stared blankly out of the sliding glass door.

At Jessica's mention of graduation, Lani's mind drifted away to the effort she had been putting into school. Lani was now a senior in college finishing her degree in Business with an emphasis in digital media. Although she loved creative and artistic endeavors, she had listened to the counsel from her high school teachers, her college professors, and her parents, to have a backup plan. The business degree would allow her to be instantly hirable while she pursued her dreams, and would be useful in any career.

The digital media classes gave her a creative outlet for her business training— telling compelling stories through film. As she proceeded through school she had found that filmmaking was indeed another passion of hers, and tied in well with her newfound desire to write. She dreamed of creating a film production company someday, and knew that business and digital media combined would prepare her well— but for now she had just been excited about graduating and celebrating with her friends. However, at the moment the upcoming ceremony felt a little hollow. Lani shook off this train of thought and forced her eyes back to the email.

She's such a poser too! Acting like she's all intercultural and stuff. Just cuz she takes a few classes doesn't make her anything! Some of us actually ARE intercultural. Anywayz, gotta run! Thanks for letting me vent! I'm getting so tired of holding all this in and pretending to be her friend. I think I'm gonna go delete her off facebook right now, lol. See ya!

Lani sniffed as she reached for the tissue box by the lamp on the end table next to the couch and dabbed her now slightly swollen eyes. Lani could only imagine that Jessica's last accusation had to do with the fact that she was also earning a minor in Polynesian Studies. It was a minor that Lani's college had just begun to offer, as an addition to the Anthropology Department, when she started school. They had modeled it after the Hawaiian Studies and Polynesian Studies programs at BYU-Hawai'i. But now, just as she was about to graduate, the funding had been cut so severely that she could only hope that it would last long enough for her to finish her degree. Unless a lot more people expressed an interest in the program, it was going to die.

Lani couldn't believe that someone could be so harsh toward another person for wanting to broaden her horizons. She had chosen her minor as a result of taking one class, as a freshman, called *Malama ka 'Aina*, which had taught her about the Hawaiians and their love for their land. It had been a love-at-first-sight kind of thing for Lani, only with a whole people, rather than with just one person. That instant affection had opened the door to the world of the Polynesian islands and each successive class made her fall even more in love with its peoples, countries, cultures, and languages.

During her exploration of everything she could learn about Polynesia, she had learned to speak Tongan, because Tonga had become her favorite of all the island nations. But she had never bragged about any of this. She simply did it. She had no idea, before this email, that Jessica felt this way about her. Now that she did know, she could not understand *why* she would feel that way. Jessica was fluent in French and Lani could only converse slowly in Tongan, at best— and even then the person she was speaking Tongan with had to be very patient with her.

Lani suddenly realized that she had finally reached the end of the vicious email. She took a deep breath and slowly typed only ten short words in response.

I don't think you meant to send this to me.

Lani hit the send button and stared out through the sliding glass door once again, holding Josiah's picture closer.

"You know none of that is true, right?" Taylor asked.

Lani jumped a little. She hadn't realized her brother had been there, and it took her a moment to realize that the question he had asked meant that he had read the entire email.

"Yes, but that doesn't make it hurt any less."

Taylor sighed and gave his sister a hug.

"Don't let her get you down, Sis. She's just jealous. She said she was just pretending to be your friend, but I know you were a true friend to her, because you always are."

"Thanks... I try to be..."

"I know you didn't just try, because I've seen how great you make your friends feel... and I know how great you make me feel as your brother. None of the stuff she said is true. School wasn't easy for you, especially in high school. You had to watch your friends take off to have fun while you stayed back to do your homework 'cuz they were so much faster than you. And don't forget that teacher who acted like it was her personal goal in life to destroy you just to teach you that not everything in life was fair! Just 'cuz you rose above the odds doesn't mean they weren't stacked against you just as much as they are against everyone else."

"Wow, that teacher... I haven't thought about her in forever. I never understood teachers like her. Aren't teachers supposed to support kids reaching for their dreams? I mean, not everybody digs in and fights when they run up against people who tell them they can't do stuff— and so lots of people have their hopes smashed before they can even get to the 'real world.' It just isn't fair."

"There you go thinking about other people again when you're crying and you're hurt! See! By the way, I've got that teacher as soon as school starts again, so you'll be avenged!"

Lani laughed a little and tried to stop crying as her brother continued.

"And, I don't know what she's talking about on those guys, 'cuz all I've seen is a bunch of losers pose as good guys long enough to get you to be their girlfriend and then stop making you the number one priority on their list as soon as they are number one on yours."

Lani considered Taylor's words. For all her ambition, she had always made time for love, no matter how busy she was. She felt strongly that love should be the top priority and that it would invariably enhance other areas of her life. Lani enjoyed relationships and she took them seriously. She truly and deeply believed in searching for and finding her other half— her soul mate.

"You treat them like kings and like they're the hottest guy on the planet, even the ones who are coyote ugly, and then they break your heart!"

"Taylor!"

"What? It's true!"

She didn't agree with Taylor that any of them had been ugly, but she knew that some of them had not been what others would call handsome. That was what was so tragic about the fact that she could never find what she was looking for. If her only requirement had been that a guy looked like a designer underwear model, one might say that maybe she got what she deserved. It was exasperating, however, to constantly keep her priorities straight and still get the same result as if she had just picked some hot guy at random.

"You just haven't been able to catch a break! She's probably just jealous 'cuz you keep putting your heart on the line even though it gets smashed again and again, and she doesn't know how to open up even once!"

"She tries…"

"And you are anything but stuck up or shallow! You think everyone is beautiful and you love everybody! Dang that stupid girl! I've seen you drop everything, even in the middle of deadlines, and drive for miles just to give someone a hug when they're sad! This chick is really ticking me off! Who is this Jessica girl, anyway? What does she know? She sounds stupid! If she wasn't a girl, I'd kick her trash for being stupid and then I'd kick the trash out of her again! Maybe I can get Michelle to do it for me! Don't listen to her Lani!"

"I think that might be the most I've ever heard you say in one go," Lani said with a laugh, as her tears started to slow.

"Yeah, well, I save it for special occasions," Taylor said, smiling and calming down a little. "But it's all true! I've never seen someone take so much garbage and keep going. You're just not normal when it comes to love."

"I'm not normal?" Lani squeaked.

She sniffed as she wiped the last tears away from her eyes and smiled at her brother's rant. She had always suspected she was a little different when it came to love. Unlike most modern girls, Lani was a hopeless romantic and saw the best in people. She really believed in true love and wanted to get married, despite the prevailing skepticism about conventional marriage.

She knew that if she wanted her happily ever after that she would have to stay true to herself and continue to give each guy a fresh chance by reminding herself that the new guy had done nothing wrong, and that the past did not equal the future. She wanted to marry her best friend and wake up each morning with someone she couldn't wait to be with— to spend every day with someone she couldn't get enough of because they connected on all levels, from spirituality and intellect to spontaneity and creativity. She knew love would be worth it in the end, but that didn't make it any easier at the moment.

"Heck no, you're not normal! But that's a good thing. Normal is dull. And normal for girls is Jessica— catty, self-absorbed, and stupid."

"Not all girls are that way… and you really shouldn't call her stupid."

"I've got other names I know you'd like less."

"No, no, we can just agree she was being mean and insensitive in that email."

"Fine, mean! She's a mean, mean, mean, mean," Taylor took a dramatically flared huge breath in, "mean, mean, mean, mean, mean, mean, mean, mean, mean, girl with a less than genius IQ."

"Okay... I'll take it," Lani laughed. "Thanks for the pep talk, Tay-Tay. You know, you're growing up to be quite an awesome guy. You're only seventeen and you know more about how to cheer a girl up than a lot of the older guys I've dated. Michelle's a lucky girl."

"I know, right?" Taylor said with a laugh. "Now if you promise me not to listen to that stu- I mean, that... oh heck with it— that stupid chick! If you promise me not to let that psycho get into your head, I'm gonna go raid the fridge. I'm starving! You want anything? And more importantly, do you promise?"

"Yes, I promise that I'll try to not think about it. And, no thank you, I just ate a little while ago."

"Okay, I'll come check on you in a sec then, Sis."

Taylor bounded off to the kitchen. Lani sighed and kept her promise to try and push Jessica's words from her mind. Her brother was right— it wouldn't do any good to dwell on them. Lani left the chaos of memory lane behind her as she pulled out the notebook she used to jot down notes on her novel, picked up one of her favorite books, and grabbed her laptop to go outside and work on her story in the fresh air under the tree she loved more than any other.

"Whatcha doing, Sis?" Taylor asked.

As usual Lani jumped and her computer nearly fell off her lap. She knew he had promised to come check on her, but it had seemed as if no time had passed and he was suddenly here, chomping down on a gigantic turkey sub.

"I'm writing a book. That's why I'm off this summer. I decided I wanted to devote some real time to working on it so I can get it going."

Taylor's full mouth fell open and a couple of crumbs flew out of his mouth as he laughed.

"I dunno why I'm surprised," Taylor said, somewhat indistinctly between bites. "After all, it is you... So whussit gonna bebout?"

"Well... you know what you were saying about how I try really hard to treat my friends really well, and especially the guys I date, right?"

Taylor swallowed his food and continued at an enthusiastic volume.

"Yeah, for realz! And most of them don't deserve it! Especially whoever that Jessica chick is and ultra especially that stupid Josiah—"

"Taylor!"

"Well he is! But anyway, yeah I know what you're talking about, Sis. Soooo?"

"So, the novel I am writing is a magical explanation for why people have treated me, and even others, so badly— giving them the excuse of a master villain who uses magic spells to make them change drastically and act horribly, instead of whatever the real reason might be."

In actuality Lani had no idea what made people behave this way. She couldn't even explain the things *she* did. But she was sure that in real life, everyone had control over his or her own actions.

"Interesting. Sounds like you still can't get Josiah off your brain."

"Be nice. Actually it *will* be a way for me to explain why I can't stop looking for my soul mate. And yes, I will be trying to explain why I can't let Josiah go too."

She sighed. People always asked her why she didn't simply take a break from dating. She had no real answer for them other than the cliché saying of, "You gotta kiss a lot of frogs to find a prince," to which she would add with a laugh, "and I'd like to get the frog kissing part over with as quickly as possible." But she was as baffled as they were at her constant need to find someone to share her life with.

"Well at least you being under some magic spell would explain why you even give that jerk a second thought."

"*Taylor!*"

"Alright, alright! I was just leaving to pick up Michelle anyway. Good luck, Sis."

"Thank you."

Taylor shoved the last bite of his gargantuan sandwich into his mouth, leaned down to give Lani a quick hug, and left. Lani laughed as she watched him run off and got back to her computer to contemplate chapter two. The novel was to be about the search for the true love she so desperately wished to find— the kind that was worth fighting for, living for, and even dying for.

However, she intended it to be much more than a romance novel. She loved all genres of books and movies, including sci-fi, mystery, fantasy, adventure, and comedy— and wanted to somehow incorporate them all. Usually, the ideas came to her so quickly that she could barely get them to paper fast enough. It was like she was watching a movie and trying to transcribe everything as she watched it— almost like she wasn't the one writing it. In just a day or two, she had already finished the prologue and the first chapter and was about to begin the second. She called the novel *Half-Hearts*.

Back in the Forest of Kar, Jharate sat deep in thought. His piercing brown eyes stared out into the thick impenetrable darkness created by the surrounding trees. He was breathing fast as if he had just run for hours and cold beads of sweat adorned his troubled brow. His mind kept replaying the scene he had just witnessed. Jharate knew his gift was extremely rare and precious, but at this moment it felt more like a curse. He was experienced enough to discern between his visions of the past, the present, and the future, and he knew for certain that his only brother had literally just died before his eyes.

His brother's death continued to play over and over in his mind until it was more than he could bear. The screams of pain and Khanye's final warning to stay away echoed in one continuous round. Jharate's heart felt as if it had frozen and every beat was a struggle to break through the ice. His stomach felt as if it had turned to stone. He desperately wanted the power to travel back in time to his brother in order to save him. Failing that, to at least avenge him, or die trying. However, Jharate knew that was impossible— especially with the knowledge he had just received through that same hellish vision. Jharate had discovered that he too was a Half-Heart.

The weight of the responsibility that this entailed slowly settled upon Jharate. Revenge would have to take second place now. He could not fail Alamea for the sake of personal redress. He focused on his duty and tried to force the images of Khanye's death out of his mind. How was he to complete this mission? He had gained an advantage because he now knew that he was a Half-Heart— but how was he to even *find* a female Half-Heart? Let alone recognize her, fall into complete and true love with her, and marry her?

Lani's grandma had once told her not to worry because someday her Prince Charming was going to come— to which Lani had replied, "I don't want a Prince Charming! He couldn't even recognize his woman when she was right in front of him without making her try on a *shoe*! And Snow White's guy didn't have to work for her at all! He just stumbled across her in the forest one day and kissed her. What kind of freak does that?

"I want a Prince Phillip. I want a guy who can recognize what he has right in front of him, and knows that she is worth doing anything for. Phillip had to defy his father, escape the evil enchantress, cut through thorns the size of his horse, and then fight a dragon! When that was all over, did he sit down and think about what to do next because he didn't want to rush into a commitment? No! He ran up a million stairs to the topmost part of the castle, kissed the girl to break the spell and married her! I'm tired of all the dead bodies strewn around my metaphorical castle of the would-be princes who died from a horrible case of quitting!"

Her grandmother had burst out laughing and had said that it was good that Lani knew what she wanted, but that she had never quite thought of those fairytales in that way before. Lani wasn't sure why that memory had just popped into her head. Maybe it was all the Josiah drama. Maybe writing her novel brought it to mind or maybe it was prompted by the book she was currently reading— or maybe it was just because she was a diehard hopeless romantic looking for a glimmer of hope in a world full of broken hearts. Whatever the reason, she was grateful for the laugh it had provided her.

Lani returned to reading Jane Austen's *Persuasion,* one of several classic romantic books she loved to experience again and again. She was still sitting outside curled up in a chair under her favorite tree, but she had abandoned her own writing after staring at the blinking cursor on her computer screen for quite some time. She had been unable to even write the first sentence of chapter two and was now immersing herself in somebody else's writing in order to clear her head.

Lani jumped as her cell phone rang. Her active imagination allowed her to see everything as she read it, and it was always disorienting for her to be pulled out of her fictional world by a noise from the real one.

Ring, Ring!

The phone rang out again as if it were somehow growing impatient. Lani looked at the screen to see who it was, but it only showed the number. She stared at it for a moment, as if trying to will the name to appear, but finally picked up the phone on what seemed to be the last ring it was willing to give.

"Hello?"

"Hey Lani, guess who?"

"JUSTIN!"

"Well that didn't take long. Yeah, it's me!"

"When did you get back?!"

"Like thirty minutes ago! So good to be back in the U.S. of A! I'm at the cell phone store! I had a cheap phone in Japan that doesn't work here anyway, so I begged my mom to drive me here straight from the airport so I could buy a new phone. I broke my old one just before I left so I lost all my numbers and I had to get your number from my mom. Glad you didn't change it while I was gone or I might have had to drive over there to get it myself."

"And we wouldn't want that now, would we? It's not like we haven't seen each other except on Facebook for two years. Oh wait, ha, ha! It is! And how many phones is that you've broken now?"

"Shhhhh! Never mind how many. And don't get offended that I haven't driven over there yet. You're the first one I'm calling!"

"Okay, you're forgiven," Lani said with an audible smile.

"I heard Raoul got back a little before me and is still having trouble adapting to the fact that he doesn't need to be in and off the streets by ten o'clock at night!"

"It's true. His brothers have a really hard time pulling him out of his house to go have fun, and they say he's even worse at night. Some things never change, especially when it comes to Raoul."

"Well Imma have to change *that*. Ten o'clock is RIDICULOUS for a twenty-three year old dude! That reminds me— I need to call him after I talk to you, but I called for a reason besides just letting you know I'm back. I've got an epic idea! Wait for it…"

Lani's eyes widened slightly as she waited for him to elaborate. She knew Justin too well to not get at least a little worried when he had an "epic idea."

"*Yesss?*"

"You. Me. Raoul. Disney World. Leave tomorrow!"

"Are you serious?!"

She couldn't help feeling excited about the prospect of going, but she was still cautious. Justin's dad was always giving him extraordinarily extravagant gifts, and so what he was saying was not out of the realm of possibility. But Justin loved to tease her, and had found her gullibility hysterical, so she wasn't going to let herself believe him completely just yet.

"Yes I'm serious! Booyah! My dad's trying to make me like him again. Trying to make up for 'lost time' I guess. As if he could make up for abandoning his seven-year-old son and his five-year-old daughter… He's been giving bigger gifts ever since about six months before I turned eighteen 'cuz he knew the court couldn't make me go see him anymore…

"Anywhooo… if he wants to try to buy my affection, who am I to say no? He owes me far more than that. And my mom too! He nearly let us starve to death for ten years! That loser never paid half the child support he was supposed to and we all knew he had the money. He just wouldn't cough it up! But he had plenty of money for his *new* wife and kids in New York!

"ANYWAY… you know all that. I don't even know why I told you again. Soooo back to the fun part! He sent airline tickets for me and four friends *and* paid for two hotel rooms in a hotel inside the park WITH the meal plan, and get this— everything is paid for, for a whole week! We're talkin' free admission to all the parks *plus* he gave me two *thousand dollars* for souvenirs!"

"That's awesome!" Lani squealed. "I'm assuming I get my own room, right?"

"I thought Raoul would and you and I could share…"

"JUSTIN!"

"Just kidding! Take it easy girl. Of course you get your own room, silly. It wouldn't be decent otherwise."

"Good. Don't joke about stuff like that. You remember how old-fashioned I am," she said, just in case the two years away from her had damaged his memory.

"Yeah, no worries I haven't changed either. I picked my mom as one of the people to go, just to tick him off, and then I chose my sister for the last ticket, so everything will be perfectly proper. The down side is you will have roommates."

"Cool! I love your mom and your sister! I know I can trust you and Raoul, but that makes me feel even better about telling my parents I'm going and also makes it look better to anyone else who might ask. Thank you so much for doing that!"

"I thought you might like that," Justin said laughing, in a loving way but also in a way that she could almost hear his eyes rolling. "Don't get too attached to your roomies, though. I told my mom I want to separate and have the three of us go off on our own most the time so that it will feel like it's just us. She was just excited to spend time with my sister and get a trip on my father's dime so she's cool with that."

"Well, I love being with them too but that sounds great to me! Thanks again for arranging it that way— 'perfectly proper,' as you put it."

"And they say chivalry is dead! Anyways, get packing. The plane leaves at seven-thirty in the morning!"

"Sounds good! Pick me up tomorrow at four-fifteen, okay?"

"Yep, you got it! Raoul and I will be there and we'll meet up with my mom and Jezzy at the airport."

Jezzy was the nickname Justin had given to his twenty-year-old sister, Jeshelle. He took a quick breath and then continued with enthusiastic volume.

"*This* is going to be *AWESOME!* The three of us haven't been together for ages!"

"I *know*, right?! Well I better start packing! Bye, Justin!"

"*BUH-BYE!*"

Lani screamed for joy and jumped up and down as she hung up the phone. When she finally calmed down she looked at the time. Three-thirty! She ran inside, rushed up the stairs to her room and hurried to her closet, which she flung open. She reached up onto the top shelf and pulled down a suitcase, narrowly avoiding knocking herself out with it as it more or less fell down while she tried to control its descent. She began to pack as quickly as she could. Seven days' worth of shirts, pants, underwear, and swimwear found their way into the case in no time.

Lani's cream-colored cat, which she had rescued from the local Humane Society just days before she would have been put down, jumped up on her bed and peered quizzically into the suitcase.

"Okay, Portia so maybe it's more like fourteen days' worth, but you never know when you might need to change!"

Portia looked up at her and meowed.

"Don't judge me! Just because you don't have to change!"

Portia jumped into the suitcase and curled up on one of Lani's blouses, keeping her eyes on Lani and meowing once more.

"No, you can't come with me, baby. It's okay though— I'll be back soon. And you need to stay off the bed and out of my suitcase. You know kitties belong on the floor and in their own beds."

Lani snapped her fingers and pointed at the floor. Portia meowed, jumped down, and walked away with her tail high in the air. Lani smiled and shook her head at her adorable cat's attitude. She momentarily flashed back on the day that she had picked her out. There had been an adorable kindle of Burmese kittens with big blue eyes that had drawn her attention immediately. She had walked over to their cage and was about to ask to hold one, when she heard the unlikely sound of purring above all the other sounds in the room. She turned her head and had instantly fallen in love with the then six-month-old Portia, who had somehow been overlooked by every other visitor since the day she was born. The loud purring is why Lani had named her Portia, after the car, but with Shakespeare's spelling.

Shortly after taking her home, Lani discovered that her new kitty had an affinity for playing in water. Portia especially loved watching the mini-whirlpool that formed as the bathtub emptied and would jump into the two or three inches of water to play with it as it swirled down the drain. A couple of days later, Portia was keeping Lani's dad company in their vegetable garden in the backyard, when she began pouncing on the over-ripe tomatoes that he threw over his shoulder to till back into the ground. To everyone's surprise, Portia enjoyed lapping up the juices from the squashed red fruit, and would even eat some of the tomato meat.

Lani laughed at the memory and went back to the task before her. She packed a modest, simple, yet still stunning black evening dress and another modestly cut and equally stunning fuchsia satin one, and two matching pairs of heels in case they went to a nice restaurant.

Various items of jewelry, assorted hair accessories, and other necessities came next, followed by the assorted toiletries she would need on her trip, however, there was relatively no make-up packed. She loved doing dramatic make-up when she dressed up in costumes for Halloween or midnight movie premieres and the like— but as far as the every day went, she had always felt it was more important for people to see the real her than to see her artistic ability displayed on her face. Additionally, she had her dad's lips and make-up took too much time to trouble with so, with the exception of some college dances, when she knew the flash from the cameras might wash her out and ruin the professional pictures of her and her date, she didn't bother. Even then, she only put on just enough so that after the flash washed her out a little in the photo, she would still just look like she naturally did in person.

Most importantly, she packed a notebook and a pen so that she could write if something she saw inspired her. Maybe this trip was just what she needed to kick out the small bit of writer's block she was experiencing.

"What are you doing?"

Lani was once again startled by her brother's entry, and nearly knocked her suitcase onto the floor. Taylor stood in the doorway looking at the chaos in front of him with a confused expression.

"Taylor you scared me! Oh, right, I forgot to tell you. I'm going to Disney World tomorrow with Raoul, Justin, his mom, and his sister."

"TOMORROW? I didn't even know Justin was back!"

"I know, right?! I just found out when he called me like five minutes ago. He's been home like less than an hour! Wow, that jet lag is gonna kill him. No, wait a minute— it's Justin. He'll be more awake than Raoul and I will be! Can you go get mom for me so I can tell her? Oh, and can you grab my laptop please? I left it outside!"

"Sure thing, Sis! MOM!"

Lani laughed as Taylor ran screaming from the room. She thought about how much fun she was about to have and wished that there was one more ticket for Taylor. She and her family had been planning to go to Disney World and on the Disney Cruise in the not-too-distant future and Taylor had been just as excited about the prospect as she was, and that was hard to do. They both loved Disneyland so much that they had annual passes and never got tired of it, and they couldn't wait to see the other parks in Disney World. She really wanted to take him with her now. He had been such a rock for her lately. But she knew Taylor wouldn't begrudge her going with Justin and Raoul and also that she would still have the time of her life— and, she was sure that the family could go together soon.

This trip would be the first time that she, Raoul, and Justin would be able to spend that much time together since they had graduated from high school. Lani suddenly remembered the fateful twist in Raoul's life that had occurred the day that he was held back in elementary school. That, coupled with the fact that she had skipped a grade, had put all three of them in the same grade level rather than being separated into three completely different ones. She didn't believe in coincidence and was sure that the Universe had arranged things to bring them together. They met in ninth grade and had been inseparable from that day on. Even within their larger group of friends, Raoul, Justin, and Lani had always been the very best of friends, referring to themselves the three musketeers.

Justin and Lani had always shared the additional bond of both being adopted children. Like Lani, Justin had never taken up the crusade to find his biological parents, but not quite for the same reasons. He was very happy with his mom and although he could have passed on his dad, Justin figured it was too much work to track down parents he didn't have names for. He didn't even know what race he was for sure, but as Lani and many others had always told him he looked like Will Smith and Tiger Woods, he figured he had to be at least part African-American.

However, Justin also thought there was a strong possibility he was the same mix of races as his stunning younger sister, who was his adoptive parents' biological child, because the resemblance between them was quite uncanny, right down to the gorgeous eyes and lashes that gave other girls fits of jealousy when they looked at her. His adoptive mother was half-Japanese and half-Caucasian, and his adoptive father was from Fiji. Justin had decided early on to roll with it, and had made up his own name for the mix of cultures he was guessing flowed through his veins— Fijapcasian.

Raoul, on the other hand, was the youngest of eight children and looked as if he were at least part Mexican to people who did not know his family. His mother was from Japan and had a bit of Filipina blood. His father was of Danish and French ancestry. The family resemblance was so strong between Raoul and his brothers that some people thought he and his brother Koji, who was just a couple years older than he was, were twins. Everyone who lived in the community would always ask Raoul, "Are you one of the Evans kids?" He would always beam with happiness and pride as he answered that he was.

Lani's cell phone rang again. This time the screen told her that it was Raoul.

"Hey Raoul, perfect timing! I was just thinking about you!"

"Lani, are you sitting down?" Raoul asked in a low hushed voice.

"Yes, Raoul, I'm sitting down."

Lani had seated herself on her bed in order to answer him honestly and was biting her lip to keep from laughing. Raoul's tone was so serious and she already knew why he was calling.

"I know that this is not much notice, and I know you like notice… so I hope this won't upset you too much."

Lani decided to play this out with a worried tone and go with whatever he said. Partly for entertainment, but also to spare his feelings and allow him to report what he felt he needed to report to her. She was barely able to contain herself as she answered him with concern in her voice.

"What is it, Raoul?"

"We have to leave tomorrow."

"Leave?"

"Yes. Tomorrow."

"Whatever for?" Lani said, biting her lip harder and pulling one of her throw pillows to her face to muffle any unintended sounds.

"Justin's dad is making him go to Florida."

"Oh no! But we just barely got all of us back here again!"

"I know, I know… it's quite sudden. I knew that might be upsetting to you so I wanted to be the one to tell you. I want you to know it will be okay, Lani. He says we can go with him. So don't worry. He has tickets for all of us tomorrow and he'll pick us up."

"Yay! That is gonna be so fun! Well I better let you go so you can pack. You don't want to forget anything."

"Oh yeah! I have to pack! Bye, Lani!" Raoul exclaimed in a panicked voice.

He didn't even wait for her to say goodbye. He was gone. Lani laughed until she nearly cried. Her mind flashed back to the three years in high school it had taken her to be able to get him to do something as simple as going to the beach at a moment's notice. Before she and Justin had worked on him for all that time, he would stand in the doorway like a deer caught in the headlights for up to half an hour, trying to decide what to do, unsure of how he could possibly deal with the spontaneity before him— even if his schedule was completely free. He and Justin couldn't be less alike. Come to think of it, the three of them were all completely different from each other. And yet as friends they were perfect together.

After high school, all three of them had gone on to attend UCSD, but both of the boys had taken two years out to dedicate to service abroad. Raoul had gone off to serve with the Peace Corps in Indonesia, teaching English and building schools, while Justin had gone off to Japan to teach children English and music, as a volunteer. Lani missed them terribly while they were gone, but she was very proud of them for being willing to serve others. And now that they were back, she couldn't wait for morning to come!

Jharate jumped slightly as he woke from his musing state. He had not been asleep, but he had been so deep in thought that he had almost forgotten where he truly was. He thought he had just seen a maiden— a beautiful young maiden with long flowing hair. She was not in the forest with him. She was in his mind. Her surroundings were strange to him. She was standing outside on a narrow and unusually-smooth cream-colored pathway. She had a strange nearly-rectangular box on the ground behind her that looked as though it might be made of cloth, despite its shape.

She stood on the pathway, looking out at what seemed to be a road. However, it was like no road Jharate had ever seen. It was pitch black and again, unusually smooth. Strange carriages rushed past her on the unfamiliar ebony surface. No animals drew them forward and they appeared to be forged from metal. The carriages had been fashioned into diverse shapes, sizes, and colors and seemed to have eyes that gleamed brighter than torches as they illuminated the way ahead of them through the darkness, which felt like the darkness just before sunrise.

Jharate marveled as one of the carriages stopped. It was black and had no roof. It bore the image of a horse crafted in silver on the front of it. There were two men inside the carriage. He watched as they got out to help the mysterious maiden to her seat. They picked up her box and put it inside a hidden compartment in the back. Although it was dark outside, there was some light coming from tall metal pillars, which allowed Jharate to vaguely see strange looking dwellings that stood close together— and then he could see no more.

He wondered what it all meant. Truly hers was a strange land. Did such a place exist? Did such a maiden exist? He could not be sure. However, it seemed real. It had felt like a vision— but was it? It was nothing akin to anything he had ever seen prior to this instance. Perhaps it was merely his imagination. Still, he could not shake the feeling that it had been a vision, nor could he remove her face from his mind. She was uncommonly alluring and he felt a burning desire to meet her emanating from his very soul, if only he could find her.

He suddenly became aware of how heavy his eyelids were and decided that it was wise to attempt to rest before the sun came up, which would not be long now. He lay back down, thinking of the fair maiden, and pictured her gentle face until he finally drifted off to sleep.

AND A LITTLE BIT OF PIXIE DUST...

"Thank you for choosing to fly with us today on flight 245 to Orlando. We hope you had an enjoyable flight and will choose us the next time you travel. Please wait until the captain turns off the fasten-your-seatbelt sign before un-fastening your seatbelts."

"Ding!" Justin said aloud, in flawless imitation, five seconds before the fasten-your-seatbelt light actually went off with a ding.

The clickety-clack of hundreds of people undoing their seatbelts sounded like a thousand mousetraps going off at once.

"Lani," Justin began, "Laaani... Wake up!"

Justin nudged Lani awake in an unceremonious manner and she sat bolt upright, blinking slowly as she sleepily surveyed her surroundings. Seeing his mischief was complete with Lani, he stood up, quietly unscrewed the cap of his water bottle, and proceeded to dump the contents onto Raoul's head.

"HEY!"

"Rise and shine you two lazy bums! We're here!"

"And you couldn't think of a better way to wake me up?"

"Reeeeelax will yah, Raoul? Sheesh!"

"Grow up, Justin," Jeschelle said, shoving Justin so hard that he almost fell on top of Lani, as she and her mom passed by to go get their carry-ons out of the overhead bins, taking her long curly hair out of a bun as she walked.

"Grow up, Justin," Justin mimicked under his breath.

Lani had been watching the scene in a half dazed state. Justin's impolite manner of waking her had thrown her off. She hadn't thought she was asleep. She had been in an unfamiliar forest looking for someone. She remembered the feeling most of all— wanting, no, *needing* to find someone. But she had no idea who she was searching for.

It had been so real. It was nighttime... and unusually dark... and she was completely alone. Stumbling upon a campsite, she had seen someone sitting up in the darkness. He was a well-muscled man with brown skin, but she could not see his face. She had been startled at first, but felt no fear in venturing forward to determine his identity. It was at this moment that Justin had chosen to rip her from her dream and back to reality. The odd thing was... it hadn't felt like a dream at all.

Lani shrugged it off— thankful that at least it wasn't the strange mirror nightmare she had been having over and over again. That dream had been bothering her for ages and she struggled to find the meaning. She thought maybe it could make interesting material for her book if only her dream would continue past the part where she stood frozen, looking at herself in the mirror, while a menacing electric current surged around her.

"Hellooooo," Justin said, waving his hand in front of Lani's eyes. "We're still here you know. Remember us? The living? You know— your best friends since forever? Wakey wakey... let's *GO!*"

Lani playfully shoved his hand out of her face with a great big smile and proceeded to pick up her things so they could exit the plane.

A young woman in her mid-twenties, with olive skin and auburn hair that was pulled back into a ponytail, awoke slowly on a cold green marble floor. She wore a fawn brown shirt with billowing sleeves underneath a brown leather corset. Formfitting high-waisted tweed pants vanished into knee-high brown leather boots. She heard crackling, like pine logs burning in a fire, but the sound was coming from above her.

As she opened her eyes, the rippling blue electric bubble that encircled her came into focus. She jumped to her feet and peered out into the dimly lit room around her, keeping a careful distance from the edges of the bubble. She reached for her back and found that her shoulder-strapped sheaths were still there, but that both of her swords were missing. Her body was sore and her head ached as if she had suffered a blow. She closed her eyes and put both hands to her temples as she tried to work out the events that had led up to this moment.

A few hazy fragments flashed through her mind. She had been outside the castle on a mission... Prince Khanye... A patrol of maybe fifty of Vranah's soldiers had spotted her in a wooded area outside the fortress... Her memory became more cohesive from this point. She remembered how she hadn't even drawn her swords. Amidst so many trees and such abundant and diverse foliage, she shouldn't have needed them.

With a subtle motion of her hands, she had commanded the ivy to lift her ten feet in the air in order to give her a better vantage point of the battle. Still more ivy tripped, enveloped, and immobilized several of the men as they advanced towards her— twisting around their bodies and then tightening its hold. With mere glances, she enlisted every branch around them to pummel some repeatedly and catapult others deep into the forest. Seven of the men were killed during the attack and the rest had been rendered inert. She was sure she had everything well in hand and would be free to rescue Prince Khanye momentarily.

Then Drakne had arrived. Every branch that reached toward him stopped abruptly, just short of touching him. The ivy that attempted to bind him was incinerated on contact as Drakne advanced forward slowly, unblinking. He calmly struck her down with an electric current from his hand and simultaneously reduced the ivy holding her aloft to ashes. Everything in her world had gone black in that instant, before she even began to fall.

The woman opened her eyes again and paced wildly within the energy field she now found herself trapped in, repeatedly going over the details that had led to her capture. The fall she must have endured explained the pain she was feeling, but that was the least of her problems now. She was well aware that her fate was to become a martyr, but felt quite irritated by the time it was taking and wanted to get it over with. She wondered why Drakne had not just killed her in the forest. He had definitely had the opportunity. No doubt Vranah found some sick pleasure in killing victims himself. Either that, or he wished to torture her for information. Well, at least she could be sure he would get none from her.

She turned her head and squinted to locate the source of the voices she now heard, conversing, and saw two figures standing near the thrones of the former king and queen. There was no mistaking the identities of the two men. Drakne stepped aside and out of Vranah's path. Vranah walked out of the shadows and into clear view, just outside of her enclosure.

"Well, well, well, Narah, you should not have come here."

"Yes, well, it wasn't my intention to come *here*. Your *pet* over there is the one to blame for this."

She spat out the word "pet" like dirt had entered her mouth. Drakne's eyes narrowed and his black leather gloves creaked as he slowly clenched his hands into tight fists— but he simply faced his lord, bowed, and strode out of the room.

"My 'pet' as you say, has served me well. He has brought me you— Narah Deskarin, the *famous* warrior from Destavnia, known for her beauty as well as for her skills in battle, although no one could say which is her stronger attribute. My, my, you truly are beautiful..."

Narah's stomach turned over as he complimented her beauty. How dare he talk of her this way? Vranah continued to stare at her as though he were magically enchanted.

"It really is too bad. I could have had a great use for you... It would have been much more enjoyable... but you are a liability and I cannot permit you to live."

"I figured as much, you disgusting degenerate— so let's get on with it, shall we? I'd rather die than continue this conversation any longer."

"*Such spirit!* Such spirit, and yet... *no curiosity*. You have no desire to know why I cannot keep you alive?"

"No, not really."

Her breathing and heart rate remained steady and calm. There was no fear in her eyes or in her voice. She knew that he had no power over her in death. She also knew that there were fates far worse than death and that the sooner he killed her, the less likely she would have to endure one.

"Very well— then die, Half-Heart," he said with a smile as he waved his hand— and with one smooth motion in her direction, she crumpled to the floor and lay still.

Death had come instantly to her, but not before she had learned what she was. For the tiniest instant a strong desire to live had returned to her, yet in that same instant she died.

"Drakne!"

Drakne returned through the doors, from which he had exited, with impressive speed, and bowed.

"Take her to her coffin."

Drakne nodded acquiescence and snapped his fingers to levitate her corpse.

"Good work, Drakne. She truly was a formidable adversary. You will be greatly rewarded."

"Thank you, my lord."

Drakne bowed out of the room as he guided Narah's body in front of him.

"Three dead, twenty-one remain," Vranah mused to himself, confident that it would not be long now.

Disney's Magical Express pulled up the drive into what Lani felt had to be the finest hotel on the Disney World property— The Grand Floridian! It reminded Lani of her favorite hotel in San Diego, the Hotel del Coronado, with its red gabled roofs and white exterior. The Victorian architecture combined with 1920's elegance was mesmerizing. An old carriage was visible near the entrance, as well as a vintage 1929 Cadillac. The Disney staff, dressed in perfect 1920's period wear, completed the illusion. The sense of being transported into another time had a surprisingly relaxing effect.

As the bus pulled to a stop, directly across from the double door entrance, Justin made the "Pssshhh" noise along with the air breaks.

"We're here!" Justin exclaimed. "We're here! We're here! We're here! We're here! We're here!"

"We get it," Jeschelle said sleepily. "We're here. Yay."

"Stop acting like you're older than me, Jezzy!"

"Start acting like you're older than me!"

"Start acting like you're older than me," Justin mimicked loudly.

"Yeah, real mature."

"It's DISNEY WORLD! The one place you don't have to act like a grown up! Your Disney age is the two numbers of your age added together. So I'm four!" Justin held up four fingers awkwardly, like he had just learned how, and shoved them in her face.

"Okay, okay," she said, shooing him away with her hands, "...just don't stand too close to me."

"That's an easy promise!"

"Be nice," Raoul chided.

"Thank you, Raoul," Jeschelle said with a smile.

"No problem."

"Let's get off the bus!" Lani exclaimed, bouncing on her toes.

Justin's mom, Jeschelle, Raoul, Lani, and Justin made their way off the bus and down to where the driver was unloading their bags, curbside. They quickly found the bags that belonged to them, and pulled them out of the pile.

"Lani, Justin, get over in front of that old car and I'll take your picture!" Raoul exclaimed.

"I'll take it," Jeschelle offered. "That way you can be in the picture with them."

"Thanks Jezzy," Raoul smiled, as he hurried over to Lani and Justin.

"Say cheese!"

"Cheese!"

Jeschelle clicked the button on the camera and the flash went off under the shaded porte-cochere.

"Thanks Jezzy," Lani said.

"No problem."

"Come help me with our bags, Jeschelle," Justin's mom called.

Jeschelle handed the camera back to Raoul and returned to her mother. The three friends picked up their things and headed inside. Going through the doors of the hotel, Lani and her friends gasped as they looked around. The lobby glowed. In fact the very word hotel seemed inadequate at best. It was more a palace than a hotel.

The ceiling was extremely high with intricate woodwork and exquisite dome-shaped skylights that let the sunlight flood in. Each floor was open with railings so that you could see the lobby from any level. The final touch was the pair of chandeliers that resembled the one from Disney's *Beauty and the Beast*. They hung majestically from the ceiling in the center of two of the three Tiffany-inspired skylights.

Lani had been so enveloped by the beauty of the hotel, that she was yet again startled by Justin, who informed her with a couple snaps in front of her face that she was indeed on Earth, and not in Heaven.

"I checked us in while you were off floating on cloud nine! Do you think you could come back to *this* planet now so that we can go get our stuff to our rooms and then jet off to the rides? Mom and Jezzy are already over there by the elevator, and one week isn't as long as it seems you know! We have to get going now! The monorail comes right through this hotel on the second floor, so we can go straight into the parks. The last park closes at 1am tonight for us so that only gives us eight hours!"

"What do you mean for us?" Raoul asked.

"Resort guests get 'Magic Hours' so it's open earlier for us on some days and later for us on other days and they kick everybody else out! HA!"

"That's cool! But now I feel bad for the other people..."

"Get over it! Anyway, let's go Lani. Lani? Lani!"

Lani's feet were still planted on the floor. Her eyes had left Justin as quickly as he had managed to get them focused on him, and were gazing around at the lobby with a wonderstruck look in them. Justin tickled her to try to bring her back and she laughed.

"COME *ON* GIRL! MOVE!"

Justin's normal hyper-energetic state seemed to have been amped up a couple of notches to another never-before-seen level— and they hadn't even gotten into the parks yet! Lani snapped back into reality and headed off in the direction of the elevator without saying a word to Justin and Raoul. Her sudden departure was so unexpected that the two of them had to jog in order to catch up with her.

The days that followed were more magical than even Lani could have ever dreamed. The world that Walt Disney had imagined truly *was* its own world. Here time seemed to fly but not matter at the same time. Since they were staying on the Disney World property, they never had to leave the fantasy that had been created for them. No skyscrapers. No housing. No supermarkets. No malls. Nothing but Disney as far as the eye could see for all forty-seven square miles. This escape from reality suited the writer in Lani because it was like walking through another author's book, and it provided inspiration for her own.

It was day five when they ventured into Disney's Hollywood Studios. They raced around the park, trying to get a taste of everything. They darted from the *Indiana Jones Stunt Spectacular*, to the *Lights, Motors, Action! Extreme Stunt Show*, whipped through *The Great Movie Ride*, *The Twilight Zone Tower of Terror*, and *Rock 'n' Roller Coaster*, starring Aerosmith, in no time at all thanks to Lani reminding them about the "Taylor Johnson strategy for navigating theme parks," combined with using fast passes. As the day began to draw to a close, they found themselves running once again toward the Tower of Terror for what would be the fifth time that day, mostly because neither Lani nor Raoul could resist Justin's begging them to do so. It was completely dark outside already, but they knew where they were going as they rushed beneath the streetlights of Disney's Sunset Boulevard.

"Come on! There's no line right now! Run you guys!! Faster!!!"

Justin was already thirty yards in front of them. Raoul spoke to Lani in an out-of-breath voice as they ran.

"I think... I think Justin has been lying to us... He's not really human... He's just been *masquerading* as a human for twenty-two years... He's... the energizer bunny!"

Lani laughed happily and ran with Raoul through the rope-lined maze of the empty Tower of Terror line to catch up with Justin who had already reached the small queue. He turned to look impatiently at them, tapping his watchless wrist to indicate the slowness of their approach. When they had still not come fast enough for his liking, he pulled out his brand new golden Mickey Mouse pocket watch that he had purchased at Mouse Gears in Epcot, when Lani had bought the identical watch for Taylor, and swung it back and forth like a pendulum to emphasize the fact that time was passing. When they finally reached Justin, he put the watch back in his pocket and shook his head. Lani ignored him and pulled out her cell phone to make a quick call before they got on the ride— again.

"Hello?"

"Hey, Chicky! How's Hawai'i?"

"Oh hi, Lani! It's wonderful!"

"Are you seriously getting on the phone *now*? You just called Taylor *and* your mom *and* your dad *and* Jenna like five minutes ago! Who *is* that?!" Justin interrupted.

"Shhhhh! I happen to love my family, and it wasn't five minutes ago. I just want to make sure she's having fun. I'll be off in plenty of time to get on the ride. Sorry, Kendra, you were saying?"

"You're talking to *Kendra*?!"

Lani held up her right index finger to indicate that Justin was to wait.

"No problem, Lani! Tell Justin I said 'grow up,' ha ha! No for realz though, we are staying at this to-die-for place at Turtle Bay on O'ahu. It's these ritzy ocean villas on the north shore next to the hotel, and guess what?" Kendra didn't wait for Lani to guess. Lani smiled widely as Kendra blurted, "We have our own three-bedroom villa! These things are like *right on the beach!* No seriously, we can just walk outside and poof! There you are! And you know *I* claimed the master bedroom because it has an awesome ocean view!"

"*Stole* is more like it!" Lani heard a voice interrupt Kendra.

"Shut up, Jonn-Jonn. Can I help it if I was born a princess? No!" Kendra laughed. "Anyway, Lani, it feels like a complete tropical getaway to our own private island out where we're staying! I wish you could see it! There's even a helicopter ride you can walk to! We're gonna check that out tomorrow. Oh, and we're at the Polynesian Cultural Center right now— there just aren't words enough to describe how cool it is! Sorry, here I am bragging about my trip. How's Disney World going?"

"No problem," Lani giggled. "I am glad you are having fun. And Disney World is fantastic! Everything I ever hoped for! Justin is as hyper as ever, only more so, if you can believe it! We're in line to ride the Tower of Terror for the *fifth* time."

"Wow! Justin *more* hyper? That must be scary. Five times? Are you crazy?! I don't even think I could make it through once!"

"Ha ha, I know, right?"

"Get off the phone, Lani!"

"Let her finish, Justin."

Justin ignored Raoul's suggestion and reached for Lani's phone, trying to pry it out of her hands as Lani struggled to finish the conversation gracefully.

"We're about to go in now, Chicky! I gotta go before Justin kills my phone! You have a great time in Hawai'i!"

"So iritz that boy! Anyway, have fun! Bye!"

"Bye!"

"FINALLY!"

"Justin!" Lani exclaimed.

"What? Look, they're opening the doors! Let's go already!"

Lani laughed as she and Raoul followed Justin excitedly through the staging area where the Twilight Zone themed movie once again told the story of the legendary characters who had supposedly disappeared while riding the passenger lift in this same hotel decades before. Once the movie ended, the three friends hurried through the ancient looking boiler room and waited behind a yellow line painted on the floor, outside the service elevator doors, where a creepy looking bellhop stood and began to speak.

"Ladies and gentlemen, a warm and gracious welcome to The Hollywood Tower Hotel. In just a few moments, your elevator will come to take you to your rooms. When the elevator arrives, we will board one row at a time."

The "ding" of the elevator arriving rang out. The doors opened and the bellhop guided the guests in row by row. Lani, Justin, and Raoul were guided to the front row on the right side. Lani sat down between Justin and Raoul and nervously buckled her seatbelt. She felt her heart beating fast with dread, despite her multiple times on this ride— or maybe because of them. She pulled up on the yellow strap as instructed by the bellhop to make sure she was secured in and listened as he continued.

"On this elevator, we ask that there be no eating, drinking, smoking, video taping, or flash photography because we have several movie stars staying with us and they wish to have their privacy. Also, we ask that you hang on to any loose items that you might wish to keep such as hats, glasses, cameras... and small *children*."

The bellhop glanced enthusiastically at the few frightened kids in the elevator car, with a twisted smile.

"Are there any questions? No? Well, if you need anything, just scream. Ah, ha, ha, ha, ha! We do hope you enjoy your stay here. Please feel free to *drop* in again."

The bellhop reversed out of the car with a quiet maniacal chuckle, still smiling fiendishly as the doors closed in front of him— preventing any escape. The elevator lurched up and stopped, opening in the Twilight Zone and then closing again. Once more the elevator lurched upward and stopped abruptly. This time when the doors opened, the car moved forward! Lani was always both amazed and horrified at this feat of engineering, no matter how many times she experienced it. It ripped any semblance of safety away and threw it right out the window because elevator cars weren't supposed to do that!

After twisting and turning through the dark, the ride reached the familiar point on the thirteenth story, where they open the doors to the outside world for you to see just how high you are right before they drop you repeatedly. Lani listened carefully to the clanking sound of the ride shifting into place. She clamped her hands onto Raoul's and Justin's arms and held her breath as she waited for what was coming. Less than a second later the ride plunged them into the darkness below. Rod Serling's voice echoed through the elevator car as it finally made its way toward the exit of The Tower of Terror.

"A warm welcome back to those of you who made it, and a friendly word of warning— something you won't find in any guidebook. The next time you check into a deserted hotel on the dark side of Hollywood, make sure you know just what kind of vacancy you're filling... or you may find yourself a permanent resident of... The Twilight Zone."

The lights came back up and the doors opened— revealing three empty seats in the front row.

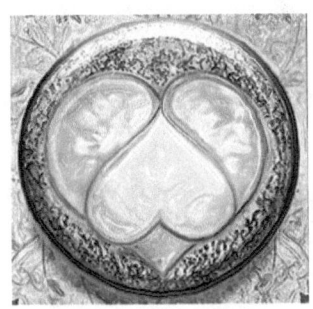

ALOHA MEANS... WHAT?

"Who was that on the phone, Kendra?" asked a tall boy with blonde hair and hazel eyes.

"Lani," Kendra said, as she put her cell phone back in her pocket and pulled her long golden brown hair, which fell to the middle of her back, up into a high ponytail.

"Oh cool. They must be having fun, huh? I was just talking to Kara."

"Really? I haven't heard from her in ages. How is she?"

Kendra shaded her eyes from the blazing Hawaiian sun so that she could look up into Erik's face as he replied.

"Oh, she's good. She's in France looking for her mom right now. She thinks she might have a new lead."

"What?! Are you stinkin' kidding me, Erik?! Alone?! Is she nuts?! Hasn't she seen the movie *Taken*?! What an idiot!"

"What?"

"Oh, never mind. It's a movie I watched on our ClearPlay. Let's just say that it didn't end well for those girls to be traveling on their own."

Kendra shook her head in disbelief. She could understand *why* Kara would feel the need to go search for her mom. After all,

Kara was an only child, and although her father spoiled her, her mother was a self-absorbed model who had not taken to being a mother at all— mostly because she missed her glamorous single life. One day, when Kara was sixteen years old, her mother ran off with a French male model and was never heard from again. But for a gorgeous, five-foot-nothing, twenty-two-year-old girl to go to Paris *alone*, on a whim, to follow a handful of clues in hopes of finding her mother again— Kendra had always known that Kara wasn't very wise, but this was stupid even for her.

"How's Lani?" inquired Erik.

"Oh she's good— probably worn out though. Justin is dragging her and Raoul around like a maniac. They're on the Tower of Terror right now for the FIFTH time! Crazy!"

"That sounds awesome! I wish I was there…"

"Well *I* am *much* more interested in being *here*. The Polynesian Cultural Center is awesome! I have always loved learning about other cultures and this place really brings the islands to life! I mean, if we were at Disney World, all we would be doing is going on rides— but here, we are learning about the way people actually live and about their heritage."

"Epcot teaches you about other cultures and stuff…"

"Shut up, Erik! I don't want to hear any more about stupid Florida! We're in Hawai'i! Besides that, you can really feel the spirit of Aloha that they keep talking about. They might think they are in a magical kingdom but you can tell that the Islands of the Pacific are a *real* magical place. Oh look! They have a canoe ride!"

"I want to go on a canoe!"

"Let's go find out where to get on!"

"You guys go ahead, I need to run to the men's room," Kendra's brother Jonn said suddenly.

"NOW?"

"I'll catch up with you, I have a cell phone you know, it's not that hard," he said, waving it in the air as he walked away and rolled his eyes at his sister.

"Fine Jonn-Jonn! But you're gonna miss out! Sheesh that boy! And that's my *favorite* brother!"

Kendra watched as her little brother ran off in search of a restroom. His normally tan skin was even darker, due to the few days they had already been in Hawai'i. Kendra felt a little jealous of his tan. Their mother was Caucasian, and their father was Filipino, which had given all of her seven brothers a nice blended caramel brown skin color, making her the only fair-skinned child in the family. She knew she had been adopted after the first three children had turned out to be boys, but despite the fact that they treated her as if she had been born into the family, the inability to blend in with her brothers always made her feel a little left out.

As Jonn disappeared from sight, Kendra turned with Erik to look at the map of the park. They discovered that the canoe tours loaded passengers at the end of the meandering lagoon nearest the IMAX Theater, and set off together.

Meanwhile, in the Forest of Kar, Jharate awoke to the sound of birds chirping happily in the trees. It was a new day and the forest was slowly coming to life. The light had barely appeared in its blue-greenish hue, and his eyes had to adjust to be able to see. No one else in the camp of nearly three-dozen people had risen yet. He scanned the area and noticed his cousin, Arante, with her back against a tree, asleep at her post. It had been her turn to watch the camp. Jharate knew it was very unlike her to make such a mistake— however, the last few days had been exceptionally trying and he knew she was exhausted.

Jharate would normally have been quite angry for this offense, but at the moment he was simply glad that she was there. Arante had definitely been blessed with great beauty and a strong resemblance to the rest of their family— and that made him feel somewhat less alone. With her rich dark-caramel-colored skin, her brown eyes that were so dark they were almost black, and her perfect ebony ringlets that fell just below her shoulder blades when she let her hair down, she looked very much like his father's twin sister. Currently, Arante's hair was in a neat ponytail with the ringlets cascading around her neck and shoulders.

Jharate mused over his cousin's unique sense of style. Arante was always dressed ready for battle, but with a decidedly feminine flair— to the point of sometimes being impractical, to his thinking. The sleeves of her white cotton shirt flowed gracefully to her wrists in a pirate style. She wore a black leather corset over her shirt with lacing in the center of the front and the back. Black formfitting pants showed under a black knee-length skirt that consisted of many one-inch leather strips. Each strip came to a point at the bottom where a gold diamond-shaped stud served as a weight to make them hang properly. The skirt moved as she did. Long, high-heeled, black leather boots came up to her knees and completed her outfit.

A tooled black leather sheath was attached to her upper leg and held her jewel-encrusted, golden-handled dagger, which was usually concealed by her skirt. However, at the moment the dagger was partially visible, as some of the leather strips had fallen to the side. Her matching leather quiver was still on her back, with the strap over her shoulder, and her bow was in hand, ready for trouble— had she been awake.

Jharate decided not to wake her. There was no point now. He was awake and would not sleep again. He would watch the camp. Jharate moved slowly, packing up his things so quietly that one would never know he was there. He rolled up his makeshift bed that he had used for the night and packed his leather-bound journal back inside the bag where his few other cherished belongings were.

The only clothes Jharate had now were on his back. A simple V-necked, short-sleeved, linen beige shirt was partially visible under a short-sleeved dark-brown leather vest, which was open in the front. The thick leather that made up his vest protected a few inches of his shoulders and covered the very short shirtsleeves entirely, but left his arms free, as he preferred to keep his arms unencumbered by armor, or even by long sleeves, during battle. Instead he wore leather wrist guards that reached from his wrists almost to his elbows. The vest also covered most of the matching leather belt, which held his scabbard, and brown pants covered all but the toes of his dark-brown leather boots. Although his outfit was monochromatic and quite cohesive, each item varied slightly in shade and texture.

Images of the hectic moments that had led him here flashed through Jharate's mind. The sounds of the battle lines retreating toward the castle and the screams of men dying as they sacrificed themselves to give others a chance to get away were burned into his memory. The blurring of the hallways as he ran with Arante and the others, at his father's command, felt as dizzying in the reliving of it as it had the first time. He remembered the feeling of trying to race an hourglass that he could not see and hoping they would escape before the baleful sands ran out, as he hurriedly organized and coordinated his people to ensure they had all the essential supplies necessary for their evacuation and survival— including a large amount of gold and jewels. He remembered the aching feeling as he left the items dearest to his heart behind, with the hope that perhaps someday he could return home to reclaim them. And that was nothing compared to the wrenching feeling of leaving his father behind and the panic of not knowing where his brother was.

As Jharate had saddled his varsin, he had looked up expectantly at the doors to the stables every few moments for Khanye. Finally, when all of the varsins had been saddled and all of the supplies had been loaded, Jharate had mounted his own varsin to take the lead. He had spurred his chestnut brown steed on and galloped away from the castle, towards the Forest of Kar at full speed, with a pit in his stomach, as he tried to comfort himself. He had left the last two varsins, which personally belonged to Khanye and Sarana, behind in their stalls, despite the danger of the varsins falling into the hands of the enemy— hoping that they would be behind him shortly and that they would reunite in the forest at their rendezvous point.

Jharate tried not to think of home, but his efforts proved useless. He missed his family. He was now the only surviving member of the Inihma royal line because his father, Karahn, had four married sisters and no brothers— and so Karahn had been the only male heir. *My father. If only I could have your guidance now!*

Karahn had always felt that knowledge of one's roots grounded one's mind and soul in the power of "the ancestors." Because of this, he had taught Jharate everything he knew of the Trisaknen history and culture. Jharate thought that maybe if he recalled the things his father had taught him all his life, now in this horrible moment of crisis, that perhaps the ties to the past would help him find a way to hold onto the future.

Jharate knew that he had the blood of two strong cultures running through his veins to help him through this, the worst of times. His father was Kelamosan by blood, as the Trisaknen royal line always had been, ever since an adventurous group of Kelamosans settled previously uninhabited Trisakne, millennia ago. Jharate remembered his father teaching him about those first settlers and how they had been a diverse people, with their main culture being a mix of the Native Kelamosans and Alamean Islanders who had left their islands to come to Kelamosa. They were joined later by immigrants from Tofan. Jharate had been taught that this unique mix created a blended, but very strong cultural identity for Trisakne. Jharate's mother, Karsenia, was a descendant of those who had come from Tofan, so both sides of Jharate's family could be traced back to the beginnings of Trisakne itself.

His mother had died inexplicably twenty years ago when Jharate was just five years old. No one knew what had happened to her. Her body had been found near a river in Trisakne— unbruised, unbroken, and she had obviously not drowned.

There was not much Jharate remembered about his mother— only that she was beautiful and that her love for his younger brother and for himself was more than any he had ever felt in his life, past or present. Khanye had been only two years old when Karsenia had died, and so he had asked Jharate about her constantly, desperately hoping to share the treasured glimpses of memory his elder brother had of their mother. And although she had been gone for most of his life, Jharate still missed her every day.

Jharate's mind moved back to the sharpest and most current heartbreak— the loss of his father. He knew that the task to measure up to Karahn's legacy was monumental, and he also knew that it was his duty to do so. His father had been a great leader and a brilliant military commander whose keen mind for strategy had kept their kingdom from falling for so long. He had fought valiantly to drive back the attacks against Trisakne from the beginning, as the first Kingdoms of Tofan, Kresar, and Lanas began to fall, and had continued to fight even after Zenastra and Kelamosa fell, leaving Trisakne surrounded and cut off from any outside help or supplies for five more years. Jharate's first challenge would be to reclaim the kingdom that had just been stolen from his father.

But beyond being a gifted military strategist, Karahn had the righteousness of a saint. He had kept the kingdom strong internally as he ruled with justice and fairness. Even more impressive was that he had been as good a father as he had been a king. He had taught his sons everything that they needed to know, not only to become great leaders, but also to become great men. The challenge to live up to that birthright would be a lifelong pursuit.

Not long after Jharate and his people had been forced to abandon the noble varsins and continue on foot into a denser part of the Forest of Kar, Jharate had watched helplessly as a vision showed his father dying by the sword, in a daring effort to help his sons and a remnant of loyal subjects escape into the forest so that they could make a run for Destavnia. Jharate felt wracked with guilt as he remembered that vision. If only he had stayed to fight by his father's side... Jharate sighed. Had he stayed, he would have died with his father, and his father's sacrifice would have been in vain. Cruelly, that same vision had also given Jharate hope, as he witnessed Khanye getting out of the castle in the last moments of their father's life. Jharate had felt sure in that instant that Khanye and Sarana would make it to their varsins.

However, less than eight hours after Jharate had received that first harrowing vision, he had also been forced to watch the death of his only sibling. Both visions had continued to plague Jharate in the days that had since passed. Jharate felt so alone. He had no time to deal with these agonizing losses. How could he? He had been on the run for days. He and the other refugees had been forced to make camp in the great forest every night— barely surviving on what food they could hunt or gather, as the kitchens were located at the end of the castle that had already been breached the night of the fall.

Jharate's culture had rich customs surrounding death, which helped the grieving to find expression for the grief inside them. These rituals were a luxury that he could not afford now. Not only was there no time, but he also lacked the resources to perform them. The loneliness in his heart consumed him. He felt as if he would never be made whole again. However, he knew he must go on, for though the battle was lost for Trisakne, the War for the Kingdoms was still raging— and he must aid Destavnia in that fight.

Jharate had grown up with war surrounding him all his life. Karahn had trained him well in the skills of a warrior and thus he was skilled with all weapons— however, from an early age the sword had called to him. It felt at home in his hands as if it were not simply an object, but rather an extension of his body. He wore it always at his side in a leather sheath. He had never been bested in any competition, or in any battle either— although that did not stop him from feeling powerless at this moment. He had been unable to save those closest to him. What good was all his skill if he could not protect the ones he loved most?

A sudden ear-splitting bang came from the shadows surrounding him. Jharate jolted from his thoughts, drew his sword and reeled around, now completely alert. His eyes carefully swept the area and his ears analyzed all around him in order to discover the source of the noise, but he saw nothing.

The noise had also startled Arante awake. In a single swift motion she stood up, pulled out an arrow, and armed her bow. She stood near her cousin, tensed and ready to let the arrow fly, peering into the early morning haze. Several others of Jharate's camp had been shaken awake by the noise as well, and jumped to their feet, weapons ready. They stood there facing an invisible foe, waiting for another sound to give up the position of their hidden enemy.

Kendra and Erik jumped onto the last row of seats in the canoe just before the guide pushed it away from the dock and they glided into the greenish water of the winding lagoon. The guide spoke to them in an energetic tone, welcoming them with a great big "ALOOOOHA!"

All the tourists joined in repeating "ALOOOOHA!" back to him. The handsome guide was a very strong and tall young man with chocolate brown skin and an island accent. He was dressed in a bright blue aloha shirt, a black sulu that covered his knees, and black sandals with a strap around the back of his ankles. He stood on the stern of the canoe, and his dark bronze muscles flexed as he pushed a long sturdy pole down to the bottom of the lagoon, propelling the canoe forward like a gondola.

"My name is Kalepo and I am from a place far, far away from here, called Samoa. I came here to study at the Brigham Young University of Hawai'i and I work here at the Polynesian Cultural Center to pay the bills." He paused for a moment and resumed with a joking tone, "My major is math, with a minor in canoe pushing."

The tourists laughed as Kalepo smiled and continued to push the canoe forward.

"On the right you will see the Samoan Village. That is where I come from. Actually, not that village there— the islands it represents."

Everyone laughed again and Kalepo looked as though he were trying to keep a straight face, but failing.

"And now we're going under a bridge. Please, remain seated, and don't panic if I fall off. The canoe will keep going."

The tourists laughed again, and a few of them found themselves ducking with him, despite the fact that it was tall enough that anyone sitting wouldn't even come close to hitting it. A couple of the tourists, who realized this, reached their hands up and tried to touch the bottom of the bridge, with only the tallest among them succeeding.

"Don't touch the bridge!" Kalepo said urgently, making the tourists who had reached for it jerk their hands back quickly. "It will get mad," he finished with a laugh.

The tourists laughed heartily at the joke and he smiled widely as they passed completely under the bridge.

"You see this plant over here? You know what they call this plant?"

"What?" asked a couple of the tourists.

"I don't know. I was asking you," he said. "You guys have the smart phones— tell them to be smart and give you the answer."

Kendra leaned close to Erik and whispered in his ear, "This guy is hysterical."

"Totally," Erik answered with a grin.

"Listen up, my friends," Kalepo began, "You see this bridge we're coming up to? That one right there that connects Aotearoa with Tonga— it's very low. That means you need to duck. I don't want to have to take any of you to the emergency room because you didn't listen to me."

They all obeyed and as they finished passing under the bridge, everyone sat up again and the tour continued— but with two less passengers than they had started with.

"Hey! Where'd the two back here go?" Kalepo asked.

The other tourists in the canoe seemed confused but looked behind them instinctively.

"I don't think there was anyone in that row," one of the tourists answered.

"Yeah, I think we were the last ones on," said another in the second to the last row.

Kalepo shook his head a little and looked down at the empty seats. There was no one there, but there had been no splash, no thud, no nothing. The wake of the canoe behind him was the only pattern in the water, and they couldn't have just disappeared.

"Forgive me, I think I've been in the sun too long today. Anyway, where was I? Oh yes, see that canoe coming up on the right? It's a Maori war canoe, so you better behave and say you like Maoris. Everyone say it with me, 'I like Maoris!'"

"I like Maoris," said many of the tourists, laughing.

"We like you too! Ha, ha!" called another tall young man who was standing by the war canoe.

All the tourists laughed harder. Kalepo proceeded with the tour and tried to forget about his minor hallucination. As soon as he finished, he gave the canoe to Sione, one of his co-workers, so that Sione could take the next group of tourists around the lagoon, while Kalepo left to get some much needed water and some shade.

Touring Paris and enjoying the lights of the city near the Eiffel Tower, Kara and her new friend, Henri, laughed happily as they walked down the street, hand in hand. They split for just a moment in order to go around a tree that was in their pathway. Henri quickly popped around the tree to the other side to smile at Kara— but he didn't see her there. He rounded the tree several times and looked up and down the dark and nearly empty streets.

"Kara? Kara? Where have you gone? KARA?!"

He continued to frantically call her out her name as he now ran through the street, alone and distraught.

The band of rebels heard another loud crack, like a cannon being fired. It echoed through the surrounding hills so that it was hard to determine where it had come from. This time, however, they noticed a flash of rainbow-colored light far away in the forest. Jharate and his party set off quickly in that direction, leaving only a handful of people to guard the camp.

Six people lay unconscious on the forest floor in near-darkness as the light of the coming dawn struggled to reach the clearing. They were arranged on the ground in two distinct groups. One was comprised of two girls and one boy, and the other of two boys and one girl— all in their early twenties.

A pair of glittering green eyes peered at them suspiciously from the shadows between the trees and watched intently as the girl, amongst the two boys, began to stir. The awakening girl's blue eyes opened and she blinked slowly as she pushed herself up into a sitting position. Her eyes widened as she looked at the tall trees surrounding her.

As the young woman with the blue eyes awoke, she surveyed the surrounding forest and wondered if she were somehow dreaming. *Where am I? Why is it so hard to move? Why is the sun coming up?* She looked to her right and saw the two young men next to her on the ground, unconscious. She gasped as she recognized them.

"What on Earth?" the woman asked as she moved closer to them and quickly started shaking one of the men awake. "Come on, Justin! Wake up!"

The glittering green eyes that had been watching her carefully retreated into the thickness of the dense forest before anyone could discover their presence.

"Five more minutes, mom…"

"Wake up, Justin!"

"Okay, okay, I'm up! What the—?"

Justin rubbed his eyes and looked again, as if rubbing them would change what he saw. He no longer looked sleepy.

"What the heck happened?" Justin asked.

"I don't know... One moment we were on the Tower of Terror and the next... Where are we anyway?" Lani asked.

Justin rubbed the back of his head and winced.

"I don't know. It appears to be a forest of some kind. Raoul, wake up!"

Raoul jolted awake as Justin slapped his back with an open palm.

"What? Whoa... Where are we?"

"That's our question, Mr. Eagle Scout," Justin said. "Where do you think we are?"

"I don't know... and hey! You're an Eagle Scout too, and that's a *cool* thing. Why are you acting like it's weird or something? It's not weird. I'm not weird. But the fact that we're in some eerie forest *is* weird."

"Just kidding, Raoul, just kidding. You can relax now."

"How can I relax when we don't know where we—"

Raoul broke off as a groan came from about ten yards away. The three friends whipped around toward the noise. Lani jumped back slightly, wide-eyed, as she saw another girl staggering to her feet.

"Kendra?!" Lani exclaimed as Justin, Raoul, and she ran over to Kendra and finally noticed the other two people who were still lying on the ground nearby.

"And Kara?!" Justin added. "And who's that other dude?"

"What are you guys doing here?" Raoul asked.

Kendra answered while she and Justin shook Erik and Kara awake.

"I don't know what we're doing here, and this 'dude' is Erik. I met him on a study abroad trip in Italy and found out that he lived like only fifteen minutes away from us in California the whole time!"

"Nice to meet you," Erik said, with a groggy voice as he sat up and offered his hand to Justin.

Justin shook Erik's hand and helped him up as he answered, "Nice to meet you too."

"The last thing I remember," Kendra began, "I got off the phone with Lani, and Erik got off the phone with Kara... and we were on the canoe tour at the Polynesian Cultural Center and then... we were here... How is this possible?"

Lani answered Kendra in a placid tone, hoping to help her friends stay calm, "I don't know. We were on the Tower of Terror and then just like you said— we were here."

"Henri and I were by the Eiffel Tower last I knew, and he was about to show me where the Paris Opera House was..."

Kara started to cry.

"This is way bizarre guys," was all that Erik could manage to say, as he looked around with wide eyes.

"I know! I'm really starting to freak out here!" Kara squeaked.

"I know it's hard, but try to stay calm, Kara. Nothing good can come of freaking out. Now let's think... You guys were in Hawai'i. Kara was in France," Lani put her arm around Kara and then indicated Justin and Raoul as she continued, "and we were in Florida. Now somehow... Justin, can I see your watch please?" Justin handed her his watch. "Thank you. Now somehow, according to Justin's watch here, in a grand total of maybe about fifteen minutes from the time Kendra and I hung up the phone, when we were six thousand miles apart... somehow in that small amount of time we all ended up in the same place... wherever this is."

"I blame aliens!" shouted Justin as he began to laugh hysterically.

Lani shook her head and smiled slightly as she handed his watch back to him. Laughing was always Justin's response to stress. He laughed when things were scary, he laughed in the doctors office when he got shots, he simply laughed whenever things became too much.

"This is no time for jokes!" Raoul's quick retort and very serious tone made Lani want to laugh as well, just because it was *so* Raoul.

"Sorrrrreee!" Justin exclaimed.

"This really doesn't seem to be possible. Maybe one of us is dreaming. OUCH!" Kendra screamed as Erik pinched her, with a smirk on his face.

"You're welcome," Erik grinned.

"Did I *ask* you to pinch me? I don't think so, Erik! Anyways it was a better guess than *ALIENS*!"

"Whoa, calm down," Erik said, slightly scared.

"Hey can you guys do this with your fingers?" Raoul asked, making his right pinky finger and left thumb point the same direction with all the other fingers balled into a fist and then switching abruptly to make his right thumb and left pinky point the same direction with all the other fingers pulled into a fist and repeating the process over and over and faster and faster.

"Stop doing that, Raoul!" Kendra demanded.

"HEY! My aliens theory is more plausible than your dream idea now, Kendra!"

Lani sighed. She had half hoped Raoul's distraction technique would work, but deep down she had known it would not. Kendra, Erik, Justin, and Kara were now arguing hopelessly while Raoul tried to break up the fight. Lani tried to gently pull

Justin back, but he wouldn't budge. When that failed, she tried to quietly guide Raoul out of the fray, but he too could not be moved. Lani had tried to assist in Raoul's peacekeeping efforts between Kendra and Justin enough times before to know better than to try to do anything more about it now.

She exhaled softly in defeat. Anytime Kendra and Justin went at it, Kara would get involved, and then the situation was virtually unstoppable. Apparently their newer friend Erik didn't mind getting involved either, as he was being just as loud as the rest of them. Raoul was tense, as he always was in these situations, while he tried to remind everyone that they were all friends and that fighting did nothing. Lani sighed once more and walked a little ways away to look around the forest as the battle raged on between Kendra and Justin.

"HOW IS *ALIENS* MORE PLAUSIBLE THAN A DREAM?"

"WELL WE ALL KNOW YOU'RE AWAKE NOW, DON'T WE? I'M SURE YOU'RE A MUCH NICER PERSON IN YOUR *DREAMS*— I DON'T KNOW! MAYBE THE ALIENS WANTED A BUNCH OF ADOPTED KIDS TO RUN EXPERIMENTS ON!"

"GROW UP, JUSTIN! YOU'RE SO STUPID! YOU AND ME AND LANI ARE THE ONLY ADOPTED ONES SO THAT MAKES NO SENSE AT ALL!"

"NO YOU GROW UP! ALIENS MAKE MORE SENSE THAN ANYTHING!"

"THIS IS PROBABLY ALL *YOUR* FAULT!"

"YEAH— I SECRETLY MOVED US ALL THOUSANDS OF MILES IN TWO SECONDS JUST TO GET YOU MAD!"

"IT WOULDN'T BE THE FIRST TIME YOU HAD A DUMB IDEA!"

"THINK ABOUT IT! HOW COULD I *DO* THAT? I DON'T HAVE MAGICAL POWERS!"

"UNLESS YOU COUNT BEING ANNOYING AS ONE, YOU'RE RIGHT!"

"DON'T EVEN GO THERE KENDRA!"

Lani heard them yelling as she continued to explore. Kara and Erik kept supporting their side with "Yeah!" and "Uh-huh." It was the girls vs. the boys. Lani could also hear Raoul, in the loudest quiet voice he had, saying things like, "Come on you guys, stop arguing." She was astonished by their complete lack of curiosity.

Their voices became more distant as Lani ventured farther into the woods. The light was growing stronger now and she knew she would be able to find them again. Even if she did get lost, she could always just follow the noise of the argument.

Back in the clearing, her friends were so caught up in their boisterous bickering that they were completely unaware of being methodically surrounded by a group of people who had weapons ready and were hidden skillfully behind the trees, logs, and bushes that encompassed the small glade. They watched carefully while the strangers in front of them continued to fight. A slight movement in the trees caught the eye of the leader of the armed group and caused him to look away from the five strangely attired people. He briefly saw a young female heading off deeper into the woods and left quietly to follow her.

A tall woman with a ponytail of ebony ringlets reached for his arm to stop him, but he was gone too quickly. She sighed and returned her attention to the loud strangers. She signaled to her people with her hands and then jumped out from behind the tree that was concealing her, with her bow drawn back, ready to fire three arrows at once.

"Surrender!"

At Arante's command, the others of Jharate's party came out of hiding in a circle around the friends, weapons drawn. The dispute stopped immediately as the five stunned and now silent friends slowly raised their hands in the air. Justin's mouth was open. The eyes of the others were wide, and they all took a few slow steps back from the people who surrounded them, and huddled together.

"Tie their hands together and take them to camp! Once you have them there, bind their feet as well. Move out!"

Arante's cool clear voice resonated in everyone's ears. The five friends remained silent and cast uncertain sideways glances at each other as their arms were pulled down in front of them and bound tightly. Once all of their hands had been bound, they worked hard not to stumble as they were marched off in the direction of the camp. Arante, however, did not follow her people. She turned and sprinted off into the trees to go after Jharate.

Lani froze in place as she realized that the perfect silence of the forest around her meant that the arguing had stopped. She turned around abruptly to go back to her friends, and jumped at the sight of a strange man standing right in front of her. Her hand flew to her heart and she inhaled sharply. He had been so quiet that she had not heard him at all.

Her eyes were wide, and every muscle in her body was tense as she regarded him—but then she saw his face. It was still too dark to be certain, but she was sure that she knew him from somewhere—but where? It wasn't possible. She didn't even know where she was, but she did know that she had never been here before. Lani was equally positive that she had never met him prior to this moment, and yet there was something very familiar about him. Her muscles relaxed and her face softened— her eyes stared intently into his and the corners of her mouth turned up slightly.

The man had stopped dead in his tracks as well. He looked surprised that she had caught him. He said nothing— he simply stared at her with a flat expression. His eyes watched her every reaction as if searching her features for something that would identify her. She wondered what he was thinking or feeling as she stood there, still staring at him. It felt to her as if the whole world had stopped around them. Neither one moved or made a sound.

Lani let out a frightened gasp as she felt a hand grab her left arm and pull it behind her at the same instant that a knife was pressed carefully against her throat. Her muscles tensed up as she tried to keep perfectly still, tightening her neck to try to keep it away from the blade, and her breathing continued on in strained shallow inhales and exhales.

"You ought to be more careful, cousin. You are the last of your line and we cannot afford to have you killed in the forest."

The woman's voice was extremely cold and full of irritation. Lani remained as still as possible as she looked toward the man, with a pleading gaze. The man looked away from her and turned his focus to the woman whom Lani could not see. His expression hardened and his jaw set firmly as he addressed her.

"I had the situation under control. I am my father's son, after all. Take her to the camp with the others, cousin. I will meet you there."

"As you wish, Your Highness."

The man seemed to ignore the woman's angry tone. He turned suddenly and silently vanished into the trees. His disappearance was so quick that Lani thought his exit was more like that of a ghost, rather than that of a man. As the knife lowered from her throat, Lani stared at the spot where the man had stood. Her mind wandered back to the moment they had just shared. She wasn't sure what it meant, or even exactly what had happened. It had felt peaceful and exhilarating, quiet and explosive, soothing and yet awakening! It hadn't felt possible at all, and yet, it had happened.

"Move!"

Arante's forceful tone brought Lani's mind back to her current situation. She had been so caught up in her daydreams that she hadn't even noticed that Arante had already tied her hands behind her back. She wondered what her fate would be, but for some reason that she couldn't explain, she was not particularly worried. She had a feeling that whoever that man was, he would not hurt her.

A DASH OF STOCKHOLM SYNDROME

L ani and the others sat in complete silence against a fallen tree, with their hands and feet bound tightly. Terrifying thoughts galloped through their minds, which manifested in their worried expressions as they shifted nervously. Lani, however, was quite still, with a serene expression on her face and a far-off look in her eyes— her thoughts focused on the man she had come across in the forest. She was dying to know who he was and trying to understand why she was so sure she knew him. There was something mysterious and wonderful about him that she simply could not figure out.

Arante sat nearby, keeping a watchful eye on them at all times, sharpening her dagger methodically all the while. Her expression was flat and stern, and her eyes held a promise to harm the first one with the audacity to cause trouble. However, every once in a while, her face seemed to soften slightly into a quizzical gaze as she looked at Erik. Erik hoped he wasn't imagining things, but every so often he swore he caught a slight smile on her beautiful face that he barely even dared to dream was for him.

Time passed by slowly, and nearly felt as if it were stuck at times. The trees above were tall and thick, and the breeze gently whispered through them. Every now and again a leaf would fall, floating down to the ground slowly— more slowly than seemed possible. The sun was high up in the sky and though the canopy of branches and leaves shaded the area sufficiently enough to make it comfortable, there was now adequate light to see well. Two guards suddenly appeared from another part of the camp and spoke to Arante, pointing at Lani in a definitive manner.

"What do you think they want?"

Justin's whispered question went unanswered. Lost in her own thoughts, Lani did not hear him. Her brain would not stop thinking about the man from the forest. She flinched a little and looked up at Arante as she cut the ropes that held her feet— she hadn't even noticed her approach. Arante pointed her dagger at Lani.

"You! Don't try anything or, so help me, I *will* kill you."

Arante stood up, turned to the guards, and gestured towards Lani.

"She's all yours. Take her away."

"NO!" screamed Justin in unison with Raoul as they both lunged forward in protest.

"Over my dead body!" Justin added.

"That can be arranged," Arante said, coolly turning her dagger from Lani to Justin.

"No! I'll go. He won't give you any more trouble."

Lani gave Justin a pointed and pleading look. He slumped back against the log again. His countenance fell and his shoulders drooped as he looked down aimlessly at the ground and then up again at Lani— his brow knit into deep worried lines.

"I'll be *fine*. I promise. You two just stay calm and don't get killed."

Justin and Raoul nodded slowly as they watched helplessly. The two guards each grabbed one of Lani's upper arms and lifted her to her feet. Arante sliced the ropes, which had bound Lani's hands behind her back, with her dagger, muttering angrily about the sanity of her cousin, and then marched back to where she had been sitting. She began sharpening her blade once more, but this time the repetitive motion was quicker, more vigorous, and slightly less controlled.

The guards held onto Lani's arms tightly. They pushed and pulled her out of the main area of the camp and through the trees for a short distance until they came across a large supply tent. One of the men let go of her and opened the flap of the tent, while the other pushed her inside. She staggered a little as she tried not to lose her balance and the tent flap shut behind her.

Lani blinked as her eyes tried to adjust to the minimal light given off by a bronze, glass-paneled lantern that lit the darkened space. As things slowly came into focus, she saw the man she had met in the forest. He was sitting there just like— just like the man in her dream on the plane! That was it! She knew him from her *dream*. It was an odd feeling to meet someone you had known only in a dream— like deja vu, but even stranger. She decided to keep it to herself. It was probably best not to let her captor think she was crazy— at least not unless it worked to her advantage at some point.

Her eyes studied his very manly, clean-shaven, smooth, brown skin and she quivered as she explored his uncommonly handsome features. All she could do at the moment was stare at him and look into his captivating dark-brown eyes. Lani had grown up in a very culturally diverse area and had become very good at guessing the heritage of the people she met, before they could even tell her. If she were back in her neighborhood and was guessing his ethnicity, she would have guessed that he was mostly Tongan— and one hundred percent gorgeous! She could tell, even while he was sitting down, that he was tall— probably about six foot three. His arm muscles bulged between the very short sleeve of his leather vest and the arm guards on his forearms, and although she wondered about his very different style of dress, it definitely suited him.

However, the feeling of his character piqued her interest even more. She knew that would sound stupid to some people if she said it out loud, but she could often feel things about people that proved to be true as she got to know them. What she felt about this man's inner self was so gentle and so strong and so... rare. His looks were dazzling to her eyes but whatever it was that this guy had inside his heart was what truly intrigued her. She felt inexplicably and powerfully drawn to him as if there were a magnet inside his soul that called to her own.

Lani nervously pulled a few strands of loose hair behind her ears. She wished there was more she could do to clean up her appearance. Her long light brown hair was in a braided ponytail that fell past her waist, but some of her hair had been knocked loose from her long day of riding roller coasters— not to mention the mind-boggling experience of being mysteriously transported into a forest. There was some dirt on her face and arms where she had fallen unconscious to the ground. She desperately wanted to brush it away, but felt that trying to remove it was not only hopeless without water, but would probably also look more awkward than it was worth. Likewise, trying to pull out the few leaves and blades of grass that had imbedded themselves in her hair would be awkward and possibly useless, as they were very likely tangled beyond the point of simple extraction. She stood up as straight as she could, and continued to stare at him, hoping that he wasn't noticing her untidy look.

The man had risen to his feet as she entered, seemingly out of respect for her as a lady. The movement had appeared to be quite natural and instinctive, as if it had been ingrained in him from childhood that this was the proper way to behave when a lady came into a room. His shoulders were back and he was standing perfectly straight with a regal bearing. However, he still said nothing. His eyes were locked on hers, barely even blinking. His breaths were controlled, but perhaps too controlled. She dearly wished that she could read his mind. He opened his mouth to speak several times, but never did.

An intoxicating scent, which had begun to waft in Lani's direction the moment he had stood up for her, now reached her. She automatically breathed deeply to drink it in. She could almost taste it. It was subtle yet hypnotic, as if his fragrance were capable of subduing her. She could feel it wrapping around her. She planted her feet firmly on the ground to restrain herself. She closed her eyes for a moment. She had to think of something— anything to change her focus. She wondered what the effect might be if she got closer to him, if this was what happened from ten feet away.

"Um…. Excuse me… but… wow… I was just wondering… I was wondering if you could tell me… Where am I?"

Lani sighed quietly. She had to fight the urge to smack her forehead with her palm. She couldn't believe her current inability to speak. She was normally so self-assured— so matter of fact.

She almost always knew what to say. Men didn't usually throw her— and yet there she was feeling like a high school freshman who couldn't talk to the senior she had a crush on.

The man's eyes widened and he blinked once or twice when he heard her speak. The corners of his mouth turned up slightly, but only enough to make Lani question if she was imagining it.

"You, my dear lady, are in the Forest of Kar, on the border of the once mighty Kingdoms of Trisakne and Kelamosa. Now, if you will excuse my asking— what is your purpose here?"

His voice was deep and commanding, but he was so quiet that she barely heard him.

"Honestly, we have no purpose. I have no idea how we got here. My friends Raoul and Justin and I were in Florida, and Kendra and Erik were in Hawai'i and Kara was in Paris. We just suddenly appeared here at nearly the same time and we have no idea how or why... If you wouldn't mind, what are *you* doing out here? I heard the girl who captured me back there refer to you as 'Your Highness.' If you are royalty, why are you out in the forest like this? You seem more like refugees... I'm sorry... I didn't mean to be rude... I don't know why I feel like I can talk to you this way... sorry."

One of Jharate's eyebrows rose slightly as he continued to regard her.

"I have not heard of those lands before."

"You've *never heard* of Florida or Hawai'i or *Paris?* Where in the world *are* we?"

"Allow me to answer all of your questions, fair lady. I am indeed royalty, as you have rightly discerned. My kingdom has been stolen by the great and evil force who has slowly been taking over all of our lands. He is known as Vranah. My kingdom has been fighting him and his forces for decades. We were able to withstand his invasions for most of that time, as all of the kingdoms surrounding ours fell one by one.

"Eventually the prolonged conflict dwindled our numbers and weakened our borders. Mere days ago, he finally conquered my kingdom. I am the eldest son of the former King and Queen of Trisakne. Trisakne is the kingdom in which you now find yourself. My father was killed and my brother was murdered during the overthrow. I alone escaped. My party and I are on our way to Destavnia, which is the only kingdom that has not fallen. We must join their fight to defeat Vranah before it is too late. Destavnia is truly our last hope."

Lani sighed gently and cocked her head slightly to the side as she listened to him with rapt attention. The way he spoke was so impressive, so eloquent— and that accent! She had always loved listening to Tongans from New Zealand, and he had the most irresistible blended Tongan Maori accent she had ever heard. Lani was melting inside. All of a sudden, it clicked.

Wait a minute… Lani thought to herself. *Of course! I should have realized when he said the names of the kingdoms. Those places are not New Zealand! They are in Alamea! This is my book! This is what I have been writing… Did I hit my head harder than I thought? Or am I really here and my book is actually true?* If it were true, she wished she knew how the rest of her book went so that she could prepare for it. She suddenly felt very strongly that she was, in fact, awake— and that all of this was really happening. Her jaw nearly dropped at this realization, but she fought to ensure that she showed no astonishment outwardly and decided not to reveal her shocking discovery to him— not just yet, anyway. She decided that the best course of action was to ask another question instead.

"How did I get here?"

"I do not know the answer to that question, dear lady. We heard a great noise in the forest, like a monstrous crack of thunder, and then another. The second occurrence of this sound brought with it a bright flash of light, which held all the colors of the rainbow within it. We marked where it had been, and journeyed forth until we found the six of you. I followed you and the rest of my party went after your… friends?"

"Yes, they are my friends."

"You discovered my presence and then… I believe you met my cousin, Arante. She is overly concerned about my wellbeing at times."

"Yes. I could see that."

Lani smiled nervously, and the man smiled back. His smile set a thousand butterflies fluttering through her stomach. A new moment of quiet passed between them as they continued to stare at each other. Lani again felt that time had somehow slowed around them as they both stayed perfectly still, not even shifting their weight from one foot to another. After an unknown passage of time, the man took a steady breath in, and broke the silence.

"I do not even know your name."

"My name is Lani, Lani Johnson."

"What an exotic and lovely name. A pleasure to make your acquaintance, Lani Johnson."

Lani's cheeks turned pink as he said her name and she flashed a shy smile in his direction. Her smile changed from shy to playful as she felt a sudden wave of mischievousness rush through her body and vibrate out through her vocal chords.

"You must be Prince Jharate."

Her eyes twinkled with satisfaction and she positively beamed as she saw that her words had indeed had the effect that she had hoped they would. Jharate's eyes were wide with surprise, and intrigue.

"Yes… That is my name… Prince Jharate Inihma— at least that is part of my title. However, you may call me Jharate… How did you— how could you know that, Lani Johnson? Did someone speak my name in your presence?"

"Oh please call me Lani, and no, they did not."

"As you desire, Lani. Please tell me how you came to know my name."

"Well this is going to sound crazy, but in the world that I come from, I was writing a novel. I titled it *Half-Hearts*, and you were one of the people I was writing about. I had only just finished the prologue and chapter one before I went on vacation with my friends. But I had no idea until now that it was a true story!"

"Please, continue."

Lani took a deep breath and thought back to the words that she had written. Though it felt like it had been ages since the moment she last wrote, the story was as burned into her mind as if she had witnessed the events herself. She told him everything that she had written in her book so far, being extremely tactful when relating her awareness of how his brother, Khanye, had died. Jharate listened intently without interruption. The only place his amazement concerning the extent of her knowledge showed was in his eyes, which responded to each key fact that she related to him as she spoke.

As Lani finally finished sharing all of the details about the coffin room at the end of her first chapter, including the threats contained in Drakne's last thoughts, she took another deep breath in and sighed— watching Jharate to see if he was alright. Jharate folded his muscular arms and looked down at the ground for a brief moment. When he looked up again, his magnetic eyes met Lani's and she could see a deep intensity and a profound sincerity within them— and she could also somehow *feel* it from his heart.

"I must ask you never to reveal the fact that I am a Half-Heart. That information could be deadly."

"Of course not! I would never even dream of doing such a thing! And... Jharate?"

"Yes, Lani?"

"I am so terribly sorry about Khanye and your father."

"Thank you for your kindness, Lani."

Lani smiled gently. Once again she found herself wishing she could read his mind as he looked at her. She hoped he was feeling the same desire to close the distance between them that she was, but there was no way to tell. She diverted her thoughts from her dreams and tried to think of something else to say, but the only thoughts that were coming to her mind right now were unhelpful at best.

She paused for a minute and decided *not* to tell him that he, Jharate, was a character whom she had previously thought she had based on Josiah Harding. Nor did she think it a good idea to tell Jharate that he and Josiah could be identical twins, if it weren't for a few minor details, such as the fact that Josiah bleached his hair and wore it longer. Once again, she figured it was best just to ask another question.

"How is it possible that I wrote about all of this?"

"I do not know for certain. It is possible that you have the gift of vision. However, I am nonetheless stunned by the scope of what you have seen and written about."

"I have the gift of vision?"

"Yes, I believe so. It would be the only plausible explanation. As you know, it is a gift I myself possess. I too have seen you before."

"Really? What did you see?"

"For a long time I saw only you. The visions were quite brief. At times I saw you gazing through a window. Other times I saw you reading in various locales. By and by the visions became longer and more vivid. I saw you walking out into the darkness of early morning on a smooth pathway near a line of tall yellow lamps, where a carriage with no horses, made of black armor, arrived and stopped before a peculiar dwelling. You climbed inside with two young men and were carried to a place with flying carriages made of armor of many colors.

"I continued to see more and more until I found you in the forest. Everything I beheld was strange to me. I have never seen anything that compares to your world. I have learned of Earth in our history— however, it seems that our two worlds have diverged greatly in the millennia of separation and independence since that time when our ancestors, whom you referred to as the Ancient Alameans, initially closed the portals with your Ancient Egyptians. What do you call the magical flying metal carriages?"

"Oh, those are airplanes, and the ones on the ground are cars. And they aren't magic— they're just machines we use to go places."

"Fascinating. We have some machines here, although nothing of that design. In your account, you mentioned that Vranah opened the portals and linked our worlds together again, which caused an event you called Vietnam. Was that event recent, or is that time far gone?"

"Many years before I was born."

"I see. And Earth has been suffering as we suffered, unaware of their destiny being chained to ours ever since that time?"

"Yes— even I didn't know, and I was writing it! We think we're causing all of our own problems."

"I still do not understand how you arrived here. The knowledge of how to travel through the portals has been lost to us, and I assumed that Earth had long forgotten as well."

"I don't know either. I wish I could tell you. Like I said before, we were there, and then we were here."

"This is all quite remarkable. Our world was as sure that Earth was no longer a part of our existence as your world was sure that we did not exist."

"What does all this mean?"

"I do not know. Nevertheless, it is astonishing and I wish very much to hear more of your world— Oh, I am so dreadfully sorry!"

Jharate dashed towards her and in an instant was at her side. Lani gasped as she felt a rush of heat race through her, originating at her heart and flooding to all her extremities. It took her a moment to realize what he was apologizing for— and why he was suddenly so near her. He gently raised her forearms, just below the wrists, so that he could inspect them more closely. The tender touch of his skin on hers made her shiver with an electric desire and she worked hard to control her breath and remain still. Lani looked at her wrists to see what he was studying so intently. They were quite swollen.

"Oh... I forgot about that."

Jharate carefully released his hold of her arms, placed his hand on the small of her back, and guided her to where she could sit down. He was so near her that as Jharate exhaled, she felt his warm breath on the back of her neck and shuddered as the hairs there stood up and sent a shockwave of tingles through her body. She could feel her cheeks burning and hoped that the dim light would not reveal her deep blush. As the heat inside her intensified, Lani wondered how long she had been holding her breath.

Jharate stepped away from her momentarily and quickly rummaged through the supplies surrounding them. As he was searching, Lani reminded herself to breathe again, while his distance momentarily diminished his delicious scent, and worked on regaining her composure as she brought her wrists slowly in front of her to see more clearly what had happened to them. She again noticed the swelling, but this time she also saw the purple streaks where the ropes had dug deeply into her skin. They were even bleeding a little.

Jharate returned with a clean white cloth and poured some water out of a canteen onto it. He knelt by her side and gently pressed the cloth to her wrists. As he continued to aid her, he felt a strong impression come to him. It was not from his mind, or even his heart. He was sure this feeling was coming from somewhere beyond the physical realm. It was a feeling of urgency… as if Lani's safety depended on him.

He was worried as to how this would sound to her, or if he should share this with Lani at all. The feeling became stronger and more urgent, as if refusing to be ignored. Jharate knew he had to tell her, but still he did not know how. He did not want to frighten her. And then the words became perfectly clear, as if someone had spoken them in his ear, and he spoke them aloud as they came to him.

"Lani, I have two more promises that I must ask you to keep, in addition to your word that you have already given me concerning the secrecy of my identity as a Half-Heart."

"What are they?"

"First, I ask you to vow that you will not run away— and second, I ask that you tell no one of this promise. Do we have a pact?"

Lani blinked and cocked her head almost imperceptibly to one side as her eyes narrowed slightly. She looked deeply into his eyes, and again saw the sincerity contained within them. She was confused but very intrigued. Although she found his request odd, she felt no desire to run away. It was hard to explain, but she never wanted to leave his side again. She finally nodded.

"Agreed. You have my word."

Jharate nodded his head once and the corners of his mouth turned up a little. His eyes twinkled ever so slightly as he looked up at her again. Her heart did a cartwheel in response. That small answer from her was all he had needed to hear. He hadn't asked her if she was sure. He hadn't asked if she could be trusted. He had just taken her word at face value, despite knowing her for such a short time. For him to treat her as trustworthy that quickly could only mean that he was very trustworthy himself. She smiled at the thought.

Lani watched him intently, as he attended to her, and breathed deeply. She felt safe and protected as Jharate continued to care for her injured wrists. She was struck by how gently he held her hands and how carefully he touched the cloth to her wounds as he cleaned them. She could tell from his strong bronze muscles and the heavy sword that he carried, as well as from what she knew of his country's history, that he was a strong man who had probably seen much battle. It would be easy for a man of his strength to hurt her, even by accident, in the process of helping her. However, he seemed to be a man who worked hard to use his power to protect others— and he was treating her as if she were made of glass and could break at any moment.

She could feel the beating of her heart against her chest so strong and loud that she feared he would be able to hear it. All those feelings she had been afraid she would never feel again came flooding into her heart and soul. She now knew how she felt about him, but she decided in that instant to recommit to herself to always let the man be a man and express his feelings first— so she would not be the first one to say it. She felt a rising surge of hope that he felt the same way too and that maybe one day he would have the courage to tell her himself. For now, everything was right with the world and absolutely nothing was going to ruin it.

NOT FOR THE FAINT OF HEART

"WHAT?! No! How could this happen?! GET OUT! OUT! ALL OF YOU!"

Vranah stormed about his stolen throne room, hurling glowing red electric power-balls, which materialized from his hand, at several of his servants. They darted frantically in every direction to avoid being hit. Each narrow miss was punctuated with a disturbing crackling sound and an explosion against whatever object it touched. Although these particular spell-balls did no damage to the inanimate objects, other than leaving behind a burst of sooty residue, one unlucky servant failed to move quickly enough and died before his body could hit the cold marble floor.

"This cannot BE! IT CANNOT BE! What magic is this?!"

As the great doors to the throne room opened suddenly, Vranah's surviving servants fled and Drakne entered. The room echoed as the frantic servants pulled the doors shut behind them. Drakne stood perfectly still in the center of the room on the purple carpet with a flat expression and a bored dullness in his eyes. Vranah was now standing in front of the thrones, and still had his back to Drakne.

"You called for me, my lord?"

"WHAT?!"

Vranah spun around and launched a red power-ball at Drakne before he realized who it was. Drakne's hand rose quickly to the level of his eye. He calmly caught the ball in his hand and fluidly closed one finger at a time to absorb its energy. The bright red color faded, and the ball broke apart into small light streams that wrapped around his hand and wrist before completely disappearing into his body. Drakne returned his hand to his side and waited.

"Oh, it's you, Drakne. There has been a change of plans due to a small problem that has just arisen."

"My lord?"

"I have felt an alteration in the balance of power. One of the strongest Half-Hearts ever born has returned to our world."

"Returned, my lord?"

"Yes, Drakne. You know very little of my previous nemesis, whose hometown I have recently destroyed, and I have never told you why she merited so much attention from me. Many years ago, that confounded woman, Karsenia, became quite a problem. She possessed the gift of vision and had learned that the portals had been reopened. She then began to discover the identities of the Half-Hearts.

"I did not have as much power as I do now, nor as many spies, as I had not yet taken over the bulk of the kingdoms. Consequently, she was able to sneak several of the Half-Hearts through the portals to the parallel world undetected. Additionally, she took hundreds of non-Half-Heart children through in order to make it more difficult for me to find them later. She was finally discovered, by one of my most loyal subjects, and was subsequently killed as she returned from what would be her last trip through one of the seven gateways to Earth.

"I decided not to pursue the matter further because, to depart through a portal, one must be in close proximity of the portal itself— however, where you arrive on the other side can have a vast variance, depending on the skill of the traveler. With the children's names changed and their whereabouts unknown, it would have been a tremendous waste of energy as I would have had to personally assess each child within an immense radius to determine whether they were a Half-Heart or not.

"I assumed that they were too young to have any chance of knowing how to make their way back to their original homes, and knew that no marriage they could ever enter into on Earth could possibly have any effect on the balance of power, as they have to be here in Alamea for that. I chose to ignore them until I had dealt with all the ones in *this* world, and then would have found them only so as to finish my collection. But, *somehow*, one of them has returned, along with some companions. I can sense her presence, but would not recognize her now as it was twenty years ago that she was taken through the portal."

Drakne's eyes lit up with interest as he listened intently. He had always known of Earth's existence, but was surprised that anyone had taken Half-Hearts there. It had been a clever plan indeed! He, however, did not share his master's annoyance at their return. Being here would only make them easier to find.

"I therefore have a new mission for you, Drakne. We must forget about the prince for now. You may destroy the replica of Khanye. It is of no use to us anymore. Jharate is nothing compared to this particular female Half-Heart! As you may or may not know, there is one portal to Earth in each of the seven

Kingdoms of Alamea… but I have a feeling that she is not far from here—"

Vranah closed his eyes in concentration. "No— not far at all. She is *very* close. Take some soldiers with you and head for the Forest of Kar. Go and kill her. Kill every woman you find in that blasted forest— just be sure that *she* dies! Once she is dead the immediate threat will be neutralized. However, if you find the prince while you are gone, bring him to me alive. I want answers from him now! But he is *not* the priority. Do you understand?"

"I do, my lord, and it will be done."

Drakne bowed to his master and turned to walk down the luxurious amethyst-colored carpet toward the doors. As he turned, his face changed from the obedient flat expression it had held to a deep scowl. His eyes narrowed and he clenched his jaw to remain silent. He hated it when Vranah spoke to him like a child. Of course he understood! And Khanye's copy was a masterpiece and should not be cast aside on a mere whim! He was glad his master could not read minds as he marched out of the room faster than he had entered in order to complete his tasks. Snapping his fingers, he flung the doors open and listened as the doors shut behind him with an echoing thud.

The composure Vranah had affected while conversing with Drakne shattered and he returned to his frantic pacing about the room with a deep frown on his face. He thought he had solved this problem years ago by having that blasted interfering woman killed. The Half-Hearts Karsenia had taken through could not possibly have had the knowledge to activate the portals by themselves. They were mere toddlers and infants when she took them to Earth. Something or some*one* had to be helping them— but who?

CHAPTER SEVEN

Karsenia had acted alone in her plan to rescue the Half-Hearts, of that he was sure. She hadn't told anyone— not even her own husband. If Vranah's most loyal subject had not been keeping such close tabs on her, Karsenia might never have been found out. She was their only help then and she could not be helping now. No, she was dead and she was going to stay dead— *and the dead cannot help the living to that degree.*

He continued to attempt to reassure himself of this fact, but his apprehension remained. Even though he had beaten her in the end, he still felt a slight twinge of fear concerning Karsenia. Goodness that strong did not occur often in people in this or any other world and it was a force to be reckoned with— much more powerful than he wanted to acknowledge. Karsenia had turned down an unprecedented offer once… one he was sure she would take… one any other woman *would have* taken— but that was no matter now.

The paramount priority at this moment was to find the girl Karsenia had saved— and to kill her. Vranah smiled with malicious joy in his eyes as he thrilled at the thought of Drakne's return with her body. He would know if Drakne had eliminated the correct girl. He could sense Half-Hearts within close proximity, dead or alive, even if their names and identities had been changed… it was odd that he could sense this one so far away— especially in his current condition.

Vranah's smile fell flat. His most recent expenditure of power in Kellinsi had been unfortunate. Had he not let his revenge supersede all else, it would have been easy to find this girl himself. For the smallest moment, he wished he had paid more attention to the escaped Half-Hearts and attempted to find them years ago. But the moment passed and one of the corners of his mouth lifted into a snarl. *It will not be long now,* he thought, looking out the window at the dreary grey cloudy sky, as a particularly large lightning bolt struck the ground.

Jharate and Lani emerged from the trees into the main area of the camp. Arante stood up quickly and pointed her dagger at Lani. Jharate's jaw set tight and his muscles flexed as he stepped in between his cousin and Lani and glowered at Arante.

"You will wait for my orders concerning these captives, Arante. I am entirely capable of protecting myself and I am confident in the wisdom of my decisions. I have determined that she and her friends are no threat to us and I have come to extend an offer to them. After that, they shall be released to do whatever they shall choose."

Arante took a couple of steps backwards. Her eyes widened and her lips parted slightly. A split second later she narrowed her eyes and clenched her jaw as she roughly sheathed her dagger, glaring at Jharate and Lani as they passed her. However, she remained close by. Jharate and Lani stopped just in front of the rest of the friends who were still tied up and sitting against the fallen tree.

"I am Prince Jharate Inihma, heir to the stolen throne of Trisakne. Lani has been kind enough to relate all of the details of your arrival. I realize that what I am about to reveal to you will be shocking. Please forgive me for having to tell you so indelicately— you are no longer in your home world of Earth."

Kara gasped aloud.

"I do not know precisely how you have come to be here, nor do I know how to help you return. What I do know is that you have come to a perilous place at a tumultuous time. This is the Forest of Kar. We are on the border of Trisakne and Kelamosa, our noble neighbors to the east. They too, were conquered by the most evil force this world has ever known. We are on our way to Destavnia now— the only free land remaining. We will allow you to travel there in our company and under our protection, if you will do your share of the work and help to defend against attacks, when necessary. Are we agreed?"

"Booyah! Talk about RPG's!"

Justin's face lit up like a kid's on the night before Christmas. He sat up straighter against the log with eyes so full of enthusiasm it was nearly palpable. Raoul also straightened up and looked at Justin with excitement bursting out of him.

"Yeah you're right, Justin!" Raoul exclaimed. "We can take what we learned from playing Final Fantasy and use it here— plus think of all the practice we got fighting with the kendo sticks and my family's katana swords in the backyard!"

Lani worked hard to suppress a laugh. She should have known Raoul and Justin would be totally down with this situation. She and Jharate both looked to the three who had not yet spoken, and waited for them to answer.

"Yeah okay," Erik said.

"What choice do we have?" Kendra asked with a shrug. "I'll help."

Kara was silent a long time. All eyes were on her and even the birds seemed to have stopped their songs as if straining to hear what she would say. Her countenance fell, her eyes welled up with tears, and the second she blinked they streamed down her face.

"I just want to go home…"

"If I possessed the knowledge to aid you in doing so, I would certainly do everything within my power to return you safely to your homes. However, I do not. Truly, your best chance, and very likely your only chance, is to come with us. If personal safety is not enough incentive for you to join us, you may want to consider what I have come to understand, while listening to what Lani has relayed concerning her book. If our world falls *so does your own.* All else in the story, which Lani has been writing, has been remarkably accurate— deadly accurate, to be more precise. The lives of everyone on your planet, including the lives of each and every member of your families, are in danger."

All eyes turned to Lani as Justin asked the question everyone was thinking.

"What does he mean by that, Lani?"

"He's talking about the book I've been writing. I'm sorry I didn't tell you about it before, but I didn't feel like it was ready to share with anyone yet. But in my book, I wrote that every major cataclysmic event since the Vietnam War has been in direct response to things happening here in Alamea. Life for life. The wars, the famines, accidents, assassinations— everything. In fact, no death is natural anymore and nothing is a coincidence. Every time someone dies here on Alamea, so does someone on Earth— someone like that person. Bad for bad and good for good."

"No! It's not possible! It's just a book! If you wrote it, it's not real!"

"I wish it was just a book, Kendra. But every single thing I have written so far has turned out to be true in every detail. Apparently I was having visions of actual events and writing them down from what I thought were only dreams and imagination. But it is *all* real. Earth itself even reacts to the death toll on Alamea to the point where it triggers natural disasters like tsunamis, hurricanes, earthquakes— you name it. That's why there has been so much more of those kinds of things since the sixties. If Vranah gets Destavnia, that's over two billion good people who could die here…"

"And two billion good people who would die there…"

Raoul's eyes lowered and his voice trailed off. The entire group sat in silence. Only the crackling of a nearby campfire let them know that life was still happening. Jharate watched carefully. He opened his mouth to speak, then hesitated briefly before deciding he must continue.

"As you have no doubt gathered by now, your entire planet is in danger— and joining with us to defeat Vranah may be the *only* way to help your people."

Kara nodded her head slowly, closing her eyes as a few more large tears slid quietly down her cheeks.

"Very well then. Arante, release them and familiarize them with the camp! Assign them their duties and inform four of the other warriors that I wish each of them to take an apprentice, in order to teach the newcomers how to fight."

Arante stomped briskly toward the captives without saying a word. She placed her dagger in-between the hands and feet of each person one at a time and yanked it up in a sharp motion until everyone was freed from their bonds. They rubbed their wrists subconsciously despite the fact that none of them had been injured as Lani had been. Arante stood up straight, flipped her ponytail back behind her with her free hand, and jerked her head to direct the five friends to follow her. Justin, Raoul, Kara, Erik, and Kendra had to jump up and jog for a short distance to catch up with her. Soon Jharate and Lani were alone again.

"What about me?"

"I will teach you the combat skills that you need and I will also teach you how to use your gift, since we are alike in that way."

Lani felt her heart do a back flip and her stomach beginning to flutter at the prospect of spending time with him. There was no stopping the huge smile that spread across her face.

"Alright. But I should tell you that the only thing I have ever done that even comes close to real fighting is sport fencing."

"What manner of sword did you use?"

"It's called a foil where I come from. It is a long, skinny, lightweight blade, no thicker than… than this stick right here." Lani selected a stick from the ground about the width of a pencil and approximately three feet long. Jharate laughed a little before he realized he had done so, but quickly caught himself and tried to look serious again. Lani flashed a sly smile.

"Want to challenge me with another stick like this one for fun?"

Jharate raised one eyebrow slightly as he regarded her. He nodded his head once in his quiet but definitive way. He found a stick similar to hers and held it with both hands, ready to fight. Lani giggled.

"No, no, no. You only get to use your *right* hand. And your right foot always has to stay in front of the left."

She gestured to his foot and then gently took his left arm and showed him how to hold it up and out of the way. She paused before letting go of his arm as she caught his eyes. Lani felt a slight but thrilling shudder within and the corners of her closed lips curved up as she turned her face to hide her blush. She stepped away from him and assumed a fencing stance as he followed her lead.

"Very well then, fair lady. Shall we begin?"

CHAPTER SEVEN

"Now!"

She advanced with cat-like speed. In one quick motion she parried his "blade" away from him; and with a touch lighter than a ladybug, tapped his chest where his heart was and held the stick there triumphantly— a grin lighting up her face.

"You appear to have won, dear lady."

Lani was sure she had forgotten more than one breath cycle as a result of hearing his deep voice speak those simple words of praise. She knew her success had mainly come because Jharate was not familiar with this form of fighting. But all that Lani had wanted was to earn his respect, and she got the sense that perhaps she had. Again she would have given anything to read his mind. She withdrew her makeshift sword, put it vertically up to her forehead, pulled it down swiftly to her side to complete the fencing salute, and smiled brilliantly at him.

Jharate smiled in return, lowering his head in a respectful nod of acknowledgement.

"The style in which I will be instructing you is quite different from the one you have just taught to me. The sword will no doubt be challenging and unwieldy for you at first. You must ignore many of the rules of your former training and ingrain the new training until it becomes instinct rather than rehearsal. However, if you pay close attention and practice often, I have confidence that you will learn. Here is my sword."

Jharate drew his spectacular broadsword from its sheath and passed it to her, hilt first. She was struck by its beauty as she took it cautiously in both of her hands. The rapier that the character Inigo Montoya had in the movie *The Princess Bride* was no more awe-inspiring. She had never seen a sword like this in real life and it took her breath away. The smooth, cold steel of the blade felt powerful as she laid it carefully across the flat of her open palm.

The inlaid rubies on the golden hilt in her other hand mesmerized her as they sparkled in the rays of sunlight that reached down, through the tops of the trees, to touch them.

Surely a master had crafted this exquisite object! But it had been designed even more for its practical use than for its decorative appeal. She loved the weight of Jharate's sword. It had a balance that was unlike anything she had ever felt. She took the hilt into both of her hands and sliced it through the air, amazed at how it handled. It was, however, extremely heavy, and it was a strain to maneuver it.

Jharate pulled out yet another sword that Lani had not noticed before, and she wondered when he had gotten it. This new sword was still sheathed as he handed it to her and simultaneously retrieved his own, sheathing it back in its rightful place at his side. He observed Lani as she looked inquisitively at the sword she now held.

"That will be your sword. It is made from the rarest and strongest metal known to my world and can do battle with a sword three times its size without any damage to the blade whatsoever."

Lani's eyes brightened and her mouth fell open slightly as she looked up at him. She quickly returned her glance to the sword and enthusiastically unsheathed it half way so that she could see the blade. Its metal was even shinier than the metal of Jharate's blade and reflected anything near it, almost as well as a mirror. Scrolling etchings of delicate leaf and floral patterns made their way down one side of the blade, and wove themselves around a long, thin, twisting dragon. Magnificent and elegant, it resembled a Katana sword in both size and shape.

Emeralds, rather than rubies, adorned its ornate hilt and glistened in the sunlight. Lani marveled at the fact that though the hilt appeared to be made out of a golden-colored mother of pearl, she could tell that it was some kind of metal. To her great relief, her sword was much lighter than Jharate's. It would still take two hands to control, but it would be much more practical for her in a real battle. Although the techniques for this new form of swordplay would take some getting used to, she loved it already!

"Thank you so much! It's so much more than I ever could have imagined! It's gorgeous!"

"Not as lovely as the lady who is holding it. Shall we begin?"

Heat rushed from Lani's heart to her cheeks.

"Yes please!"

Raoul had been assigned as an apprentice to Jaresh, an expert on the use of the crossbow. Jaresh was a tall, fair-skinned man in his early forties who had a deep tan, exceedingly large muscles, and light blonde hair that fell to his shoulders. The word "wow" escaped Raoul's mouth. As Raoul strained his neck to look up at Jaresh, he was sure that Jaresh could have been the real life *Terminator* and had to fight his urge to say, "Come with me if you want to live." To Raoul's infinite relief, Jaresh smiled warmly and offered his hand in greeting.

"My name is Jaresh, and I will be happy to pass on my knowledge of the crossbow to you. I am a demanding teacher, but I am also fair. Give your all, each and every day, and we will have no problems."

"Oh no, I wouldn't give someone like you trouble— uh, I didn't mean that in a— I mean I don't give teachers trouble ever, but especially not you because... Hi, I'm Raoul."

Jaresh laughed heartily as he shook Raoul's hand and slapped him playfully on the back. Raoul stepped forward to keep from falling and laughed nervously along with Jaresh. As the days wore on, it turned out that Raoul was a natural when it came to the crossbow. Lani caught glimpses of him from time to time in-between her own training. There was never a time that his crossbow bolt didn't hit at least part of the target he was aiming at, and the number of exact hits was growing exponentially. She marveled at his skill, and wondered if all this ability could have started when he earned his archery badge in scouts.

Justin was learning to use an axe that looked like a medieval weapon from Earth. When his trainer first handed him the weapon, his mouth had fallen open wide and a rolling, nearly maniacal, laugh erupted from deep in his throat as he exclaimed, "Are you *serious?!*" He had turned the axe over and over in his hands, inspecting every inch of it. His weapon had so many options for defending against a foe in close combat. The main large blade was in front, with a five-inch pick-like point directly behind, and it also had a sharp spike on the bottom of the handle.

Every time Lani saw Justin training, he had a grin on his face from ear-to-ear. He looked just like he had back in high school when they were having a blast making home movies. If Lani knew him as well as she thought she did, he was not thinking ahead at all about how he might actually have to use these skills. However, he was so serious about play, he was progressing just as quickly as if he *were* thinking ahead.

"Hey, Justin! Where'd you learn to fight like that? Video games?"

Justin ducked as his trainer took advantage of Lani's interruption.

"Hey, Lani! Where'd you learn to swordfight like that? Watching *Highlander*?"

Justin ducked once again, narrowly avoiding a fierce blow from his trainer's staff.

"You know I knew how to fence already!"

"Yeah but what you've been doing ain't fencing! It's real sword fighting!"

Justin dodged his trainer once more and angrily swung his battle-axe so that his trainer had to tuck and roll to avoid injury.

"Do you mind? I'm trying to have a conversation with my friend here? Can you give me just a second, Ke'arn?"

"No. In real battle you have to be able to fight during any distraction."

"True dat. Hey Lani, I'm kinda busy right now. Can we talk later?"

"Sure. Sorry, ha ha! Thanks for the comparison to Duncan MacLeod!"

"Don't let it go to your head. Fighting like a TV character isn't going to help y— Ow!"

"Concentrate!" Lani laughed.

"I'll concentrate a lot better once you're gone!"

"Okay, okay, I'll go back to my training then! See you later, Justin!"

Lani cracked up. She figured that there was no reason to try to focus Justin on the reality of upcoming battles and facing death. Ke'arn could attempt to do that if he wished. For now she would rather not think about it herself.

Erik was being instructed in the ways of the broadsword. His attitude was quite different from Raoul's and Justin's. His reaction to his weapon had been to raise his eyebrows and nod in a chilled-out kind of way, pursing his lips in a thoughtful manner, as if to say that the sword would do. Although Erik was probably the most naturally gifted of all of his friends from Earth and possibly more gifted than half of the Alameans in the camp, he was not really disciplined or focused in trying to improve his skills.

Erik had never really applied himself in school, or in life for that matter, and he wasn't about to change that about himself now. However, like most guys, he enjoyed the swordplay, and an occasional muted smile would cross his face whenever he managed to get a new move down correctly. But, if he ever saw Arante looking his way, his technique suddenly became more accurate and concise and his fighting amped up in intensity— pushing his muscles past the point of fatigue.

Kendra was given a quarterstaff, which had sharp metal points at both ends. From the moment it entered her hands she had felt that it belonged in them. She had passed it back and forth in quick motions between her left and right hand, and twirled it rapidly before bringing one end to a rest on the ground with a quick approving nod, as if praising the stick itself. When the rebels had finally broken into their mini-camps for lunch that day, Kendra had run to find Lani, and dragged her back to show her what she had learned. Lani watched with rapt attention as Kendra and her trainer demonstrated her new skills.

"Wow!" Lani exclaimed.

Kendra was already such a feisty little thing naturally, even without a weapon, that now she was downright formidable. That, combined with the fact that Kendra was a black belt, made her a force to be reckoned with. On more than one occasion, she surprised her trainer by out-maneuvering him.

"You go, Chicky!" Lani exclaimed.

"Thanks!" Kendra beamed.

Kara had frowned upon receiving the news that Arante had chosen her to be her apprentice. Kara's eyes had searched the area as if looking for another trainer to rescue her, and it seemed as though she might cry again. Arante rolled her eyes and shoved a bow and a quiver full of arrows into Kara's hands so roughly that Kara had to take a few steps back to keep from falling over. The days crawled by for Kara as Arante continued to push her to become a better archer.

"No, no, no, no, *no!* You're not even trying! *All* of your other friends are doing better than you are!"

"Look, I'm doing the best I can! I've never used any kind of weapon before! I wasn't obsessed with video games and Japanese weapons like Justin and Raoul, I'm not super strong like Erik, I never fenced like Lani did, and I never took karate like Kendra! I was trying to become an actress where the closest thing to fighting I would have had to do would have been to argue with the director about my character's motivation!"

"Your biggest problem is that you are weak and spineless and have more desire to go home than to learn how to save your family and your friends! Using a bow and arrow is all about practicing to refine your skills and subtle technique! You don't need any of the strengths your friends have, other than their drive to work through pain and to access their courage!"

"That's not fair!"

"It's perfectly fair! Now try again!"

Kara sighed in aggravation. She yanked a new arrow from her quiver, strung it, hauled it back, and let the arrow fly.

"Look out!" Arante yelled.

Erik turned around and flinched as the arrow narrowly missed his head and hit the tree behind him. His face turned red and his cheeks undulated with anger as he saw the look on Kara's face. He inhaled to yell, but stopped as he saw Arante. Instead, he exhaled and forced a smile as he called back cheerfully to her.

"Thanks!"

"You're welcome!" Arante called with the corners of her mouth slightly upturned.

Erik turned away before his urge to yell at Kara could get the better of him, and he and his trainer disappeared into the trees out of her range. Arante's slight smile transformed into a frown and she rounded on Kara with sheer fury emanating from her eyes. Kara took several hurried steps backwards in retreat.

"But Erik wouldn't *need* to be thanking me now, Kara, if you had been anywhere *near* the target you are *supposed* to be hitting!"

"I'm sorry! It was an accident!"

"He was thirty feet from the target!"

Kara started to cry and Arante stormed off.

Lani and Jharate often found clearings away from the rest of the rebels where they could practice alone. Lani hung on Jharate's every instruction and did her best to get each move memorized by the second or third try, often wishing she could do everything right the first time. She gave no leeway when she made mistakes— demanding perfection of herself. It felt like she was reliving the time in eighth grade when she had joined the orchestra at her new school. All the other students in that class had been learning progressively since sixth grade.

Though the activities were different, the feelings were extremely familiar. She thought back to the adrenaline that had seemingly filled the pit of her stomach as she asked for special permission from the instructor to join the class in the first place, when she didn't even know how to play a stringed instrument. She recalled the dizzying feeling in her brain as she tried to learn where all the notes were on the violin within a week's time, while simultaneously trying to get used to the feeling of the bow crossing the strings. The way she had seen it, she was in eighth grade so she should be at an eighth grade level. The memory of the pain in the fingertips of her left hand, as her body gained the calluses needed for playing, flashed through her mind frequently— as did the did the memory of the feeling of overwhelm from trying to keep up with students two years ahead of her on pieces like *Brandenburg Concerto No. 5 in D Major,* that were well beyond her comfort level, which was more along the lines of *Twinkle, Twinkle, Little Star.*

Only this time, the pain of learning involved every muscle in her body and she was trying to catch up with a master who had practically studied since the day he took his first step. Not to mention the extremely real possibility that her life could very well depend on the skills she was learning now. That same attitude of feeling as though she should be at the level she would have been at her age, had she been in training her whole life, coupled with extra hard work, was paying off— as the blisters on her hands changed to calluses, the fatigue in her muscles grew into strength and stamina, and her memorization and constant internal evaluation in her brain turned into intuition.

As the fighting became more instinctive, Lani and Jharate were able to have normal conversations as they fought. They also talked during almost every break they got, discussing every subject under the sun, until they inevitably became the best of friends. But Lani was dying to know if there was more. She thought she had caught subtle hints that maybe she wasn't alone in her feelings, but it was never conclusive. Jharate began to hum out loud from time to time when he was in her presence and smiles became a frequent reaction when she perfected a new move he had given her to learn. But was he singing just because... or because of her? And were those the smiles of a proud trainer? Or those of an interested man? His face retained its dignified air whenever they were amongst the others in the camp. But again Lani wondered if this was simply the action of a prince who felt it better not to look like a starry-eyed youth in front of his people or if it was an indication that he wasn't into her... It seemed like everything he did, which gave her hope that he might have feelings for her, could also be interpreted another way.

One particular night stood out in her memory. She and Jharate had been practicing long and hard that day, and as the sun began to set, Jharate had looked at her intently. She had felt a rush in her heart as she waited for him to tell her what was on his mind.

"As night is falling, perhaps we should build a fire here."

Lani's heart leapt! A romantic fire for just the two of them— it was the sign she had been waiting for! Lani and Jharate both sheathed their swords and she got to work helping him build the fire. He insisted that she only get the kindling and that he would handle the heavy work— another sign! The moment they finished, a horn sounded in the distance with a low tone announcing that dinner was ready. Lani turned to go, but Jharate lifted his hand to indicate that she should wait. She stopped and looked at him, waiting for him to speak.

"You need not go, Lani. You have been working very hard this day. I will go and bring back food for both of us. Wait for me here."

"Thank you," Lani sighed, as her arm muscles twitched with fatigue.

Jharate disappeared as Lani sat down against a tree near the fire and stared happily at the dancing flames. She was tired but thrilled because this was going to be the first time they were alone together for an evening meal— this was their first real date! She unbraided her hair and fingered through the wavy cascades and bit her lips to make them redder. Jharate reappeared in no time at all with their food, politely handed hers to her, and sat down next to her. Her stomach jumped with excitement for the food before she even got the first bite into her mouth and her heart fluttered in anticipation of what Jharate would do next.

"I am pleased that you are such a hard worker. Many people would not have had your enthusiasm for hard work after dinner."

"Work?"

"I am glad you do not feel that training is work. That is very commendable! Thank you for helping me to build the fire so that we will have enough light to continue to practice into the dark hours."

"No problem..."

Lani's heart sank, and she fought to keep her face from falling with it. She forced a smile in response to Jharate's praise. *That's* why he had wanted to build the fire? Seriously? Not that she minded the practice, but her hopes had sailed way past work and into love. The two of them sat there, eating quietly. Jharate finished before she did and stood up.

"We will need more light. I will return in a moment with more wood to stoke the fire."

"Thank you. That sounds good. It will give me a chance to work on that one move thingy you just taught me..."

Lani trailed off. That sentence had completely gotten away from her— not that she had really known where she was going with it in the first place. While Jharate was gone, she quickly re-braided her hair for training. When the fire was sufficiently stoked, they returned to practice, and Lani tried hard to ignore the frustrated thoughts that rushed through her head. After another hour of training in the dark the horn rang out again, much to Lani's surprise. Jharate answered her question before she could ask it.

"Jaresh found a jhana tree and has prepared a customary Trisaknen hot drink. The fruit of the jhana tree has healing properties and is very soothing. It will be an excellent way to end the night after our long day of training. I will return shortly."

Lani sat down once again, grateful that training was finally over, and irritated that this whole thing had been about just that— training! On the other hand it was very sweet of Jharate to bring her food and then to bring her the drink that would help her aching muscles. She had a feeling she would sleep very well that night. She leaned against the same tree and stared into the wild flames. Jharate returned and handed her a tin cup.

"Careful. It is still quite hot."

"Thank you."

She held the cup to her lips, blew carefully across the surface of the amber liquid, and sipped it slowly.

"Yum! This tastes kind of like hot apple cider with cinnamon, which is a traditional drink for my family during the winter months."

"I am pleased that you like it."

They sat there enjoying their drinks and listening to the sounds of the night. Again, Jharate finished before her but did not rush her. Instead, he started to sing. It was the first time Lani had ever heard Jharate do so. Her heart fluttered as he began and she quietly unbraided her hair. His crystal clear baritone voice rang out in a hypnotic otherworldly quality. A shiver ran up her spine and goose bumps formed on her arms. She closed her eyes, trying to absorb the sound.

Jharate finished his song, but it took her a moment to awake from the trance his voice had put her into. Her eyes opened slowly and she gazed at him with a dreamy look. She jumped as she realized that her iPod was still in her pocket. Quickly, nearly frantically, she pulled it out and turned it on, hoping there was still some battery left. She was glad that she had charged it before they had started running around the theme park the day that they had disappeared from the Tower of Terror. Because she hadn't turned it on since then, she dared to hope that there might be a few good hours left.

Lani unwrapped the headphones from around the outside of the iPod and gave one to Jharate. He looked at it curiously and she smiled, placing the other one in her right ear. She scooted a little closer to him and pointed to his left ear. He raised an eyebrow, and mimicked her action, placing the ear bud carefully inside his ear. Lani scrolled to one of her favorite songs, *I Wanna Hold You* by Na Drua. She giggled as Jharate sat bolt upright, his eyes wide as he pulled the ear bud out of his ear. After examining it carefully, he placed it back in his ear and smiled as he listened intently.

As the song played, Lani watched the expressions on Jharate's face. When the song ended, she realized that she had only heard the melody as a background to the music video in her head, starring Jharate, with frequent close-ups on his deep brown eyes. Despite the fact that she loved the song and knew every word, she hadn't registered any of the lyrics this time as her own thoughts had overridden them. She pulled some of her recently unbraided hair back behind her ear and looked shyly down at the ground.

"That is a magnificent song. I thank you for sharing it with me. This is truly an extraordinary device. How is the music performed inside my very mind? Is it magic?"

"Oh, it's nothing as amazing as magic. Earth only has machines for stuff like this. We use science— we don't even believe in magic there."

"Perhaps the two are not as separate as we think."

"Oooh! I like that. It reminds me of a quote I read by Arthur C. Clarke. He believed that, 'Any sufficiently advanced technology is indistinguishable from magic.' So maybe you're right— maybe our technology has a few magical elements after all."

"Does this device contain more than one song within it?"

"Oh yes," Lani giggled with a twinkle in her eyes. "It *definitely* has more than one. There are close to a thousand in this one, but they can hold a lot more."

"Astonishing! Would you be so kind as to share more with me? I would be particularly interested to hear another similar to the song you have just shared. I cannot explain to you in what manner it does so, nevertheless, the feeling your song evokes reminds me very much of the songs from my kingdom— and of happier times."

"I'd be glad to share more with you!" Lani exclaimed, as she started searching gleefully through her list. "That genre is one of my favorites too! It comes from some of the island peoples of Earth— specifically the Pacific Islanders. I fell in love with their music when I got introduced to it in college by some of my friends who are actually from those islands. The battery will

eventually die on this thing though— that's the power source—
and then it won't work anymore."

"Then let us make the most of it."

Lani lit up as she scrolled through her play lists to all of her
favorite songs. They spent the rest of that evening listening to
some of the music from the island music groups Hoʻokoa, Fiji,
Ekolu, Koaʻuka, Israel "IZ" Kamakawiwoʻole and Rebel
Souljahz. *With This Ring* by Kaulana Pakele and *Windward Skies* by
Ten Feet became additional favorites for Jharate as, like the song
by Na Drua, they somehow reminded him of his homeland of
Trisakne. Lani also shared a few of her favorite classic rock
ballads and some of the old school music by Louis Armstrong
and Sinatra. One of the songs he asked her to play more than
once was an instrumental called *Labyrinth* by Lisa Linsky.

"The song you call *Labyrinth* reminds me very much of the
journey to Destavnia that we are currently undertaking— with
hope for a better future."

"I can totally see that! That song does feel like a journey. I
never really thought of it that way before— well I guess I never
imagined being lost in a forest and making my way across enemy
lines before either."

Lani giggled again. She loved that Jharate enjoyed discussing
what he liked about the songs with her and that even when she
offered to let him have both earpieces to listen, he always handed
one of them back to her so that they could listen together. It was
so different from many of the friends she had on Earth who
disconnected once they "plugged in" and didn't have the desire
to share anything— Justin for instance. That boy disappeared the
moment technology came within a fifty-foot radius. She hated
that feeling of being so completely separate when you were

supposed to be together. Conversely she loved how unity seemed to be second nature to Jharate, even in such a simple moment.

The whole night would have been perfect if she could have only known one thing. Did Jharate feel more than friendship towards her, or not? Still, it had been one of the best nights she had ever experienced and she would take what she could get— for now.

As the days passed, she thrilled when she heard him singing some of the songs she had introduced him to, from time to time, long after the iPod she had given to him as a gift had lost all of its *unusually*-long battery life. His voice seemed to cast a spell over her, and she could listen to it all day! It left her breathless and yearning for more.

And his mastery of those new songs was unfathomable! He could hear a song only once, or maybe twice, and then sing it perfectly without missing a lyric. Furthermore, his rich baritone voice could reach the unimaginably high notes of the singer, Fiji, in *Jowenna* and other Fiji songs, in a clear and angelic falsetto that left her even more entranced with him. She beamed when Jharate sang, *I Can Be the Guy* by Koa' uka one night by the fire, and was blown away by his ability to master even the rap part of any song. Another song he loved singing, and that she loved to hear him sing, was *I Don't Want to Miss a Thing* by Aerosmith. It was the ultimate rock ballad in her opinion and Jharate's singing it almost made her swoon.

Music was just one of the things that they shared. Lani and Jharate always arose to watch the sunrise together while they ate breakfast. The mornings were usually spent in silence. But there was something transcendental about their relationship that made her love these quiet moments almost as much as their conversations. She felt as if their souls spoke for them when their voices had ceased.

They also shared a love of nature and would listen to the birds singing, the wind rustling through the trees, and the sound of babbling brooks bubbling by, in preparation for their day. But as the days rolled on, Lani became more and more anxious to know how he was feeling in no uncertain terms. She didn't want to just feel like *maybe* he loved her— she wanted to know! More than once she was tempted to say something, but she frequently reminded herself of her commitment to wait until he made the first move... she knew that guys felt stronger and deeper if they could do the pursuing— but it was so frustrating!

Each day, they continued to practice their sword fighting over various terrains. Lani's favorite sparring match with Jharate occurred as they were practicing fighting over uneven and inclined surfaces. All at once her old habit of never counter-attacking kicked into overdrive. She advanced again, and again, and again, forcing Jharate to keep retreating up the steep slope until he reached the edge of a cliff.

"Jharate, stop!"

Jharate stopped and looked back into the air behind him and then down below. Lani smiled at him as he turned back to her. She addressed him in a very out-of-breath voice, with her sword still pointed at his chest.

"Do you surrender?"

Lani saw a twinkle in Jharate's eyes and watched a mischievous smile cross his face.

"Always know your terrain," he said.

Jharate turned abruptly and leapt off of the cliff. Lani screamed and rushed to the edge to look down. She placed her hand to her heart and took in a deep breath as she saw him land in a large, remarkably clear, pool of water, about twenty-five feet below— with a giant splash. As he surfaced, she yelled down to him.

"You scared me to death!"

"I have taught you a valuable lesson!" Jharate called back as he tread water to remain afloat. "You must never allow an opponent any means of escape. Had I been a spy, you would have lost me and I would now be able to recount all that I had discovered."

"Point taken."

"Now, you must jump!"

"Me?" Lani squeaked. "Are you sure it's safe?"

"I would never endanger you, Lani."

Lani looked down at the water. It seemed so far away. She knew landing wrong would hurt! She could feel her adrenaline spiking and her heart pounding in response. She took a deep breath and jumped off the cliff, screaming as she fell. Her entrance into the water was so smooth that her eyes flew open in surprise as she plunged deeper into the pool. A few colorful fish scattered around her and she thought she saw something large on the bottom, several feet below her, which looked like a brilliant electric-blue lobster. She wondered if it could be a lobster when they were in fresh water. Her musing was interrupted as she realized she was running out of air, and she swam upwards. Surfacing, she grinned as she heard Jharate's hearty laugh. She giggled and followed him as he swam for land.

One particularly sunny day, Lani and Jharate came to a river in the course of their daily training. It was hot and they had been working hard for hours. Lani looked at the cool clear water. Although trees covered much of the area, the sun was beating down on them and their training was intense. She wondered how the cold crystal liquid would feel against her hot skin. She imagined the water washing over her and replacing the glistening sweat with splashes of cool water that would return her body to its normal temperature. She looked back at Jharate with eager eyes.

"Can we take a quick break here please?"

Jharate gave his signature single nod of acknowledgement as the corners of his mouth turned up slightly. He sat down on a nearby boulder and watched her. In an instant she was wading knee-deep into the river. She leaned down, cupped her hands, and threw some of the water high above her into the air, letting the droplets fall down on her face and arms like a light summer rain. She laughed happily and looked back at Jharate. Her smile suddenly became mischievous and playful as she bent down again and splashed him before he had even noticed what she was doing.

Jharate grinned and laughed freely as he ran into the water, splashing her back as he rushed towards her. She continued to splash him as she retreated slowly, until Jharate caught up with her. He carefully grabbed her arms to keep her from splashing him further and she giggled again. All at once her giggling stopped. She could feel the warmth of his hands on her wrists. The water she had splashed in his face dripped temptingly to the corners of his lips. She wondered how they would feel pressed against her own and how they would taste. She looked up into his eyes, unable to look away.

Jharate looked intently back into her sparkling eyes with a fiery gaze. He let go of one of her arms and gently lifted her chin.

Time seemed to stop. Jharate leaned down slowly. Lani's lips burned for his and she was irresistibly drawn forward, unconsciously reaching for his ever-nearing lips, on tip-toe, when her feet slipped on the mossy river rock she was standing on and down she went. Jharate threw his arms around her to try to catch her, but it was too late. He twisted his body so that she would land on top of him, to keep her from harm, as they fell into the knee-deep water with a great big splash. Lani laughed nervously as she sat up and avoided eye contact with Jharate.

"Are you injured, Lani?"

"Just my pride. You?"

"I have not been harmed in the slightest, thank you."

Lani could have screamed. Why did she have to be so clumsy? She had just messed everything up! His lips had been inches from hers! She had been waiting for so long for that moment and in the last two seconds she had ruined it! Jharate stood up and gently helped her to her feet. They walked back to the riverbank and sat down on a nearby rock to dry off. The rock was a semi-flat boulder the size of a large coffee table that had absorbed the sun's heat.

Lani worked to quickly suppress her frustration. *At least he tried to kiss me… that's a good sign, right?* She told herself that their first kiss would come in time and got back to enjoying the day. The two of them watched and listened to the river rush by, happily waiting for all the water to evaporate from their clothing. As they sat there together, his hand barely touched hers and she held very still to ensure that *this* moment lasted.

The days quickly turned to nights, one blurring into the other— each day beginning seemingly before the last one had ended, as the six friends worked hard to learn how to use their various weapons and care for the camp. The arduous duties became routine as they constantly helped to build fires, cook food, gather wood, clean up, wash clothes in the streams, and everything else that was required. One of the hardest tasks was filling the small water tanks for the makeshift showers, but it did serve to help build up both muscle and calluses. The tanks were made of animal skins so that they could be rolled up and easily transported when not in use.

Hanging full tanks in nearby trees allowed gravity to bring the water into the folding canvas shower enclosures, which also doubled as stretcher-like devices to carry supplies from camp to camp. A pull of the rope attached to the bottom of each tank would open the spring-loaded caps so that the water could sprinkle through the multiple tiny holes that the caps covered— and releasing the rope would automatically close them again. Justin had been shocked by the level of priority placed on hygiene and Jharate had been equally shocked that Justin would not want to bathe as often as possible, simply because it was inconvenient. Jharate even managed to shave his face every day, even though he only had a straight razor to work with.

The camp moved forward every three days or so. This was necessary in order to have time for training as well as for proper rest. The woods were so thick that it was hard to make a great deal of progress in a day, especially since they had the contents of an entire camp to maneuver through it. After a month of this, they finally neared the edge of the forest in Kelamosa and travel became somewhat easier as the trees thinned out out slightly.

On this particular late afternoon, they came to a clearing that was large enough for the entire party to be able to camp together for the first time since entering these woods. As it would not be long before the sun would set anyway, they cheerfully made use of the space and quickly set up their camp. There was something about this simple pleasure that set everyone abuzz. There were more smiles, more happy chats, and more kind words between them than there had been in the entirety of the past three or four weeks. The atmosphere held within it a feeling of hope and joy for a coming success that was discernable by all.

As the camp was in the final stages of preparing for nightfall, Jharate and Arante met to discuss the strategy for the next day.

"There is a Kelamosan family who resides on the edge of Lake Helasi. They have remained secretly rebellious toward Vranah and his armies," Jharate said. "They have a small sailing ship, which they use to transport refugees to safety. It is well stocked with fresh provisions at all times, to be ever-ready when desperate travelers appear. I am confident that we can rely upon this family to have the boat in readiness with ample provisions for all of us, should we need more than we have on hand."

"Yes, I've heard of that family as well. I will have everyone ready before daybreak so that we can get out of the forest at first light and begin crossing the lake shortly after that."

"Agreed." Jharate nodded once to Arante, and she lowered her head in response. The two cousins separated to attend to their duties in preparation for the coming dawn.

As the last bit of light slipped behind the thick tree line, the six Earth friends found themselves around one of the campfires. It was the first time that they had all been together in almost two weeks. Training and taking care of the camp had been all-consuming, and the men and women slept in different areas, so they had only been able to run into each other randomly. As they realized that they were all present and accounted for, they hugged each other, grinning ear to ear, and began to swap stories about what they had been doing while they had been away from each other. Their words flew from their mouths, seemingly at the speed of light, as they ate their dinner.

"What I wouldn't give for a game of Mario Kart right now!" Justin exclaimed loudly, a split second after Raoul had finished telling his story about shooting all of his targets dead center with his crossbow, for an entire day of perfect shots.

"Back on Earth, I would have bet that you would die if you ever had to go without technology for more than a day, let alone this long!" Kendra laughed.

"Hey! There's more to me than video games and tech stuff," Justin defended.

"Yes there is," Lani smiled. "Your cheerful attitude, for one, has made this whole experience better. And although I have been loving the technology hiatus, you know I'm always down for Mario Kart. It's a classic!"

"Yeah, that's one of the things that made you such a great girlfriend! How many other girls will play Donkey Kong and Tetris and Mario Kart and Mario Party for hours on end, just because their boyfriend wants to? You really were the best…"

There was an awkward silence for a few moments as Lani tried to think of how to respond.

"I do actually *like* those games too," Lani said, blushing slightly. "I had lots of fun with those games and with Kingdom Hearts and Legend of Zelda and all the other old games—although, admittedly, on Zelda, all I really liked doing was cutting the grass with my sword, ha ha. There were times I would have played any of those games for days on end if we'd had time to in-between all of our homework."

"I sure wouldn't" Kendra interjected, trying to help Lani escape. "I hate video games. They're stupid."

"No they're not!" Erik defended.

"Are you trying to refute my point or prove it?" Kendra asked with a scoff.

"Kendra," Lani reminded gently.

"Alright, alright," Kendra said. "Have your little trip down memory lane. Why don't I just add all the other stupid stuff my brothers played with besides video games? Let's see there's Furbies, Razor Scooters, Sailor Moon, Pokémon—"

"You've gone too far now, Kendra," Justin laughed. "You know you owned one of those scooters AND a Furby. And if anybody watched Sailor Moon, am I really supposed to believe it was one of your brothers?"

"Yeah, okay," Kendra said with a sheepish grin. "I guess you got me there."

After a long chat, the conversation lagged and a comfortable silence fell amongst all the members of the group. Kara finished eating rather quickly, and then nestled her head into Raoul's shoulder. Within seconds of closing her eyes she seemed to be peacefully dreaming. Raoul was quietly doing his little hand trick, making the pinky and thumb of opposite hands point the same direction, while folding in all other digits, and abruptly changing to the opposite pinky and thumb over and over again, while keeping his shoulders very still so as not to disturb Kara. Justin and Erik continued shoveling food into their bottomless stomachs, and Kendra was thinking of starting a new conversation, but wasn't sure just yet what to say. Lani was, as usual, lost in her own thoughts, with a far-off and content look in her eyes.

Her mind was reliving every last moment she had experienced since Jharate had entered her life. She recalled the curve of his mouth when he would smile at her. She could feel the heat in her veins whenever he touched her, especially when he had stepped behind her and held her arms to help guide them through the motions that her new heavy sword demanded of her. Lani shuddered slightly as she remembered the sparks that flew within her and the way the hair of her neck had stood up. Although his method had been entirely necessary for teaching, she fancied that it was also an excuse for him to touch her and be close to her as well. Her mouth watered as she relived the anticipation of their missed kiss. And his intoxicating scent never seemed to leave her altogether, nor did the timbre of his voice or the sound of his laughter, which played in her ears like a whisper in the wind.

The compliments he had given her warmed her heart as much as the memory of his touch set her body afire. Remembering the pleased look in his eyes as he told her how impressed he was with her ability to press forward and not complain made her smile unconsciously. She appreciated the fact that he would notice how tired or sore she was without her saying a word, especially since she had tried to hide how much her arms were aching and had only rubbed them on breaks when she thought he wasn't looking. He always praised her for being ready to practice and for giving it her all each and every time. But she also loved the extra praise when she did especially well.

She knew she was still no match for Jharate, but his telling her that he now felt she stood a good chance in a real fight made her feel that she could possibly be an asset in a physical conflict rather than a potential liability. She couldn't believe that anyone like him even existed, let alone that he had somehow found his way into her life. He was so supportive and so respectful and so...

"What do you think about that, Lani?"

Lani blinked. Her daydreams evaporated and she saw her friends sitting there in front of her— the blazing firelight flaring and illuminating their expectant faces. She had completely forgotten that they were even there. She saw an impatient look on Kendra's face that obviously meant that she was waiting for Lani to weigh in on a conversation she hadn't even heard a word of. Lani swallowed hard. She wished that her gift of vision would kick in and save her by showing her the conversation she had just missed, but alas, it did not. She sighed as she realized that there was no option. Lani simply had to ask, "What?" which caused her cheeks to turn red with embarrassment that the ever-moving firelight was kind enough to hide.

Justin laughed loudly. "Helllllloooooo? Earth to Lani... or, wherever this is anyway. You're always daydreaming! You know, one day that is going to get you into trouble!"

"I was asking," Kendra said curtly and with untamed irritation, "what you think about what we have been talking about, which I am now sure you heard none of, so never mind!"

"I'm sorry... I wasn't really here... I guess it's the curse of an overactive imagination."

"Yeah, well anyways, I am getting sick and tired of this whole thing! I don't want to be here, I didn't ask to be here, and I am sick of being ordered around by everyone! Especially Arante! I cannot *stand* that woman! She is the most irritating, stuck-up, selfish, uptight, poor example of our sex that I have ever had the incredible displeasure to know!"

Kendra finished with an emphatic pounding of her right hand onto her knee. Justin sat laughing with his mouth still full of food and little bits of it sprayed out as he spoke.

"Tell us how you really feel, Kendra!"

"You don't have to work with her all day. Just be thankful for that."

Everyone's head turned sharply to look at Kara. They had all thought she was asleep. But more than that, there was an unnerving quality in the tone of her distinctly quiet voice.

"I don't know, she seems nice to me…"

Erik had spoken before he could stop himself. All eyes were now on him, and everyone froze. He looked at the faces around him and cringed, bracing himself as Kendra verbally pounced.

"*Nice? Nice?* You call that she-devil *nice?*!"

"You liiiiiike her, don't you?"

Justin prodded Erik enthusiastically in the ribs.

"Grow up, Justin!" Erik turned as red as a beet and the firelight was not as kind to him as it had been to Lani.

Kendra and Justin erupted in laughter, much to Erik's visible dismay.

"Leave him alone!" Lani blurted out. "Whom he likes or does not like is his own affair, and certainly none of your business, unless you are lucky enough to be invited into his confidence. What is this, junior high?"

"Sorreeeee! Can't you take a joke? Sheesh!" Justin exclaimed, rolling his eyes and shaking his head slightly.

Kendra's eyes narrowed at Lani.

"Yeah, don't think we haven't noticed the way you are around her cousin *Jharate*. Could you *be* more obvious? Why don't you just put up a big billboard in this stupid forest that says 'Hi, my name is Lani, and I'm desperately in love with Jharate'?

Not that it would take one— a blind man could see the way you're after him."

"Hey Kendra, be nice. We're all friends here."

"Shut up, Raoul!"

"Thank you for defending me Raoul, but maybe you better help Kara get back to her bedroll. She looks really tired. And by the way, nice job on your perfect shooting day."

"Thanks, Lani," he beamed, before turning serious again. "Are you sure I should leave you here?"

"Like we're going to kill her, Raoul— really?" Kendra scoffed as she folded her arms.

"Yes, go ahead. I'll be okay. Thank you, Raoul."

Raoul hesitated, but saw the tense looks on all the faces around him. His shoulders lowered a little and he kept his eyes on the ground as he took advantage of the temporary cease-fire. He helped Kara up and left, just as Kendra and Justin burst into laughter again. Erik shifted his shoulders uncomfortably and stared at his feet. He felt ashamed that he didn't defend Lani the way that she had defended him. But what made him feel worse was that his most overwhelming feeling was relief that he wasn't in the spotlight anymore.

Lani could feel her blood beginning to boil. She was sick of their immature behavior and was trying to keep herself from sinking to their level. It would be so easy to just fly off the handle, but she didn't want that. She'd have to apologize later for something she shouldn't have said, which would be super frustrating because that would then become the focus and obscure what had started the whole situation in the first place! She decided firmly to say nothing. She gripped her right hand into a fist where they couldn't see it, trying to contain her anger. Her jaw was clenched tight and every inch of her body was tense.

It was harder than she thought to stay quiet on this subject, especially since Justin and Kendra both continued to taunt her.

"Lani and Jharate sitting in a tree…" Justin sang.

"Oh Jharate, of course I'll marry you! Let us ride off into the sunset to your castle in the clouds!" Kendra cooed, fluttering her eyelashes.

"K-I-S-S-I-N-G! First comes love…"

"If she marries him she'll be a *princess*," Kendra laughed. "I bet you'd like that, huh, Lani?"

"… then comes marriage, then comes BABY in the baby carriage! Ha, ha!"

"Your Royal Highness," Kendra said, bowing her head low before a mocking snort escaped her.

Kendra and Justin both burst into a renewed fit of laughter. They laughed so hard, tears streamed out of their eyes, and they could barely breathe. They both took several deep breaths to try to calm down, but additional laughs continued to come, slowing only slightly. As they finally tired of their own jokes, Lani decided to speak at last. Her voice was strained but she gathered all the composure she could muster to keep a steady and even tone.

"Are you finished?"

The smirks fell from their faces and both Justin and Kendra looked around uncomfortably. Justin rubbed the back of his neck with a nervous motion before dropping his hand back onto his lap. Kendra averted her eyes. They didn't apologize, but they answered her with a quiet "Yes."

"Thank you. Now if you will excuse me, I think I am going to retire for the evening."

With that, she got up and left. The others soon followed. As they filtered off in their separate directions, the same pair of glittering green eyes that had watched them when they had first appeared in this land peered at them from behind the dark trees. When all but the assigned watch had retired to their beds, the mysterious face disappeared into the thick forest in as ghostly a manner as it had come.

Drakne and over one hundred of his men had been traveling hard and fast on horseback in order to reach the thick and troublesome Forest of Kar. Even so, it had taken days to get there from the castle, since there had been only two varsins left in the castle stables. Drakne had ordered his men to retrieve both of them for his personal use— one to ride, and the other to be brought along, un-ridden, as a spare— in case Drakne's varsin did not suit him.

However, Drakne's men were not familiar with handling varsins, and as soon as they opened their stalls to harness and saddle them, both of the animals had bolted out of the stable at full speed— uncatchable, as a varsin's speed was well beyond the speed of a normal horse. This had forced Drakne to ride along with his men on plain ordinary horses. Drakne had sent the men responsible into the castle to clean up the scorch marks from Vranah's red power-balls in the throne room and had replaced them with three soldiers from the castle.

Using trackers, they had been searching the forest for weeks now. Drakne was sure that he had to be making better time than those he sought, because the children who had grown up on Earth would have no knowledge of this land— and yet they were nowhere to be found! Because he had no intuitive powers, he had no way to know how close they really were— but they should not have been able to get even this far alone! And with this abominable forest, they could be right in front of them, or they could be on a completely different path, or, blast it all, they could have passed them already! That the trackers gave him constant assurance that they were closing in only infuriated him further.

The weeks of trudging through the trees had been chipping away at Drakne's sanity one second at a time. Drakne always did as his master bade him, but his orders were becoming a colossal pain. Tracking and hunting was work for those inferior to himself. This was not the proper use of the second-in-command. True, Vranah had given him a great responsibility in tracking the Half-Hearts, but why couldn't someone else *find* them? Then he could simply take them to his master triumphantly. He was sick of this vile forest and everything in it. The birds, the squirrels, the deer, the trees, the bushes, the streams— *everything* was driving him crazy.

"We will stop here for the night."

His men immediately spiked their torches into the ground, and dropped the loads they had been carrying as they began to set up camp. Drakne returned to his thoughts as his soldiers worked. *This forest is a problem.* They had been forced to leave the horses outside of it because the trees were too thick. *I have been traveling on foot through this elf-forsaken forest for far too long! Wait a minute… the trees.* Yes, that was the answer. He would burn a path through this wretched place. He could easily contain the flames so that the fire would not rage out of control. And if he could not, why should he care? He did not need this forest and neither did his master.

"Never mind, men— there has been a change of plans."

Drakne smiled at his own genius as his men began to quickly reverse the process they had started just moments ago. The sound of rocks sliding through the thick trees ahead caught Drakne's attention, and one eyebrow rose as he saw a girl come tumbling down a small embankment, landing directly in front of him. Drakne snapped his fingers and a force field surrounded the confused and frightened girl.

"Who are you?"

"I-I-I'm nobody, really."

The girl's eyes darted wildly as she saw the large number of men around her.

"Do not try my patience, woman!"

Drakne struck her with a small bolt of current from the cage and she screamed.

"I ask you again. Who are you?"

"My name— my name is… Kara."

"What manner of clothing is this that you are wearing? Where are you from?"

"I'm not from here. Please, all I want to do is go home! I never asked for any of this, I just want to go home!"

"*You* could not have survived this far into the forest on your own. Where are those you travel with?"

"Please… I just— I just want to go home! I JUST WANT TO GO HOME!"

"Do not make me ask you again!"

Drakne struck her with another energy bolt and this time she cried out in greater pain.

"All I know is that they are headed for the lake! I snuck out of camp while everybody was sleeping. I've been wandering for hours by myself out here trying to find a way back. Please! I just want to go home!"

"If you know the lake is there, you must be with people who know this forest... How many are in your camp?"

"I don't know! My friends and I didn't mean to come here! I just want to go home! I want to go home!"

Drakne paused. He knew his orders had been to kill any woman he saw, but this girl was *obviously* no threat. She was weak. She did not even *try* to withhold the information he needed. She could not be the one his master feared. She might also possess information that could be valuable to them later.

"Enser, Kolbin, come here!"

"Yes, sir," two voices answered in unison.

"Take this girl to our master for questioning."

"Yes, sir!"

Drakne snapped his fingers again and the force field disappeared. Enser and Kolbin each grabbed one of Kara's upper arms and pulled her to her feet. Drakne moved his hands in a circular motion around the two henchmen and the girl they held. A whirlwind formed and began to surround them. It picked up speed until it took off with its three passengers, toward Trisakne. Kara's frightened scream faded into the distance. They would be there in a very short time now. A smirk crossed Drakne's face. Things had definitely taken a turn for the better for him. He would soon have those he sought within his reach.

Drakne stretched his long, thin arms straight up and pulled them down to his sides, slowly at first, and then with a quick jerk, until they were parallel with the ground. His head went up briskly at the same time— his face to the sky. His eyes glowed for a split second with orange and yellow flames as he lowered his head to its normal position. His hands swept straight in front of him and his palms extended forward with a great push. Flames burst as if they were coming from his hands, and began to clear a path one hundred feet wide through the forest.

He felt the power surge through his body with intense force. He rolled his neck as if adjusting it and smiled. Trees exploded and nearly disintegrated in the magically-enhanced forest fire. Drakne walked forward, arms at his sides, palms facing forward at a slight distance from his body. The wall of fire no longer came from him but it obeyed his every move. The flames disappeared wherever he took a step forward and the ground magically cooled, but the fire never paused from its destructive path. His open-mouthed men stood gaping at the spectacle. One by one they forced themselves to break free from their trance, and slowly moved to march closely behind him.

OUT OF THE FRYING PAN INTO THE FIRE, OUT OF THE FIRE INTO THE...

"WAKE UP! WAKE UP EVERYONE! RUN!"
Jolted from their sleep by Arante's frantic cries, everyone scrambled to their feet. Lani scanned to locate the danger. Eyes now wide, her heart skipped more than one beat before pounding frantically like a jackhammer. Deep in the forest, a fifty-foot wall of fire was coming toward them like a blazing tidal wave. They could hear the roaring flames and the trees exploding as it advanced.

The camp fell into instant chaos as people screamed and shouted to each other. Every person ran and grabbed everything they could before following Arante. They were close to the edge of the forest and the trees were thinner here, but not thin enough. The fire came closer and closer. It seemed that no matter how fast they ran, they could not increase the distance between themselves and the flames. The fire advanced still faster, and they began to feel its heat on their necks.

"Lani!"

OUT OF THE FRYING PAN INTO THE FIRE, OUT OF THE FIRE INTO THE...

Lani turned toward Jharate's voice, but could barely see him through the now hazy darkness. He rushed to her and they ran together, dodging tree branches and rocks, trying desperately not to trip. This was a worst-case scenario for Lani. She had never been a good runner and was somewhat uncoordinated when it came to navigating around physical obstacles. And that was under the best of circumstances— with no pressure and nothing more than a chair or two to avoid. She hoped that the sheer adrenaline would keep her going and somehow give her the abilities she lacked.

It was still pitch dark and the only light they had was coming from the massive wall of fire behind them, which flickered wildly and cast moving shadows in all directions. Arante yelled that they were nearing the lake. Lani's heart beat hard from exertion and anticipation, but she still could not see her way out. She stayed close to Jharate and tried to follow his every move. The flickering firelight fooled Lani's eyes into thinking she had gotten over a twisted tree root. Instead the root grabbed her foot and held it tightly, breaking her leg as she fell to the ground. She smacked her head hard against a rock.

Jharate stopped dead in his tracks and looked back. He saw Lani lying motionless at the base of a tree. The wall of fire was just moments away and gaining. He dropped the provisions he was carrying and ran back to her. Jharate gently untangled her foot from the root that had taken it. She was unconscious and her head was bleeding profusely. He carefully lifted her limp body into his arms. Now the fire was mere seconds away. He ran and ran, ducking under tree limbs and making sure that he, himself, did not trip, while trying his best to shield her from any more damage.

The color was draining from Lani's face and she was getting cold. All Jharate could do was to keep running forward with everything he had. They had already been at the back of the group and this had left them even farther behind. No one had seen them and they were alone.

Arante cleared the forest and hurtled into the shallows of the lake, followed by everyone else. She looked back once she was waist-deep in the water and realized that Jharate and Lani were missing. A burst of panic filled her soul. She turned back and squinted to see across the dark lake. The sliver of a moon shone down dimly, almost directly, on a small sailing ship with a gas lamp hanging from the mast, about one hundred yards away. She pointed to it sharply and yelled to all around her.

"Swim for that ship, now!"

Those who were not strong swimmers kicked as they held onto the sides of the supply stretchers, which floated because of the wooden poles.

Arante ran back to the shore as the others obeyed. She shielded her eyes and strained to look into what remained of the forest, hoping that the wall of fire had not consumed them. Heat from the inferno reached her face and she held her breath as she waited… and waited. Finally, she saw their silhouettes clear the forest just before the last trees exploded spectacularly behind them. With Lani still in his arms, Jharate ran with Arante into the water.

"Arante!"

Jharate stopped, knee-deep in the water, to keep Lani's unconscious form out of the freezing cold lake. Arante's eyes widened as she turned and saw the blood seeping from Lani's head and the pallor that was overtaking her skin. Arante looked behind them and saw the fire burn out. She peered through the smoke into the scorched remains of the woods and saw the shadowy figures of scores of men by the light of the dying embers.

"We have no choice, Jharate. We have to take her into the water and swim for it. You hold her head up out of the water and I will help support her. We'll swim together."

"If we do as you say, she will die!"

"WE HAVE TO! Or we will *all* die— or worse! There are men following us right now! What do you think *they* will do to her? It's her only chance, as well as ours. MOVE!"

Jharate looked behind him for a moment. It was so dark that he could not see what she did, but he knew Arante's eyes were extremely keen and he trusted her. He grimaced with a short sigh before turning back to Arante.

"Very well."

Jharate carried Lani into the water, holding her head up with his left hand while wrapping his right arm around her waist, and began to swim, mostly with his legs. Arante swam on the other side, trying to help keep them all afloat. The water chilled their skin and the constant current made it feel as though they were making little progress. The two of them continued to push forward with everything they had, kicking their way toward the ship.

Arante felt her leather outfit pulling her down beneath the water. She kept fighting her way back to the surface and gasping for air, but each time it felt harder and harder, as if threatening to be her last.

"I can't hold her anymore, Jharate. The current is too strong. We're too close to the mouth of the river."

"Go on without us."

Arante hesitated, but finally released her hold on Lani.

"I'll send help. Just hold on!"

Arante turned away from her cousin and swam the last twenty yards to the ship. Justin and Erik pulled her aboard, but Raoul was the first to speak.

"Where's Lani? I checked with everyone on the boat and she isn't with us! Where is she?"

"She— she's," Arante said, coughing hard from all the water she had swallowed and shivering from the cold. She pointed out into the dark water, "Jhar— Jharate has her— Help him!"

Raoul dove overboard before she could even finish her sentence and swam in the direction Arante had indicated until he saw the shadows he was hunting for.

"Let me take her! You're too tired from swimming all this way with her. Let me take her in. You can catch up."

Jharate sized Raoul up before he answered.

"Agreed. Take great care as you go. Her head is bleeding profusely and I believe her leg is broken."

Jharate carefully handed Raoul Lani's motionless body. As Raoul took off through the icy water with her securely in his grasp, Jharate followed close behind, keeping his eyes fixed on Lani.

Raoul's brain frantically reviewed everything he had learned during the one summer he had spent working as a lifeguard— but he had never imagined having so precious a victim in his arms and it was hard to remain as calm as he knew he needed to be. He focused on reaching the boat, but that wasn't enough to keep the creeping doubts and fears away from his mind. What if he wasn't fast enough? What if he didn't have the resources to save her? What if he failed in this crucial moment? He felt his heart start to race faster and beat harder until there was a sharp pain in his chest. He prayed that she wouldn't die. Raoul tried to force the dread from his mind as he managed to reach the boat about five yards ahead of Jharate.

"Erik! Justin! Help!"

Erik and Justin were already waiting anxiously at the edge of the ship when Raoul arrived. They quickly leaned over the edge as far as they could without falling in and carefully pulled Lani onto the ship. Jaresh extended his enormous arm to Raoul, and as soon as Raoul saw that Justin and Erik had Lani safely aboard, he gratefully took the assistance and climbed up.

Justin and Erik struggled to keep Lani's body properly aligned as they gently laid her down on the smooth wooden deck. The moment Raoul's feet landed on the solid deck he rushed over to Lani, forcefully pushed Erik and Justin out of his way, and dropped to his knees by her side. He leaned over her body, turning his left ear toward her, and listened to hear if she was breathing. She was! Thank goodness! He placed his index and middle finger against the side of her throat and checked her pulse. It was extremely weak and thready. Worse, it was fading.

"I need a clean cloth to bandage her head. Justin, you're an Eagle Scout too, so you take care of splinting her leg. Erik, you go find blankets for her so she doesn't get hypothermia or go into shock! Come on, Lani— stay with me, now. I'm here and I'm gonna make this okay, okay? Just stay with me!"

Arante handed Raoul a long white cloth that was about six inches in width. He launched straight into action, wrapping it securely around her head a few times, trying desperately to stop the bleeding. Jharate was pulled aboard just as Raoul finished bandaging Lani's head. Jharate was out of breath and exhausted but he immediately rushed to Lani's side, grasping her hand to his heart.

Seeing that Jharate was safe, Arante called out to her people in a hoarse but booming voice, "Put out the gaslight and set sail before we are seen! NOW!"

It was done. They sailed out of the patch of moonlight and into the black of night.

Drakne reached the edge of what had previously been the forest and saw the ship just as it slipped away into the shadows.

"BLAST IT ALL!"

He turned abruptly to face his men with a deep frown on his face.

"Search for another boat!"

Drakne's men rushed off and combed the shore in both directions. Drakne knew there would be no vessels to be found, but he wanted a moment to himself in order to strategize. He regarded the ebony surface of the water in the same manner one would expect a hungry tiger to regard a raging river that stood between it and its prey. His mind raced for a possible solution. It was true that he had tremendous powers, but his powers were mostly those of great forces like electricity, wind, fire, and control over life energy. Water and earth were a different matter. These did not obey him. He could electrify the water, but all that would accomplish at this point would be to kill all of the fish and make the mermaids angry— and he did *not* want to deal with *those* creatures.

Drakne wished he had gotten a better look at exactly where they were, because then he could have teleported to them and killed them all. However, without the precise image in his head, he knew that teleportation would likely just get *him* killed. He had to be able to picture the exact destination for any of his transportation powers, but especially for teleportation, or he would just end up somewhere in the middle of the dark lake at the mercy of one of its terrible creatures, who all hated him. No, he would need a different plan.

What little color Lani had left drained into a near-ashen grey.

"NO! Don't do this to me, Lani!" Raoul exclaimed.

"What is wrong?" Jharate asked in alarm.

"Her pulse is gone and she's stopped breathing! That's what's wrong!"

Raoul placed the heel of his left hand below the lower half of Lani's breastbone, placing his right hand on top of his left while interlocking his fingers, and began to press down firmly and smoothly— compressing to one third of her chest depth. He continued pushing, keeping his elbows locked, and leaned in with his body to keep the motion steady— and to conserve his own energy. After he finished the first round of compressions, he moved over, closed her nostrils with his finger and thumb, placed his mouth over hers, and breathed into her. Her chest rose slightly in response. He finished the breath cycle and returned to giving her compressions. He continued cycle after cycle, becoming a little more frantic with each unsuccessful attempt to revive her.

Kendra and Justin had been watching intently over Raoul's shoulder ever since Justin had finished splinting Lani's leg.

Kendra grabbed onto Justin and buried her face in his chest. He put his right arm around her, running his left hand so roughly across his forehead that it moved the skin back and forth as he stared down at Lani's pale face in silence.

Raoul's movements became more and more frenzied, to the point of nearly losing it altogether, but he would not stop.

"Raoul," Justin said quietly.

"No! Don't say it! Just don't say it!"

Raoul continued to alternate between pumping her chest, and breathing into her mouth, again, and again, and again.

"Raoul, you did your best…" Justin interrupted again.

"Shut up, Justin! Just shut up! You don't know anything! You don't know *anything*!"

Raoul repeated the steps, over and over and over again, without missing a beat. He finished yet another breath cycle and moved on to pumping her chest. A small bright white light emanated from his hands. In that same instant, she started to breathe again and her pulse returned. The light faded away and Raoul's eyes flew open, wide with shock. He turned his hands over to look at his palms with a baffled gaze. There was no sign of the light.

Jharate's eyes widened and he straightened up as he looked at Raoul.

"A healer! Raoul, quickly move your hands to her head and attempt to heal the wound."

Raoul stared at Jharate, open mouthed, with fear in his eyes, and looked down again at his open hands. Being asked to repeat such a freak occurrence felt like being asked to fly. But Raoul knew that if he didn't act soon, the wound in Lani's head would kill her. He quickly moved his hands to her head and placed them gently on top, closing his eyes. He concentrated hard. He tried to picture the light coming again and the wound healing—but nothing happened. He opened his eyes and exhaled sharply.

"Aah! How do I do this?! I can't— I don't know how!"

"Focus. Take a deep breath and feel the energy from your body collecting in your hands. Allow that healing power to enter into Lani. Do not worry if you feel extremely fatigued. If you accomplish this, the healing power will drain much energy from you to give to her."

Raoul felt a Herculean hand on his shoulder.

"You can do this, Raoul," Jaresh said strongly.

Raoul took a deep breath and tried to focus all of his energy into his hands as Jharate had instructed. He held very still, and worked to keep his breathing steady and sure— clearing his mind of any thought but the thought of giving Lani the energy she needed to live. He felt something. His hands felt warm and he could feel energy leaving his body. Raoul kept his eyes closed and stayed very still, but the corners of his mouth turned up as he realized, by feelings alone, that it was working. He knew he would never be able to explain this, but he could feel Lani's life force coming back to her.

Jharate had been holding his breath as he watched. He finally exhaled as he saw the white light coming from Raoul's hands once again. Eventually, the light stopped and Raoul fell back onto the deck, onto his elbows. He opened his eyes, leaned forward again, and pulled himself closer to Lani. Jharate hadn't been kidding when he had warned him about feeling fatigued—Raoul felt utterly exhausted. But he had to know. He gently checked under the material he had wrapped around her head. He gasped as he saw what was beneath. There was nothing wrong! He carefully unwrapped the rest of the bandage. There was a little dried blood in her hair, but her scalp was perfect! There wasn't even so much as a scratch!

Raoul sighed in relief and collapsed onto his back next to her, completely drained. He had been running on sheer adrenaline to that point, and the energy transfer, or whatever it was, had finished him off. He saw Justin and Kendra still standing where they had been during the entire ordeal. They looked relieved and tranquil. Raoul barely understood Jaresh as he told him that he would return with something to help him regain his strength as soon as he could prepare it. As Jaresh left, Erik arrived and put some blankets over Lani. Justin scowled.

"Good job, Erik! My grandma could have gotten those faster! And she has a walker! Lani could have gone into shock, you idiot!"

Erik scowled back.

"Shut up, Justin! How was I supposed to know where they were? I've never been on this boat before, and someone stocked it before we got here, so I couldn't exactly ask anyone from our camp now either, could I?"

"Excuses, excuses!"

"Guys! Guys! Shouldn't we just be glad she's okay? And can you keep it down? I'm really tired from that light thing."

Raoul placed the inside of his elbow across his eyes. Erik and Justin exchanged bitter looks, but held their tongues. Justin looked around for the first time at everyone else on the boat. He saw all of the other rebels working to dry off and warm up, while also working to restore order to what was left of the supplies that they had managed to grab. Justin scanned every face to see if everybody had in fact made it aboard.

Jharate gently tucked the blankets around Lani and pulled her very carefully into his arms, making sure to not harm her splinted leg, as he leaned back against the side of the ship. He knew her leg would still be broken until Raoul had the strength to heal again, but he hoped that she would not have to wait long. He held her close and sighed deeply. He wished Raoul had been strong enough in his gift to be able to fully heal and revive a victim to instant consciousness, but they had been more than fortunate that Raoul had accessed his gift at all.

Jharate was surprised that one as old as Raoul could have lived so long without developing his gift. He had not even discovered it. Those types of gifts were innate. They often manifested before the time a child would even have left its mother's womb, and control over them ordinarily began in the first few years of life. Adolescence was usually the latest stage in life in which the more difficult gifts were mastered— and that was long ago for Raoul. Jharate looked at Lani's peaceful face as he continued to hold her in his arms, and tenderly stroked her hair as she slept. Her color was nearly back to normal and her breathing was steady and calm. Jharate inhaled deeply, grateful that at least Raoul's gift had surfaced in time.

"Where's Kara?" Justin asked as he completed his visual scan of the ship. "All that drama with Raoul should have caught her attention and I don't see her anywhere."

"I think she ran away," Arante shrugged. "I was making my rounds through the camp when I came across her bed. It had a note on it saying something about how she couldn't 'take it anymore,' and that she was going to try to find a way to get home. I was about to get someone to go find her when I saw the fire off in the distance. If she ran into the men chasing us, she has probably been captured or killed. If she somehow avoided both the men *and* the fire, then maybe she will find a way back home. There's really no way to tell."

"Well that's not very comforting," Justin retorted. "We already almost lost one of our best friends tonight."

"Wake up! Nothing about our world is comforting anymore! The sooner you deal with that fact, the better off you will all be! You have to accept that sometimes there is nothing you can do. We can't go back for her or we will *all* die. So assume the worst or assume the best— either way, our course remains unaffected."

The four conscious friends stared at Arante with their jaws nearly falling to the deck below them. They eventually blinked, shook their heads, and looked away. Erik, Kendra, and Justin walked as far apart from Arante as they could get and sat down close to each other on top of a wooden chest. They stared off into the pitch-black darkness of the night as they traveled across the lake in silence.

Raoul remained flat on his back, motionless from the fatigue, but his mind was alert and active. It all made sense now. Once, when he had been quite young, maybe ten years old or so, his father had suffered a heart attack. Raoul had panicked as his mother called for an ambulance. He shook his unconscious father and pushed on his chest to try to wake him— and all of a sudden… his father was fine. The paramedics arrived and everyone was very confused. They concluded that it must have simply been a panic attack. Raoul's father had insisted he was a calm and rational person who would never have such an attack, but could offer no other explanation. Raoul now theorized that he must not have noticed the light coming from his hands at the time because of his frantic emotional state, and because it had been daylight.

Realizing he had this gift was a strange feeling for Raoul. It was spectacular— mind-boggling. He had grown up having this wonderful power and had never known it. He had never even dreamed that something like this could even be true, and yet Jharate had recognized Raoul's gift for what it was the very instant he saw it. Raoul pondered this strange world that they had come into. He wondered if maybe they were actually better off being here in some ways. Obviously running for their lives on a daily basis was not what he considered better, but there were places on Earth where life was like that anyway. What he meant was the belief in, for lack of a better word, miracles.

The fact that Jharate had seen him healing Lani and had identified it as a gift, instead of fearing it or seeing it as something strange, said something to Raoul. What if everyone on Earth had a unique gift as special and awe-inspiring as the one he had, but none of them knew it because they were raised in societies, which taught that those things were not real— societies with no faith or dreams or beliefs, just jaded cynicism and the desire to expose anything with no basis in scientific fact. What if something like this had happened to Lani on Earth? Would he have been able to save her? No. It had taken help from Jharate. He would have lost her. The very thought made him cold— colder than he already was from being in the dark lake twice. He shuddered at this realization as he closed his eyes and drifted off to sleep.

Hours passed as the ship sailed across the calm waters of Lake Helasi. Jharate knew that there would still be at least three hours before the sun came up, and another six after that to complete the lake crossing. Lani was still in his arms. He had not slept at all as he kept a vigilant watch over her. He leaned his lips down to her forehead, and kissed it gently. As he straightened back up again, she sighed contentedly in his arms and the corners of his mouth turned up serenely.

A moment or two later, Lani's eyes slowly fluttered open. As she saw Jharate's face above her, she looked up at him, very nonplussed.

"Wh–What?"

She closed her eyes for a second and stretched her neck a little bit. It felt sore. She opened her eyes again. Where were they? The last thing she remembered was running from the fire. She opened her mouth to speak, but Jharate spoke first.

"Do not force yourself to speak just yet. You very nearly died only hours ago. Your foot became entangled in the root of a tree. Your leg broke as you fell and you hit your head on a rock. You were bleeding badly. I carried you out of the forest to the lake. To make matters worse for you, we had no choice but to bring you through the freezing water. I was— I mean— we were afraid we were going to lose you."

Lani remembered falling now and suddenly became very aware of the pain in her leg. The pain was greater than any she had ever experienced. She had never broken anything in her body before in her entire life. She blanched and lifted her hand unconsciously to her head. Her hair felt as if it had been dry for a while now and as she touched her scalp, it felt normal. She moved her hand to a few different places on her head, but again, everything felt normal. There was no lump on her head, no hint of a gash, and to her further astonishment she realized that she did not even have a headache. There was nothing wrong at all!

"I thought you— I thought you said that my head was bleeding?"

"And so it was. You are very fortunate. It seems your friend, Raoul, is a healer. He was quite surprised, as were we all. He fought hard to revive you after you stopped breathing— and suddenly, during one of his many attempts to do so, his gift surfaced on its own. You began to breathe again and, with a little guidance from myself, he was then able to heal your head. Raoul was too fatigued to heal your leg, following that effort. It could be some time before he is strong enough to finish. However, you are alive— and that is all that matters."

He said the last part softly, almost reverently, as he kissed her gently on the forehead. Lani was so shocked that she barely even noticed the sweet kiss. She had known Raoul for eight years and had never had even one clue that he might have any mystical gifts— and apparently, neither had he. Between her near-death experience and trying to process the thought of a dramatic save by a power she never knew her friend possessed, she felt dizzy. But there was one thought she liked a great deal. Jharate had stayed with her and saved her life, when it would have been much easier just to save himself.

Lani smiled as she realized Jharate truly cared for her more than he did for his own life. She felt the same way about him, but the fact that he had just proven it made her feel extremely warm and cozy despite the cold. She felt the kiss on her forehead now— and even though his lips had withdrawn moments ago, it felt warm on her cold skin. She sighed happily.

A small splash and some distant conversation caught Lani's attention. She looked to her right and noticed that Arante was leaning partway over the opposite railing of the ship, and seemed to be speaking to the water.

"What is Arante doing?"

"No doubt she is speaking with a mermaid."

"A mermaid? Really? Wow! But, she's speaking English, isn't she? Don't mermaids have their own language? Like Mermish or something?"

Lani felt a little stupid. After all, what did she know about mermaids?

"They did. As a matter of fact, all of our kingdoms had their own languages once. After a fashion, they still do."

"What do you mean?"

"Sometime after the fall of Lanas, and before the fall of Zenastra, Vranah cast a spell over all of the Kingdoms of Alamea so that everyone would understand each other. It made it easier for his men to subjugate the people when they did not have to concern themselves with finding reliable translators. It also insured that the conquered people could not work behind his minions' backs in a language they could not understand. So although everyone still speaks his or her own language, everyone understands each other as well. That is why you think I am speaking... What did you call it? English?"

"Yes. You sound like you are speaking perfect English—with a charming accent. That is truly fascinating... So you are actually speaking a different language to me right now?"

"Yes. I am speaking Trisaknen, which is the language of my kingdom, as is Arante with the mermaid, who is speaking Mermish, as you correctly called it. However, you hear us in your language just as I hear you in mine."

"Wow."

"Yes, it has its advantages— although we have lost much of our individual identities as kingdoms and cultures. So much of cultural identity is connected to language."

"That is so true. It's the same way on Earth. I think that is why it is always one of the first things that conquerors try to destroy, along with a people's artistic and dance heritage. If they can rip the heart out of a nation, it falls much more easily."

"Very wisely spoken, Lani. We have had to learn to express our uniqueness in other ways, as it is a permanent spell. In truth, I believe it would likely remain with you if you ever returned to your own world."

Lani thought of the advantages this would give her should she ever return. Before she had come to Alamea, it would have been a thrilling prospect to be able to travel all of Earth and speak every language— especially Europe and Polynesia. A six-month split between a villa in Italy and a bungalow in Tahiti as permanent residences would have sounded like a dream. Not to mention the stories and the knowledge that she could help preserve amongst cultures whose languages had all but died!

But it seemed unlikely that she would ever find a way home. And even if she found a way to go back, she would never want to leave Jharate. Lani looked up at Jharate and smiled with a gleam in her eyes. He smiled back at her and she closed her eyes happily. After a moment Lani opened up her eyes brightly and her eyelashes fluttered a little.

"You know, Jharate... I've never seen a mermaid before..."

Jharate smiled and lifted her gently into his arms, being extra careful with her splinted leg, and carried her to the edge of the ship.

Lani looked down into the black glassy waters and her eyes lit up in complete wonderment. The night was very dark and so she wouldn't normally have been able to see anyone in the water. But the mermaid glowed. She had long glossy silvery hair, with a hint of lavender color streaming through it. Her tail splashed for a moment revealing its silver scales, which phosphoresced as she moved and gave off an unearthly glow.

Her eyes gleamed in the darkness, shining like her purple fish scales, which started just below her waist where the silver scales of her tail ended, and continued upwards until they covered her chest. Strands of freshwater pearls draped across her shoulders like fallen straps. Her eyelids shimmered as if they were covered with ground up stars and her lips were a glistening icy purple color. The necklace she wore was made of freshwater pearls and assorted jewels. They were delicately intertwined to support a massive amethyst pendant, which hung just an inch or so above her cleavage against her white skin. A magnificent, three-pronged crown, studded with diamonds and amethysts, rested on her head.

"Greetings, Narani," Jharate said in a very polite and respectful tone. "Lani, this is Narani, Daughter of the King of All the Seas, Uarian the Great, and Princess of the Merpeople. Narani, this is Lani, a traveler from another world."

"It's a pleasure to meet you, Your Highness," Lani said respectfully.

The mermaid nodded in acknowledgement and returned her attention to Jharate with a mischievous grin on her face.

"She may have been *in* another world, but she is not *from* another world."

Jharate raised an eyebrow.

"Excuse me, Princess Narani, but what do you mean?" Lani asked curiously.

"You'll find out," Narani trilled with a small laugh.

"Narani was just telling me what the men on the shore were doing and who they are. Jharate, we have a problem," Arante stated gravely.

"Drakne?" Jharate guessed.

"Evidently. That explains why the wall of fire that followed us out suddenly stopped and didn't burn the whole forest down. He was controlling it the whole time."

Lani stared across the water, her head cocked to one side, immersed in thought. What had Princess Narani meant by saying that she was not *from* another world? She had been born in Southern California and adopted by the Johnson family not long after. Her birth certificate said Fallbrook, California on it. It had had no information about her biological mother and father, but it was very clear about where she had been born. Dr. Chipman had delivered her and he had signed it himself. So how could she have been from anywhere but California? She had lived there her entire life. How could— Lani suddenly went limp in Jharate's arms.

"Lani? Lani!"

Jharate quickly took her back to where she could lie down again, holding her gently in his arms. Had he allowed her to do too much too soon? He held her close, hoping it would not be long before she revived again.

Lani opened her eyes. She did a quick double take and blinked hard to make sure she was really seeing what she thought she was seeing. The green marble floor, the long purple carpet, the dark chandeliers, and the dim torches did not fade away into nothingness. *I'm in Jharate's stolen throne room!* She looked to her right and started as she saw Kara. Kara was on her hands and knees inside a force field, breathing hard, and her skin was glistening with a fine layer of sweat.

Lani tried to run to help Kara but found herself unable to do so. She looked down at her feet and tried to pull her legs up with her hands, but they would not budge. She tried harder, then frantically, but it was no use. Lani could do nothing but watch.

CHAPTER EIGHT

She looked up helplessly at Kara and this time she noticed that in front of Kara was a man. Lani knew him instantly. There was no mistaking that tall menacing figure or those cold soulless orbs. *Vranah!* Lani's heart beat rapidly as she remembered the dream she had recently had in which Vranah had burned an entire village to the ground, and realized for the first time that it hadn't been a dream at all. She looked at Kara and desperately tried to run to her again, but just as before, she was only able to observe.

"Now, answer my final question and you shall have your desire. I will send you home. I want the names of your companions from the forest. First, the names of those who are from this world, and then the names of your friends who came through the portal with you."

Lani felt a burst of panic within her for Kara. Had Lani been in Kara's place, she would have remained silent, but she knew Kara would use a different strategy. Kara was a brilliant girl with a great imagination and she was also a decent actress. She had always won whenever they had played the game Two Truths and a Lie, because she was so good at making everything sound true. But Vranah was the master of lies. Would he know when Kara gave him the wrong names? Would he be able to sense it? What would he do to her then? If she was able to pull off the ruse that Lani knew she was about to employ and Vranah somehow bought it, Lani prayed he would actually let Kara go as a reward.

Kara exhaled slowly and a single tear fell from her eye and hit the floor with a quiet splash. She bit her lip and turned her head away from Vranah, pausing for a moment. She released her lip with a pained sigh and stared at the ground as the names slipped sadly from her tongue.

"Jharate and Arante are the only ones I know from your world... and as for mine, their names are Raoul, Justin, Kendra, Erik, and Lani. Now please let me go home," she sobbed in self-loathing.

Lani gasped and shook her head in disbelief. *No, Kara... no... How could you?* Hot, despondent, double-crossed tears streaked slowly down Lani's cheeks as Vranah smiled.

"Ahhh. Drakne's work will be easy then. After he kills the girls from your world, the prince will be mine as well. Things do certainly work to my advantage at times. Ha! Willing to sell your friends' lives for a simple trip home. How delectable! Drakne was right to send you to me."

Lani felt as though the room had suddenly gotten colder. She truly hoped Vranah had meant it when he promised to send Kara home alive. But her sudden fear for everyone else came to the forefront now. She wondered what she and Kendra could have possibly done that would merit *his* attention? And what if he saw her now? Was that possible?

She had assumed this was a vision, but she had never had one like this. Everything she had seen before had always been 2D like a movie screen. This felt like she was actually in the room. *What if I am?* Was it possible that she was only moments away from her own death? And even if it was only a vision, was it possible that she could be hurt or even killed while she was within it? The sound of Kara's horrified voice pulled Lani's attention back to the moment at hand.

"K-kk-k-kill them? N-N-No, y-you can't! They're my friends! They aren't important to you! Just send them home like me!"

"Oh no, my dear, feeble, girl. You see, *you* are not important. You are not a Half-Heart, *obviously*. Even the weakest of all Half-

Hearts can put up a bigger fight under torture. But your friends... now their importance is less certain. At least one of them *is* a Half-Heart. And, as fortune would have it, that person is one of the strongest Half-Hearts ever born. Although I am not sure which one she is, or whether or not there are more Half-Hearts in the group who traveled with you to this world, I will know who she is when her body is brought before me."

"But they are my friends! Just send them back like me! They can't bother you there!"

"Oh no," Vranah chuckled. "I will not make that mistake again. But, I will keep my word. You are going to go home—now!"

Vranah snapped his fingers and she disappeared. The force field deactivated and he smiled as he looked at the vacant spot. The wind blew in from one of the throne room windows and Vranah stood frozen... completely still... waiting.

"What is this treachery?" Vranah asked, his eyes narrowing. "*Someone* is *WATCHING ME*!"

He reeled and faced the spot where Lani stood. Her eyes widened in terror and she struggled wildly to move, to run, to hide, anything— but she could not. She stopped and held her breath as Vranah neared. Vranah walked closer and closer until his downturned, sharp-featured face was a mere foot or so away from her own. He towered over her, and Lani's desire to flee became desperate.

"YOU! Whoever you are— I cannot see you, but I *know* you are here! I would not use a gift such as yours to spy on me if I were you! You do not know what I am capable of! Ah, you are with the prince. I can sense it. I told you spying on me could be dangerous. You have now betrayed him. From the moment a door is opened, it may be stepped through in either direction, you foolish girl. Perhaps *you* are the one I am looking for, perhaps not. I cannot be sure. Some magic is protecting you. But mark my words— it will not save you from me forever! Now GO!"

As he commanded her exit, he shot a stream of energy straight through her. She threw her hands up defensively, closed her eyes, and screamed.

Jharate endeavored to keep Lani from harm as she struggled against his arms harder and harder and harder, until her eyes flew open and a frenzied cry burst forth from her lips.

"You are safe, Lani!" Jharate spoke firmly to her. "You are safe now! I am here. You are safe. What happened? What did you see?"

Lani relaxed as Jharate's face came into focus before her eyes and she realized where she was. She shook her head slightly and blinked slowly, trying to clear her mind. She had never experienced anything that vivid and strong before. The intensity was so great that she didn't even notice that all of her friends were staring at her.

"I... well, it was... what? Oh my goodness...Vranah! It was Vranah! He had Kara! He tortured her to get information. She told him! She gave him your name and Arante's as well! And... the rest of my friends! And mine... I think he sent her home. Something about her not being a Half-Heart so she could live. He ordered Drakne to kill the rest of the women from my world. I guess that means Kendra and me. And he wants you! He wants to capture you! He wants the rest of my friends too! But he isn't sure why. He seems to think that at least one of us is a Half-Heart for sure but... he *saw* me!"

"Are you certain?" Jharate asked. "How is that possible?"

"Well, he didn't see me, but he sensed me. He told me not to spy on him. He told me he couldn't see me, but that he knew I was with you, and that I couldn't be safe forever. I don't understand. I've seen him before in other visions or dreams, or whatever they were, and he's never noticed me! And how could there be a chance that any of us could be a Half-Heart? I was born in California! So were all of my friends. Half-Hearts are only born in Alamea! There must be a mistake!"

Lani's friends looked very confused. They whispered to each other and looked from Lani, to Arante, who was nearest them, and back to Lani again. Kendra rolled her eyes and glanced back at Lani one more time. She stood up, threw her head back and dragged her feet the few steps between her and Arante before stopping in front of her and dropping her head dramatically to look down at the deck.

"What's a Half-Heart?"

Arante rolled her eyes and sighed before answering.

"How can you not know this yet? You've been here how long? Alright, according to legend there are twenty-four Half-Hearts born in every generation— twelve exceedingly virtuous men and twelve exceedingly virtuous women. According to one of our primal prophecies, if any man and woman, who happened to both be Half-Hearts, could fall in love and marry in a place 'magically prepared' for such a union, they would be able to tip the balance of power from evil to good, and defeat Vranah forever. Only problem is— only Vranah knows who they are."

Justin gave a long low whistle. "*Okay...*"

"That's interesting..." Kendra reflected.

Erik didn't say anything. He simply looked from one face to another, and then down at Raoul, who was now leaning against the trunk they were using as a bench. Arante's expression informed all four of them that she was not open to answering follow-up questions, and so Kendra returned to her place on the wooden chest next to Justin and Erik, and they all sat there quietly, thinking.

Jharate smiled and held Lani closer. She wrapped her arms around him and clung to him tightly, with a sharp, troubled sigh.

"You need not worry, Lani. I will protect you. He will not lay one hand on you, and neither will any of his men."

Lani loosened her hold on him, rested her head on his shoulder, and nestled into his strong muscular arms. The deep sincerity she had come to associate with him coaxed the muscles in her own body to relax one by one. She felt her eyelids getting heavier and heavier and she struggled to keep them open to see the early glow of the first rays of morning light filling the lake with shimmering sparkles, as the sun began its ascent into the heavens above. But, the Sandman finally got the better of her entirely and she fell asleep.

Jharate smiled as she slipped into peaceful rest and stroked her hair carefully, so as not to risk waking her. Raoul crawled over from where he had been sitting against the chest until he reached Lani. Jharate placed one hand on Raoul's shoulder and looked intently into Raoul's eyes to express his deep gratitude. Raoul looked away modestly and a bashful grin crossed his face as Jharate removed his hand from Raoul's shoulder and gently replaced it around Lani.

Raoul shifted a little, embarrassed by the sincerity of the thank you, and then straightened up with a determined look. Raoul took a deep breath, placed his hands lightly on Lani's leg, and closed his eyes. When he didn't feel anything, Raoul opened his eyes and looked at Jharate with a disappointed glance and a frustrated sigh. Jharate nodded encouragement to signal Raoul to try again. Raoul repeated the attempt again, and then again, and yet again, without result. Finally, the warming sensation came, as did the glowing white light.

Raoul opened his eyes with a wide grin on his face. The corners of Jharate's mouth went up in response and he bowed his head slightly in acknowledgement. Before attempting to remove the splints, Raoul examined Lani's leg carefully— there wasn't even a bruise left behind to show that her leg had been injured in any way whatsoever. A breathy laugh escaped Raoul. Only a bloody rip in Lani's jeans told the story. To be sure, he gently pressed on her leg and incrementally increased the pressure. When there was no reaction, he undid Justin's professional splint work until her leg was free. Raoul backed up a little ways and once again lay down on the deck to recuperate— but this time, happily playing his little pinky/thumb game as he rested.

The sun was high in the sky when Lani's eyes opened again. She blinked, adjusting to the light. As she realized she was still in Jharate's arms, a bright smile spread across her face. She looked deeply into his dark-chocolate-brown eyes and took note of the mystery that lay beneath the shimmering flecks of light that reflected on their surface.

"Didn't you sleep at all?"

"I did not."

"Oh, no! I hope you're going to be okay. You didn't need to stay up—"

"Do not trouble yourself, Lani. It was my privilege to watch over you."

Lani felt a deep blush burn her cheeks. She slowly pulled herself up, out of Jharate's arms, and knelt in front of him until they were at eye level with each other. She leaned in and gave him a kiss on the cheek.

"Thank you for saving me."

"You need not thank me. I am grateful that I was able to do so."

Lani could barely stand the intensity of Jharate's dark eyes peering into hers. Something felt different about the way in which he was looking at her now. She couldn't quite put her finger on it. She smiled and looked away. Through the ship's railing, she saw the shore as they sailed towards it, and then she caught a glimpse of something else.

"Oh my goodness! Look at this, Jharate!"

Lani scrambled to her feet to get a closer view with Jharate right behind her, smiling at her enthusiasm.

"I've never seen a dock anywhere *near* that beautiful!"

Lani gazed, in awe of the masterpiece, and tried to take in every last possible detail— but there was always something more to be discovered in the intricately carved woodwork. Just above the lake, the base of the dock was carved with brilliant swirls that mimicked the movement of water. Chiseled leafy vines appeared to spring from the water designs and wound around the poles until they reached the rafters on the sides and reached the tympanum, at the front end, where billowing spirals illustrated the long white clouds in the sky all the way up to the gabled roof. In-between and around these three areas of water, earth, and sky were exotic birds, tropical flowers, land and sea animals in their respective domains, and elegant figures representing humans— all in harmonious balance. With its totem-like posts and open walls, it reminded her a little of a Polynesian-styled version of a covered bridge she had seen in Lucerne, Switzerland— all of it made of a luxurious rich deep-brown wood.

"The Kelamosans are expert carvers, are they not?"

Lani nodded in response, still staring at the dock, as the ship continued its smooth approach.

"Oh yes! They truly are! I've never seen this particular style before, but it reminds me of an island people from Aotearoa, on Earth, called the Maoris. They have very sophisticated carvings, similar to these, that tell of their history and their genealogy, etcetera."

"The Kelamosans do the same. As you may already have ascertained, the carving on this dock represents the deeply held Kelamosan belief and understanding that the sky, the earth, and the waters are all connected with every living thing that lives amongst them."

"I think it speaks very highly of them that they would make such an ordinary thing so extraordinary. Especially since it's out here in the middle of nowhere."

Jharate smiled and Lani looked past the dock and studied the scenery. It was the first terrain in Alamea she had seen in daytime besides the forest and it was a very refreshing change. To the left of the dock was an immense and verdantly-green meadow, filled with tropical flowers— much like those depicted in the carvings. Thousands of bewitching butterflies and energetic hummingbirds flittered from flower to flower.

To the right were great mountains. The smell of something similar to pine trees wafted down through the air from the mountaintops, along with a crisp clean cool smell that reminded Lani of snow. It brought to mind the time she had been able to go to Big Bear with Kara during ski season. Kara's dad owned a cabin there so, although Lani's family could not afford such a luxury, she had been able to learn how to ski because of Kara. She wondered how Kara was now, and hoped that Vranah had actually kept his word and sent her home.

The ship gently bumped up against the dock, and a few of the rebels tied her off.

"Let's hurry this up, people!" Arante called out. "We lost a lot of supplies in the run, but there is more than we need on this ship. Load the supply stretchers and make sure they are complete and secure!"

"Here, Lani," Raoul said. "It's your sword."

"Oh, thank you! I was afraid I had lost it! I'm so glad it made it! And thank you so much for saving me, Raoul!"

Lani hugged Raoul and squeezed him hard with a quick kiss on his cheek. Once she released him, she buckled the belt with the attached sheathed sword back on, around her waist, with the sword on her left side.

"Well, you know…" Raoul shrugged, nervously kicking the ground before turning awkwardly and walking away.

"Erik," Justin whispered sharply. "Erik!"

Justin shoved Erik hard. Erik staggered forward a few awkward steps to keep from falling to the deck.

"What was that for?"

"'Cuz we need to get moving and you were staring at that ice queen over there. I said your name like twice, Dude!"

"Really? Arante didn't see me staring at her, did she?!"

"How am I supposed to know, Kook? Just get moving, already! Oi! Kendra! Over here!"

"I'm coming— keep your shirt on!"

"Such a cuddly kitten, that one," Justin said with a mocking snort.

"You should have seen her in Italy," Erik said. "She was a lot more relaxed then."

"Oohoo! Do I detect a hint of history?"

"What? No! Grow up, Justin!"

"Well you learned that phrase from her awfully fast."

"I learned that one on my own. I'd only known you for a couple weeks before I had to use it."

"Nah, I'm sticking to my idea that you got it from Kendra."

"Got what from me?"

"The whole 'Grow up, Justin' thing."

"Oh grow up, Justin!"

"See! See! There it is."

Kendra rolled her eyes and started helping everyone unload the approved items from the ship. She was surprised to see the amount of supplies everyone had managed to save in the mad rush of the night before— even most of the shower tanks had made it! She guessed that was more from the fact that they had been rolled up on top of the shower "stalls," which had been used as stretchers to carry the rest of the supplies out faster, rather than from someone's obsession with hygiene when a huge wall of fire was coming their way. She watched out of the corner of her eye, careful to avoid any eye contact with Arante, as Arante rushed around and rummaged through everything, casting anything unimportant to their continuing journey onto a large pile on the ship. All of this seemed to take almost no time at all as they disembarked nearly as fast as they had scrambled onto the ship in the first place.

The instant they were ashore, Lani felt Jharate's strong arm wrap around her shoulders. She leaned into his side as she looked to see where he was pointing with his other arm.

"Once we cross that meadow, it is less than a six-day walk into Destavnia."

Jharate let go of her and took the bag she was carrying, strapping it across his shoulders in addition to his own pack. Lani didn't really notice what he had done because her heart was still leaping for joy at the words he had uttered. To be that close to safety sounded like a symphony to her ears. She gazed at the trees that lined the edges of the meadow and thought of the promise that lay behind them. She and Jharate would actually get to spend some time together, while not on the run!

They had walked about fifteen yards into the lush meadow when they heard the sound of a horse trotting toward them. It stopped with a loud snort as its master began to speak.

"Put down your weapons!"

The harsh and penetrating voice belonged to a tall, sturdy looking man sitting astride a horse that was blacker than the dark lake at night. The man had quintessential brown hair, which complemented his quintessential brown eyes. Everything about this man was precise, as if his proportions were entirely symmetrical and entirely under control. Even his dress was precise, with the designs on every golden button precisely aligned and rigidly in place. The deep green jacket and black pants of his militaristic uniform were perfectly starched and the golden epaulets and cords on his shoulders were immaculate. Even his boots were perfectly shined and looked as though they never touched the ground. Below his right epaulet was a gold and green coat of arms, with a golden dragon and the motto, *For the Honor of Kresar,* embroidered below it.

But the man was not alone. The weary rebels had drawn their weapons the moment they had heard his horse coming, only to find their way barred, as a semicircle of sinister-looking men ran out from the tree-line and confronted them with weapons drawn. Lani watched fearfully as that semicircle became a complete circle. They were surrounded again. Lani turned to find Jharate for safety— but he was nowhere to be seen. Neither was Arante for that matter. Her heart dropped to the pit of her stomach like a cold rock. Where had they gone? And how had they done it so quickly?

"Asharen!" Jaresh yelled as he spat toward the dirt. "Do not hinder us."

"That's *Lord* Asharen to you. You would do well to remember that, Jaresh."

"A title gained through bloodshed and the overthrow of the rightful monarch of this land."

"But gained, nevertheless."

"We fought side by side once. In honor of that former camaraderie, let us pass. We are not important enough for you to waste your time."

"I will be the judge of that. And as for our former camaraderie when we fought together for the losing side— that was over two decades ago, before I became enlightened. Our kingdoms may have once been allies, but when mine began to fall, I had to make a choice and I chose what was best for Kresar."

"You chose evil because it was more convenient. Do not try to make your choice sound like it was out of loyalty to Kresar. If you had truly been loyal, you would have fought to your dying breath to free your people from oppression."

"Jaresh, I am tolerating your speech because you once saved my life in battle. Do not press me to the limit of my better nature. And as for choosing evil, there is no such thing. There is only power and those strong enough to keep it— and those who would rather cling to an ideal no matter what the cost. I suppose we have both found out which type we are in the years since we last met. Do not speak to me further or I will have you all killed this very instant. Now, all of you— drop your weapons."

The rebels glanced at each other and then looked to Jaresh, who still had his crossbow raised and aimed at Asharen's heart. His finger toyed with the trigger as he vacillated. He knew he could make the shot and rid Vranah's army of one of its highest-ranking members— but at the same time, he knew they were outnumbered, and the advantage was not theirs. Could he live with himself if his fellow rebels were killed because of his hasty action— especially if that action caused the death of even one of the few women among them?

"I'll not ask you again," Lord Asharen commanded with deliberate enunciation. Every syllable was treated as though it were more important than the last. "Drop your weapons to the ground."

Jaresh sighed and took his finger off the trigger. He threw his crossbow down, keeping his fierce eyes locked on Asharen. The weapons of the other rebels fell one at a time to the ground with the sad clanking thuds of surrender.

"Wise decision," Lord Asharen snarled.

Lani did everything she could to avoid looking at Lord Asharen and instead looked at the contrast of her silvery sword against the soft green grass. Her last means of defense was gone. Even running from the fire and the intense vision of Vranah had not been as terrifying as this moment was to her. She was a naturally brave person, and that bravery had sustained her to this point, but this was different. Jharate was not with her. And this man, whoever he was, was no gentleman— of that she was sure. She quietly tried to hide her face to keep from being noticed, by staying close to the others, as they were all shuffled off toward a makeshift holding cell that was hidden only a little way into the trees on the left of the meadow.

As Lord Asharen watched the rebels being herded away, he caught sight of a slender young woman among them in strange attire with braided hair falling well past her waist. As she disappeared with the others he raised an eyebrow and the right corner of his mouth twisted ever so slightly.

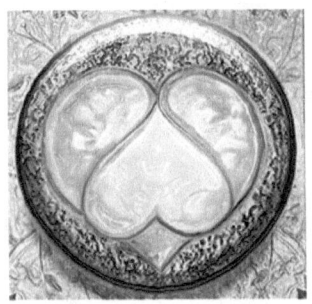

DRASTIC TIMES CALL FOR...

The holding yard was very simple, but it did the job. It stood in a man-made clearing just a few yards in from the meadow. Once inside the structure, Lani and the others had to be careful not to trip over the tree stumps Asharen's men hadn't bothered to remove. It was large enough to accommodate one hundred, but currently the close to forty members of the rebel group were the only occupants. Its four walls formed a perfect square and were made of wooden logs of exactly equal height that had been sharpened into perfectly symmetrical points at the top. Its designer had obviously been Lord Asharen. Lani shuddered at the thought of him. His very aura reeked of some foul-spirited danger.

Lani jumped as she heard the huge gate close behind her. She turned and saw that they were trapped. However, there was something comforting about that gate being closed. As long as that gate was closed it meant that she was in here and Lord Asharen was out there. That was nearly enough to make her wish that it would never open again. Lani turned her back on the gate and scanned the pen until she found Kendra and the rest of her friends, all sitting together, talking in hushed but clearly resentful tones.

"What a git!" Justin exclaimed quietly. "He full-on ditched us without a word!"

"I know!" Kendra replied angrily. "That guy! Come on! He's supposed to be this great warrior! He should have stayed to help get us out of this mess! He's been acting like he's really into Lani, and where is he?"

"I can't believe Arante could just leave like that," Erik let slip out.

"Well you better believe it! Because do you see her anywhere? NO! She's lucky these walls are holding me back and that I don't know where she is! When I see her again I am going to beat her down until her curly hair falls straight!" Kendra yelled.

"Wait," Raoul stated in a panic. "Calm down, guys. There's no use fighting."

"Just shut up, Raoul!" Kendra barked back bitterly. "No one asked you for an opinion."

Raoul started doing his pinky/thumb trick again— but this time, right in front of Kendra's face.

"Raoul is right, we need to be nice," Lani said, stepping forward and putting her hand on Raoul's shoulder as Raoul slowly lowered his hands away from Kendra. "All we've got right now is each other. If we start fighting amongst ourselves we won't stand a chance. Besides, I'm sure they'll come back for us."

Lani realized that her last sentence was a mixture of hope and belief. She wondered how two people could possibly pull off a rescue with such impossible odds of success. But she wanted to— no, she *had* to believe it was at least possible.

"Lani's half right at least," Justin said. "We do need to stick together now or we won't stand a chance."

The friends all nodded in agreement. They sat there for a few moments, each lost in their own thoughts. Kendra was still furious at their abandonment. Raoul was wondering how they would ever get out of this one. Erik was feeling betrayed by Arante and feeling stupid for having ever thought she cared for him. And Justin was trying to come up with a plan for escape.

Lani was feeling worried, confused, hopeful, and terrified, all at the same time. Where was Jharate? He had risked his own life back in the forest in order to save her and now, when she was facing death again, *or worse*, he was nowhere to be seen. She heard the monstrous gate opening behind her. The world seemed to freeze in that moment. She slowly turned her head to look over her left shoulder and swallowed hard as she saw Lord Asharen riding in on his horse through the horrid gaping maw, surrounded by his guards. Several of them sought out Jaresh and the other strongest warriors and restrained them. The remainder of the soldiers in the enclosure held the rest of the rebels back en masse.

Lani wanted to run but there was nowhere to go. She breathed silent quick breaths and could feel her heart beating faster and faster. Everything pulled into sharp focus— she could hear the sound of Asharen's horse breathing, she could taste the fear and adrenaline on the tip of her tongue, she could smell the sharp pine of the surrounding trees and the wooden scent of the fresh-cut stumps and logs that imprisoned them. She remained still, hoping to become invisible.

Lord Asharen slowly cast his eyes over the faces of the foreigners, starting with the ones closest to him and moving back until they fell upon the one he wanted. The right corner of his mouth warped up toward his high cheekbone, revealing some of his perfectly straight teeth like a snarling animal. He lifted his hand and extended his index finger directly forward as his eye twitched with a greedy glint.

"Her."

He had spoken so clearly and calmly, and yet the word echoed through Lani's head like a shotgun through a canyon. She felt all the blood rush away from her face. She felt cold and dead, but her lungs insisted on continuing to breathe, her heart to beat, and her brain to be painfully aware of every second as if the scene were playing out in slow motion. The way his eyes had made their way up and down her body made her feel as if she needed a thousand showers just to even *begin* to get the dirt off of her. Her heart turned to ice and she was paralyzed with fear.

The men reached Lani quickly and grabbed her roughly, pushing and pulling her toward the exit. She screamed! She kicked, she struggled, she dug her feet into the dirt, she pulled her arms hard underneath the grasp of the guards— but it was all in vain. There were too many of them, and each one of them alone was stronger than she was.

Justin burst forward and attacked one of the guards from behind. He locked his arm around his throat and pulled back hard, causing the guard to fall backwards on top of him as he began to choke and struggle to try and get Justin to release him. Justin snapped his neck and wrenched his way out from beneath the body to rush the men holding Lani. One of the guards holding the other rebels back lunged at Justin from behind and struck a savage blow to his head with a staff before forcefully kicking him back to his friends. Justin's face skidded across the dirt and his body settled roughly against the ground as he fell completely still. His eyes were closed and his head was bleeding badly. The guards were now more alert because of Justin's attack and quickly shoved back anyone else who dared to make a move.

"I will kill you for this," Jaresh said plainly, as he struggled against the four of Asharen's men who held him back.

"Doubtful," Asharen replied, in a bored tone.

With a barely perceptible command to his animal, Asharen turned his horse around and exited the enclosure. Raoul hurried over to Justin and knelt by his side, but kept his hands to himself and waited as one by one the soldiers left. Raoul felt his stomach turn over and an overwhelming reflex inside of him threaten to eject its contents as Lani was shoved out of the door and the gate shut behind her. Only her screams of protest and panic now resonated through his ears. His stomach started to burn as if it were on fire, scorching everything, including his heart, and then all at once everything went horrifyingly and disgustingly numb. Raoul blinked and looked down at Justin. He closed his eyes, took an agonized deep breath, and focused on healing him.

Justin snapped back into instant awareness. He jumped to his feet and glared at the wooden barrier between him and his best friend. Justin was in half-rage, half-anguish, as he tried to push out the ghastly thought of the fate Lani was about to endure. He had not been strong enough to save her! He fell to his knees— head in his hands, ripping through his hair. He suddenly stopped and looked up with hate filling his eyes.

"JHARATE!"

This was all his fault! Why hadn't he at least taken Lani with him? Would it have been that hard to make three disappear rather than just two? If he ever saw that double-crossing weasel again he would make him pay!

Kendra slowly sank onto a stump behind her, unable to look away from the gate. Erik stood in back of her, also unable to avert his gaze. The four defeated friends fell silent once again.

Lani was dragged inside another enclosure, built with more thick spikes, perfectly arranged in a rectangle. The grass inside the enclosure was so flawlessly cut that not even one blade of grass was longer than another, and not one single stump remained in the entire area. In front of a pristine tent stood several sturdy posts. With a nonchalant wave of his hand, Lord Asharen directed his men to tie Lani's hands behind her around one of these posts. The post was so wide that her wrists barely met together on the other side and she grimaced in pain. Asharen dismounted his horse and handed the reins to one of his men.

"Leave us."

The men led the horse out and shut the gate behind them. Lani was breathing fast, but her heart was beating even faster. Her brain seemed to have shut off and at the same time kicked into overdrive as she felt herself grappling for her sanity, while simultaneously wanting to give in to the urge to lose it and succumb to a complete nervous breakdown. She had sensed the personality of this man from the first glance. Her heart beat harder and harder, to the point that she thought her ribs would break trying to contain it. Her eyes were wild with terror-stricken panic. Why hadn't she died back in the forest? If Jharate was going to abandon her to a fate such as this, she wished he had never saved her life!

"You are truly beautiful," Lord Asharen said crossing over to her, one slow step following another. "It is remarkable, really."

Lani's stomach turned over. She was so revolted she couldn't even manage to throw up. He touched her face slowly with the back of his hand and let it flow down, twisting his hand at her jaw line so that his fingertips finished the trace down to her neck and rested on her clavicle. She shuddered and flinched and struggled to escape his touch. But the ropes held tight and her back was flat against the post.

"I wish I were dead!"

She cursed the day she had ever come to this world. She felt a burning rage within her against this planet. Why had Jharate left her? How could he? *How could he?!*

Lord Asharen took a half step back with a short laugh as the right side of his mouth twisted into a toothy snarl.

"Patience, patience. That can be arranged. But first..."

He sharply unclasped the belt holding the empty sheath of her sword and threw it to the ground. He then methodically undid the braid that held her hair, one strand after the other. He disappeared into his tent and quickly returned with a golden brush. He slowly brushed her hair with long strokes and then arranged the free and slightly wavy locks around her, letting them fall softly about her face and shoulders, all the way down past her hips. His eyes flashed with insatiable hunger as he saw the way her hair caught the light of the setting sun as its rays danced around her.

"You know, you should always leave your hair down. It is much more... *attractive.*"

The way he was taking his time and the relish with which he said the last word pierced Lani and generated an ever-deepening loathing for this man with each syllable he uttered. Hate surged through every vein in her body. She hated him with every fiber of her being. She had never before hated anyone in her life in this way. He raised his hand again, gently caressing her lips with his fingers. She sunk her teeth into them as hard as she could.

He yanked his hand away and looked at it, as the blood appeared on his fingers. His lips receded from his teeth with a devilish smile that looked more like a wild animal bearing its fangs than a man, and he laughed. Lani stared in disbelief, mouth slightly open in horror.

"Such spirit!"

Lani spat, trying to get the taste of his horrid hand out of her mouth. He unsheathed a dagger from his side and held it in his right hand as he approached her, leaning in extremely close, his left hand above her on the pole she was tied to, until they were face to face. She quickly turned her head as far to her left as she could and pressed her lips together to keep from crying out as she felt his hot sticky breath on her neck. She deeply wished that he would just kill her.

The bright blue V-neck t-shirt she had on was the same one she had been wearing when they were on the Tower of Terror. It had a black tank over it, with lacing down the middle in the front, like an old-fashioned peasant-style corset. Asharen stepped back from her a little and slowly cut a stitch from the top of the tank with his dagger, as he talked to her, exposing a little more of her blue shirt.

"You ought to feel honored," he said, cutting another strand.

Lani was going numb inside. She could feel herself shutting down. Fear and desperation were taking over and she was running away somewhere deep inside to try to hide from this moment, half-hoping to never return.

"I am the lord of all this land, and there are not many women whom I deem worthy of myself."

He cut yet another strand of the stitching. Lani had never imagined it would happen like this. Not even in her wildest dreams. She had always been so careful, even paranoid about potential danger, and so she had thought that she would always be safe. Whenever she was alone, she had always walked with her car keys between her fingers, so that she could slash the throat and eyeballs of any man who tried anything.

Furthermore, she never went anywhere alone at night in the first place, if she could help it, and she always took care to watch the area around her car, and to ask people to walk her to it whenever possible. She was careful about what she wore, because her mother told her that her clothing could either keep her safer or invite trouble, depending on what message it was sending. She went on double dates so that she wouldn't be alone with a boy, especially one she didn't know very well. This way she didn't have to worry about anything. And now here she was, completely defenseless. There was nothing she could have done— nothing she could do. Nothing.

He smiled as he saw the last connected string of her tank. She did not want to imagine how he planned to go about the rest.

"You really are spectacularly gorgeous," he said slowly. "I think I'm going to enjoy this more than usual."

Lani closed her eyes and tried to picture herself anywhere but here. She tried to escape, at least in her mind, since her body could not.

He ran his fingers through her hair and looked her up and down as he chuckled to himself. His knife was lifting the last strand when his smile faded. His face twisted into a grimace and he gasped for air. Hearing this, Lani opened her eyes in uncertainty.

CHAPTER NINE

Asharen looked at her with a confused expression and moved his hand down to feel his stomach, which was covered in bright red liquid. He brought his hand up slowly before his eyes to see the cherry-red stains on it. His brow knit in bewilderment, and with one final glance at Lani he fell to the ground. His eyes still stared at Lani, as his life force left his body.

Lani wanted to look up from the lifeless form to see who had run the sword through her attacker. But what if it was another of Asharen's men making a power play? What if she had just been saved only to face the same scenario again? She didn't think she could survive that, but she finally forced herself to look up.

Her eyes fell upon Jharate as he grabbed the hilt of his sword and twisted it violently. His eyes were full of a deadly rage and every muscle in his body was tense. When he exhaled, his breaths were quick and powerful, like a bull about to charge. His jaw was clenched in outrage and indignation as he placed a foot roughly on Asharen's back and wrenched his sword free. Lani had never seen Jharate this way before. She was thankful to have been saved, but was somewhat wary of his ferocious appearance.

"You came for me…"

Her eyes were glazed over and closer to grey than to their normal brilliant blue. She spoke in a quiet dead tone— unwilling or unable to completely come out of the hiding place in her mind, just in case the rescue she saw in front of her was only a figment of her terrified imagination.

"Of course I came for you."

His tone conveyed a great depth of protectiveness. His eyes fell into a softer and agonized sort of tormented gaze as he looked at her. Without another word, he ran behind her and loosened the ropes that held her.

As her hands became free they dropped limply to her sides. She closed her eyes and slid down against the post to the ground as streams of tears began to fall. She buried her face in her hands, rocking back and forth, but didn't make a sound. She didn't scream, she didn't sob, she didn't even sigh— she just kept rocking back and forth, back and forth, over and over again. Even the tears stopped falling as she sat there rocking in the same repetitive overwhelmed motion.

Jharate gently placed his arms around her but she flinched and shrank back from him. Jharate's face fell to an even more helpless expression— his brow was knit and his eyes looked tortured, but he understood. He closed his eyes for a second and turned his head away. When he opened them again he saw the empty sheath on the ground. He had found her sword on his way into the camp, and he now took a few steps, and quietly reunited the two once again.

He walked carefully back to Lani and slowly handed the belt back to her. She took it in her trembling hands and mechanically buckled it around her waist and looked up at him with her deadened gaze. He swallowed hard as he beheld the agony in her lifeless eyes and motioned for her to follow him out. She reluctantly got up, and obeyed.

They crept quietly behind Lord Asharen's tent. Jharate found the small door he was looking for, and pushed it open. The door had been camouflaged on the other side with a few wild bushes, so that it was invisible to the untrained eye. Jharate looked out to make sure there was no one there. He peered in both directions and opened the door just a little bit more. The two of them exited, and Jharate shut the door behind them.

As Jharate turned to lead the way, three of Lord Asharen's men rounded the corner. It was too late to hide. The three men drew their weapons and attacked. Jharate took on two of them, but the third had to be handled by Lani, and suddenly Lord Asharen was all she could see. His glinting hungry eyes and his twisted toothy smile taunted her until the greatest fury of her life surged through her veins.

The woman fighting now had none of Lani's composure or calm demeanor. Instead, she had the power and force of a tornado. Their swords clashed until she found the open spot and took it. She screamed wildly as she lunged forward and plunged her sword deeply into the man's stomach before violently pulling it out again. He dropped his weapon and stumbled back. In seemingly slow motion, he fell to the ground as his face transformed from that of Asharen's and back into the man he actually was.

Lani squealed in horror as she looked at the man on the ground. Realizing that she had just unleashed her vengeance on a complete stranger was more than alarming. She looked at her dripping sword and shuddered at the sight of his blood on her hands. She gasped as another kind of shock fell upon her. The point of her sword hit the ground and she stood there staring off into nothing.

Jharate had finished off the two men he was fighting just in time to see Lani kill the third. His eyes widened as he saw the wild power within her. He cautiously moved into her field of vision and motioned her forward, being careful not to get too close. He wanted to avoid provoking an attack from her because he didn't want to risk hurting her by having to stop it.

Lani picked up her sword and followed him out of the thin line of trees that hid Asharen's camp from view and they crossed the empty meadow into the surrounding trees on the other side. He slowed until he could be sure she was matching his pace. They ran together until they reached an enormous tree, dripping with long thin leafy branches that nearly touched the ground. Jharate parted the curtain of flowering limbs and held it open for Lani to walk through. Inside stood its giant trunk, which had a very large hollow. Arante was already there and standing beside it. Jharate guided Lani inside the roomy wooden chamber.

"Wait here. It will hide you while we free the others. You will be safe here. Wait for me."

Jharate looked at her with a worried expression, waiting to make sure she understood what he was telling her to do. She nodded, indicating with a vacant look that she would do as he said. He ran a short way into the woods and brought back something in his closed hand. As he opened his fingers, it flew from his palm and hovered a few feet above his head, near the roof of the hollow. It was the size of a grasshopper but looked like a small human man wearing miniature earthy-looking pants and a tunic. His nearly-clear wings sparkled with golden flecks of dust, and suddenly his entire form began to luminesce and shine, until the hollow glowed with a soft warm light.

"This is a fire pixie. They are very good beings. He will not harm you. I have asked him to stay here and give you light while I am gone. You will be safe here, Lani. I will return soon."

She nodded once more, without looking at him. Jharate placed some branches in front of the opening and then used vines that were already growing around the tree to camouflage the branches, until Lani was completely and expertly concealed to the point where not even the light of the fire pixie could be seen by an outside observer. He then turned and faced Arante.

"What hap—"

"We must go."

Arante nodded in response but hesitated. She took one last unnerved glance in Lani's direction, and then turned, running after Jharate.

Lani started rocking back and forth again. Her thoughts fluctuated rapidly between the trauma she had just endured, and the man she had just killed. Her hands trembled violently as she tried to put her tank back together. She was relieved that she had dressed conservatively, so that there had been two layers to protect her. Still, she felt extremely violated. She frantically continued her efforts to put the tank back together, as if fixing it would somehow magically undo the horrid injustice that she had just been subjected to. Her hands shook and fumbled over the severed strands until she finally realized that she could not fix it, and burst into uncontrollable sobs.

The sun had set when Jharate and Arante stole into the camp, which was now in disarray. Many of the structures and even a few of the trees that used to hide the camp were on fire and sparks were swirling through the dark night air. The deaths of Asharen and the three guards had been discovered and some of Asharen's men had immediately set off in search of the attackers. However, most had begun to quarrel amongst themselves to decide who would be the new ruler. The arguments had quickly escalated into a physical battle for control.

Jharate and Arante took advantage of the confusion and moved quietly over to the pen that held their friends captive. Jharate gripped the enormous bolt and slid it aside. His muscles flexed as he used his massive strength to force open the huge gate. Once opened, Arante motioned to the rebels to follow her and pointed to where they should go to retrieve their weapons. Each of Lani's friends glared fiercely at Jharate as they crept silently out of the enclosure.

As the rebels finally retrieved their possessions and were making their way out of the camp, those of Asharen's men who had been searching for the culprits noticed the escape. They ran toward the rebels with their weapons drawn. With a wild fury, Jharate swiftly cut down every man who came at him. Arante calmly marched forward, placing three arrows in her bow at a time and, as she let them fly, each one sank deep into the chest of each of the three men she aimed at. Erik stood agape at her superhuman archery skills until Justin smacked him upside his head and handed him his sword. Some of the other rebels also joined in the fight, but the two cousins were practically taking the entire camp down by themselves.

Every soldier who came at the rebels fell, one by one, until all who had noticed their escape lay still. The rebels ran quickly out of the burning camp, crossed the meadow, and disappeared into the woods on the other side. Not only had all of the rebels survived, but not one of them had even so much as a scratch on their arm from the battle.

The only men left alive in Asharen's camp were those who had survived fighting each other for leadership. They had been focused on that goal so fiercely that they hadn't even noticed the commotion around them. Finally, two of the three remaining men surrendered, and Brenar Kansata emerged as the winner and would-be Lord of all Kelamosa. He raised his arms in the air, sword held up high, and cheered as he looked around triumphantly. His mouth fell open and he dropped his arms as he saw the full extent of the destruction around him by the dim light of the glowing embers and the few remaining flames of the dark smoldering camp. He stood there for a moment, bewildered, as he realized that he had only two men left to serve him, but he quickly shrugged it off. After all, what did he care? There were many more soldiers where they had come from.

The rebels followed the cousins to the tree where Lani was hidden. Jharate and Arante parted the leafy curtain and beckoned everyone to come in under the massive umbrella of branches to rest for the night in the safety of the natural camouflage. There was more than enough room for all of them to sleep comfortably and the place had a quiet feeling of peace.

"Arante, would you please provide light for the camp?" Jharate asked.

"Of course."

Arante moved her hands and threw several delicate brass lanterns with etched glass into the upper area of the canopy, and then arranged more in a spiral around the trunk until there was a soft warm glow. Erik gawked at the lanterns that had materialized from her hands, and wondered why they were all slightly transparent.

"Wow, how did you do that?" Raoul asked.

"It's my gift."

"Oh, cool. They look Japanese. How long will they last?"

"Hmmm, until bedtime, I suppose. Each time is different and it depends on how much I work on it in the first place."

"That's amazing!"

"Yes it is. Thank you."

"Shut up, Raoul! Stop talking to her!" Justin exclaimed, as Arante glared back.

Justin was seething. He saw Jharate making his way towards the tree trunk. Justin's eyes narrowed, and he ran up to Jharate and punched him hard in the face. Jharate staggered back slightly.

"THAT'S FOR LEAVING LANI!"

All of Jharate's loyal subjects reached for their weapons, but Jharate held up his hand to signal that they were not to interfere in this exchange. Jharate looked directly into Arante's eyes to emphasize his wish. Arante and the others reluctantly released their grips on their weapons, but stood ready as Jharate turned again to face Justin.

"I had no choice," Jharate said. His words dripped with deep irritation, but he remained where he was and calmly wiped a little blood from the corner of his lip. "I could not have saved her *or* you otherwise."

"*Saved her?* I guess you lost count of who you saved during your *heroic* rescue. LANI'S NOT WITH US! AND YOU DIDN'T EVEN NOTICE THAT?! You acted like you loved her! I was unarmed and I killed a guard trying to save her and all you did was leave her!"

Tears spilled from Justin's eyes as he mentioned the life he had taken. Justin punched Jharate with everything he had, this time in the stomach. Again Jharate staggered back, glaring steadily at Justin. Once more, Jharate held up his hand to his people, who had grabbed hold of their weapons and stepped forward. At his command they stepped back, but glowered at Justin, unsure if they would be able to restrain themselves if another outburst occurred. Jharate stood firm. If it were not for his desire to shield Lani from further anxiety, Justin would be on his back looking up at the tree's canopy at this very moment… well maybe not *looking*.

"I did save her. I saved her *before* I helped the rest of you."

"What?"

Jharate growled his answer as he struggled to maintain control over his behavior despite his immense indignation. "Did I not just tell you? She is safe. She is physically unharmed. I did not arrive before she had to endure a monstrous ordeal— however, I assure you that Asharen did *not* get anything he desired from her before he died on my sword."

"Prove it!"

"Very well… However, you need to be silent."

Jharate had meant that everyone should keep quiet, but he shot a pointed look at Justin, who gritted his teeth and narrowed his eyes in response.

"She has been hidden here this entire time— and as she has not called out to us, she may yet be sleeping."

Jharate guided Justin around the tree to the hollow and gently moved the vines and branches that had concealed her. The fire pixie executed a salute of deference towards Jharate and glowed brighter to better illuminate Lani. There she was, asleep. Her bloodstained sword lay at her side. Her face looked uneasy. Every now and again she sighed a stressed sigh.

Seeing that his best friend was safe, Justin felt a little foolish. He wasn't ashamed of his defense of Lani, but he was feeling as if his rash reaction had caused him to insert his foot in his mouth. He felt a deep blush come across his cheeks and a desire to avoid eye contact at all costs. He turned quickly and walked away without another word.

Jharate carefully picked up Lani's sword from beside her and cleaned it so she would not be reminded of what it had been used for. He noticed that the fire pixie must have already cleaned the blood off of Lani's hands and face while she slept. Jharate gave him a grateful nod and whispered his thanks. The fire pixie bowed his head in reply. Jharate sat down against the tree just outside the entrance of the hollow and watched Lani sleep, by the light of the fire pixie, careful to keep a polite distance so that she would not be startled if she woke up unexpectedly. He felt profoundly grateful that he had gotten there in time to stop Asharen, however, his heart broke because it had really not been soon enough at all.

Jharate knew that the guard had been the first person that Lani had ever killed. Her tortured expression had given it all away. He was all too familiar with both the expression and its meaning. It was the expression that every good person has when they are forced to do something for their survival that they would never do under normal circumstances. The look conveyed that they were devastated and appalled by their own actions.

He had seen it many times on the faces of young men and women in his country during the battles they had fought over the years. He had seen it on his brother's face during their first time at war together. And Jharate had also seen it in the mirror after the first time that armed conflict had forced him to take a life. He had been only fourteen years of age at the time, and he remembered it like it was yesterday. And now he had recognized it on Lani's face. If only he had arrived earlier!

Jharate knew she would have to confront this issue sooner or later, and he would be ready to help her when she did. For now, she was asleep. He desperately wished for her sake that she would never have to face danger like this again, but he knew better than to hope for a wish like that to be granted. At a time such as this in his world, there was no safety. He knew that it would not be long before her life would be in peril again.

AFTERMATH

Drakne looked over the smoldering remains of what was left of Lord Asharen's camp in the first slivers of the coming dawn— the charcoal trees that no longer served to hide the fortress, the scorched structures collapsed onto the blackened earth, and the dead bodies of the soldiers where they had dropped. Asharen's personal quarters had only lost one wall, making a sort of morbid diorama to display his body lying on the perfect grass— his open eyes visible from a good distance. Drakne scowled as he finished scanning the wreckage. His men cringed whenever they even came close to making eye contact with him.

Drakne stepped forward deliberately and stopped in front of the newly self-proclaimed leader of Kelamosa. He paused to glower at the man and spoke slowly, with every syllable enunciated with excruciating clarity, as the man cowered before him.

"Brenar Kansata. Explain to me again how two warriors"— he held up two fingers for emphasis and his black leather gloves creaked as if they too were trying to control themselves—

"managed to kill more than *forty* of your men and escape without your even knowing in which direction they went?"

Brenar shifted his weight from one foot to the other and closed his eyes with a grimace as he forced each word out of his mouth— each sounding worse as he spoke it than it had in his head.

"It was over before we even knew they were there. We only found out what had happened from a wounded man who was left for dead. In fact, he did die, moments after relating the tale… Your Excellency. We did not see them ourselves."

"Oh," Drakne said. "You did not *see* them. Well that makes all the difference. It couldn't possibly be your fault, because you did not *see* them."

"We were, um… well you see…"

"Silence, you fool! You do not realize what you have lost through your moronic behavior! I know full well what you were doing. You were fighting amongst yourselves for who would be the next to lead. You idiots took more than fifty of your own men out for them! I assume *you* won?"

"Yes, Your Excellency… I did."

"Well, it will surely be a short-lived victory. Vranah will not be pleased by this gross incompetence," spat Drakne, nearly hissing as he turned to two of his own men. "You two take him to Lord Vranah, now!"

"No, please! Please, Your Excellency!"

Brenar fell to his knees and grabbed Drakne's boots.

"Get your hands off of me!"

Brenar instantly let go and held his palms behind him as far away from Drakne as he could while keeping his head low. Drakne scowled at Brenar. He formed a glowing yellow energy ball in his hand and dropped it calmly into Brenar's back. Brenar curled in at his midsection, as if he had been kicked in the gut, writhing and gasping for air as he clawed his fingers into the dirt beneath him.

"Touch me again and you shall die in that instant!"

Brenar nodded slowly as he recovered his breath, keeping his face low to the ground and his hands in the dirt. Drakne turned to leave just as Brenar began to speak again.

"Please! I beg of you, show mercy, Lord Drakne! Mercy!"

"*Mercy?*"

Drakne stopped in his tracks and rounded on Brenar with a twisted half-smile. His voice sounded as if merely speaking that word tasted badly.

"What do *I* know of mercy? I do my master's bidding! I am the most powerful man in this entire world next to him. Do you think I got here with mercy? Mercy is not exactly a quality Vranah prizes…"

Drakne's voice trailed off for a moment, but he quickly snapped back into his normal demeanor.

"Besides, even if mercy was something I was capable of granting, you have done nothing worthy of it. Get him out of my sight before you two meet the same end as he will!"

It was done.

"As for you…" Drakne said, referring to the last two survivors of the camp, "…you will take the place of the men who just escorted that idiot to Vranah. You should know, however, that if we do not find the escaped prisoners, or if I see any such display of ineptitude as was demonstrated here last night— you will meet a worse fate than that of your comrade's. I will not tolerate failure or cowardice in any of my men."

"Yes, sir!" the two men said in unison.

"Now get out of my sight."

The two men fell quickly into the back of Drakne's ranks.

Drakne turned his back on his men and placed two fingers of his very tense right hand against his temple. His eyes rolled closed for a brief instant and he took a deep, but livid, breath and exhaled quietly though his gritted teeth. He was always surrounded by idiots, morons, and imbeciles! He was sick of them all! He began to think that he stood a better chance of accomplishing his mission by himself.

Where have those blasted rebels gone?! It could not have been far. They would not have chosen the mountains. No, that journey would take weeks. They were less than a week away from Destavnia if they had taken the direct path beyond the meadow. However, to avoid another attack, they would not have wanted to be unprotected and in the open like that. That left only one route.

"Follow me!" Drakne ordered, as he led the way.

Lani awakened slowly as morning found its way into the hollow of the tree she had been sleeping in. She became instantly and acutely aware of her pain. She felt nauseated and dizzy. Her eyes fell on the figure of a man sitting in the entryway and she nearly scrambled to her feet in alarm. Once she realized it was Jharate, she relaxed, but her feelings toward him were still decidedly mixed. She felt deep gratitude that he had saved her, but she was still hurt over being abandoned in the first place. She knew it wasn't his fault, but she needed a place to direct some of her pain. Feeling something— anything, other than helpless violation, was a welcome distraction.

"Lani?" Jharate asked quietly. "May I come to you now?"

Tears formed in Lani's eyes from the gentle way in which he had just spoken to her. She had almost forgotten how she had shoved him away from her at the camp the night before. Had he waited all night, watching over her, just to ask her this question? Her heart melted a little. She couldn't bring herself to say anything. She simply nodded her head and scooted over slightly, so there would be room for him to sit next to her inside of the tree. She didn't want to come out yet.

Jharate quietly moved beside her and slowly put his arm protectively around her. At this, she wrapped both of her arms around him and started to cry on his shoulder. He gently stroked her hair. With his other arm he embraced her, holding her close and secure.

"You are safe now," he whispered gently. "I am here."

"But, you *weren't*," Lani sobbed.

"I am so very sorry. I never meant to leave you. It breaks my heart to know how much pain that must have caused you. Arante saw the horse before it emerged from the tree line and pulled me behind a nearby tree. It was only then that I saw you and the others being ambushed. I began to run to your side to be with you— to protect you. However, Arante seized my arm and reminded me that I could not save you if I were captured as well."

"What took— what took you so long to save me?"

"The plan was to come for all of you at nightfall to insure success. However, while we were waiting, I had a vision of the future… of the way events would unfold if I waited any longer… and of what would happen…"

"What would happen to me, you mean?" Lani asked between her sobs.

Jharate swallowed hard and his chest shuddered during his exhale. He closed his eyes and hung his head before opening them again. He hugged Lani closer and kept his arms around her as he loosened his hold a little, choking on the answer to her question.

"Yes."

An icy feeling jolted through Lani and her tears continued to fall. She was glad that Jharate had been warned of her trouble, and therefore had been able to come to her rescue, but she worried about how much he had been forced to see, and how hard that must have been on him. Had he only seen himself rescuing her before anything could really happen, or had he seen the consequence if he had failed to do so? She shook at the very thought and squeezed him in appreciation for what he had done and also to comfort him for what he had been through.

"I ignored Arante's protests and ran to save you that very instant. I knew she could not understand my actions. However, I also knew that there was no time to waste in explaining. Judging from what I observed when I arrived… I reached you just in time. Although I desperately wish I had been able to arrive faster! I cannot imagine what you must have gone through! Please forgive me for not being able to be at your side sooner."

Lani continued to cry on his shoulder, holding him tightly, her hands clutching his shirt as if she might fall. She felt badly that she had ever doubted him.

"I am here, Lani. I am here for whatever you require. Whether you wish to speak to me, or simply wish to cry, I am here."

Lani trembled in his arms.

"I can't stop seeing his face— I can't stop hearing his voice. I can't make the memory of that horrid— I can't make it go away."

Jharate closed his eyes and took a deep breath before opening them again. He opened his mouth to speak, but quickly closed it as he swallowed the words that had not come. He leaned his head down and gently kissed her on the top of her head and held her closer to his heart.

"I-I've ne-never been so scared in my entire life. I thought for sure— I thought he was going to…"

Her sobs overpowered her and prevented her from speaking further. Jharate resumed stroking her hair and held her securely as he kissed her on top of her head once again.

"I am so sorry that you were forced to wonder if help was coming to you. I promise— I will never let anything happen to you again."

"I-I believe you."

Lani's sobs continued, but slowed. Her tears kept falling, but her gasps for air and sharp sighs were slowing. The severity of her near-hysteria and the intensity of her shaking started to lessen. Her thoughts turned to the other issue that was plaguing her and filling her soul with another kind of terror.

"Jharate?"

"Yes?"

"I… I killed a man. I've never…"

"You had no choice," Jharate said firmly and with great feeling. "It was kill or be killed."

"But… You don't understand. I *wanted* to! I was so angry. I thought it was Asharen… I wanted to kill him! I…"

"That man was going to kill you, or worse, if given the chance. He was no different from Asharen."

Lani looked up at him with tears in her eyes in a way that made it clear that, in her mind, that did not matter. She lowered her eyes after meeting his gaze. She did not even feel worthy to look at Jharate. She had taken a life, and she had *wanted* to. That went against everything she had ever stood for.

Jharate gently lifted her chin so she could see his eyes again, and stared at her intently.

"Listen to me, Lani. You are *not* a murderer. You did not kill him for a foul or self-serving reason or with any malice aforethought. You were simply acting in defense of your own life and virtue, and rightly so. That man would have done the same as Asharen attempted to do, if given the opportunity. You were acting by instinct alone. You are not a murderer. I have been forced to kill many people in my life. In the heat of battle you must focus on survival— and everything in your body and mind prepares you to do so. You *want* to kill your attacker. However, the difference between people like you and myself and people like those we fight, is that we are acting in defense of ourselves, our country, and to preserve the lives of others.

"We do not feel fulfilled by killing. It is deeply scarring to us. Our conscience tells us that we are doing a horrible thing. People similar to the two of us would never kill anyone for anything so trivial as money, power, or any other such worldly reasons. We believe in the sanctity of human life, and even more in the nobility of the human soul. We are striving to reach our most elevated state. We want to be *truly* good. We only kill when we absolutely must, and then we regret having to do so. You are a good person, Lani. In fact, after having the privilege of talking with you at length and of beginning to discover who you truly are over the past weeks, it is now my sincere opinion that you are the best person that I have ever had the honor to know."

Jharate paused for a moment. He let go of her chin and smoothed her hair behind her ear. He looked from her hair, to her eyes, to her soft full lips. He felt a lump in his throat and his voice changed from a determined tone to a gentle and sincere near-whisper.

"You are also the most beautiful woman I have ever seen in my life. Your eyes are the sapphire blue of the Manaleina Ocean at twilight, your lips have the magenta hue of a Kelamosan dawn flower, and your own fragrance is just as intoxicating. Furthermore, just as any flower blossoms in the sun, when its rays kiss your skin and turn it golden brown, it sets your creamy white skin aglow. When I first saw you, I was astonished to find that you were even more beautiful than my previous visions of you had led me to believe, and you grow more beautiful each day.

"When I learned that your morality and intelligence surpassed your beauty, I was dumfounded. You are forthright and articulate and witty and the sound of your laugh fairly takes my breath away. From the moment I met you, I knew my heart would never be in my possession again. It has belonged to you ever since that first day and you will continue to hold it for eternity. I should have told you all of this long ago. I suppose what I am attempting to say, Lani, is… I love you."

Lani's eyelashes fluttered in surprise. She felt happily dazed by his words. A warm feeling surrounded her wounded heart like a blanket on a cold night. For one glorious moment, she forgot all of the pain that she had just been through.

"I love you too, Jharate."

Exhilaration rushed through her entire body. It seemed as though she had been aching to hear those words and to say them back forever— from long before she ever knew he existed. She saw the love brimming in his eyes.

He watched as her eyes sparkled blue again and her ruby lips formed a smile. Jharate kissed her forehead gently, then her cheek, and then the other cheek. Lani could feel his heart racing and heard his breathing become slow, almost to the point of not breathing at all, as he held his lips on her soft, smooth cheek before letting them drag slowly to her cherry lips. They kissed.

Passion such as Lani had never felt erupted within her in a fantastic wave of heat. But there was something more— Lani felt warmth inside her soul. There was something about his kiss. It was so gentle and loving, so selfless, so protective, so every nice thing there ever was about love. She felt that she had finally found her Prince Phillip, her other half, the one person in the world who would do anything for her, and love her back with as much love as she had to give. She kissed him back fervently. When their lips parted she rested her forehead against his and giggled softly.

Jharate smiled at her and leaned in for a second kiss. His kiss warmed her from her head to her toes. She felt as if she could fly if she wanted to. Her heart had entwined with his forever. She wished this moment would never end.

"Ah-hem."

Arante cleared her throat to announce her arrival. The happy couple started, surprised that there was anyone on the planet besides the two of them.

"I'm sorry to, hmm— interrupt," she said, looking at them in a slightly irritated manner that matched her tone, "but we have to move. Drakne and his men have reached Asharen's camp. It is only a matter of time before they set out to look for us."

"Thank you, Arante," Jharate said coolly. "We will be joining you shortly."

Arante nodded her head once, looked down at the ground, and turned to leave the two lovebirds alone again.

"She has perfect timing."

"That's okay," Lani said. "She's right. We probably do need to go."

Jharate kissed her sweetly, once more, on the lips.

"Shall we go then, my darling?"

Jharate stood up and offered his brawny hand to her. She took it and followed him out of the hollow. She stopped for a moment to look back as she stretched daintily. This little place had suddenly become quite lovely to her. As they turned to go, the fire pixie hovered a few feet in front of them, as if asking permission to be dismissed.

"Your light made a very bad time more bearable for me. Thank you so much!"

"Think nothing of it, dear lady!"

"I am deeply grateful to you for watching over her when I could not."

The fire pixie bowed graciously to Jharate.

"My pleasure, Your Highness."

The fire pixie bowed once more and flew quickly away into the forest. Lani noticed her perfectly clean sword and smiled. She took it and placed it back in its sheath.

"Thank you for cleaning my sword."

Jharate took her hand and kissed it gently as he moved his hand to intertwine his fingers with hers. They looked at each other and smiled happily, as if they would never let go. Despite his hands being much larger than hers, it wasn't awkward or uncomfortable at all. It was as if her hand had been made to fit into his. Jharate leaned down to kiss her one last time before the two of them rounded the trunk of the tree to join the others, who were now ready to go.

Lani now marveled at the flowering canopy above her as she took it in for the first time. How she wished they could stay here! Arante handed Jharate's bag to him with a peeved look on her face. Jharate returned her look with a determined stare and she looked away. Lani noticed, but was grateful because she was pretty sure that Arante was going to keep whatever her feelings were to herself. Maybe she could even become friends with Arante someday.

Lani could see that Jharate sensed Arante's disapproval as well, but that he truly could not have cared less. That was what was most important in her eyes. She sincerely believed in respecting parents and other family members. However, she admired men who could stand up for true love against their family's well-meaning opinions and advice. A man who could do that with his family, respectfully, while never letting his woman doubt his feelings or alliance with her, even for a moment, was a rare man indeed.

In Lani's mind, love was no place for diplomacy. Trying to please everyone would only hurt the one who truly deserved the respect and loyalty, which was being spread too thinly amongst others to be recognized as such any more. She had always put her man first and it felt wonderful to have Jharate do the same for her. Once Arante had looked away, Jharate carefully squeezed Lani's hand and looked down at her with a smile. Lani smiled back happily.

"Alright," Arante spoke loudly. "Drakne and his men have reached our shores. Drakne is obviously not an idiot like Asharen. *And* Drakne has a much clearer chain of command, should anything happen to him, which we all know is more than unlikely. We need to move quickly and change routes as much as possible. Ten to one he has ruled out the direct path, so it may be best to start there."

Everyone nodded. It sounded logical to try to do the one thing that someone on the outside would not expect, even if it left them out in the open. They began their journey, using the direct route. Off in the shadows, the same glittering green eyes that had been intently staring at them deep in the Forest of Kar were again watching them now. As the group came closer the eyes turned and sped off ahead of them.

Lani and Jharate stayed at the back of the group and continued holding hands as they walked. Lani could still feel the glowing feelings that the kiss had generated inside her heart. She found it kind of funny that though the kiss had been wonderful, it had somehow rendered the two of them a little less talkative than usual. She kept looking up at Jharate, and he kept looking at her, and the two of them both smiled every time their eyes met as they walked. After a while, Lani attempted to start a conversation.

"Soooo, what do you do for fun? I mean, when you're not running for your life and saving damsels in distress."

"I have always enjoyed playing a Trisaknen sport we call Tarsi, between battles that is."

"What is Tarsi?"

"Tarsi is played with two teams. Each team attempts to carry the ball to the opposite side in order to score a goal, while the other team attempts to stop them from doing so. The players may kick the ball, or carry it, or throw it between themselves and their teammates. If they are tackled, they must let go of the ball and move out of the way in order for the other players to keep the ball in play. The game continues until the hourglass runs out. Whichever team scores the most goals, wins. I enjoy it immensely because of the fast pace and the physical exertion. It is truly exhilarating."

"You're kidding me! That sounds just like rugby!"

"Rugby?"

"Yes. Rugby is a game in my world that is exactly like that! We have another one kind of like it too, American football— but they wear a bunch of protective pads and helmets and uniforms and stuff and the game keeps stopping with every tackle and things like that."

"Are these boys who play the game you speak of?"

"Well they start when they are younger, but the men are the ones who play it professionally."

"Why would grown men need protective uniforms to play a game?"

"I don't know… hmmm… Well, I always did say that 'Real men play rugby,' but then again, I did have a lot of friends who played football, and they were very tough, so I probably shouldn't say that."

Lani laughed nervously. She felt stupid. She was rambling and she couldn't seem to stop. She hoped that Jharate wouldn't notice how silly she was being right now.

"What were your favorite diversions before you were pulled into this perilous world?"

"Oh, wow! There are so many things I like to do! I love the beach and swimming and snorkeling and surfing. I love reading and playing the piano. I like drawing and sculpture and building things out of various objects from nature, like the boat I made one time from debris I found on the beach, but painting is my fave! I obviously like writing too. I mean, I told you about the book I was writing, called Half-Hearts. I never thought it was real though. I really like fencing. I love doing anything outdoors like hiking and things like that. Oh, and I absolutely love watching movies."

"Movies?"

"Oh, I wasn't thinking. You wouldn't know what they are. Well, do you have plays in your world, or theatre?"

"Yes, my love, of course we do."

"'My love'... I love that! Okay, well, a movie is kind of like a play— but it's performed ahead of time and a thing called a camera records the image and it can be projected so that it can be seen again later, in many places across our world at the same time, without the actors having to be there anymore. But you can see the performances, exactly as they were originally performed."

"I see. I believe I understand. It sounds somewhat similar to Arante's gift."

"What is her gift?"

"She can conjure images of things and events, which have happened in a particular area. For instance, if something had occurred here, where we are walking, she could recreate it whether it was hours ago or even days ago— sometimes longer. She can also create false images to fool others. Sometimes she can do it very convincingly, but most of the time her images are at least partially transparent. Such was the case with the lanterns Arante conjured in the canopy of the tree, to give us light, last night while you were sleeping. The lanterns disappeared by themselves by the time the camp had settled in for the night. However, she could have removed them instantly with her gift, had we needed her to do so."

"That's sensational! I wish I hadn't missed it! I would love to see her do that! That's like something we only have in our fictional stories. We need computers to create anything close to a phenomenon like that!"

This reminded her of something she had been meaning to ask Jharate. She spoke before Jharate even had a chance to ask her what computers were. He laughed quietly and smiled an angelic smile as she continued and blushed happily back.

"Remember how you said you would teach me how to use my gift, because we are similar?"

"Yes, of course."

"Is there any way to control it? Like, to get a vision of something on demand? And is there any way to send messages or send a vision to someone else? Are there any other things that go with it?"

Jharate pressed his lips together, but his laughter burst forth, despite his effort. Lani's cheeks deepened in color as she realized why he was chuckling.

"I'm talking too much and too fast, aren't I? I do that sometimes, you know. I just don't seem to have an off switch."

"No, no, I love it. You are utterly delightful when you are enthusiastic," Jharate said, still laughing. Once he regained composure, he smiled as he continued in a clear voice, "I will try to answer all of your questions. Our gift is highly intuitive. It is not so easily controlled as those similar to Raoul's and Arante's gifts. They can be immersed completely in anger, fear, or frustration, and still have the ability to use their gifts once they have mastered them.

"Ours, however, will only work when the soul is balanced. No matter how long you or I have studied and practiced our gift, there must not be any significant disruption to our inner peace if we want any control over it. That is not so say that you can never receive a vision under those circumstances, nevertheless, you will definitely not be able to receive one 'on demand,' as you put it."

Lani listened intently, taking every word into her mind purposefully where it would never be lost.

"To receive a vision at will, you must focus and relax. You must clear your mind of any worries, thoughts, or feelings. You must be at complete peace with your life and with your surroundings. Then, and only then, are you able to ask questions in your mind. If you have achieved this state, you will often receive an answer in vision, or sometimes simply through a feeling.

"As for sending messages or visions to someone who is not expecting a vision, nor prepared to receive one— I have heard of it occurring. However, I have never experienced it myself. I have been told that it is extremely difficult and nearly impossible to do intentionally.

"Now, as for what else you can do with our gift, that is highly individual. There are many possibilities. Some can share emotions or memories with another individual and some can show their vision to others. Occasionally, someone with the gift of vision can feel another's emotions or sense things about character that would not be visible to the physical eye. As I have mentioned, there are limitless possibilities, and it depends on the individual. Personally, I am able to share memories with others."

"That's wonderful! Could you share one with me?"

"I see no reason why not."

Jharate grinned. He stopped and turned to face Lani.

"We will need to stop for a moment."

As she stopped and faced him, he took her left hand and lifted it to his right temple. He then took his left hand to her right temple.

"Here. You must hold my right hand in your right hand like this," he said, as he clasped her hand like he was about to shake it in greeting.

It reminded Lani of a science project she had made in fourth grade, which demonstrated closing an electrical circuit. This was much more fun, though! She felt a thrill of excitement flow through her as they connected.

"Close your eyes and take a deep breath."

She closed her eyes and breathed as instructed, and he followed after her.

Everything was just black for a moment. Then she saw a small light as if it were at the end of a tunnel. She watched as the light came closer and closer. Suddenly, the light enveloped them and they were in an exquisite golden room. There was a huge, king-size bed, with four posts and cream-colored satin draping from the wall behind it.

A crystal chandelier hung from the center of the room. Near the window, in a decorative rocking chair, sat a lovely woman. Her skin was a creamy white. She had rich brown curly hair that fell to the middle of her back. She held a newborn infant in her arms while her three-year-old son tugged at her intricately embroidered dress, trying to see the baby. The woman smiled at the interest that her small son had in his new sibling.

"Come Jharate, sit on the window seat so that you can see your new baby brother."

Young Jharate did as he was told, scrambling up awkwardly onto the window seat, which seemed too high for him. His mother laughed happily as she watched him climb.

"There," Karsenia said, as she positioned the infant so that Jharate could see. "What do you think, my love?"

"What is his name, Mother?"

"His name is Khanye."

"Khani?"

Karsenia smiled.

"No, sweetheart— Khanye."

"That's a *hard* name!" Jharate said in his adorable three-year-old voice that made Lani giggle with delight.

As the great door of this bedroom opened, a man came into the room. He was tall and strong, with rich brown skin that was a few shades darker than Jharate's. He was ruggedly handsome and very large in stature. His muscles were enormous. Lani figured he must be Jharate's father. He crossed the room to his wife and kissed her lovingly on the lips.

"How is the most beautiful woman in the world today?"

Karsenia positively beamed.

"Wonderful, my handsome husband, simply wonderful."

"And how are my two fine sons doing?"

Karahn picked up Jharate effortlessly and swung him atop his shoulders. Jharate giggled freely as he answered.

"Very well, Father."

"That is so good to hear. Did you know that you three are the most prized possessions I have? I love you all more than anything in this world, and I would do anything for any one of you."

"I know *that*," Jharate chortled happily, rolling his eyes with a big grin. "You tell us *all the time*."

"That is because your father is a very good man. One day when you grow up and find a wife, you must remember his example. Treat her like the queen that she will be, and treat your children like the princes and princesses they will be."

"I will, Mother," Jharate assured, suddenly very serious.

Young Jharate squealed joyfully, as his father swung him off his shoulders and down into his arms to tickle him.

Lani smiled gently. The room began to fade away down the long tunnel again into darkness. Once she realized that she was staring at the back of her eyelids, she opened her eyes with a soft flutter.

"That was a beautiful memory, Jharate. I feel honored that you shared it with me. Thank you…"

Lani brought her hand down from his temple as Jharate did the same, but they kept their right hands together. Jharate became more serious now and he lowered his gaze to the ground. Lani brought her other hand up so that his right hand was now sandwiched between both of hers, and squeezed it.

"It is my most precious memory. She died just two years later. It broke my father's heart. He continued to be an outstanding father, yet there was an empty space that I could always sense. He loved her so dearly, and to have her gone so young… Well, he is with her now."

"I'm so sorry…"

Lani felt a lump rise in her throat. She knew her words were inadequate at best, but she had no idea what else to say. She gently caressed his arm. The corners of his mouth turned up ever so slightly, and he squeezed her hand tenderly in return.

"I miss them very much," he almost whispered.

"I understand. I'm sure they are watching over you now though. They are so loving. You are probably never alone."

"Thank you. I know they are always with me. It feels as though I can almost hear them at times."

Lani sighed gently as she reached to cradle his cheek in her hand. He closed his eyes and took a deep breath. He brought her other hand up to his lips and gently kissed her palm, and the inside of her wrist.

"As much as it pains me to say this, I think we must hurry to join the others, my love."

Jharate turned her hand over and kissed the top of it gently, and with one smooth motion guided her back to where they could hold hands again, side by side.

Lani could still feel his lips on her wrist and she suddenly felt as if her legs were made of Jell-O. She pushed forward, forcing herself to walk normally until the feeling of solidness returned to her legs. Her heart was twittering around inside of her like a caged bird. She was deeply touched by Jharate's candor and willingness to be so vulnerable. She knew that memory was a huge part of himself.

So much of what she had seen of his parents was reflected in his own actions. His father and mother had both been equally responsible in showing Jharate what a relationship should be like. If that memory was any indication of what she and Jharate might have if they married, she was more than ready for it. She knew now that they were forging an indestructible bond. She couldn't wait to share more with him. She wanted to know everything about him and for him to know everything about her.

They had fallen quite a ways behind the others and had to walk quickly to catch up. Even with their hastened speed, it took them a while to find the back of the line. Lani noticed that once again, the two of them did not feel the need to speak to each other for a long while. It seemed that the ever-deepening feeling of love they were sharing, and compassion for one another, had caused their connection to grow to the point where they could feel each other's spirits. Lani continued to ponder what he had shared with her. She knew that it was her turn to open up now and to allow herself to be as vulnerable as he had done for her. Why was this such a hard thing to do? He had obviously been through more than she had, and yet she felt nervous. She took a deep breath, and jumped straight into the heart of her biggest insecurity.

"You know, I have never lost anyone to death, but I have lost people that I loved dearly in other ways. The men I love have always left me or betrayed me. I know that the past does not equal the future— and I tried to tell myself that it never affected me, but it did. I became terrified of relationships, even though I desperately wanted one. The road just got too hard somewhere along the line. I don't even know what I am saying. I guess I just feel like I can really be myself around you."

"And you always can be. I will always be true to you, and I will never leave you."

Lani beamed and her eyes filled with joy. She could feel that the love in her heart was healing her, inside and out. Lani watched Jharate as he looked at her, his eyes falling on her features, one by one. She blushed yet again, and smiled.

"What?" Lani asked with a cheerful tone.

"I am merely wondering how you are becoming more beautiful before my very eyes."

Lani's blush turned scarlet. She closed her lips, but the inevitable smile parted them once more as she looked away from his gaze.

"I think what you are seeing is just the fact that you are making me so happy. I haven't been this happy in a long time."

"Lani, my love, this is only the beginning. If your beauty increases every time you become happier, it may become hard to behold you with mortal eyes in the future."

"Oh no! That's not exactly what I meant," Lani giggled. "You sure know what to say though. Wow! My heart is racing!"

"I mean every word I utter."

"I know... *That* is what is so amazing! Thank you for your compliments, Jharate. I appreciate them, even if I'm not sure I quite live up to them. You, on the other hand— there aren't words enough to tell you how handsome I think you are. I had a list of things I'd been waiting to tell you, but now that you're actually holding my hand, and I'm free to say the things I'm feeling... the perfect words just ran away. But your brown skin is the most gorgeous color I have ever seen, and I could stare into your eyes all day."

"Thank you, Lani. You are very kind."

"It's true though. You are the most handsome man I have ever laid eyes on."

Jharate smiled and looked down at his feet. Suddenly, he threw his arms around her and tickled her. Lani squealed and struggled to break free of his gentle hold, giggling the whole time. He laughed freely as she tickled him in return, and finally swept her up into his arms and carried her, running to catch up with the rest, who had left them behind yet again. Lani laughed in surprise and delight. Once they caught up, he gently placed her feet back on the ground, and took her hand in his. He smiled sweetly at her and she smiled back at him, while they caught their breath from all of the laughter and play, as another comfortable silence overtook them.

Neither Lani nor Jharate noticed the glittering green eyes that were once again peering at them through the trees as they walked. The eyes watched for a few more seconds and, remaining under the cover of the thick trees, quickly but quietly ran ahead of the entire group of rebels without being seen.

FALSE SENSE OF SECURITY

The rebels reached a small clearing where they set up camp for the night. The air was filled with a sweet fragrance resembling night jasmine and the tranquil sound of crickets beginning their evening songs. They had inexplicably made much better time than had been expected. Destavnia was a mere three or four days away at this rate, rather than the planned six or more. Everyone was so excited to be this near the final destination that no further thought was given to that minor mystery. Instead, there was animated discussion, while they ate around a delightful fire, about how magnificent Destavnia was and how blissful it would be to arrive there soon.

Hopeful talk of the future was followed by legends of the days of old when all the lands were free and Alamea was a safe and relatively untroubled world. Lani was captivated by the change in the rebels. She was surprised by how much they could laugh in a time of war and uncertainty— and impressed by their faith that things would eventually get better again. One fable in particular grabbed her attention, and she hung on every word as Jaresh spun the tale like the master storyteller he was.

CHAPTER ELEVEN

"It is said that many hundreds of years ago a sickness plagued our fair kingdom. As it moved its black hand across the land, the people of Trisakne began to fall one by one— wives, husbands, mothers, fathers, daughters, sons. No house remained unaffected. Many family lines were lost altogether. It seemed that nothing could stop this contagion— and indeed, one day it reached the castle walls. First one princess fell, then the other, next The Queen, and then The Heir Apparent— and finally The King.

"Only one member of the royal Inihma line survived because he had traveled to the northern regions of Kresar to meet his betrothed. His name was Jhoran. By the time word of the misfortune in his homeland reached him, it was too late for anything to be done. The King and Queen of Kresar called off Jhoran's betrothal to their beautiful daughter and commanded that Jhoran leave their borders immediately, lest their kingdom be infected by his presence.

"Devastated by the news of his family, Jhoran left that instant. Since he had not been the eldest son, his marriage had been intended as a political gesture, and held no real importance. Therefore, he was more than happy to be excused from that burden, as he had always wanted to marry a woman from his own beloved land. But he had never imagined that his freedom would come at such a price. In the weeks that it took for him to wander back to Trisakne, his mind wandered as well, and a heavy guilt weighed down upon him— threatening to crush him. He believed it was his desperate prayer to be saved from his arranged marriage that had led to the death of all whom he held dear. By the time he reached the western corner of Trisakne, in the hills that divide us from Lanas, a fever had overcome him, as well as a madness.

"He stumbled through the hills until he could go no further and finally dragged himself into the shade of a small number of trees next to a clear trickling brook and drank thirstily, for he had been without water for days. In his madness he saw each member of his family begging him to live. He told them that he wished to do as they asked, but that he could not save himself and that no one knew where he was. He told them how much he missed them and that he would have given his life if he could have saved them, but the images of his family never came to him again. His condition worsened and his hallucinations increased in frequency and intensity until he did not know what was real and what was nightmare.

"The end had come for Jhoran and he prepared for death, when suddenly a tall thin man with dark hair appeared before him. Jhoran pled with the man to help him as the man passed by. Jhoran's voice was so weak by this time that he was not sure if the man could hear him. Twice he cried out as the man continued in his path and got further and further away. Jhoran's third cry was the last cry he could make and the weakest of the three. But somehow, the man stopped and came back in Jhoran's direction. When he saw Jhoran, he ran to his side to attend to him. The foreign man told him in a strangely cheerful voice that he was the son of a physician and that, although his skills paled in comparison to those of his father, he would do what he could to try to save him.

"Jhoran thanked him repeatedly and told the young doctor that if he succeeded in saving his life, he could have any honor in the Kingdom of Trisakne that he desired. The man refused, insisting that there could be no greater honor than to save a life. That was the last thing Jhoran remembered. When he awoke he found that his strength had returned. Jhoran did not know how much time he had passed in his delirium. Stranger still was that as he sought out the man who had saved his life in order to thank him, Jhoran found that the man had disappeared without a trace.

"To this day, no one knows if there truly was a man who saved Jhoran, or if it was a spirit sent by his ancestors to help him, or if the doctor had merely been a figment of a troubled brain trying to save itself. However, the one thing that Jhoran certainly taught us is that the line of the Inihma royal family is strong. It was diminished in the past until there was only one surviving member left, and it rose to become a strong and prosperous line for hundreds of years after that— and it will rise again one day as Jharate returns to the Kingdom of Trisakne to reclaim it. Long live Trisakne!"

"Long live Trisakne!" the rebels answered proudly.

"And long live our Prince Jharate, to whom we will give our last breaths to protect."

All of the rebels made their right hands into fists and placed them over their hearts, fervently repeating Jaresh's words. Jharate lowered his head in acknowledgement and as he raised it, they relaxed and returned to their meals.

Lani watched Jharate carefully. The look on his face tugged at her heartstrings. He heaved a troubled sigh and his shoulders fell ever so slightly. He had done so well at keeping his reaction to a minimum that she was sure that no one else had noticed. She placed her hand on his and gave it a tight squeeze. Jharate looked at her and smiled. The burden was still there in his eyes, but they twinkled for her.

As soon as she and Jharate both finished their meals, Jharate led her by the hand to the edge of the camp and the two of them sat side by side near one of the smaller campfires. A fallen tree served as their backrest.

"Are you okay, Jharate?"

"I am."

"Are you sure?"

"Yes. How could anything be wrong when I have your love?"

Lani smiled, but she searched beyond Jharate's smile and found stress still lingering in his eyes and so she waited quietly. He sighed and looked down at the ground.

"Perhaps you are right, Lani. Perhaps I am not quite myself at present. I heard the tale of Jhoran many times as a boy. However, I never imagined I would become him. When I think of his story, my heart feels heavy, as does the burden on my shoulders. I only hope that one day when my story is told, it will not be said that 'Jharate was the Inihma who lost Trisakne forever.'"

"That will not happen, Jharate. I have every faith in you that you will get your homelands back."

"With you at my side?"

"There is nowhere else I would rather be."

"Lani, you are truly unique. I have never met another like you. I wonder if…"

"Yes?"

Jharate opened his mouth to answer her, but closed it. Lani watched him closely. She had a feeling he was trying to choose his words very carefully, but she couldn't understand why. She waited patiently as a few more moments passed.

"I wonder if our love was meant to be."

"I would say so. I mean, I was pulled from another world and you just happened to be the first person I met when I could have landed anywhere. That feels like the Universe was trying to get us together somehow, doesn't it?"

Lani smiled, but Jharate's expression remained serious. She heard him whisper something.

"I'm sorry, I didn't hear you. What did you say?"

"My apologies, Lani. I was saying—"

"Jharate! I would like a word with you, please," Arante's voice rang out.

Jharate sighed. He closed his eyes and did not move.

"It's *very* important!" Arante pressed.

Jharate opened his eyes and looked at Lani.

"Please excuse me for a moment, my love."

"Of course."

Lani sighed as Jharate left. She watched him as he stood up and crossed over to Arante, who was by her own fire, sharpening her weapons, with a stern look on her face. Lani strained to hear what they were saying, but she couldn't make it out. She guessed that it was about her. She was all but certain that she was correct in her guess when she saw Arante's dagger pointed in her direction. Arante was probably trying to talk him out of the relationship. Lani felt the tiniest twinge of panic, but then quickly reassured herself that Jharate was strong enough to make up his own mind about whom he wanted to be with. Still, she desperately wished she could hear what they were saying.

Lani's mind raced over what Jharate had said just before he left. Why had his demeanor gotten so serious when he asked her if she thought their love was meant to be? What had he whispered after she had answered him? She thought she heard the words "other world." She had just mentioned how she thought the Universe had brought them together... Had he been musing over that? She wished Arante had waited one more minute before calling Jharate so she could have been sure. Then again there was the much larger issue of—

Lani was suddenly distracted from her thoughts by Arante's voice, which had risen to the point that Lani could hear one sentence. Only one. It traveled on the wind to Lani's ears with a ghostly echo. *If you continue this way, you might mislead her into thinking something she shouldn't!* A chill ran down Lani's spine. What did that mean? Lani looked up and saw Arante glaring at Jharate in disbelief. Lani's brain tried to find an answer. Was Jharate not as in love with her as he had seemed? Was he leading her on? Was she a pity case? Her heart felt a sharp twang. No! She was doing it again. This is how she had messed Josiah and her up— and she wasn't going to make that same mistake twice. No, she would just believe in Jharate. She pushed her worries away where they would not bother her again.

"Lani?"

She jumped a bit. She had not noticed that Jharate had returned and was already sitting next to her. Arante had disappeared as well.

"Oh! I didn't hear you come back. You scared me a little. You're really quiet sometimes... Did you know that?"

"Yes. I apologize for startling you. And I apologize on Arante's behalf for interrupting us."

"That's okay... Jharate?"

"Yes?"

"Your gift... can you see a memory if I want to share one with you?"

"Yes I can."

Jharate smiled widely. It warmed her to see his smile again. She felt the lock click on the hiding place for her doubts.

"I have some things I want to share with you about myself, and I think the quickest way would be to show you some of the moments in my life. They are nothing as special as what you shared with me, of course, but they are part of me. Just to warn you my mind jumps a lot and you already know I talk too much sometimes, so my memories might be a little disjointed and may be too long— so I'm sorry in advance if they are."

"I am honored to see anything about you, Lani. I love you, and if I could, I would spend all day long listening to you or looking at your memories. You can never 'talk too much' and the privilege of looking at your past could never last too long."

He said this so sincerely that Lani's heart swelled with love and gratitude. She couldn't believe that a man like this existed!

"Close your eyes and visualize the first memory. When you are finished with that one, visualize the next one you desire to share. I will be able to see what you see. Simply picture black when the memories that you wish to show have concluded."

They did the "closed circuit" grasp again and he closed his eyes. She closed her eyes after him. She knew exactly where she was going to take him to in her mind. She started with the first day that she had met Raoul. Lani felt a rush as she easily directed the memory. Everything was in 3D living color! And she could see herself too. She wondered how that was possible because when she had lived through it the first time she obviously hadn't seen herself, and now she was curious if Jharate had been able to see his younger self, as well— perhaps it was just the way his gift worked. It was trippy but awesome at the same time.

She and Jharate watched as the younger versions of Lani and Raoul stood outside of Vista High School waiting for the school bus to take them home. Raoul's thick curly hair had been longer at the time and stuck almost straight up in the air. He wore baggy white pants with an oversized t-shirt, both much too big for his body, and carried a grey and yellow backpack.

"Do you wanna get shocked?" Raoul asked the young girl he saw in front of him.

Lani was even shorter than she was now. Her hair was cut to her shoulders and she had a teal backpack on. She looked at the boy curiously and warily at the same time— as if she wasn't really sure if she had heard him correctly.

"What?"

"Do you wanna get shocked? See this thing right here?" he asked as he pointed to a small black object in his other hand. "If you touch it, you'll get shocked."

"No thanks," Lani said, as she took a couple of slow and easy steps back while keeping her eyes locked on him.

"Okay!" he shrugged. "My name is Raoul. Nice to meet you."

"Nice to meet you too," Lani said cautiously.

Lani concentrated on the next memory she wanted to share. It was a few months later. The background phased from the schoolyard into a classroom, full of desks and books, with a middle-aged-hippie-looking woman sitting at her desk grading papers. The younger versions of Lani and Raoul sat in two of the desks, eating lunch across from a group of boys who had pulled their desks into a circle and were concentrating hard on their card game. The cards had drawings of men and fantasy creatures and had lots of writing on them— all in medieval style.

Within that group was the young version of Justin, whose incontrovertible energy made him stand out from the rest of the crowd. He was tall and super skinny, with a slight Afro, and he was speaking like a punk.

"Moted!" Justin yelled at the top of his lungs to one of the boys as he threw his card down in victory. "You just got moted!"

Justin noticed Lani and Raoul across the room and crossed over to them.

"Hey, my name's Justin. Who are you?"

"I'm Lani, and this is Raoul."

"Nice to meet you. Hey Lani, you wanna play chess? I have my own set."

"Sure."

Justin reached into his pocket and pulled out an extremely small chess set.

"Look, it's magnetic!"

"Cool," Lani giggled. "Raoul, you want to play on my team?"

"Yeah! Thanks, Lani!"

The three of them began to play.

The classroom now changed to reveal Lani's living room. Justin, Raoul, and she were all sitting on the couch. Justin was staring at the ceiling and making popping sounds with his lips. Raoul kept nodding off and when his chin would fall to meet his chest he would jump up and say, "I'm awake... I'm awake." And Lani had her history book in her lap, trying to finish the last page of her assigned chapter.

Suddenly, Lani clapped her book shut and left the room silently. Raoul and Justin both looked at each other curiously and cranked their heads to see where she had gone. When she came back into view she was holding an extremely tall stack of white paper cups with purple flowers on them. Once she set them down on the hardwood floor, the stack came nearly to her waist. She looked at Justin and Raoul with a mischievous smile rising on her face. They jumped up and ran for cover as she proceeded to throw the cups at them. Justin and Raoul did fantastic dodges and flips, acting like they had "The Matrix" skills, and grabbed the fallen cups, launching them straight back at her, while she ran for cover, firing back the whole time.

Lani laughed to herself as she watched this memory. She couldn't help but miss the way their friendship had been in those days. It had been so long since they had done anything like that. She realized that she needed to get off the fun nostalgia and get on with the uncomfortable stuff, but there was still a little bit more that Jharate would need to know of her background with Raoul and Justin for the rest of it to make any sense.

She took a deep breath and suddenly they were outside Lani's house. Lani's younger self stood on her porch and Raoul was close by, standing on the grass. They were a little older now— Lani was about sixteen, making Raoul somewhere around eighteen. Both of them had tense and uncomfortable expressions. Raoul was gesturing wildly and Lani's arms were crossed.

"But *I* asked you to junior prom!" Raoul said angrily.

"Yes, you did. But then you told me that you wanted to ask Jennifer, so I let you. It isn't my fault that Justin asked me once you decided not to take me."

"But Jennifer said no!"

"I'm sorry, but there's nothing I can do about that. You can't tell me you are going to ask someone else and then expect me to wait around just in case your first choice doesn't work out."

"Yeah, well have fun with Justin! I can find another date!"

"You go do that."

That memory was almost as painful for Lani to relive, as it had been the first go around, because she and Raoul did not speak for six months after that. Lani wondered what Jharate was thinking about all of this, but figured she had better try to speed things up, just in case this was getting too lengthy.

Lani's junior prom was held in a country club ballroom with large chandeliers. Lani became acutely aware that she could now smell all of the food in the memory— even the chocolate fountain. She wondered how interactive a memory could get, or if such a thing were possible. Lani focused on the sights surrounding her first date once again and noticed that her sixteen-year-old self looked more like she did now than the other younger versions of her had. She wore a simple raspberry-colored satin dress, which was fitted at the bodice to the point of being almost corset-like, with an extremely full and flowing floor-length skirt and butterfly sleeves.

She smiled as she saw herself wearing her first-ever imitation diamond tiara. It glittered beneath the light and the small, interspersed white faux pearls glimmered. Her sun-kissed golden brown hair, which now flowed to the small of her back, was half-up and half-down. Lani was holding onto Justin's offered arm. He looked sharp in his black tuxedo and he had matched his bowtie and cummerbund to her dress. Justin was smiling from ear to ear. Lani noticed that she looked very happy too, as she and Justin began to dance.

Lani jumped to the next memory, which was about a year later. The three musketeers had been reunited again. Raoul had been back with them for a while at this point and the three of them were each dressed in a cap and gown, walking to their graduation. Lani laughed quietly as she watched her seventeen-year-old self nervously reciting her speech.

"I hope you're not *nervous*," Justin said with a laugh.

"Thanks a lot, Justin!"

"What, it's not like you're about to give a valedictory speech in front of over two thousand people... oh wait, you are!"

Justin laughed harder this time. Raoul bit his lip to keep from joining in.

"Very funny," Lani said as she lightly pushed his shoulder.

"Just don't choke!" Justin exclaimed, as he put his hands to his throat and pretended to choke, and then laughed again. "Remember, since you're my girlfriend, what you do reflects on me too, ha, ha!"

"I'll try to remember that," Lani said, rolling her eyes, but still smiling.

"Nah, just kidding. You know I love you no matter what, and I'm always proud of you."

"Ohhh! You can be really sweet when you want to. I love you too."

Lani kissed Justin on the cheek.

"PICTURE TIME!" Raoul exclaimed.

Raoul set the camera on a low wall and set the timer. He ran into the frame, between Lani and Justin, and the three friends posed with huge happy grins on their faces— their eyes looking excitedly toward the future. Lani concentrated and skipped the memory to the end of her speech.

"...and stay true to yourself and to your own values no matter what the world says. Always follow your dreams and never sacrifice your integrity to get what you want."

Lani sighed a stressed-out sigh as she directed her mind to reconstruct the next memory. She didn't want to go here. This was the beginning of all her ferocious luck— but her whole purpose for sharing this with Jharate was to open up, not to hide from him or even from herself. She wanted to follow Jharate's example. She watched anxiously as her living room appeared before them once again. This time it was only Lani and Justin sitting on the couch, facing each other. Justin looked worried and Lani looked tense and nervous.

"Justin, I was waiting right there for you at the graduation party just like you asked me to. You said that you'd be right back, but I waited alone for *five hours*. You didn't even answer your phone, and you had my money so I couldn't even play arcade games while I was waiting for you. I was afraid to leave because I thought we wouldn't be able to find each other again in that huge crowd! You got there like five minutes before the buses came to take us home again! I can't believe you did this to me.

"And I could totally let even that slide with a good apology, if it had been the only thing that had happened lately. But you've been taking me for granted for the past six months— ever since you asked me to senior prom. It should have been even better than the first prom because we are in love with each other! Everything was so great the first six months of our relationship! I could have stayed with you forever... But I can't just keep begging you to treat me right and to go back to the way things were. If you wanted to fix things, you would have done it by now. I keep trying to make this work but it's obvious that you aren't willing to do what it takes to have a relationship."

"What are you saying, Lani?"

"I'm saying... I'm saying I can't do this anymore, Justin. I will always be your best friend, but I can't be your girlfriend."

Justin's face fell and his body language said the rest. He looked totally devastated. He ran his hand nervously through his hair and looked around, avoiding eye contact at all cost.

"Fair enough. I need to go... I'll talk to you soon though, okay?"

Justin kissed her on the cheek and walked out without waiting for an answer. Lani stayed where she was on the couch and hugged a pillow as the tears began to fall freely down her cheeks.

Lani tried to ignore the kick in her gut that reliving this memory had just caused, and skipped through memories with increasing speed now, showing one boyfriend after the other. She figured if she went fast, like a quick montage in a movie, it wouldn't hurt as much, and so she picked the shortest "snapshots" she could.

The first of these "snapshots" was of her second boyfriend. He was shorter and darker than Justin and the memory showed Lani walking in on him kissing another girl and Lani running away crying. She cut that memory there and jumped to a curb at the airport when she was saying goodbye to Justin and Raoul as they went off for their service abroad— Justin to Japan and Raoul to Indonesia. She looked at her eighteen-year-old self with pity. She didn't know that this moment meant that she wouldn't have her two best friends to help her through what was coming next. Lani started picturing the memories faster and faster. No matter how fast she relived it, there was still a gut-wrenching twang, or a jolt to her heart, but she pressed on, determined to get through this so that her heart would be completely on the line for Jharate.

The next memory showed Lani on a date with a boy who tried to pressure her to do more than just kiss him. Lani said no because she was saving that for her wedding night, and ran away from him when he refused to listen. A few other disjointed fragments showed the guys who had insisted that she was perfect for them and then promptly tried to change and control her after they got her to be their girlfriend. Another memory showed a man pinching her rear end in the hallway at college and her slapping him in the face instinctively before she walked away.

Lani cringed as she saw three of the guys get down on one knee and ask her to be their wife, and flipped faster and faster through the memories attached to each man. The first one left her crying four days before the wedding with a stunning pure-white wedding dress hanging from her door, tons of papers with details for Lani to take care of, and hundreds of well wishers congratulating her on a wedding no longer happening. The second one proposed one day and then said that it was "too soon" the next day— even though *he* had proposed to her. And finally the third one broke up with her because he was jealous of Raoul and Justin, even though Lani assured him that they were just friends, and reminded him that they weren't even in the country! Lani bit her lip and sighed sharply. In-between those bitter fragments, she showed a few different moments of her family members comforting her.

"Why would he leave me, Taylor? Why? What did I do to deserve this?"

Lani saw the love in her brother's eyes for her, as he held his sobbing sister, and his anger against the man who had hurt her. She smiled. Taylor was the best little brother in the world.

"I don't understand, Mom… Why would he ask me to marry him and then take it back the very next day?"

Her mother held her tenderly and Lani felt a tear fall down her face as she watched this memory. She missed her family so much! She wanted to detour her memories to several wonderful family moments, but that wasn't the point, and she could share those later if Jharate wanted her to. She had to get this over with. The memories just kept coming. This time Lani was talking to her sister Jenna right after a break up.

"My heart keeps getting broken. But I can get over it and keep going. What I *really* hate is what it's making me look like! I look like I jump from one guy to the next and can't stay committed! It makes me look like a flake!"

"Anyone who knows you won't think that, Lani. You are such a one-man woman. If it had been up to you, you would have married Justin. You're just smart enough not to marry someone just because you're invested in the relationship and everyone else thinks you should marry them. I've seen too many people make that mistake. You're right to hold out for your Prince Phillip."

"I agree... But the problem is my reputation is being ruined. That could keep me from getting to meet him."

"I wouldn't worry about it. I really think that people who are worth your time aren't going to judge you like that. So maybe if it does keep some people away, it's a good thing. It's just weeding them out for you."

"Maybe. But this process is so painful. It seems like each new guy comes up with a new way to impersonate a prince— and then, as soon as I believe, he pulls the rug out from underneath me and says, 'Surprise! Ribbit, ribbit!' It's getting harder to wait the more times I come 'close' to finding him. It's like I'm Sleeping Beauty without the benefits of anesthesia!"

Jenna laughed at her sister's sense of humor, which helped Lani to laugh too. The memory faded into the next and Lani was at Jenna's wedding, standing next to her. They were in the reception line together when Jenna leaned over and whispered to Lani.

"You'll find your guy too. You deserve the best. Don't ever settle for less. It's so worth it!"

Jenna threw the bouquet and Lani caught it with a smile on her face.

Lani took a deep breath in. The memory of the wedding hung there for a second, as if a remote was malfunctioning and hitting the pause button and the play button over and over again. There was one final destination she had to take Jharate to if she was going to be completely open with him. She exhaled hard and the memory switched to one more quick montage, but this time every moment revolved around one man.

Lani zoomed quickly through many lighthearted, joyful, and playful moments between Josiah and herself. She then jumped to the moment she had misunderstood Josiah's feelings and broken up with him because she did not know that he loved her. She zipped past her countless efforts to make up with Josiah and then to a progression in the mending of their relationship, to the point where it seemed as if they would reconcile. Josiah beamed every time he saw Lani and both of them looked incredibly happy, but Lani and Josiah had only been seeing each other on campus and at church until the next memory when Josiah accepted Lani's invitation to his own birthday party at her house.

Lani watched herself as she joyfully shopped for the birthday/reunion and spent a great deal of money getting Josiah's favorite foods and making everything perfect for his first time back to her house since their break up. Her dad got off work early to make his famous spaghetti that Josiah loved so much and Lani decorated the house and made a cake. Once she had finished everything for the party she sat down to wait. She waited. And waited. And waited. Josiah never came.

Lani took the deepest breath yet and let it out forcefully. She still had one last memory of Josiah left to share. Lani and Josiah stood in one of the campus parking lots together near Josiah's car. Only the yellow glow of the parking lot lights kept them from being surrounded by complete blackness. The smell of delicious food and the sound of college students laughing floated through the air in-between the booming music from the international student festival where Josiah and Lani had just run into each other. She asked him why he didn't come to his birthday party. The light was completely gone from Josiah's eyes— they were now cold, harsh, and distant.

"I remembered what you did to me and I'm not going to give you another chance to hurt me."

"Please don't think that way. We didn't cheat on each other or do anything irreparable. All we did was have a big misunderstanding. I didn't realize that you loved me before, Josiah. Now that I know, I promise I will never leave you again."

She touched his arm in reassurance. He yanked it away from her. She pleaded with him to stay and work things out. His face was like stone and he refused coldly. Tears welled up in her eyes. He turned his back on her to walk away. She was crying so hard that she couldn't see as she tried to follow him. She stumbled and fell to her knees.

"Josiah! Please! Please forgive me! Josiah!"

He left her without a word. The last thing she saw were his headlights, swimming through her tears, as he backed his car out of the space he was parked in, and left her there in the dark, alone. Pain, regret, and anguish crashed over her as she realized nothing was going to be fixed— ever. It would never be fixed because Josiah had made it clear there was no forgiveness. Everything around her was still a blur and she realized that she was in no condition to drive. She called her friend, Maika, and he drove her home, with her sobbing all the way.

Somehow this last memory had seemed as if Lani were living it from both her original perspective as well as that of an observer. Although she no longer wanted anyone but Jharate, the memory was still sharp. Lani exhaled hard. She knew that the worst was finally over. She figured she'd better show Jharate one more thing, just so it wouldn't appear as if all she ever did was cry all the time— but this had been going on for so long now that she didn't want to make him wade through another montage of memories. She thought hard and remembered a conversation with Kendra not long ago that she felt would best sum up what she wanted him to know about her. The image of the dark parking lot melted into her warmly lit bedroom with Kendra and Lani both sitting on her bed eating chocolate.

"You just need to get over him!" Kendra stated emphatically. "He's not good enough for you. Maybe you should take a break from dating for a while."

"Thanks. I think you're right that I should try to move on— but I'm not sure how. I thought he was the one..."

"That's why I'm more careful about which relationships I get into. You give your whole heart every time."

"Yeah, but you know, all relationships fail until the last one— and when it *is* the last one, I don't want to ruin it by starting it out wrong. I know you wouldn't want to lose the man of your dreams by holding back when he needed to see your heart either, so be careful not to have too many walls. I've always said that 'I'd rather be a hopeless romantic than a skeptic, because while the hopeless romantic may get burned many times, the skeptic will never really experience love.'"

"I don't know how you do that."

"Do what?"

"Keep your positive outlook when you've been through so much. Not only that, but you go on and you help others feel better, and you achieve all these crazy things most people don't even do when they're happy! I haven't had half the drama you have in the dating arena, and I don't even have that much hope."

"Hold out for it, Chicky. It'll be worth it in the end. Don't stop believing in love."

"Yeah, but our country has a horrible divorce rate. I mean, think about it— of all our friends, Justin's parents are divorced, Kara's parents are divorced, and even our newest friend Erik's parents are divorced. That leaves your family, Raoul's, and mine that are still together. And those are the ones that even made it to having a family. A lot of marriages end in the first couple of years— sometimes in the first couple of months nowadays. I don't want to get married just to go through a divorce."

"Well, even if worse comes to worst, it's better to have had two marriages than none. We can't live in fear unless we want to end up living alone. And do you think Erik's, Justin's, or Kara's parents would give up the kids they got just to avoid the pain of divorce?"

"Of course not! They all love their kids. But do you think you could give me just one-tenth of your optimism— like a happiness transfusion or something?" Kendra asked with a laugh.

"Sure. They just discovered that it's transferred through pillows!"

Lani smacked Kendra in the face with her big fluffy pillow. Kendra grabbed the matching pillow off the opposite bed and the two girls squealed in delight and giggled together as the eight-year span of memories came to a close and Lani finally pictured black.

As Jharate and Lani slowly re-entered the real world, Lani took in a shuddering breath and exhaled. It felt better to have her deepest darkest fears out in the open now, but she also couldn't help feeling like she'd just been run over by an emotional freight train. And now, she was vulnerable. She wiped a few tears away from her eyes, refusing to make Jharate watch her cry one more time, and took another deep breath. Lani searched Jharate's face, trying to read it. She saw shock in his eyes for sure. She held her breath as she waited for him to say something… anything. Jharate put his arms around her and pulled her close to him, in a strong protective hug.

"Thank you for opening your past to me. I am deeply honored that you have entrusted me with that knowledge. I am astonished that you have endured so many heartbreaks— and yet, you are so willing to give your heart to me."

Lani felt heat rushing into her cheeks and a deep blush came over her face. She was glad Jharate was still holding her close so that he couldn't see it. She smiled and breathed in deeply, enjoying his wonderful scent— feeling safe and secure.

"I do not know why Josiah would not forgive you, Lani. However, his thoughtless loss is truly my gain. I would never behave in such a cold-hearted and foolish manner. My love for you is unconditional and will grow each day. You are truly extraordinary and deserve to be treated as a queen. I will never treat you in the manner in which the men from your past treated you. They do not know what they have lost."

Lani pulled away from him slightly so that she could look into his eyes. They were so sincere. She smiled and sighed happily.

"I feel like I have known you my whole life, Jharate."

"You are not alone in that feeling."

Jharate pulled her to him once again, held her tight, and kissed her sweetly on the top of her head. Lani beamed as a wave of love swept over her and she held very still, enjoying this moment in his strong arms. She fought to stifle a yawn and suddenly realized how tired she was. She was sure that she had been sharing her memories with him for well over an hour.

"Wow," she said. "I didn't notice how late it had gotten."

"Perhaps you should retire for the evening, my love."

"As much as I am loving our time together, I think I might have to. I'll see you in the morning. No, don't get up, sweetheart. I'm just going to bed. Thank you so much, Jharate."

"Nonsense, my sweet. A gentleman always rises when a lady rises. I love you, Lani."

"I love you, Jharate."

Lani stood on her tiptoes and kissed him tenderly on the cheek. He turned her face gently toward him and kissed her softly on the lips, then kissed her hand with a sweet and passionate kiss as she began to walk slowly over to her bedroll. He held her hand with both of his until she gently slipped away. She walked several yards and then smiled at him over her shoulder. She knew she would sleep well tonight. She turned and walked the rest of the way until Jharate was out of sight. She reached her bedroll, and saw Kendra already laying on the one next to hers.

"Hey," Kendra said softly.

Lani sat on top of her own bedroll and smiled as she replied, "Hey."

"You okay? I mean, you don't have to talk about it if you don't want to— it's just I haven't gotten to talk to you since the— well, you know."

"Yes, I know. I don't really feel like talking about it in detail, but nothing serious happened, and I'm okay. Jharate saved me. And we're in love."

Kendra smiled as she whispered back.

"I'm so glad you're okay and that he saved you, and I wish you luck with him and hope you are very happy. Heaven knows you've been through it all when it comes to—"

Lani jumped up and screamed. Her shrill frantic cry pierced through the air, quickly joined by Kendra's. Lani felt Jharate's hand on her arm in an instant.

"What is it, my love?"

"A spider!"

Lani rushed behind Jharate and pointed where the giant furry arachnid was crawling on her bedroll. Kendra perched herself on a stump to try to avoid the horrid hairy black thing, and was screaming something about its eyes. Jharate bit his lip to keep from laughing.

"What's wrong?" Arante asked, as she and several others rushed to join them.

Jharate answered quickly before any of them could even see the spider. "I have the situation in hand."

Many inquisitive and unsatisfied looks were exchanged between the newcomers, but seeing the adamant look on Jharate's face, they left.

"It is all right, my love. Diamondback spiders are not venomous."

"I still really, really, really don't like them! Can you get rid of it for me, please?"

"Yes! Take it away and kill it!" Kendra exclaimed.

"Of course I will remove it. I would have done so already. However, first, you will have to release your hold on me, Lani."

Lani had not realized how tight of a grip she had on his shirt. She now let go with a nervous giggle and gave him a wide berth as he picked up the furry grapefruit-sized creature with ease, and took it far away into the trees where it would not bother her again, before returning to her side.

"You are safe now, Lani."

"Thank you. I feel kind of stupid, actually."

"Do not feel that way. We all have our fears. Get some rest, my love. I will see you in the morning."

Jharate kissed Lani gently on the lips one more time and went back to the log where they had been sitting earlier. Lani felt her heartbeat slowly returning to normal, and after scanning the area for any possible relatives of that stupid arachnid, and waiting a few additional seconds, she and Kendra slipped into their bedrolls.

"Well I never want to see another one of those things again!" Kendra insisted.

"I second that motion," Lani said with a laugh.

Kendra giggled. "What is this? Model U.N.?"

"Ha, ha! I don't know. It just sounded like something to say."

"The chair recognizes the delegate from Earth."

Lani and Kendra looked at each other and burst out laughing.

"Thank you, Madam Chairperson. Those were the days, weren't they, Kendra?"

"For realz! I still remember that one kid in Justin's and Raoul's delegation. What was his name? Johnny... no ... Aaron? No, that's not it either. Well anyway, you know the one I'm talking about, right?"

"The one we all thought was going to marry Angela one day?"

"Yeah, that's the one! I wonder if they ever did get hitched. Anyway, remember the year they were representing Pakistan, and during one of the breaks he pulled out his ridiculous wanna-be accent that sounded more Indian than it did Pakistani and he was all like, 'There are three reasons why you should vote for my bill. Number one, I come all the way from my country to be here. Number two, I take the time to learn your language. And number three, what do you think I have in this briefcase, *papers*?' and then he shook his briefcase like a madman. I thought I was going to die laughing! It was so inappropriate and yet, somehow, totally hysterical!"

"True," Lani said, laughing with Kendra. "Half the stuff he said was inappropriate— and when any one of us would try to get him to stop, he'd just amp it up, so I always tried to laugh at the funny parts and ignore the other things. I remember when his voicemail recording was him doing an Osama Bin Laden impression, talking to the CIA knocking outside his door, saying, 'I'm not home! ... and I'm armed!' That kid was a riot! I wonder what ever happened to him."

"I dunno," Kendra replied, still laughing. "I think he moved to Alaska or something like that— somewhere really off the map."

"Like us?"

"Ha! Yeah, seriously, right? But for realz, Lani, if I was gonna have to get stranded on an alien planet, I'm glad it was with you, Raoul, Justin, and even Erik."

"Thanks, Minxy. I'm glad you're here too."

Kendra yawned loudly. "I'm getting tired. I think I'm gonna sign off now, Chicky."

"Me too. Sweet dreams."

"Sweet dreams."

Lani listened as Kendra rolled over and settled in for the night. She thought of Jharate— his sweet smile, his angelic voice, and his fiercely protective nature. He was so wonderful. She couldn't believe that he had somehow ended up in her life. She closed her eyes and pictured his enchanting eyes and his luscious lips and fell asleep with his image securely in her subconscious.

Morning came and Jharate quickly found Lani. He held both of his hands behind his back with a gleam in his eyes.

"Choose a hand."

Lani looked at him curiously and searched his face for a clue as to which hand she should pick. She leaned as far left as she could, but he moved to make it so she could not see. She smiled and leaned to her right in the same way, but again he blocked her view.

"No peeking," Jharate chuckled.

Lani bit her lip with a smile, closed her eyes, and pointed at his left hand. She opened them again and watched as he pulled the chosen hand forward. There, in his palm, was a tropical-looking ruby-red flower with five large satiny petals.

"Oh! It's beautiful!"

Lani reached for the flower, but Jharate pulled it back just out of reach. She looked at him with a quizzical gaze.

"May I?" Jharate asked, gesturing toward her ear with his right hand.

"Yes, of course," Lani answered with a blush.

Jharate took the flower in his right hand and placed it carefully behind her left ear. Lani could smell a heavenly fragrance, similar to plumerias, as it passed near her face.

"In both the Trisaknen and Kelamosan cultures, it is customary for a taken woman to wear a flower over her left ear."

"Thank you so much!" Lani stood on her tiptoes and gave Jharate a kiss. "Earth has a similar tradition among the Polynesian Islanders, where the music you love so much is from. So, what would have happened if I had picked the other hand?"

"Both of my hands held the flower," Jharate grinned.

"Ha! You're so adorable!"

Jharate leaned down and kissed her once more.

"Time to go!" Arante's voice called out.

"There's that timing again," Lani giggled.

"Indeed," laughed Jharate.

Lani and Jharate worked side by side to help pack up the camp and set off for the day's journey. The terrain was changing slightly now. The seldom-used path they had chosen was getting rockier and much less level. It was also becoming narrower. This was made worse by the overgrowth of many different kinds of bushes and trees. They eventually came to a fairly large river and quickly located the shallowest point they could find. However, it was still about three feet deep and a hundred feet wide, and the water was flowing briskly.

Arante led the way. Lani followed Jharate closely. She had to grab onto him several times because her natural lack of balance, combined with the current, was trying to knock her over every other second. But with his help, she managed to make it successfully without falling in. Once everyone had reached the other side, there was an instant cheerfulness in the ranks.

"We're almost there!" Arante shouted with an unusually carefree tone.

Lani and Jharate squeezed each other's hand tightly and looked at each other uneasily.

"*That* is where you are wrong. You are not going anywhere."

Drakne and his men appeared out of the willow-like trees, weapons raised, pointing towards the weary refugees, who quickly drew their own weapons. A small army stood blocking their way to Destavnia. They were practically surrounded, yet again. Lani could not believe it and apparently, neither could Arante.

"You have *got* to be kidding me! How did you get here before us?"

"Clearly you underestimated me. I have my ways. But that is beside the point…"

Drakne turned to address the entire crowd.

"You need not all die. Just give us the travelers from the other world, and your former prince, Jharate, and we will simply let the rest of you go. You can walk straight ahead through these trees and into the valley that leads into Destavnia, and there you will all obtain the freedom you so desperately want."

"I don't think so!" Arante barked back.

"Anyone else feel differently?" Drakne drawled, pausing for a moment. "No? Then have it your way."

Drakne's lips curled into a malicious grin.

THE PURE OF HEART

Drakne had over one hundred men, and they were much more skilled than Asharen's. The rebels numbered only forty, including the five from Earth. Arante kept Drakne's men back as far as she could with her bow and arrow. She targeted three at a time, but found that someone on Drakne's side was using deflecting powers. Changing tactics, she found that aiming at one man at a time systematically allowed her to take out the ones who had no shielding powers. Next, she focused on targeting their archers to minimize the number of arrows flying at her people. Raoul and Jaresh stood near her with their crossbows, skillfully doing the same.

Erik, Lani, and Jharate fought the opposing swordsmen. Lani was doing almost as well as Jharate now as she crossed blades with the men who attacked her. One of Drakne's men lunged toward Erik, who parried the blade away from his chest, and the soldier sliced Erik's left arm instead. Erik groaned as he felt the sharp searing pain, but as his anger grew, his groan transformed into a furious yell. He rushed his attacker, slashing his arm in return. The man redoubled his efforts against Erik and they continued to engage furiously. Finally Erik's sword slashed across his opponent's stomach and he emerged as the victor.

Justin struggled as four men came at him, one after another. He planted his feet firmly on the ground, a shoulder-width apart. With sweat pouring down his face he met the first attacker whose blade clanked wildly against his axe. Justin used the top of his weapon to slice one attacker as he maneuvered the pick on the bottom into the stomach of another man behind him, who fell to the ground. He pulled his weapon out and ferociously swung at the next two men who came to face him, fatally wounding both of them. The last of the four men rushed Justin from behind but tripped over the falling body of one of his comrades as Justin yanked his weapon backwards, accidentally impaling the man as he fell. Breathing hard, Justin braced his foot on the man's chest and pulled his battle-axe out quickly.

"I could use a little help!" Justin called to Erik as five more men came his way.

Erik rushed over. The two working together managed to keep the five at bay. Kendra aggressively used her martial arts skills and her staff with deadly effect. She had just finished knocking a handful of Drakne's men senseless, when an arrow came zooming towards her. She saw the archer, far across the battlefield, pulling back his bow and aiming to pierce her heart— but by the time that registered in her brain, he had already let the arrow fly and it was only a few feet away from her.

Kendra dropped her staff as she raised her hands instinctively to protect herself. The arrow glanced off, as if it had hit a stone, and fell to the ground. Kendra's eyes widened and her mouth fell open as two more arrows did the same. She could now see a distorted bubble around her. She lowered her hands and concentrated on the bubble disappearing— and it did. She quickly raised her hands again and focused on making the bubble reappear. It did! She laughed jubilantly, relishing her newfound talent. She dropped the force field and put it back up a few more times to make sure that she had command of it in case she needed it again. Satisfied, she picked up her staff and continued to fight on the offensive.

Drakne rubbed his right temple as he looked at his men. This was completely unacceptable. His over one hundred men had now dwindled to about seventy, and the rebels had only lost seven people, none of whom were important enough for him to care about. He scanned the battlefield thoughtfully. He refused to walk away from this incident without the prizes he sought.

His eyes fell upon a woman fighting wildly with her sword near the edge of the fight. Her strange clothes gave her away as one of the travelers he was after. Her skills with the blade were impressive, but she would stand no chance against his power. Drakne took a sure step in her direction. Using his powers to repel any objects that got close enough to hit him, he strolled through the chaos unharmed.

Drakne reached the woman and a large red energy ball materialized in his hands. He raised his arms to throw it at her. She had just finished killing another one of his men when she turned around and saw him. A surprisingly appropriate amount of fear registered in her eyes as she pointed her sword at him defensively, trying to keep him at a distance, watching his every move without blinking. As Drakne saw her face— he *hesitated*. The ball stayed suspended between his hands and he simply stared at her.

Their eyes locked. It was as if time had stopped for the two of them. The battle seemed to rage around them in slow motion with muted sound. Drakne's eyebrows rose, both of his eyes widened subtly, and his mouth opened slightly as he saw glowing white flames flickering where the blue in her eyes had been. The flames disappeared almost as quickly as they had come, but now Drakne felt something happening to *him*— something that had never happened before. He received a vision!

He saw this same girl in another place and time wearing a supernaturally white dress with flowing sleeves. The light coming from the dress was too bright to see any of the details of its design and it contrasted sharply with the black background behind her that spread out in every direction. Her eyes flickered with the same white flames he had just seen and her skin and hair began to glow with a golden white light. She glowed brighter and brighter until a shockwave emitted from her waist, parallel to the ground, and expanded, lightning fast, out into the infinite reaches of the blackness that surrounded her— like a star going supernova.

Drakne stood there dazed as reality came back into focus and he blinked in confusion as his vision of the girl disappeared. Jharate pulled the girl down and shielded her with his own body, breaking their eye contact. In that same second, Drakne lost control of the magical ball and it dropped to the ground. The energy had built up so high during his hesitation, and the ball had become so large, that it exploded against the dirt in a huge cloud of dust and reddish smoke.

"RUN FOR THE MOUNTAINS!" Arante screamed.

Baffled, Drakne stood still as he heard the sounds of the rebels scrambling away through the smoke screen. Why had he hesitated? How had he, who had never had a vision, seen something about this girl whom he had never encountered before? And what did the vision mean? He shook his head deliberately. These questions would have to wait. He had to get to her before they escaped.

"FOLLOW THEM YOU FOOLS!" Drakne screamed to his sixty remaining men.

The twenty surviving rebels rounded the corner into the Trazanian Mountain Pass until they came to a manmade arch in the mountain wall on their right, just inside the entrance of the pass itself. About twenty feet inside this cave-like opening, there was a ring-shaped object, reminiscent of a mirror. It seemed as if it were filled with brilliantly sparkling liquid, resembling colored glitter, rather than glass. If it had been turned horizontally it would have been a pool. The ring was suspended in mid-air about two feet above the ground and was about seven feet in diameter. Words began to spell themselves out on its glittery surface with a slight rippling effect, as a metallic female voice spoke the written words to them in rhyme, in what sounded to Lani like an upper-class British accent, with a New Zealand twist.

Ye need not be perfect
But evil take heed
This ring is not harmless
To those who deceive

"Yeah, yeah, we know the rules of the sanctuary," Arante hurried the voice. "We are in danger! Can we skip this part, *please?*"

"Very well. But consider yourself warned."

The words disappeared and the rainbow colors of the glittery surface changed to blinding silver. Arante ran through the ring and disappeared within it.

"Yeah, *that* looks safe!" Justin exclaimed.

"What choice have we got?" Erik asked.

"Move!" Kendra ordered.

Kendra, Justin, Raoul, and Erik followed hard upon the heels of the rebels vanishing through the ring in front of them, before jumping through themselves. Jharate and Lani were the last ones left. Jharate squeezed Lani's hand firmly as he led her through the portal, immediately behind the others.

Drakne rounded the corner into the tunnel and quickly shot a glowing purple ball at the woman who had spawned that uncomfortable vision, a moment before she could clear the liquid-like surface. It disappeared inside of her back just as she vanished into the portal. Drakne straightened himself up and walked toward the ring, regarding it with a cautious eye. He approached it carefully, keeping a good three-foot distance, and listened as the powerful echoing voice of the portal began to speak.

Ye need not be perfect
But evil take heed
This ring is not harmless
To those who deceive

You will never break through it
Unless pure of heart
For my magic detects frauds
And splits them apart

So if evil is friend to you
And deceit is your brother
Your feet will go one way
Your head quite another

But if you are pure
In your heart and your soul
You will not be harmed
And I charge you no toll

So pure of heart enter
And take your respite
Safety is granted
To those who do right

"BLAST IT ALL!"

"Watch your language," retorted the voice.

Drakne shot a dirty look at the portal. This was what he had feared— blasted sanctuary! He hated this kind of good magic. It was as strong as the magic that protected the rooms in the castles. The only way to get through it was with *goodness*. Bah! It was time for a new plan. He sharply turned his back on the ring and glared at what was left of his incompetent platoon.

"Since you are of no use to me whatsoever, I will be going on alone from this point. Rutghar, go back to Vranah and tell him that I will soon have what he seeks. Get there faster than *humanly* possible. As for the rest of you, half of you will walk just outside of this tunnel back to the exit of this pass, where they were headed before we cut them off, and remain there. Face the valley to the northeast that leads to Destavnia so that they will be forced south through the main canyon between Destavnia and

Trisakne. Do not engage them. Let them think that they have crept past you unawares. Just make sure that they have no option but to go south through these mountains.

"The other half of you moronic oxygen thieves will go around the mountains the other way, along the eastern shores of Lake Helasi, and through Trisakne into Zenastra. Cut the rebels off when they come through into Zenastra, before they can reach the river that tunnels through the Zenastran Mountains into Destavnia. You had better hurry because you will be going the long way… WHY ARE YOU ALL STILL STANDING HERE?! GO!"

All but one of his men ran to carry out his orders. As the others fled, Rutghar shrank in size while his grey ponytail and thick armor morphed into supernaturally silver feathers until he became a sleek and sinister looking hawk. Rutghar flew off with a shrill cry and was soon out of sight.

Drakne grabbed his hair in irritation. He had been chasing these people for far too long! They were having too much luck. Someone must be helping them. He wondered again— why had he not been able to kill the girl? Why had he hesitated? She *was* beautiful. Could he have been so weak as to be blinded by something so common as beauty? No, that could not be it. Could it?

She must be more powerful then she looked. The vision he had seen of her disturbed him. The power he had sensed from her was beyond imagination. He was not intuitive and had never experienced an intuitive gift before. He did not like it at all. It made him *feel,* and he tried to stay neutral and in absolute control at all times. It must have come from her somehow. Was it possible that she was too powerful for him to kill in a direct attack? Although that idea was incomprehensible, at the same time it *felt* correct— maybe it would take something more subtle.

After all, even his master feared a woman. Perhaps she was the one. He needed to change his tactics. He needed to study her carefully before making his next move in order to avoid another incident like the one he had just experienced. He was sure that the purple spell ball he had thrown at her would start to weaken her protection rapidly, even though he had not been able to hit her heart. He considered the matter for a moment. The right corner of Drakne's mouth went up into a smirk. Did this woman really think that she could beat him? He scoffed at her arrogance. It was weeks to the nearest town, now that he had diverted them from the direct route, and that meant that he would have plenty of time to break her— if the spell did not finish the job for him.

Lani came through the portal into the sanctuary and doubled over, grabbing her lower back. She took a couple of deep breaths and rubbed the area slowly.

"Ouch! Does that portal always hurt that much?"

"I have never experienced anything similar to stepping through this enchanted ring, and I feel no pain, myself. However, it is quite disorienting. Are you all right, my love?"

"Yes, I think so. My back just hurts a little."

Lani smiled as Jharate tenderly caressed her back. She loved how attentive he was. She relaxed and allowed the pain to drift away beneath his touch. The expressions on the faces of all around her turned Lani's attention to the surroundings, and she joined them in their awe as she took in the intricacies of their refuge. They were in a vast and magnificent cave. Its walls luminesced and looked as though they were made of abalone shell with some unseen source of light within them.

The air was fresh and pleasantly cool and both she and Jharate took deep, satisfying breaths in. She smiled at the wonderment in his eyes as he beheld the cave as well. A bubbling spring burst forth from the center of the main cavern and emerged from a large white marble bowl atop a matching five-foot tall pedestal. As the water filled this bowl, it flowed steadily over its sides and formed a dome-like sheet of water that fell continuously into the pool below. Its water was as crystal-clear as the twenty equidistant sparkling goblets set around the fountain's green marble rim, which was wide enough to sit on comfortably.

At the far end of the cave was a large and graceful waterfall. It sparkled like sapphires and flowed into a pond full of fish. Many delicious-looking fruits and vegetables grew near this pond. Lani laugh quietly as she noticed what Justin was discovering. He grabbed a nearby net and scooped out a bright lavender fish. The moment the fish was out of the water, an identical fish popped out of nowhere in midair and splashed into the water below it to swim happily with the others!

Justin laughed much louder than Lani did as he found that whatever he took was immediately replaced and his giant grin seemed almost permanent, as he got busy with his plans for a meal.

"This is awesome! Anybody see a frying pan or a knife?"

Everyone else was wandering around and too engrossed in the cave to answer and so he searched on his own. Lani didn't see anything either, and felt her stomach turn over a little as she saw him eyeing his battle-axe! It was completely clean and shiny— she found that odd, but stranger things had happened— but magical clean or no, that was totally gross.

"Justin, don't you dare!" Lani called out.

"I know, I know! I'll find something else."

Lani sighed in relief.

"Should I offer him the use of my knife?" Jharate asked.

"Thank you, darling, but he'll have a lot more fun on his own. And he's a lot of fun to watch when he gets this way."

"As you wish, my love."

Lani kissed Jharate's cheek and returned to watching as Justin's eyes fell on an empty fire pit surrounded by a low stone circular wall with a very wide flat ledge on top of it. There sat several copper wire baskets stacked neatly on top of each other. The shiny spit had multiple tines for these baskets to attach to, and a crank to turn the mechanism for even cooking. In one giant and energetic leap, Justin was beside the fire pit.

He took the fish out of the net and put it in one of the wire baskets and set it back on the wall. Before he could take another step he blinked and shook his head vigorously. His eyes opened wide.

"What is it, Justin?" Lani called.

"Whoa! The fish is boned and filleted!"

A fire burst into a perfect blaze inside the fire pit, ready to broil the fish.

"*AWESOME!* I may never leave!" Justin laughed to himself.

He ran and grabbed two fistfuls of vegetables straight out of the ground. He put them, as is, in the basket and watched expectantly.

"Haha! Julienned to perfection! Holy cow! And I didn't even have to clean them! This place is too good to be true!"

Lani laughed at Justin's exuberance. She loved seeing him this happy.

"Are cows considered holy in your world?" Jharate asked Lani, as he handed her a goblet full of the crystal clear water.

"No. I mean, yes— in some places. Not where we're from though. It's just an expression meant to convey surprise or excitement."

"I see."

"Thank you for the water, my love," she said as she sipped the ultra-refreshing liquid gratefully.

"It is always my pleasure to serve you, Lani."

Lani giggled and finally looked away from the joyful spectacle that was Justin, as fresh tropical-looking pink, purple, blue, and white flowers, which grew near the waterfall, caught her eye. Their wonderful perfume floated through the air. She inhaled deeply and felt an instant sense of peace. Next she noticed a double ring of trees and counted twenty silver hammocks strung between them— which happened to be the exact number of the remaining rebels.

Lani turned to Jharate and her eyes widened slightly again. He seemed different. She looked down at herself and she, too, was different. They had been completely cleaned. They were more than clean. There wasn't a smudge or smear from the battle left on them. Their clothes were as if they were brand new and had just been washed, dried, and ironed. Every last scratch they had received in battle had healed. Even Lani's tank had repaired itself!

She looked quickly around the main room and saw Raoul double and triple checking Erik's arm. Amazement was apparent on both of their faces as they noticed that there wasn't even a bloodstain or tear in his shirt. In addition to all of this, everyone had perfectly styled hair. Kendra was complimenting one of the female rebels on this very detail.

"You look so beautiful, Te'era! You should wear your hair like that more often."

"Thank you, but it is not very practical for battles."

"Kendra is right though. You look absolutely gorgeous!" Lani chimed in.

At that very moment, Lani caught a reflection of herself and discovered that her hair, too, was silky and shiny and straight. She looked as if she had just had her hair washed and blown dry at a salon, where they had then proceeded to brush her hair a thousand times and finished it off with a hair-shine product. The rest of the band of rebels looked as if they might be ready for a costume party back on Earth, or a movie poster photo shoot, rather than having come straight from a battlefield in Alamea.

Even more impressive than the physical changes was the general feeling of emotional wellbeing— everyone seemed peaceful, relaxed, and in Justin's case, even playful. It was as though the terrible losses from the battle had not been incurred— like the burden of grief had been removed for now.

"What *is* this place?" Lani asked, musing.

Arante was quick to answer with a proud smile on her face.

"This is the fabled Pure of Heart Sanctuary. The entrance only reveals itself when good people are in danger. If we had passed by under normal circumstances, we would have only seen the mountain wall. I haven't ever known anyone personally who has been inside of it, so I was desperately hoping that it actually existed when we retreated from the battlefield. Luckily, it is real! Only people with a pure heart may enter. Any evil thing that attempts to come inside will be punished, just for trying."

"How long can we stay here?"

"Well, that's the trick… According to legend, you can stay indefinitely. There is no time limit. However, there comes a point where if you stay too long, your heart will not remain pure, because it is selfish to stay longer than necessary. Good people are needed to win a war, right? And if all the good people could just run in here and stay forever, evil would win on the outside. It was designed to give righteous warriors a respite long enough to heal, and to give them some much needed food, rejuvenation, and sleep, but not to be a permanent sanctuary."

"So what happens if someone tries to stay too long?"

"It depends. If you just stay too long unknowingly, then it will eventually just kick you out when it is safe enough to venture outside. But, if you purposely try to stay for too long, you will meet the same end as if you were not pure of heart when you stepped through the ring in the first place."

"Forgive me for not knowing, but what end would that be?"

"The sanctuary will literally split your body in two and spit you out"

"Oh..." Lani said, slightly taken aback. "Well then..."

Lani suddenly felt extremely dizzy and staggered back. Jharate caught her to keep her from falling and handed his goblet to Arante so that he could free his other hand. Arante took Lani's glass as well.

"Thank you, Arante," Lani said, as she shook her head gently and blinked to get her bearings again.

"No problem, Lani. You look like you need to rest. I'll just take these back to where they belong. You are in good hands with my cousin."

"Thank you, Arante," Jharate added.

"No prob, Cuz," Arante said as she left.

"What's wrong with me?"

"I believe that you are simply exhausted. You have fought well this day, my love."

"But everyone else seems fine."

"*You* are not 'everyone else' and I am grateful for that fact."

Jharate easily scooped her up in his arms and carried her toward the hammocks. She felt a rush of excitement as her feet left the ground and she leaned her head against his chest as he walked. He gently set her down in one of the silvery hammocks. It was impossibly comfortable! Even the ropes felt more like clouds than cords. Lani sighed happily as all of the weight seemed to disappear from her body.

She looked to her left at the center space within the smaller ring of trees and saw that it was lush and grassy and dotted with clusters of the same fragrant flowers that she had noticed earlier, near the waterfall. A pair of snow-white peacocks strolled peacefully amidst them— the male fanning his tail from time to time. The sound from the rest of the cave was slightly muted, which would allow for more uninterrupted sleep, and it was warmer here— but a gentle breeze kissed her skin. Jharate took the hammock next to hers and took her hand as they both lay in their own hammocks, staring at the ceiling above the trees, which resembled the Alamean night sky, even though it was still daytime.

"Jharate?"

"Yes, Lani?"

"How did I ever get so lucky as to find you?"

She gazed at the fake stars above her with a smile on her face and waited for his answer. He always said the sweetest things, and she was excited to hear what he would come up with next. She waited and waited and waited. He didn't answer. She looked at him out of the corner of her eye, and he didn't show the slightest sign of response. In fact, it didn't even seem as if he thought he had been asked a question. Maybe the muted acoustics had somehow combined with the fact that she had whispered her question and therefore he just hadn't heard her. She looked back up at the pseudo sky, replaced the smile on her face, and tried again.

"I said, how did I ever get so lucky as to find you?"

Again there was no answer. She frowned slightly. She was sure she had been loud enough to be heard that time. Maybe he just didn't know how to answer that question modestly. She forced the smile back onto her face as she continued to look above her and tried something else.

"I love you, Jharate."

Silence. *Okay... that* she *knew* he knew how to answer. And she was equally sure that she had said it loudly enough. What was going on? She turned to look at him. His eyes were open— so there went the possibility that he had just fallen asleep. He was just lying there, still looking at the ceiling, but he wouldn't answer her. Why?

A jolt of terror seized Lani's heart. This moment was getting far too close to resembling one of the many things that Josiah had done. But Jharate was far beyond Josiah in maturity and had already done so many of the right things at the right times. Jharate had never let her doubt his love before, so what could this mean? Was the magic of their relationship already fading for him? He had always responded instantly prior to this moment. Well, at least he was still holding her hand. That had to be a sign, right? The very second she thought this, he pulled his hand away from her so quickly it made her jump.

Another icy jolt struck Lani's heart. Why had Jharate done that? Was it something she had said? She didn't understand. Again she was reminded of Josiah Harding. He had pulled his hand away from her in public, because he was too shy to handle being seen. But Jharate had been fine holding her hand in front of everyone. What was happening?

"Do you even care about me?"

Jharate was still lying on his back, staring at the ceiling with a flat expression on his face. Lani saw lavender ripples in the air around Jharate and his hammock, but she blinked and they disappeared. Her heart beat a little faster. She felt sick to her stomach and she swallowed hard before speaking again.

"If you don't care about me, why don't you just say so and get it over with?" Lani stated more than asked. "I'm a big girl and I've taken a lot worse. Why don't you just tell me?"

Jharate did nothing. She could feel stinging tears forming in her eyes but blinked hard to prevent them from coming. A dizzying sensation came once again and she closed her eyes tight, hoping that if she couldn't see, that maybe the world would stop spinning. When the vertigo ceased, she opened her eyes one more time to see if maybe Jharate had snapped out of whatever his problem was. But he was still lying on his back, staring up at the ceiling, with that same flat expression and wholly unworried eyes. *How dare he do this to me?*

"Never mind, Jharate— just never mind!"

She rolled over on the hammock and slammed her eyes shut in an effort to keep the threat of tears at bay. Because of her fatigue and the near perfect comfort of her surroundings, she fell asleep instantly.

In a different chamber of the cave, Kendra laughed merrily as she played with her newfound ability. One of the greatest mysteries in her life had now been explained. When she was eight years old she had been playing outside and had ended up in a driveway, just as a car was backing out. It had knocked her down and the back tire had run completely over her chest. But when the frantic people responsible for the accident got out to see what had happened, there wasn't even a bruise on her.

Her mother had looked up from the dishes she had been washing and out through the kitchen window just in time to see the incident from across the cul-de-sac. She dropped the glass casserole dish she was drying in her rush to run to Kendra's side. She was just as shocked as everyone else to find her unharmed, but was so happy that Kendra was okay that she didn't question why or how. Kendra was now sure that she had somehow activated her shield without realizing it.

The space Kendra had chosen for her practice room was huge and perfect for what she wanted to do. She just needed one more thing. There were quite a number of stones near the entrance of the main cave, arranged artistically like a small rock garden. Each stone was different from the rest. There were multiple shades of green, grey and blue. Some rocks had all three colors while others had rings of white around them or little starburst patterns. They were different shapes and sizes but they were all extraordinarily smooth.

"Justin, Raoul— grab some of those rocks and bring them over here for me!"

"What's the magic word?"

"Grow up, Justin!"

"Wrong!"

"Now!"

"That'll work. But just this once."

Justin and Raoul did as she commanded, and came back with a huge pile of rocks.

"Okay, so Justin, I want you to throw those rocks at me, as hard as you can, and I'll deflect them."

"I thought you'd never ask!"

Justin laughed maniacally as he chucked each rock as hard as he could in her direction. He aimed for places that wouldn't hurt too much if she failed to protect herself, but he was not holding back in speed at all. Every time he ran out of rocks to throw, he quickly dashed around to pick up some of the deflected ones, and re-launched them immediately.

Erik and some of the other rebels watched them from the main room near the entrance of the cave— safely out of the way.

"Faster!" Kendra ordered gleefully. "Faster!"

"I'm going as fast as I can, Kendra!"

Justin ran quickly for one of the rocks that had just ricocheted off of her shield and had landed about twenty feet away.

"It's kinda hard playing fetch with twenty rocks at a time you know."

"Use the Force, you must!" Raoul chimed in, in his best Yoda impersonation. "Not ready, are you."

Raoul burst out laughing as Justin ducked to avoid one of the five rocks he had just chucked all at once at Kendra, as the other four whizzed off fifty feet in every direction— one of which smashed a crystal goblet out in the main chamber of the cave. The broken goblet instantly vanished and a new one appeared in its place. Raoul started doing his pinky/thumb trick quickly and moving his shoulders from side to side with a motion that only made him laugh harder, until he couldn't do it anymore.

"Yeah, you could help, you know!" Justin said as he shot Raoul a pointed look.

Raoul was laughing too hard to answer, let alone move.

"Well?" Kendra demanded impatiently. "Go get them!"

"As you wish, My Lady," Justin said, faking a curtsy.

Justin didn't have any intention of giving her the satisfaction of running after those stupid rocks again. Instead he stood there and closed his eyes with his best imitation of Luke Skywalker trying to raise the X-wing fighter out of the swamplands of Dagobah. Raoul erupted with a renewed fit of laughter— louder and longer than his last. Justin had seen that movie one too many times. The imitation was almost perfect, with one minor exception— Luke had failed. Five small rocks came floating gracefully back to Justin and landed at his feet. Justin opened his eyes and looked down. He leapt back in surprise.

"WHOA! Did I? How did? Really? ARE YOU SERIOUS?!"

Justin jumped up and down for joy and punched the air triumphantly.

"I'm telekinetic! Wahooooo! The only thing that could top this would be having the Force for realz! Ye-ah!"

As Justin stopped jumping, he tried to make the rocks move again, on purpose this time, and laughed exuberantly as he began to master this unexpected gift by swirling a solitary pebble through the air.

"Yeah baby! Look at me and my *rad* self! Uh-huh, uh-huh! Uh-huh, uh-huh, uh-huh! YEE-AH!"

Raoul and Kendra stared at him open mouthed. They had never seen any hint of this before in all of the time that they had known him. Neither had he. Unlike Kendra and Raoul, there were no unexplainable mysteries in his life. He had progressed to this point quite free of anything supernatural or extraordinary.

"Great!" Erik muttered bitterly. "Now I'm the only one without some special ability."

Erik had been secretly trying to activate some power for days. He knew about Lani because he had been there when she received her vision on the ship. He knew about Raoul because of the healing he had done. Kendra had been obvious about her gift. And now Justin had one! He felt cosmically left out.

"That's okay," Justin said. "You still have your super brooding power."

"Justin!" Kendra said sharply.

"Sorry, Mom!" Justin said, giving Kendra a teenage boy look. "Erik, I really am sorry man— that wasn't nice of me. We cool?"

Justin smacked Erik hard on the back.

"Yeah. I just wish I had something special too, you know?"

"Well, you're crazy good with that sword. I mean you haven't hurt yourself yet, just other people. That's good, right?"

Erik smiled faintly. He turned to look at Arante and sighed. She was so beautiful, sitting there, letting her gorgeous legs dangle into the fishpond. She had been on his mind nonstop since the first time he laid eyes on her, but she always seemed just out of reach.

"Why don't you just go over there and talk to her?" Kendra prodded.

"What?" Erik said, snapping out of his trance. "No! I mean... Her? She's so out of my league."

"Yes, I see your point," Justin said, oh-so-helpfully. "But you know, some girls don't mind dating down. You seem like a decent fellow to settle for."

Kendra gave Justin a dirty look. He stuck his tongue out at her, but kept quiet.

"No, really," Kendra said, shooting one more warning look at Justin before continuing. "Go talk to her. You're a great guy and I think I've seen her looking at you more than once."

"Really?"

"Yep."

Kendra shoved him off in Arante's direction.

"Now go, get lost, and get your woman!"

Erik straightened up, puffed out his chest and threw his shoulders back— but his footsteps were careful and tentative as he slowly approached Arante.

"Arante?"

"Yes?" Arante replied, slightly softer than usual. She looked up at him, doe-eyed, and gently batted her eyelashes twice as her full lips curled into a slight smile.

"G-Good job out there. I mean, today, ah-hem— in the battle."

Erik was kicking himself on the inside. He wanted to throw his head back and rip his hands through his hair, but he resisted the urge. He felt so stupid. He couldn't talk to her. He had been an idiot for even trying. He turned to go find a hole to crawl into and die in, when Arante spoke.

"No, wait! Don't go."

Erik stopped dead in his tracks and slowly swiveled back to look at her, his eyes wide and his mouth slightly ajar. Had he heard what he just thought he had heard? Had the most gorgeous woman in the world— make that both worlds, actually— just asked him to stay?

"Really?"

"Yes. Sit down. Tell me of your world. What is it like?"

"Well, it's different, that's for sure."

Arante giggled and batted her eyelashes at him again.

"You're really pretty," Erik said before he could stop himself.

"Thank you! You're not so bad yourself."

Erik grinned so widely that he thought his face would break if his smile were to stretch any further.

"YUCK!" Justin exclaimed from a distance.

Neither Erik nor Arante heard him. Kendra, however, slapped him on the back of his head.

"Ow!"

"SHHHHHHH! Let them have their time! You left Lani and Jharate alone."

"Yeah well that's different! She— He— Well they just— I don't know, they just don't bother me as much."

"Excellent defense."

"Well, how come *you're* okay with it? We all know how little you think of Arante. How come it doesn't bother you?"

"Probably because I never liked Erik that much either. They belong together."

Kendra was only half kidding. She liked Erik when he was happy, but whenever he felt stressed or depressed he was too much of a whiner for her taste.

"AH!" Justin said, sighing with a mischievous look in his eyes. "Who cares about them anyway? Let's get talking about you and me, Kendra."

Justin slid up next to her as she moved to put more space between them.

"What do you mean *you and me?*"

Justin closed the distance between them once again. He continued advancing until he had her backed up against a wall. He leaned against the wall with his right arm above Kendra and put his left hand on her waist. Kendra's eyes flew wide open with fear and she swallowed hard. He leaned in like he was going to kiss her but swerved suddenly to whisper in her ear, simultaneously smoothing a bit of her hair behind her ear with his left hand.

"Don't you know? Can't you tell? I mean the way we always argue all the time. The way I'm always teasing you? Don't tell me you could have misread the signs. My heart belongs to you Kendra. Don't break it— just take it and kiss me. Kiss me, Kendra!"

He closed his eyes and puckered up his already full lips, a mere two inches away from hers.

"Oh brother!" Raoul said, rolling his eyes.

"WHAT?" Kendra shouted, shaking her head nervously. "No way, no, uh-uh! Never ever! We're just friends and that is how it is going to stay forever! Not even if you were the last man on Earth would I ev—"

"Ah, but we aren't *on Earth* now, are we?" Justin asked as he opened his eyes back up with a smirk on his face.

"Oh grow up!"

Kendra finally caught on and shoved him away from her.

"You're so stupid sometimes, Justin."

"I know. It's a gift. Let's see, that is one for Justin…" he said, drawing an invisible tally mark in the air, "… and, oh I'm so sorry, *none* for Kendra— but thanks for playing! We have some lovely consolation prizes!"

Kendra punched Justin in the shoulder hard enough to leave an impression that he had better not push her any farther, but soft enough to let him know she was still just playing with him.

"OW, ow, ow!"

Justin fell to the ground as if she had really hurt him, grabbing his shoulder in agony.

"Oh the pain! I see a light at the end of the tunnel. Grandma? Grandma, is that you? I'm coming, Grandma! Wait! Don't go! I brought sushi!"

Kendra sighed in frustration, and gently kicked him, as she turned and walked away to go get some food. She could smell the heavenly aroma of some sort of fish cooking in the fire pit. Justin burst into hysterical laughter as she left, rolling from side to side on the ground. He laughed so hard his sides ached. Raoul couldn't help but laugh too. He always tried super hard not to laugh when Justin got really immature, but he rarely succeeded.

Outside the sanctuary, Drakne stormed out of the entrance tunnel. He knew that the rebels would be in there for a while, and he needed to leave so that the sanctuary would believe the occupants were safe enough to allow them to exit. The sooner he was out of range, the less time he would have to wait for them.

Drakne made his way back to the opening of the pass and walked between two of his guards, who were in a line facing away from him, toward the valley in the northeast, as ordered. He strode through without a word— unaware that he was being observed by anyone other than his own men. He continued further, past the guards and back through the trees, into the area where the battle had just taken place.

The pair of glittering green eyes, which had been following the rebels since the Forest of Kar, watched him leave. This time, however, the mystical green eyes were not alone. A pair of glittering brown eyes was close by, and now two pairs of eyes watched as Drakne disappeared around the corner of the entrance to the pass. With one last glance at the Pure of Heart Sanctuary, the mysterious spies disappeared into the mountains.

Once outside of the pass and away from his men, Drakne muttered a few ancient and powerful words to himself. The light bent around him, starting at his head, and flowed down his body until it disappeared into the ground. He looked at his hands and, as expected, they were still visible to his eyes. He needed to be sure— anything less than perfection in this spell would lead to disastrous consequences for his plan.

He walked back to where his men were guarding the entrance to the mountain pass. They were spaced evenly apart to cover the width of it. Nothing could get past them unseen. He approached the soldiers quietly and stopped in front of one of them. Drakne acted as if he were ready to throw a spell ball. The guard did not flinch or make any sign of having seen him. Drakne took a couple of steps to his left and stopped just short of punching another of his men in the face. Again, there was no reaction.

"Perfect," Drakne whispered to himself.

The second guard looked around as though he might have heard something, but saw only the other guards. Drakne froze, remaining perfectly still and silent until the guard who had heard him shrugged off the sound and stopped looking for its source. Satisfied, Drakne quietly crept through one of the spaces between the rest of his guards and back into the mountain pass with a smile on his face. No one would be able to see him until he undid this magic— not even the cave itself would be able to detect him with this enchantment. And it was obvious from Jharate's actions that he was in love with that girl, so although the former prince was well known for his gift of vision, Drakne doubted that Jharate would be able to sense anything once the spell truly did its work and chaos ensued.

Drakne thought about cloaking his sound as well as an extra measure— but there would be no fun if there were no danger in the game. Rather than entering the manmade tunnel of the sanctuary, he sat on a boulder across from the entrance to wait. They couldn't stay in there forever.

"Okay, listen up, everybody," Arante's voice rang out. "I'm sure that Drakne is well versed in the lore surrounding the Pure of Heart Sanctuary and knows that it will protect us until it is safe outside. That means that Drakne will have no choice but to pull his men off at some point. He is not a man known for his patience, so he has more than likely already sent his men away, making it so that we can leave at any moment now.

"But, obviously, he isn't going to let us take the easy way back through the valley to Destavnia. He will be sure to post guards to block our way there and force us to make our way south through the mountain pass into Zenastra. I'm sure he's hoping that we will just try to force our way through, but I don't want to give him that satisfaction for the same reason that he would like it. He is hoping we will lose Jharate, because he knows what a blow that would be to our people and to Alamea as a whole. And, according to Lani's vision on the ship, we have at least one Half-Heart among us— possibly more than one. We can't take a risk of losing even one Half-Heart just to get to Destavnia faster, even if we could win the battle against Drakne's men— which we would.

"Drakne will probably have the rest of his men go back along the shore of Lake Helasi and through the Trisaknen side so that he can fool the sanctuary into thinking that we are safe. As the mountains here are too steep to safely travel over directly into Destavnia, it will basically be a foot race to see which party can get to Zenastra first. If Drakne and his men arrive before we do, it will mean another battle. Luckily the Trisaknen way is about two or three days longer than the journey through the Trazanian Pass so we should get there first.

"Long story short, in order to ensure that we keep this slight advantage, we should probably only stay one night to enjoy the safety of this sanctuary. So make the most of it. That is all. As you were."

Arante sat back down to dangle her legs in the pool again and looked up as Erik came back to her side. He had just picked some fresh flowers for her. He brought them over with an embarrassed look on his face, looking down at his feet and shifting his weight as he handed them to her. She accepted them with a warm smile, and delicately inhaled their scent. She suddenly stood up, dropped the flowers, grabbed his shirt by the collar with both hands, and pulled him in for a passionate kiss.

"Wow," Erik muttered as their lips parted.

Erik staggered back, falling. Arante still had a hold on his shirt and the two of them tumbled together into the pond with a huge splash, sending the fish into a frenzied chaos. When they resurfaced, Arante laughed happily and kissed him again, as they knelt in the water together. As they exited, the water sheeted off of them like they were made of glass.

Arante turned and flashed a flirtatious smile at Erik, who took a misstep and fell back again into the shallow water. This time Arante did not fall down with him. She laughed freely like she had not laughed since she was a child. She leaned over and offered her hand to help him get out. He took it and stepped out of the pond. There were stars in his hazel eyes as he gazed at her. Erik had never expected this kind of luck in his entire life. He barely noticed that they were instantly dry the moment they stepped out onto the solid ground again. He leaned in and kissed her on the lips, his right hand gently holding the nape of her neck, with his left cradling her waist.

As their lips parted this time, Arante jogged away with a giggle and a girlish smile until she found a good climbing tree and beckoned for Erik to follow her. They climbed up to one of the topmost sturdy branches and sat on it together. She lifted his arm around her and put her head on his shoulder and they sat there for a long time. Arante conjured up an image of some fireflies to float around them as they cuddled. They sat quietly, simply enjoying each other's company. After a while, Arante abruptly broke the silence between them.

"I think I want to go with you to your world."

"Really? But, this is your home."

"Yes, but I want something new. Everyone knows me here. I am part of the royal family of Trisakne and I am always recognized everywhere I go. I can never hide in a crowd. This would have to be after we find a way to defeat Vranah, of course. I could never abandon my world in a time such as this. But once the Kingdom of Trisakne is returned to Jharate, there will be very little for me to do. I want to go with you if you ever find a way back home."

"Well, I'd love to have you come with me," Erik beamed, wondering if he was dreaming.

"Tell me of your family on Earth. What are they like?"

"I'm the youngest of four— the rest are all girls, which made me the victim of countless chick flick marathons and hairstyling sessions growing up."

"Chick flick?"

"Never mind, it's kind of hard to explain. They just did a lot of girly things to me, but I love them."

"What about your parents?"

"Well… my parents aren't together anymore."

"Oh, I'm sorry! Which one of them died?"

"Neither of them died. They just split up. They aren't married anymore."

"What?!" Arante asked in shock. "How is that possible?"

"They're divorced."

"Divorced? What does that mean?"

"You guys don't have divorce? Oh wow, well um… it's a legal way to end a marriage on Earth. The two can split and not be together anymore… like, be single again."

Arante pulled Erik closer to her, and held on tightly.

"That's terrible! I'm so sorry, Erik."

"Yeah, well, it was a long time ago. I was like fourteen. I was the youngest and I think they were going to try to wait until I was eighteen so it wouldn't be so traumatic, but they couldn't hack it. My three older sisters were surprised it lasted as long as it did. I guess I never saw it coming. It was hard, but yeah. Whatcha gonna do? I'm over it now… mostly anyway."

Arante turned her lips up to his and kissed him gently, smiling sweetly at him. He grinned from ear to ear and squeezed her close, feeling better than he ever had before.

Justin, Raoul, and Kendra were so shocked that they were completely silent.

Lani slowly opened her eyes, blinking carefully. She wondered how long she had been asleep. She looked around her surroundings, feeling very confused. Where had all these hammocks come from? Was that a white peacock?! She saw Jharate sitting upright in the hammock next to her, looking at her with a worried expression on his face. She put her hand against her right temple and blinked hard a few times as she tried to adjust her neck.

"I have a huge headache…"

"I am sorry, my love. Are you well otherwise?"

"I think so. What happened? I remember a huge pain in my back coming through the portal and then… nothing. Did I black out?"

"Not precisely… You truly remember nothing?"

"Nothing… Wait, now I do. I was pouring my heart out to you and you weren't answering. Why wouldn't you answer me?"

Lani waited for him to answer, but he only stared back at her.

"Why aren't you answering me now?"

"What is wrong with you, Lani?"

"What's wrong with me? What's *wrong with ME*? I don't know. Maybe I like being answered when I tell someone I love them!"

All the fears and pain that she had felt from every relationship came rushing back to her, swirling through her mind like a giant storm. She felt betrayed. She felt abandoned. She felt rejected. She felt taken for granted. She felt stupid for believing he was different! A deep anger began to rise from the ashes of her broken heart.

"Now you aren't answering me again? Great! If you're angry with me, you could at least tell me what I did! This is not only childish— it is cruel!"

"Why are you behaving like this, Lani? I did nothing to you."

"THAT'S the problem! You didn't do *anything!* You won't answer me! You pulled your hand away from me! It's like you don't love me at all! I heard Arante telling you not to 'mislead' me by letting me think 'something' I 'shouldn't.' What was the secret? That you don't care about me? That you were just taking pity on me?"

"I do not know why you could *ever* think that I love you, Lani."

"Maybe this wasn't such a good idea…"

The acid tears came all at once, falling in large streams. His harsh and mocking tone still burned in her ears. She felt as if the walls were closing in on her, threatening to crush or suffocate her, whichever came first. She couldn't stand it anymore— not another minute with someone who could be so cavalier about her feelings. She couldn't breathe! She grabbed onto the hilt of her sword, still sheathed at her side, jumped out of the hammock, and ran out through the portal.

"Lani, NO!"

Jharate sprang to his feet and ran after her, disappearing through the glittering ring.

Those left behind in the cave looked at the portal Jharate and Lani had just run through, completely bewildered. Arante, however, looked extremely annoyed. She sighed a frustrated sigh. She supposed it was probably about time anyway. She gave Erik a quick kiss on the cheek and did a back flip out of the tree— landing on the ground with the grace of a cat.

"Alright everyone, let's start packing up! I want seven people to come with me right now for a quick patrol— the rest of you stay here and get things ready so that the sanctuary will remain open. We'll be back to help soon. Do not leave under any circumstances until we return. *All* of the Earth people stay here."

"No way are we staying here when Lani's out there! Besides, didn't you say that the portal won't let us out unless it's safe? So it's safe!" Justin insisted.

"Oh alright," Arante relented in an exasperated tone.

All of the Earth friends came to Arante's side along with three of Lani's new rebel friends— including Jaresh and Ka'ern. Everyone else started packing up as Arante turned to face the portal, and led the way out.

Outside, Drakne looked up and watched with a smile, as he saw Lani run out crying, followed by a most distressed Jharate.

"Please, Lani, I—"

"Just leave me alone!"

"I do not understand."

"That's part of the problem! You just don't understand. I thought maybe if you saw what I had been through you would understand that I *need to know I am loved*. But you just made it very clear that you don't love me anyway, so fine! I don't need this. I am done with dead end relationships. I want a serious one. One that will last... forever! Just let me go!"

"Lani, you will die if you venture off alone."

"I don't care! Death isn't the worst thing in life! Besides, I can take care of myself for five minutes! Leave me alone!"

Arante and the others came out of the sanctuary now. They glanced from Lani to Jharate and back again, completely confused. They hadn't heard what Jharate had said, but no one expected the two of them to have problems of any kind. They were so perfect for each other. Lani turned and walked off alone, crying. The walk turned into a jog, which turned into a run. Jharate stood, dumfounded, until she vanished from his sight.

She ran for a short time until she was sure she was by herself. She slowed her steps and turned off the main part of the pass into a box canyon. It was stark and empty, like she felt. She walked over the jagged pebbles and small boulders up to a lone dead tree near the entrance to another cave in one of the canyon walls. She regarded it for a moment, not sure what she was thinking or even knowing exactly what she was feeling. She pulled her sword out of its sheath and let out a primal scream, which echoed against the walls and back again, as she swung it down on one of the dead tree's thick branches— cleaving it in two with the force of her blow.

Drakne had stepped into the canyon in time to see the power of her rage. He lifted an eyebrow at her exhibition of strength.

Lani breathed hard as some of the adrenaline left her. She looked into the cave and gasped in fear as she saw two glowing yellow eyes the size of trashcan lids staring back at her. She backed up quickly toward the other wall of the canyon, but moved too fast. Again, her klutziness betrayed her as she tripped and fell onto the rocks, suffering several cuts and bruises. She hurried her hair out of her face and looked up in terror, just as an enormous dragon emerged with a great roar from the darkness of the cave and looked down on her with its giant nostrils flaring.

Drakne watched with interest. Perhaps his work was about to be done for him.

TOO LATE FOR *THIS* INFORMATION!!!

Scraped and bleeding and face to face with a ferocious beast, Lani was paralyzed with fear. This day just kept getting worse and worse! Now to top it all off, she was about to be dinner for a dragon. Fantastic! A dragon! Of all the ways she had ever imagined that she would die, a *dragon* had never even made it on the list! She stayed very still hoping that maybe dragons were like T-Rex's, which were supposed to be unable to see you if you didn't move.

Wait— how could anyone know how a T-Rex behaved? What was she even *thinking* believing she had great tips on T-Rex behavior at her disposal to apply to a *dragon?* She was being stupid! Not only was she about to die, but now she was also going to die with ridiculous dying thoughts. She'd get to the other side and when they asked about her death, she'd have no choice but to say, "I got eaten by a dragon because I thought he would be like a T-Rex, and so I stayed still and made it easy for him."

The dragon reared its head and inhaled deeply. After a moment, it lowered its face— closer and closer, eyes trained on Lani. She braced herself and threw her arms over her eyes, waiting for the inevitable. Nothing happened. She was still alive. She barely dared to open her eyes again— but when she did, she saw Jharate standing between her and the dragon. Flames were blasting out in all directions off the charmed shield he held in his hands. Although it diverted the fire away from them and provided a bubble of safety, Lani's face felt like she was being sunburned. The heat swirled tempestuously around them and the air was almost too hot to breathe.

"RUN!"

Lani obeyed and ran about a hundred feet away to the opposite canyon wall, and then turned to watch for Jharate. Without the shield, even at this distance, the flames were blinding and the heat was so intense that it almost burned her. She couldn't see Jharate anymore. All she could see was the gargantuan beast wading through a sea of fire. Its black scales seemed to be pulsing with anticipation and rage, almost as if they had a life of their own. Lani's heart nearly stopped until she finally located Jharate again. She breathed a sigh of relief as she saw him emerge from the torrent of fire, which receded as the dragon took another breath. The shield was diverting the fire but Lani didn't think that any human could withstand the overpowering heat much longer, magic shield or no.

Drakne's eyes lit up and he laughed. Still invisible to all around him, he lifted his hands from his sides toward the sky, arms bent slightly, with his palms facing upward. As he did so, he rose one hundred feet into the air and set himself down on a ledge where he could have a bird's-eye view of the battle in the canyon below. The exhilaration Drakne felt made him wish that he could do more than just levitate himself vertically. His black cape fluttered in the wind as he stood on the ledge. From this vantage point, he could also see into the main pass where Arante and a few of the other rebels were running toward the commotion. He smiled as he snapped his fingers.

Two enormous bolts of lightning struck opposite sides of the main pass. The rebels stopped dead in their tracks as they heard a low rumbling sound and the ground began to shake. An avalanche of hundreds of boulders and rocks of all sizes plummeted from above as the mountainside crumbled. Arante threw her hands up in front of her face as she scrambled backwards. Kendra concentrated on extending her shield around Arante. The rocks and debris bounced off Kendra's shield and protected her, but everyone watched in horror as Arante disappeared from sight. They found themselves stuck only twenty yards from the entrance of the box canyon, where Lani and Jharate were trapped, with Arante now buried beneath the rubble.

"That ought to keep you busy," Drakne said aloud.

"ARANTE!"

Erik rushed with Kendra, Raoul, Justin, and the other rebels who had exited the sanctuary to the hundred-foot-tall pile of rubble and started clawing fiercely at its base. Arante was under what had to be at least three feet of debris. Every time they pulled some off, more would slide down on top of her. Even with Jaresh's phenomenal strength, the rock pile kept defeating them in their efforts to uncover Arante.

"Justin, use your gift and move some of the rocks off!" Kendra exclaimed.

"I am!"

"Use it better!"

"Why don't you open your shield from inside where she is and lift the rocks off of her?!"

"Stop the rocks from falling at least! I already tried to put a shield around her when it started to fall! It didn't work!"

"Try again!"

The dragon continued to spew great shafts of fire. Jharate dodged the beast's attacks but did not attempt to flee. He kept drawing the dragon's attention to himself, to keep it from remembering that Lani was there too. The dragon was blocking the entrance, so Jharate could only retreat up the steep rocky terrain at the closed end of the box canyon. Jharate enticed the dragon to attack him as he climbed higher and higher until he was level with the top of the dragon's fifty-foot-tall legs.

Jharate could now have scrambled to the lip of the canyon and escaped up the mountainside. However, he showed no sign of retreating. He slashed at the dragon, dodging its attacks. He slashed again, and again, and again at the dragon's head and arms to keep it at bay. Jharate waited until the dragon started to inhale once more. As it did so, he dropped his shield so that he could hold his sword high above his head with both hands, and raced over the rocks toward the dragon's soft underbelly. With an impossible leap, he flew into the air and plunged his sword deep into the dragon's chest.

The dragon howled in anguish and smacked Jharate onto the rocky ground with one of its claws, before crashing to its death. As its head hit the ground, a huge blast of fire escaped the dragon's nostrils directly towards Lani. She ran desperately to avoid being scorched, but she had run out of space. She turned around to see what was happening, but could not bring herself to look. Instead she closed her eyes tight and flattened herself against the wall— hoping she had somehow outrun the fire. Her heart beat frantically as she waited for the flames, and when they did not come, she took a deep smoke-filled breath and coughed as she slowly opened her eyes again.

The silence that followed as the smoke and dust settled was almost more frightening than the roars of the dragon. The only sound was the crackling of the remains of the single tree by the dragon's cave, which had been charred in lieu of Lani. The haze slowly faded until Lani could see what had happened. Jharate's sword was deep in the dragon's chest. Her eyes searched wildly through the wreckage until she found Jharate. He lay motionless on the ground.

Lani's heart jolted. A searing pain ripped through her head and she felt as though it would literally split her skull in two. She fell to her knees in agony, cradling her throbbing head in her hands. She cried out in a blood-curdling scream and smacked the ground with both fists. Her headache disappeared. Breathing hard, she was covered in cuts and bruises, and her hands and knees were bleeding— but losing the headache was liberating. It was as if she had been imprisoned somewhere inside herself. It was the oddest feeling she had ever had— and all at once it was gone. Looking up, she saw that Jharate still had not moved. She flew to his side and desperately pulled him into her arms.

"No! Please, no! Come on, stay with me! Jharate, please!"

Drakne's mouth fell open.

"Not possible!" he whispered to himself.

He had never seen *anyone* do that before. His power had always been stronger than his victim and no one had ever escaped the effects of any of his spells on their own. She was indeed much more powerful than she looked. What a fascinating development. He couldn't even take her down with magic! Well, no matter. He was starting to think that he would like to study her more before killing her anyway. It had been so long since anything had been challenging for him— and the fact that she had been such an unlikely threat only made things more interesting. Drakne moved his palms slowly downward as he floated effortlessly back to the ground. A thin smile stretched across his face as he spoke to himself.

"Let's see how well Jharate fares with the same challenge."

Lani's tears blinded her. Drakne was sure that she couldn't even see Jharate anymore, let alone anything around her. Now was his chance. He threw a purple pulsing energy ball, directly into Jharate's heart.

The rebels finally uncovered Arante enough for Erik and Justin to pull her limp body out from under the rubble and lay her down on the solid ground. Tears ran down Erik's face.

"Hurry, Raoul!"

"I'm on it!"

Raoul knelt at Arante's side, took a deep breath, and went to work. He started with her head, and then her heart— keeping his eyes open as he continued, so that he could see when he was done with one spot and needed to move to another. Arante's injuries were extensive and it took a great deal of energy out of Raoul, but he pressed on until she revived.

"Thank you, Raoul," Erik said with a great sigh of relief.

"No problem."

Raoul sat down on the ground to rest, breathing hard. Erik helped Arante up and held her close. She hugged him in return, but soon pushed him back a couple of inches and froze with her hands still on his chest.

"Wait," Arante almost whispered. "Do you hear that?"

"I don't hear anything," Justin answered.

"Exactly! I hope we're not too late! Follow me!"

Arante led them up the gigantic pile of rocks as quickly as they could go. Tired as Raoul was, he jumped up and began to scale the rockslide with the others.

Jharate was in bad shape. The dragon had scratched him deeply across his chest and stomach when it threw him off, and Jharate had landed on the rocks. He was bleeding profusely from several places and there was sure to be internal injuries as well. Lani sobbed and shook as she clutched him closer.

"RAOUL!"

Her agonized voice echoed through the canyon walls as she continued to plead in-between sobs.

"RAOUL! HELP ME! PLEASE!"

Raoul heard her call. It echoed through his ears. He could hear her from anywhere. Even though he was already fatigued from the energy needed to heal Arante, he was fueled with a massive adrenaline rush. He hurried over the landslide harder and faster, overtaking everyone else and leaving them far behind. He quickly slid down the other side and jumped the last six feet to ground. He cleared the rock pile, ran around a corner toward Lani's anguished cries, and came to a skidding halt as he saw the enormous corpse of the dragon.

"Whoa! What happened?"

"Talk later! Heal now! Please! I think he might be dead!"

Raoul saw Jharate for the first time. His eyes went wide with horror. He knew he couldn't say this to Lani, but he feared it might be too late. He ran to Jharate's side, and began to heal his badly broken body. He started by stopping the bleeding at Jharate's head. Just as Raoul did so, a death rattle shuddered through Jharate's throat and he fell silent— his breathing stopped completely. Raoul quickly put his hands on Jharate's chest. One minute. Two minutes. Three minutes. Raoul still could not bring him to consciousness, but finally Jharate inhaled sharply and started to breathe again. Lani felt as if she had begun to breathe for the first time in minutes as well.

Raoul now moved his hands over the torn flesh and broken bones in Jharate's body until everything was as good as new. Jharate's eyes flew open and he saw Lani. Tears of relief and love streamed down her face. She was kneeling and holding one of his hands in both of hers. He knit his brow and his lips stretched tight. He yanked his hand away from her roughly, stood up, and walked over to the dragon. Without a word Jharate wrenched his sword from the lifeless beast and walked away.

Lani lost her balance and fell back slightly. She stared at him open-mouthed, in silence, with tears still running down her cheeks— blinking in disbelief. A heavy weight pressed down on her heart as she choked on her breath. Collapsing across a rock, she buried her face in her arms and convulsed with sobs.

"What have I done?!"

Lani's heart beat hard against her ribs and her gut clenched tight as she sobbed. She remembered now. Every moment. Every word. Every look. Every touch. Everything. She heard all of the words in her head— words that only minutes ago she had been unable to hear. Oh his words! They now echoed through her mind. *I love you more than the air that I breathe. Did you not hear me?* She cried harder and harder as the missing words kept coming. *I do love you, Lani. You are the most important person in the entire world to me. I value your life above my own. What is wrong, Lani?*

"What have I done?!"

Lani wailed as the words continued to come into her mind. *I do love you, Lani. You know that. I have told you that every time that you have asked. Why is this not sufficient for you? What is wrong? What must I say to make you happy? Name it, and I will say it. What must I do? Tell me what you want for proof and I shall give it to you! Lani, what must I do?* And Jharate's fatal sentence that had spurred her to run away had not been how she had heard it at all. *No, of course not! I do not know why you could ever think that... I love you, Lani.* How could inflection, vocal tone, and a small pause make such a crucial difference? And how had she not heard it? Jharate had constantly reassured her. He hadn't yanked his hand away— she had! He had been perfect! How had she missed it all? How could she have been so dense? What had possessed her?

"What have I *DONE?!*"

Raoul felt horribly lost. His eyes shot from Lani to Jharate. What on Earth had happened in that sanctuary? Raoul watched as Jharate cleaned his sword without so much as a glance at Lani, who was obviously in tremendous pain. Raoul narrowed his eyes, marched over, and looked up at Jharate, who towered more than a foot above him. Raoul's jaw was set firmly and his index finger pointed up at Jharate's face.

"I don't care who you are, or what she did. You shouldn't leave her like that! No man should let a woman cry like that, no matter what his 'reasons' are!"

Jharate looked down at Raoul calmly with no sign of emotion visible on his forbidding face. No anger, no frustration, no compassion, no regret— nothing at all.

"Thank you for saving my life, but I will handle my own affairs."

Jharate walked away from Raoul toward Arante, who had just arrived with everyone else. The seven newcomers had the same looks on their faces that Raoul had just had on his. Everyone looked from Jharate to Lani and back again.

Now that all was silent, Drakne had to put his fist in front of his mouth to hold in his laughter. He was suddenly glad that he hadn't been able to kill the girl immediately. This was so much more fun. No, more than that— this was perfect!

"We must depart," Jharate said coldly.

Arante saw the unyielding look on Jharate's face and knew better than to try to talk to him right now. She had seen it before. It meant that he had made up his mind and there was no changing it. But there was something unnerving about it— some foreign visage was there that shouldn't be— or rather, something familiar that *wasn't* there. It was too cold and distant— lifeless might be a better description. It startled her to see him like this. She wanted to know what had happened between the two of them that could account for this disconcerting change. She dropped her gaze and he marched past her, toward the landslide. She slowly turned and followed him.

Justin and Kendra looked hesitantly from Lani to the rest of the party that was heading back. Raoul insistently jerked his head toward those leaving. When Justin and Kendra didn't leave immediately, Raoul pointed definitively for them to go. They quietly turned and left, following the others.

The glint of Lani's sword caught Raoul's eye. He walked over near the smoldering dead tree and picked it up off the ground. He brought it back to her and carefully put it back in its sheath at her side. He leaned down, put his arms around her, and helped her up.

"It'll be alright, Lani," Raoul said rather helplessly.

Lani didn't answer. The words had entered her brain but they didn't ring true. Her tears kept falling and her sobs were making her sides ache. She slowly stood up with Raoul's prompting, unconscious of the fact that she was even doing it. He kept his hold on her and guided her out toward the rockslide. Raoul helped her one step at a time as they plugged forward behind the others.

Tears fell silently from Lani's swollen eyes as she climbed over the rubble. The sobs slowly subsided but a few rapid breathy shudders overcame her every now and again. The quiet tears kept coming and coming with no sign of stopping. Seeing her like this nearly made Raoul cry himself. To fend off that possibility, he distracted himself by trying to think of what he could do to help her now. He attempted to heal any physical wounds that he could reach as they walked without letting her know he was doing it, because he knew she was blaming herself and would not want to feel better. Even though he knew the sanctuary would soon heal her completely, he couldn't stand to let her suffer any pain that he could take away now.

Drakne followed Lani and Raoul with an amused smirk on his face. This had become his very own private puppet show. Jharate was doing *exactly* what he wanted him to do. HA! Jharate was not stronger than a woman! This was too good! He knew he was going to enjoy the coming weeks as this pathetic ensemble tried to reach Zenastra before his men.

In fact, Drakne no longer cared if his men even made it at all. Knowing those dimwits, they probably wouldn't. It didn't matter anymore. He could follow these rebel fools straight into

Destavnia if he had to. They would never sense him. Not now that he had successfully neutralized Jharate. He could enjoy watching this drama play out and still have time to kill them all before they could reach safety. He was no longer in a hurry. After all, he had been working so hard for so very long. He deserved to have some fun.

Vranah was sitting on the king's throne. He felt weary. It took so much energy for him just to be able to sit on a physical object without passing through it, but even with all that work, at the moment, it was still easier than standing. And what was his alternative? Give in to his metaphysical spirit and float? *Never!* He was stronger than that— he was more than that!

He wondered how long it would take him to recover his normal stamina. He couldn't sleep the way that mortals could when they needed to heal. He couldn't eat nourishing foods or drink restorative potions. All he could do was to try to conserve his energy by not using magic as much as possible and wait! How he despised waiting.

Once more Vranah wished that he had allowed Drakne to take care of that vile little village of Kellinsi. His sporadic and feeble ability to exercise magic was making it very hard to manage his affairs. He was not used to being this immobile. Worse, he had to constantly hide his dysfunction so that no one would dare challenge his authority. Drakne was the only one who knew about his condition. It was absolutely imperative that this secret remained solely between Drakne and himself.

And where was Drakne? He had been gone many weeks now chasing after the women from Earth and those who had been helping them. Why was it taking so long? He had other matters that needed tending to and was having to use those less capable for the work. Vranah heard the shrill cry of a hawk outside the window and stood up abruptly, throwing his shoulders back and standing tall as the hawk seized a mouse that had been creeping along the window ledge and began to swallow it whole.

The hawk morphed into the tall, sturdy battle-dressed figure of Rutghar, with his shiny silver-haired ponytail. The tail of the mouse was still hanging from his mouth. He slurped it in as he took to one knee. He placed his right fist over his heart, and his left hand behind his back and bowed his head.

"My Liege, I have news from Lord Drakne."

"Proceed."

"Lord Drakne wishes to inform Your Excellency that he has gone after those you seek alone. His soldiers have been divided and sent ahead of the rebels to prevent their entry into Destavnia."

"Very well. You are dismissed."

"Thank you, Your Excellency."

Rutghar morphed back into the silver hawk and flew out of the window into the grey sky with another shrill cry. Vranah staggered slightly but forced himself to stand straight again.

"What are you up to, Drakne?" Vranah asked quietly as he looked out the window.

Vranah paused for a moment. He was not entirely sure how he felt about this change in Drakne's plans. He found it foolish on one level, but brilliant on another. He assumed that all this had to be mostly about Drakne's ego and his love for games with worthy opponents. Now was not the time for such tactics, but he also knew that Drakne always had a reason for his actions.

Vranah decided to let the matter go. Drakne had never failed him before. He would trust him for now. He could always command him to return if need be. Until then, he would have to make do with the next one in his hierarchy. She too, had great expertise in certain kinds of magic. However, Drakne had an amazing aptitude for power that she did not. One simply had to be born with that kind of ability and there was no making up for it no matter how much a person studied. Vranah turned to face the door.

"Zarkania, come to me!"

The doors of the throne room were thrown open as if they had long been waiting for the excuse to do so, and an exceedingly pale woman with midnight-brown curls that fell to her waist entered the room. Her perfectly arranged hair bounced as she sashayed forth in her classic and neatly pressed emerald taffeta dress, which swayed with her every move. She glided up before her master and bowed her head as she curtsied low.

"You called, my lord?"

"I have a mission for you."

Zarkania smiled brightly. "Yes, my lord?"

"I need you to take care of securing this kingdom. Seek out those who are still loyal to Jharate and dispatch them."

"It will be done!"

Zarkania looked as though she were a cat being told to kill all the mice in a pet shop. She turned and left swiftly.

Wonderful woman, Vranah thought to himself as the doors shut behind her and he carefully sat back down on his throne. If only her sister had been like that...

❖ 321 ❖

Days passed in stony silence between Lani and Jharate. He went well out of his way to ensure that they never got close enough to be able to talk as they traveled through the mountain pass on their way to Zenastra. The awkwardness between them was oppressive, even to those around them. Not only did he seem oblivious to the pained longing in Lani's eyes— he never even acknowledged her existence. It was as if she wasn't even there.

Lani was far off and distant herself. Not toward Jharate, but toward her friends. The only one she let near her was Raoul. She didn't want to answer questions, and she knew Raoul was the only one who wouldn't ask. He always let her come to him with her worries, rather than trying to pry them out of her. She knew she couldn't keep her secret forever, but even just a couple of days would be enough. It would give her time to wrap her mind around it and accept it before she would have to talk about it with anyone.

"This isn't right," Justin said.

"What isn't?" Erik asked.

"Lani— she isn't acting like herself. I'm starting to get worried."

"I know, me too," Kendra said quietly.

"She just got her heart broken or something," Erik offered. "I think her actions are normal."

"Yeah for you," Kendra said curtly. "But Lani isn't like you. And she's never avoided Justin and me like this. She didn't even ignore Justin after she broke up with *Justin!* Half of me wants to go chase her down and make her talk, but the more rational half wants to give her a little more time."

"Yeah, it never took more than a few questions before to get her to pour her heart out to us and tell us everything that was wrong," Justin affirmed.

"Give her some time," Raoul said. "She needs it right now."

"But I mean, look at her!" Kendra exclaimed. "She's in complete denial. She's going forward, performing all of her duties, and helping everyone who needs her. She even tries to force smiles— but it's like a part of her is missing!"

"I know," Raoul agreed. "It's scaring me too. But I think pushing her will only make her worse. Give her some time."

"I should just go beat Jharate up!" Justin growled.

"Yeah, I think Arante would kill you if you did," Kendra said. "I think the only reason you survived last time was because Jharate was in love with Lani. You saw him signal them all to stay out of it when you punched him. With whatever his current malfunction is, I don't think he'll save you this time."

"This is messed up!" Justin exclaimed.

"Again, guys, just give her some time," Raoul insisted.

"Fine!" Justin relented.

"Okay, I guess," Kendra sighed.

Arante had been listening to their conversation. She too, had been watching Lani carefully as they traveled. She was impressed with how much Lani kept going despite the pain in her eyes. But what had caused it? Arante had watched her cousin as well. The odd stillness that had overtaken him after the dragon incident had not subsided. If anything, it had intensified. It frightened Arante to see him like that. Arante knew Lani's friends were right, but she also knew that she wouldn't get anywhere in a conversation with Jharate, so she watched and waited for her chance.

The next evening, after they set up camp for the night, just before dusk, Arante saw her opportunity. Lani had separated herself, even from Raoul at the moment, and Arante jumped in before anyone could notice.

"Lani, may I speak with you for a moment?"

"Sure."

Lani exhaled more than spoke the word. Everything hurt her now, no matter how minor. Speaking, eating— even sleeping hurt. She didn't even look at Arante as she quietly got up and followed her around a corner where the two of them could be alone.

"What happened between you and my cousin?"

Tears welled up in Lani's eyes, but did not fall.

"I wish I knew!"

Lani sighed, and Arante could tell from the look on her face that the wall she had placed around herself to protect her heart from feeling the pain was crumbling. The memories were invading Lani's mind, and now was the time to discuss them. Arante hesitated for a moment— but she needed to get her answers.

"Try to explain then."

It was as if a dam had broken and both tears and words gushed forth from Lani.

"I... well, it was in the sanctuary. I mean... I kept telling Jharate I loved him and things like that, and it was like he never answered. I saw him yank his hand from mine. And then later— it was weird. I only heard parts of what he was saying like 'What's wrong with you, Lani?' and 'I do not know why you could ever think that I love you, Lani.' And earlier, back by the meadow, when you called him away to talk to him by your campfire, I thought you were trying to tell him not to lead me on or something like that... when you said he might make me think 'something' I 'shouldn't.' I felt his actions were proof of that possibility.

"It was all so strange. I ran out feeling betrayed, hurt, and alone. Well, you know the rest. He saved my life. Right after that, things felt even stranger. My head hurt like crazy— like it was going to split in two. I was afraid for a moment that it would. I screamed and hit the ground, and as I did, it was like I came back to myself. I heard all the missing pieces of the conversation from earlier, about how much he loved me, but it was too late. He won't forgive me now. I don't know how to explain to him that I sincerely thought he didn't love me. Maybe he really doesn't now..."

"I know he loves you. What we were talking about in the forest— well, maybe you don't want to know now."

"Oh no, I do. Please!"

"Well, when I said he might 'mislead' you, it was because he wasn't planning on telling you what he wanted for a while. I was afraid if he took too long, you would think he wasn't interested in you. I am very straightforward about things, especially relationships, and well, as you can see, my cousin is not. But he was telling me that he intended to marry you."

Great, Lani thought to herself, as her world spun downward, it was Josiah all over again— only worse because Jharate had been doing everything right. It was officially too late for this information. Her heart sank into the pit of her stomach. She had met the love of her life. He had fallen for her. *And* he was intending to make her his bride. And what had she done? She had gone and lost it all. What on Earth could have possessed her?

No sooner had she asked the question in her mind, when she gasped. She closed her eyes and her body lurched forward slightly. When she opened her eyes again, she saw that Arante had helped to stabilize her so she wouldn't fall.

"Maybe you should sit down."

"Yes, maybe. Arante, I think I just figured out what happened!"

"What? How?"

"A vision."

"What did you see?"

"It was right before Jharate and I entered through the portal. Drakne came behind us. He threw something that looked like a glowing purple ball of energy into my back. It disappeared inside of me. That must be why my back hurt so badly when we entered the sanctuary. It wasn't the portal at all. It was that purple ball. Could that have done something else to me? I mean, besides just making my back ache?"

Arante narrowed her eyes and regarded Lani.

"That must be why you couldn't see or hear things. It sounds like some sort of spell. The confusing thing is that Drakne was close enough to hit you. Why did he hex you instead of just killing you then and there? You said Vranah wanted the women of your world dead. But, then again, Drakne has done odd things before. When your head hurt, that must have been when you snapped out of the effects. It makes sense, actually. Although I have never heard of people breaking out of spells as powerful as the ones Drakne uses."

"If only Jharate would listen to me, maybe I could tell him that it wasn't my fault! But he won't listen to me— he won't even look at me."

Lani sighed. She felt like a lost cause.

"I'll talk to him. I'm sure he will forgive you. After all, it wasn't really you."

"Oh thank you! How can I ever repay you?"

Lani threw her arms around Arante and hugged her. Arante patted Lani's back.

"Don't worry, I'm sure something will come up."

Arante flashed a girlish smile and walked off to find Jharate. Lani couldn't help but notice that Erik had definitely had a profound effect on Arante. She had become much more warm, friendly, and feminine since they had become a couple. Lani allowed the warming glow of hope to enter her heart. *Maybe there is still a chance,* she thought, as she walked back to the makeshift camp.

As she rounded the corner, she saw Kendra and Justin at the very edge of the camp, away from everyone. Lani's mouth fell open. Justin was apparently hurling everything he could manage at Kendra— without touching any of the objects that he threw. *Justin is telekinetic? When did that happen?* Lani decided that for their safety, and hers, she should keep quiet, but her eyes widened in amazement as she watched, unseen in the shadows.

Justin launched objects with increasing amounts of strength, and everything from pebbles to dried up logs flew through the air. Kendra blocked them with her shield. She was practicing influencing the size and shape of her shield in order to best defend against different types of threats, as well as working on how to direct where the things she deflected went. Kendra could land the objects where she wanted nine times out of ten now. What Kendra didn't realize, was that the one time out of the ten that she failed to deflect the object in the direction of her aim, was actually Justin's fault. He moved whatever object she deflected off her shield with his own ability, mid-trajectory, to make her miss.

Justin yawned, as if he was getting bored with the status quo. Suddenly, a giant grin crossed his face. A boulder the size of a Volkswagen Bug began to hover above the ground, three feet in the air.

"No! Uh-uh!"

Kendra shook her head vigorously while motioning for him to put the rock down, but the grin remained on Justin's face and he showed no signs of obedience.

"Come on! Don't be so boring!"

"I don't want to try that one, Justin. Justin! Don't you *dare*!"

"Oh, you had to say the magic words!"

"JUSTIN!"

The rock sailed toward her at what seemed like Mach Five. She reacted defensively with the largest dome-shaped shield she had ever managed to create. It was as large as an R.V. The rock shattered, upon impact, and the debris sprayed everywhere, like a heavy rainstorm. Justin ducked behind another boulder in order to avoid getting hit by the rocky shrapnel, laughing his head off all the while.

"JUSTIN YOU IDIOT! YOU COULD HAVE KILLED ME!"

"*Reeelax!* I wouldn't have killed you... and besides that's what we have Raoul for, right?"

Kendra squealed in anger as her hands formed fists at her sides and she shook as she glowered at Justin. She continued to glare as Justin stood up and brushed himself off. Kendra narrowed her eyes and her lips went tight as she activated her shield, this time in a flat, wall shape, and walked towards him.

"Now, now, Kendra... Remember we're friends!"

Kendra advanced slowly and purposefully, never taking her eyes off her target. Justin scrambled until his back was against the granite surface behind him. She pressed forward until he was trapped against the canyon wall.

"Well this feels odd," Justin mumbled with his lips squished sideways against the invisible force field, which kept him trapped and flattened against the rock surface.

"Have you learned your lesson yet?"

A smirk spread across Justin's smooshed face.

"No, I don't think I have."

Justin concentrated with his mind and pictured her shield moving backwards. Kendra dug her feet into the ground to brace herself, but she slid backwards as if she were trying to push a car uphill on a gravel road. He backed her up until she was against the wall on the other side of the canyon. Her own shield now trapped her.

"Stop being so ornery all the time, Kendra!"

"Stop being so stupid and reckless all the time! *Grow up, Justin!*"

Kendra pushed her hands forward and outward as she greatly expanded her force field, now back in its normal bubble form. Justin had to back up twenty feet fast to avoid being knocked over, and with his last step he swiveled out on one foot and then jumped onto the other until he regained his balance. He turned on Kendra and puffed his chest out, letting his arms fly out to the sides of him.

"What? Is that the best you got? Huh, Kendra?"

Kendra narrowed her eyes still further and pulled her hands back, ready to throw them forward to slam Justin against the wall— but Raoul's voice called out calmly to them as he walked towards his two friends and interrupted her before she got the chance.

"Okay you two show-offs. I think it's time to call a truce. You are both obviously powerful, and it seems like you are equally matched. So, shake hands and stop shoving each other around."

Kendra looked at Raoul as he continued his approach and then back at Justin. She rolled her eyes and dropped the force field. She marched toward Justin and shook his hand roughly before shoving him one more time, hands only.

"Alright," Justin said, sad that his fun had been cut off prematurely. "But I could have taken her."

"Oh *really*? Don't forget I have seven brothers! I could take you with or without my shield."

"Just keep telling yourself that, darling," Justin said with a bow.

The three friends sat down on a flat rock in front of one of the campfires. The sun was almost down in the dark grey sky and the screech of a lone hawk rang through the stark and empty pass. The canyon wind blew strong and the air began to cool enough that they huddled a little closer together. They allowed several minutes to pass silently as they watched the flickering flames and listened to the crackle of the fire. Raoul unconsciously did his pinky/thumb trick as thoughts he'd been avoiding raced through his mind.

"I wonder what's happening back home in our world," Raoul reflected, as his hands finally stilled.

The words felt strange falling out of his mouth and they felt even more foreign as they flowed into the ears of his friends. It was the first time they had really allowed themselves to think about it in over a month. The hypnotic silence fell between them again as each of them thought about the sentence that had been uttered.

"Do you think Earth time runs the same as here?" Kendra asked, the sound of her own voice feeling to her as if she had just yelled inside an empty cathedral, despite her quiet tone. "Because if it does, I bet our families are really worried."

"Yeah," Justin said, "I can just picture the employees at Disney World showing the police the photo of the Tower of Terror and wondering where the three people in the front disappeared to."

This time Justin's eyes didn't light up the way they normally did when he joked.

"I miss my family," Kendra said, her voice cracking a little. "I mean, will I ever see them again?"

"I don't know," Justin replied calmly. "I never see my dad much anyways so I don't really care so much about him. But I do miss my mom… and maybe even Jezzy."

"You know, it's kind of funny. I always thought I wanted to get away from home and have an adventure, like I did for my study abroad trip, but now I miss my brothers and my parents way more than I ever thought I would."

"I really miss my family too, but I don't see how we can ever get home," added Raoul. "I mean, we don't even know how we got here, and neither does anyone else with us. We might have to just accept the fact that we're stuck here for good."

"I guess," Kendra said sadly, her voice getting a little higher in pitch and her eyes struggling to hold back the tears welling up inside them. "But I don't like it."

"Don't worry," Justin said genuinely. "We're here for you. We got your back. We'll just be a new family."

Justin threw his arms around his friend and gave her a really warm hug. Raoul leaned in too, rubbing her back compassionately as Justin let go.

"Thanks," Kendra said, sniffing, but with a smile. "So this is really it, huh?"

"What do you mean?" Raoul asked.

"I mean, we're staying now… we're really giving up on all of our hopes and dreams back home."

"I know," Justin said. "I was going to compose music. I was hoping to become the next John Williams."

"I was going to produce movies," Raoul said, rather sadly.

"Well, at least you two knew what you were going to do. I was still trying to find that one thing that I loved doing above all other things."

"Well look at the bright side, Kendra" Justin said. "That makes you better off here. I mean, you didn't have your plans set yet, so you should be able to adapt the best of all of us."

"But I'm sick of running for my life! I may have not known what I wanted to do, but war and danger was never on the list—that's for sure. If I wanted this kind of life I could have joined the military!"

"I think we're all sick of that," Raoul said gently.

"Well, again, look at the bright side. Maybe the Half-Heart legend is true. Maybe two people will find each other and get married and then this world won't be so bad," Justin suggested.

"That's wishful thinking," Kendra said. "I mean, Arante told us back on the boat that no one knows who they are but their 'Great-Evil' guy. So that's not really good odds. Plus there are only twenty-four, so that's even worse."

"Maybe one of us is a Half-Heart. Lani was wondering if one of us could be," Justin said. "If I am, where's my other Half-Heart?"

"Exactly. Even if *one* of us is a Half-Heart, it's still just that— *one*. You need two," Kendra answered.

"Well, I think we should just make the best of things and have hope," Raoul determined.

"There's really no other option," Justin said in agreement.

"Oh, no worries," Kendra replied. "I intend to make the best of it, it's just… It's just hard sometimes."

"We know," Raoul said understandingly. "But we will all be here to help each other through it. That's what friends do."

"Thanks," Kendra said again, with a slight smile as her two friends squeezed her between them in a group hug.

Lani had been careful to remain in the shadows where she wouldn't be seen. But she knew she had to go over there. They had been waiting patiently for answers for days. She figured that while she was waiting to see what Jharate would do, once he found out what had actually happened, was as good a time as any. The hope Arante had given her would be enough to help her through the questions they were bound to ask. She took a deep breath and walked over to sit next to them.

They stared at her in surprise, waiting for her to say something.

"I saw your stunt show," Lani said with a smile.

It was the first time she had truly smiled in days. It felt nice.

"Awesome wasn't it?" Justin stated more than asked.

"Yes. It was *way* cool."

"I noticed Arante pulling you aside earlier. So what did she want?" Kendra inquired.

"Oh, she just wanted to know what happened between me and Jharate."

"Well we'd kind of like to know... you know. If you're ready, that is," Raoul started but it was Justin who finished, "Tell us what happened too."

"Alright."

Lani inhaled deeply. She backed up all the way to what had happened on the battlefield with Drakne and proceeded to tell them what she and Arante had discovered about the spell Lani had been under, and the damage that the spell had caused, as quickly as she could. Her friends remained perfectly quiet, with only their faces showing the thoughts on their minds, until she finished the entire story and exhaled, dropping her shoulders slightly as she did.

"Oh you poor thing!" Kendra said sympathetically.

"Why would Drakne do something like that?" Raoul asked.

"Because he's a jealous idiot!"

Drakne turned and shot a dirty look at Justin. Had he not been determined to remain undetected, he would have killed him where he stood for such a comment. To think that he, Drakne, could have a weakness so frail as jealousy! It was insulting to a man with his almost limitless power.

"I highly doubt that! Not *everybody* falls in love with Lani, present company excluded," Kendra said, ignoring the looks from Justin, Lani, and Raoul as she continued. "A man of his obvious power doesn't have time for crushes on passing strangers. I mean, he did try to kill her before out on the battlefield. That's not exactly a love note."

Drakne smiled. At least Kendra knew what she was talking about.

"Sounds like you might be crushing on Drakne," Justin scoffed.

"Oh grow up, Justin!" Kendra retorted.

"Ha, ha! That's funny!" Raoul exclaimed.

"I don't know why he didn't kill me. He certainly had plenty of time before Jharate was able to pull me out of the way," said Lani, choosing to ignore the rest of what Kendra had said. "I am sure he was about to. But then it was like we connected for a moment. I felt his power, and it was almost like I could see into his soul… so what I do know is that he is definitely no one to be trifled with."

Drakne smiled again. He was glad that she appreciated his power. He was surprised she had been able to read him though. It was an unsettling thought.

"Anyway, I don't know why he bothered putting me under a spell to break us up. It seems like an odd thing to do when he obviously wants me dead. I mean if he had time to hit me with that spell, why didn't he just hit me with something that would kill me? Not that I'm complaining."

Drakne raised an eyebrow in thought. That was a good question. Drakne could not answer that. The only explanation at the moment was that he had felt her power. He knew that trying to kill her directly was useless somehow, but he could not explain it. He had never had an intuitive ability before and so he wondered why he trusted this feeling so implicitly. It was definitely more fun this way though.

A more pressing matter caught his attention. He saw Arante approaching Jharate as he passed into the same area where Lani and Arante had just met. Drakne knew what she was going to try. He strolled over to watch her fail or, if necessary, to ensure that she failed if Jharate seemed to be breaking out of the spell.

"Jharate, I want to talk to you."

"If it is concerning Lani, you had better save your breath."

"It *is* concerning Lani and you *are* going to listen to me!"

"I would not wager to that effect."

Jharate turned and started to walk back towards the camp. Arante threw her hands forward and conjured an image of Lani to block his path. The holographic Lani now stood directly in front of him. He stopped dead in his tracks and turned around to face Arante.

"I do not wish to see her face and I will thank you for *not* placing her in front of me. I am already forced to expend a great deal of energy to ignore her every moment of every day."

"Then you had better listen to me, or so help me that won't be the worst thing I do to you. I know you too well, cousin. I know your fears. I can make them *all* come to life in living color everywhere you turn!"

"Very well," he growled. "Make it brief."

"That's more like it. She was under a spell, Jharate."

"That was succinct. Why would I believe that?"

"She had a vision after she snapped back to herself. She saw Drakne throw a purple ball at her as she passed through the portal. That's why she was in pain on the other side. It wasn't just the normal effects of the portal, it was more— we just didn't notice because none of us had ever been through it before."

"*Lani* had a vision. How *convenient.*"

"You know she has visions, Jharate!"

"Yes, she does. However, how do I know that she did not fabricate this particular one for her own purposes?"

Drakne smiled. Jharate was so smug, judgmental, and self-righteous. He didn't have to do a thing. The spell was holding full power over Jharate's heart.

"Jharate! I know that girl. She's *not* a liar. And for some reason that I am starting to think is completely irrational, she loves you!"

"She has a superb way of demonstrating her affection!"

"*She* was *under* a *SPELL!*" Arante yelled.

"Then perhaps she should have been stronger. Perhaps she should have resisted it!"

Drakne bit the knuckle of his glove to keep from bursting out in laughter. The irony of that statement was really too delightful!

"Oh yeah, that's right, the girl from *another world,* who didn't even know she had a gift until about a month or so ago, and, who didn't even know spells *existed* and who had never faced Drakne before, should have been able to resist a spell that hit her *in the back*?! Are you *listening* to yourself, Jharate? You should be giving her massive amounts of respect for being able to get out of it *at all!* How many people do you know, whom Drakne has cursed, that have *ever* come out of it, unless he released them? HMMM? I'll tell you how many. None! I've never heard of one. NOT ONE! Until now, and that's Lani!"

"You act as though I should care. It was a mistake to plan a union with her in the first place. I need to focus on my destiny, and I was wrong to think she could have been a part of it."

"What *destiny*?"

"I am a Half-Heart!"

Arante was dumfounded. Her eyes went wide and her mouth hung open. Drakne's mouth fell open as well— only Vranah was supposed to have that knowledge. How had Jharate discovered this?

"How do you know that?"

Jharate got very quiet and very serious. Tears formed in his eyes and he tried to choke them back as he spoke.

"I had a vision while in the Forest of Kar. I witnessed Vranah inform Khanye that he is... that he was a Half-Heart, and that I am a Half-Heart as well. Vranah said that he was coming for me next and then he— he killed my only brother in front of my very eyes."

Drakne realized that would explain it. Perhaps the gift of vision was a more useful gift than he had given it credit for in the past.

"I am so sorry that you had to see that. But there's nothing you could have done. If you had been captured with him, you would be dead by now too."

"I am aware of that fact. I simply detest the helplessness I felt then. And then Lani came. She healed me. She healed my heart. I felt safe with her. I wanted to protect her and to be with her forever... That dream has been destroyed now. She inflicted a greater wound on my heart than any other could have ever done. She cannot be the one. I must focus on finding another Half-Heart now so that we may end this war once and for all. I must forget her."

Arante remained silent for a moment and looked away pensively. Suddenly, she looked back up at Jharate as if she had just had an epiphany.

"But Jharate! What if Lani *is* another Half-Heart? You have no way of knowing. Think about it! You have wanted to get married for years. You feel that desire keenly, and yet you haven't been able to find anyone. Your father brought how many women before you to try to find a suitable companion? Let's see there was Princesse Selana of Destavnia—"

Arante waved her hand and a holographic image of the past Karahn, Jharate, and Princesse Selana stood before them. The Princesse had light skin and black hair that was curled into perfect ringlets. She stood with exquisite grace and carried herself perfectly.

"She was beautiful and accomplished— a woman that any prince would have sought after. And what was wrong with her?" Arante asked.

The past image of Jharate whispered to the image of Karahn, saying, "She is far too vain, Father."

"And then there was Contessa Regianna whose family had run to Trisakne years before, for safety, when Lanas fell."

A slender brunette stood before the same two holographic men. She had olive skin and sparkling green eyes.

"She was gorgeous and sweet-natured! But she wasn't good enough for you!"

"Father, the woman cares nothing for the enlightening of the mind. We have nothing in common."

"And thus, Contessa Regianna was dismissed. Then there was Vikontessa Tesha of Kresar, whose family also gained asylum in our land."

A new woman appeared. She had auburn hair that was half up and half down. It cascaded down past her shoulders and stopped just above the waist. She had hazel eyes, and a warm smile.

"Father, she does not fit. I do not know how to explain that fact, as there is nothing obviously wrong with her— we simply do not match."

"You gave the same answer for the dark-skinned angel from Kelamosa, Princess Karani'oka'are, not two days later. She was brilliant, sweet, kind, playful, spiritual, and had every attribute you could possibly ask for in a future wife— in fact, every trait you had ever listed. But for some reason, she didn't 'match' you either!"

The woman Arante was referring to appeared in front of him. She was by far the most beautiful of the four. Her black hair fell down to the middle of her thighs, and she had a tropical red flower above her right ear, indicating the fact that she was a single woman.

"Then there were all of *these* women whose claims to nobility, beauty, poise, and charms were all equal, and yet..."

Nearly twenty more women flashed in, as Arante created them one at a time. They stood in a ring around Jharate until he was surrounded. Jharate cringed when one of the women he particularly disliked appeared nearly in his face. Each time, the holographic Jharate said the same thing.

"I apologize, Father. She does not fit. I can feel that there is something very important missing."

"Hmmmm. So none of these girls fit you? *None?* Any other prince would have jumped at the opportunities that you had handed to you, and yet you held out. Looking back it's a wonder I didn't figure out you were a Half-Heart! You just didn't 'fit' anyone else. But what did you tell me just the other night?"

The ring of women disappeared as Arante conjured an image of Lani sitting against the log where Jharate had left her at Arante's beckoning. The holographic images of Arante and Jharate repeated their conversation.

"I do not know how to explain it, Arante. Lani simply fits me. We feel right together. It feels as if we are two halves of one whole. I believe it is destiny."

"And, if you needed any further proof, which really you shouldn't at this point, but if you do— remember Drakne wanted the travelers from another world. It was one of his demands. Why would he *specifically* ask for them? How would he even know about them? Why would he care unless they posed a threat? Wouldn't that go along with Lani's vision that she received on the ship? Vranah says that one of the Earth girls is a Half-Heart. Wouldn't that mean there is an even greater chance that Lani *is* one? In my mind that means the chances are *huge!* Lani is your best bet! I'm sure Kendra isn't one! And no one knows who the other Half-Hearts are— no one but Vranah, and I doubt he'll tell you."

Drakne motioned toward Arante with his hand and nodded as he cocked his head slightly, as if conceding her point. She had presented a very compelling argument. He himself felt that Lani was the most likely candidate. Drakne readied himself and watched carefully in case this insightful reasoning started to take hold in Jharate's mind.

Jharate paused for a moment. He looked straight at Arante as if considering the evidence she had put forth. There was a slight glimmer in his eye. But the fleck of light disappeared and the coldness returned. He stood up straighter, and every muscle tensed as he looked down on Arante. When he finally spoke, his voice was measured, but a sting of rage accented each word that he uttered.

"I doubt that *she* is a Half-Heart."

"HOW COULD YOU SAY THAT AFTER EVERYTHING I JUST POINTED OUT?! YOU CAN'T KNOW THAT!"

"Yes, and you cannot know that she is one. So unless you have found irrefutable proof that she is indeed a Half-Heart, I will bid you goodnight!"

Jharate walked away from her before she could counter. Drakne took a very elaborate bow for his handiwork and mouthed a couple silent thank you's. His power was so extraordinary he even surprised himself.

"YOU DON'T DESERVE HER!" Arante yelled after Jharate, shaking with anger.

Drakne agreed. Jharate did not deserve Lani, although she would not live long enough to find someone who truly did.

Lani heard the last two things that Arante had yelled. She saw Jharate storming away from Arante, and Arante stomping angrily after him but turning, instead, to head toward Erik, who greeted her with a comforting hug. Lani sighed heavily. It was no use. She was just going to have to get used to being alone. She sunk into a deep melancholy. She excused herself quietly and walked over to her bedroll. She closed her eyes and went to sleep, feeling so hurt that she couldn't feel anything at all. Her heart was shattered, and she now knew it was going to stay that way.

ISN'T IT SUPPOSED TO BE *DAMSELS* IN DISTRESS?

The next morning Lani stood frozen in her steps as she stared at the wide black mouth of the cavern that they were about to enter. She swallowed hard and kept her eyes locked on the darkened hole. Arante saw her hesitation and crossed over to her.

"It's okay, Lani. This is a well-known passageway and I promise there are no dragons inside. I have never even heard of a dragon attack in this particular area. It tunnels through the mountain and cuts two weeks of hiking off our trek. If we did not take this shortcut, the mountains are so steep here that we would have to travel extremely slowly just to stay alive and we would never make it to Zenastra before Drakne's men."

With this reassurance, Lani nodded and followed Arante inside. Jharate led the group with a great torch. Behind Jharate, Erik kept close to Arante, as had become usual. Lani was directly behind them. Drakne, still invisible, walked behind her but had to be very careful not to bump into her because of the close proximity. Raoul held another torch behind Lani, and Justin and

Kendra were directly behind him. The other thirteen warriors made up the back with two more torches spaced between them.

Lani felt her sense of adventure flooding back into her soul despite her inner turmoil. Her heart beat excitedly and little butterflies flew inside her stomach. She could only see as far as the torches cast light before them. Beyond that was a pitch black so pure, it was as if she had never seen darkness before this moment. The cold air had a crisp, clean, slightly earthy smell and a gentle feel on her skin that refreshed her like a cold shower.

The water trickling down the cave walls contributed to the damp, fresh scent. Lani breathed it in deeply. The only sounds that broke the profound silence were their footsteps, the echoing pitter-patter and dripping of water droplets falling from the ceiling onto the rock surfaces and into the puddles, and the quiet hiss of the cool, fresh airflow. There was a deep and fulfilling silence that reminded her of diving eight feet down under water and staying there, immersed in tranquility, until she had to swim up for oxygen.

The terrain was uneven. The jaggedness of the lava had been smoothed by the elements over time and so the rock tube had a quality that was both smooth and rough at the same time. It was a little wet and Lani had to be extra careful where she stepped, so that she did not slip, but she loved the feel of the varied surface beneath her feet.

As they trekked deeper into the cave, Lani's emotions played with her even more. She felt a sense of mystery, wonder, excitement, and even safety in a fearless kind of way. Perhaps even stranger was the feeling that she was disconnected from time itself. This spellbinding place was almost enough to make her forget the pain from Jharate's iciness, even if only for a few blessed moments at a time.

ISN'T IT SUPPOSED TO BE *DAMSELS* IN DISTRESS?

Drakne watched Lani carefully and with great interest. He had never seen a girl quite like her before. The excitement she was deriving from exploring this cave was highly visible, even now, after having lost more hope, just last night, when Arante had failed to intercede successfully with Jharate. Drakne wondered how she had gotten so strong. She hadn't grown up *here*— and from what he knew of Earth, it wasn't a hard place to live in. How had she become so tough, while at the same time remaining so sensitive? Who was she?

He knew that she had been born into this world originally, because of what Vranah had told him, and he found himself deeply curious concerning her mysterious past. Perhaps the key to defeating her now, lay in knowing who she once was. As he pondered all of this, they rounded a bend in the cave and he noticed that torchlight definitely suited Lani. Her skin luminesced and her braided long hair glimmered like copper. Drakne wondered if any part of Jharate knew what he was giving up. Drakne hoped so. He hoped it was torturing him.

Lani stopped suddenly. Drakne had to flatten himself against the cave wall so that Raoul would not smash him into Lani. Raoul quickly raised the torch high in the air, so as not to burn her. She turned to her right and looked straight at Drakne. He held his breath and did not move a muscle.

"Lani, what is it?" Raoul asked.

Lani did not answer. Raoul followed her line of sight and saw only the cave wall.

"Raoul, we need to keep our pace," Jharate said.

Jharate's voice, and the fact that he had so blatantly overlooked her, and had chosen instead to speak to Raoul, broke Lani's concentration. She blinked and regarded the wall with confusion. She wasn't sure what she was doing. Why had she stopped to look at a section of the cave wall that was so obviously devoid of anything out of the ordinary? Why had she felt it was so— Lani caught a glimpse of Jharate and saw a most impatient look on his face. She felt a clinch in her stomach. He was staring over her, looking only at Raoul, as if he could see straight through her— again as if she did not exist.

"Is everything okay, Lani?" Arante asked.

At the sound of Arante's voice Lani looked back at the spot where Drakne stood frozen, trying to see or feel whatever it was she had felt, but now she felt nothing and all she saw was an empty wall. A sudden wave of embarrassment swept over her. Now she wished she truly was as invisible as Jharate was making her feel.

"Nothing I guess… I just thought— never mind."

Lani started walking again rather abruptly to catch up. Drakne breathed a muted sigh of relief, but had to act quickly to jump back into the line and maintain his place behind her. That was close— too close. She shouldn't have been able to feel anything with as much heartbreak as she was experiencing. Another minute and his game would have been forced to come to an abrupt end. Drakne found himself quite glad that Jharate had broken her concentration, and hoped that Jharate's spell-induced idiocy would be enough to ensure that she didn't come that close to sensing him again. He looked derisively at Jharate and reassured himself that he was safe.

Lani acutely felt every last feeling Jharate had meant to convey from the tone he had used with Raoul. It was obvious that he wished to forget her and act as if she had never come into his life and that he was determined to turn any ache he might be feeling into a dull apathetic numbness. She exhaled sharply and felt one more stabbing pain in her heart. But she did not wish to dwell on any of this any longer. She inhaled deeply, forced the corners of her lips up slightly, and opened her eyes a little wider as she focused on keeping her footing and enjoying the cave while they continued their long march.

"Okayyy! *That's* not comforting!"

Justin's voice echoed through the tunnel and made everyone snap out of his or her reverie. No one had spoken for what seemed like hours and it was strange to hear a human voice. It was almost as if you *couldn't* speak in this cave— like your voice had been checked at the entrance. The sudden agitation of the profound tranquility was both disorienting and jarring, like a very large rock being hurled into a glassy lake.

Lani saw what Justin was referring to immediately. There, lying against the cave wall was a pair of human skeletons. As Lani looked more closely at the skeletons, she thought it was both romantic and sad. The skeletons were embracing one another. Nearby their remains was a torch that had burned out centuries ago. Lani guessed that when the torch had gone out, they had simply never been able to find their way out of the blackness, but Justin was thinking something much more horrific had happened to them.

"Ewww!" Kendra said, as she finally saw their bones.

Raoul felt an unsettling gurgle in his stomach and gulped quietly at the sight of them. It was too late to turn back now though. So he shook his head and averted his eyes, pressing forward with the rest, trying to forget what he had seen.

"How were these caves formed, Arante?"

Lani knew full well that they must be made of lava, but she wanted to get everyone's mind on something other than the eerie pair of skeletons.

"Oh, they are actually lava tubes. This mountain was once an active volcano."

"Really? That's fascinating."

"When we get out of this cave, we will come to a beautiful clear pool fed by a hot spring. It is heated by underground rivers of lava that still flow. We will probably stop there to rest when we reach it. It is a great place for swimming— one of the best in all of Alamea in fact. Jharate and I went there once when he was fifteen and I was fourteen. My parents served as the Trisaknen ambassadors to Zenastra, before it fell, and they took us with them on one of their trips. Lanas had already fallen, so this was the only safe route to travel there to avoid meeting up with Vranah's troops. *Remember that, Jharate?*"

"Yes, Arante, I do remember."

"Well anyway, Lani, I think you will love it."

Arante smiled warmly at Lani. Lani smiled back. Arante had been extra nice to her lately. Lani thought maybe part of her kindness might stem out of a feeling of obligation because Jharate was her cousin. But it was nice. Lani felt a leap of excitement within her as she thought of the unusual place Arante had just described. A good swim was just what she needed! She loved the water, and only now realized how exhausted she was from all the running and fighting and emotional pain. Oh how she longed for a break. The very idea of it fueled her with the energy she needed to continue, like the sight of a lighthouse across a stormy sea.

Jharate stopped abruptly. This forced everyone behind him to come skidding to a halt as well. Yet again Drakne had to sidestep to avoid being bumped into, but the tunnel was a foot or so wider here and so he did not need to flatten himself against the wall this time. The vantage point he gained from this small move to the side allowed him to see what had made Jharate stop. The right side of his mouth curled into a malicious smirk. Drakne muttered a few carefully chosen powerful words under his breath. There was a rippling in the air around everyone's feet, except for Jharate's. The ripples quickly vanished into the ground, unseen by the rebels. Drakne's smirk widened as he sat back and waited to see what Lani would do in *this* situation.

Jharate stared forward intently. He saw his mother standing directly in front of him with a gentle smile on her face. She beckoned with her hand, bidding him come forward. He hesitated, but the invitation was irresistible. He thought he might be having a vision. He felt his legs move unconsciously beneath him. Closer and closer, he moved toward the apparition ahead of him with a glowing thrill of joy within his heart.

"NO! JHARATE STOP!"

Jharate did not respond to Arante's cries. Arante struggled harder and harder to move forward, but could not. She pulled at her legs with her arms and wrenched her body violently, trying to move forward, but her feet remained firmly planted on the ground.

"What's wrong?" Lani asked, panicked by Arante's reaction.

"He's headed straight for a mountain siren! They survive by stealing youth from other beings! It's how they keep their eternal beauty! They have the greatest power over men, but I can't move for some reason!"

Lani tried to move her own feet. She, like Arante, struggled against the invisible bonds with everything she had, but couldn't even get her legs to budge. Lani's eyes suddenly fell upon the siren. She felt her heart drop with an icy plummet as Jharate was drawn forward. The siren was tall and looked quite young. Her hair was a fiery red and her sparkly eyes glowed in a matching color, which would normally look ugly to Lani but somehow looked beautiful in an otherworldly way. Her skin was unnaturally white, like one who had never seen the sun. Her body was voluptuous but her face was somewhat thin. She wore an extraordinary dress, which looked as if it were made of silk that had been dipped into a puddle of red stars. It seemed as if sparks flew up from the material as it floated in the gentle breeze.

All of the men were silent, with dreamy looks in their eyes. Each quietly tried to move forward but Drakne's spell held their feet tightly in place. Their arms swung and their shoulders ebbed and flowed back and forth abnormally, as they continued to try to walk.

"Justin?" Kendra asked. "Why can't we move? Justin! Snap out of it! You're freaking me out! Justin!"

Justin showed no sign of having heard Kendra and kept staring at the siren and trying ineffectively to move forward, just like the rest of the men.

The song of the siren reached Lani's ears and caused a preternatural chill to run up her spine. The voice of the temptress resonated with the volume of a chime but penetrated with the power of a cathedral bell. Lani felt a renewed surge of panic as she watched Jharate continue forward, completely entranced. She desperately struggled against whatever force held her captive to run to Jharate and stop him, but again to no avail.

Jharate walked closer, one hypnotic step after another, to reach his angelic mother, her brown hair flowing in the breeze, as she called to him to come and join her and Khanye and Karahn. He followed, gripped in a trance.

ISN'T IT SUPPOSED TO BE *DAMSELS* IN DISTRESS?

"She'll kill him!" Arante screamed frantically. "JHARATE! STOP!"

Tears streamed down both Lani's and Arante's faces as they struggled to break loose and save him. Jharate hesitated for a moment, feeling more than hearing Arante's desperation. The siren raised the volume of her song ever so slightly, and the notion soon passed. He pressed forward until he was directly in front of the siren, only about six feet away. Jharate mechanically dropped his torch and knelt before her.

Drakne muttered a few quiet words, and the rippling effect reversed from the ground and away from Lani's feet only, and blew away into nothingness in the gentle breeze of the cave. The moment the ripples dissipated, Lani tripped and fell forward against Erik. She quickly struggled to regain her balance and gasped in hope as she realized that she could move! She instantly pushed between Erik and Arante and ran in front of Jharate, putting her body between him and the siren. In one quick and fluid motion she drew her sword defensively.

"Now, now," the siren said calmly, in a surreal and unnerving tone that sent frosty shivers through Lani's body, "though your bravery is commendable, I would not harm me if I were you."

"Well you are not me! Give me one good reason why I shouldn't run you through right now!"

"If you kill me while I still have control over the minds of all the men in your party, well, they will be as good as dead. They will never regain possession of their minds unless I release them— so if I die, their condition will become permanent. Besides, I only need one life— the rest of you will live."

"No, there must be some other way! Please don't hurt him!"

Lani dropped her sword, unsure of what she was doing. The siren looked at her searchingly.

"Why shouldn't I take him? He is by far the most worthy of your companions, and I need youth or I shall die."

"Because I love him."

"Interesting… Well, there is *one* other way. You see, one year of life willingly given is much stronger than an entire life forcefully taken. It is especially strong when given selflessly. Would you be willing to lose a year of your life to save this man?"

"Take it."

"My, my," sang the siren, smiling brightly, "your loyalty is quite impressive… not even a moment's hesitation. There are few people willing to sacrifice even part of their own life to save another. There will be immense pain involved. Are you still willing to proceed?"

"Yes."

"Intriguing! You are so willing to take his place. You do not even know if I am telling you the truth about taking just one year from you or if, in reality, I have just tricked you into sacrificing your entire life."

"I don't need to know. All I know is that I love him and I would rather die than watch him lose his life when there is something I can do to stop it."

"You truly love this boy…"

The siren cocked her head to one side. She looked from Lani to Jharate and then back to Lani once more with a quizzical gaze.

"I have never encountered such undaunted loyalty. I have likewise never seen a woman so fiercely protective of a man before— and I have been around for centuries! You will be able to stop the process at any point if you change your mind. Your life truly must be given freely for it to have power— one year of it that is. All you have to do is tell me to stop and I will cease instantly and your pain will be relieved. However, I will then revert to my original plan and will take his life instead."

"I will not ask you to stop."

"Very well. Kneel before me."

Lani did so, directly in front of Jharate. She breathed in deeply to try to calm her racing heart. She exhaled slowly through her mouth and braced herself for whatever was about to come.

"Now close your eyes."

Lani obeyed with a quiet swallow and waited in uncertainty for the promised agony. The siren put her hand to Lani's forehead and touched it gently— so gently it could barely even be called a touch. Pain such as Lani had never experienced jolted through her body instantly. It was as if someone had one needle for every square inch of her body and had slammed them all in with great force simultaneously.

Lani had to fight not to scream for the siren to stop as a reflex from the pain, but there was never even the smallest thought in her mind to actually do so. Jharate was everything to her. She stifled an anguished scream as the torture continued. Her blood raced through her veins with a stinging sensation, and her lungs throbbed as if all of the oxygen was being sucked out of them.

Worst of all was the pain in her forehead, as a silver white orb began to materialize and emerge from it. Now Lani's entire body felt as if she were being electrocuted, but the siren's power kept her perfectly still and on her knees. Only tears streaming from her closed eyes indicated what was happening, as Lani stifled any sounds that could emerge from her lips. The orb exited Lani's head and floated above her in the air. The pain stopped and Lani crumpled to the ground quietly. She remained conscious, gasping for air— completely drained of every particle of energy.

"Brilliant!" the siren trilled. "Who *are* you?"

The siren did not wait for an answer.

"This is the strongest life force I have ever felt! I have only taken a year, as I promised, but I will be able to go at least *three hundred years* with this energy alone!"

The siren opened the sparkling-red heart-shaped locket that hung around her neck and placed the orb inside it. It glowed so brightly that it lit the entire cave surrounding where she stood. A rush of air burst around her as she closed the locket and the siren's beauty intensified as some color returned to her skin and fullness returned to her cheeks.

"Release them now," Lani strained to say. "I kept my end of the bargain."

"Yes you did!" the siren said in admiration. "Very well."

The siren made no motion of any kind, but the men were instantly released from their stupor, blinking and shaking their heads. Some ran their fingers through their hair as they came out of the daze. Drakne muttered the same words that had freed Lani, releasing everyone else's legs at that same moment in order to maintain the illusion that the siren had been responsible for holding them each in place as well.

"I shall never forget this," the siren said, as if she owed Lani a favor.

The siren turned and disappeared. The men shook their heads more vigorously, wondering what had just happened to them. None of them had seen the siren. Each man had beheld what he wanted to see most in the world. Jharate missed his family, and so he had seen his mother. Justin had always wished his life had been different when it came to his family, and this longing had conjured up his father calling him to a family picnic, where he and Justin's mother were happily married. Although Erik's deepest wish might have been much like Justin's, recent events had changed things— Erik had seen Arante smiling at him, dressed in a breathtaking white wedding gown. Raoul looked the most uncomfortable of them all as his illusion faded from his eyes. He vowed to himself that he would not tell anyone what he had seen.

"What happened?" Justin asked.

"You men were under the power of a mountain siren," Arante explained. "Lani saved you all by willingly giving up one year of her own life. It was an excruciating process."

It was only then that Raoul and Justin noticed Lani on the ground. They ran toward her. Jharate heard what Arante had said. He looked down on Lani and saw that she was still in tremendous pain.

From where she lay on the ground, Lani caught a glimpse of warmth in Jharate's eyes, and smiled weakly as she managed to whisper to him.

"I love you, Jharate."

As Justin and Raoul rushed to her side, the line of sight between Jharate and Lani was broken. Jharate blinked. His eyes grew instantly cold and distant again. Every muscle in his body tensed as he got up and walked back to Arante, without a word.

Lani blinked back the tears that wanted to fall. A prickling, dizzying sensation moved throughout her body. She felt like she was falling from a great height and waited indifferently to feel the thud of her body hitting the ground. But the thud never came.

Instead, Jharate's stab to her heart, combined with what she had just gone through physically, caused her to lose consciousness. Her eyes closed and her head rolled to one side so that her cheek pressed against the cold damp ground, as she fell completely still.

Drakne tried to blink away his surprise as he stared openmouthed at Lani. He could have sworn, no, he was sure—right before Lani's eyes had closed, he had seen white flames flicker in them once more. He looked at Justin and Raoul, but their faces registered nothing out of the ordinary. He searched every other face. No one was reacting to this phenomenon. Had they not seen it? Drakne watched expectantly as Raoul handed Justin his torch and began his attempt to heal Lani.

"Come on, Lani," Raoul said quietly. "Wake up."

Arante looked from Lani's motionless form to Jharate. An angry scowl crossed her face and, before she could even think, she slapped her cousin hard across the face.

"She saved your life by sacrificing some of hers, you idiot!"

"I did not ask that of her."

Arante's mouth fell open and she shook her head slowly in disbelief. She tried to say something in response, but only a few quiet indistinct sounds came from her throat.

Kendra's eyes narrowed as Jharate uttered his harsh statement and she jumped as high as she could, and decked Jharate. Jharate staggered back and fell against the cave wall, mainly because he had not expected it. Kendra turned and walked away from him, cradling her broken hand and hoping that her punch would leave a mark to at least compensate her a little bit for the excruciating pain she was now experiencing. She realized she should have given him a roundhouse to the stomach instead, but at least Raoul could heal her hand later.

Jharate took both the slap and the punch without reacting. He had been raised to never even lift a hand toward a woman in anger. He had never done so, and would not begin today. He simply turned his back on his cousin and prepared to leave.

Jharate's people had seen Arante and Kendra attack him, but quickly busied themselves with picking up the few items that had been dropped during the hypnotic episode— pretending they had seen nothing. They knew from what Arante had said that they all owed Lani a debt, and were more than confused by Jharate's dishonorable behavior. He had not even thanked her! They continued to avert their eyes from Jharate in order to continue the illusion of not having noticed, and thus remain out of a potentially problematic loyalty issue.

Arante shook her head yet again with her mouth still hanging open in shock. She felt like she couldn't possibly be awake. This was the worst thing she had ever seen Jharate do in her entire life. This was not him. It could not be him! And yet, he had done it. She had heard it, and she had seen it with her own eyes. He was dishonoring his family name and dishonoring her and dishonoring all that was right. She couldn't bear to look at him. She walked briskly past him and over to where Raoul was still trying to heal Lani. She placed her hand gently on Raoul's shoulder and spoke quietly.

"I'm sorry, Raoul. You cannot heal her from this. A loss of life is permanent. She gave it up for him. She will never get it back."

"She won't wake up," Raoul said softly, still trying.

"She probably won't for a while. I have never known anyone personally who has gone through this. In fact, I have only heard of it in fairy tales. I didn't even know it was possible until today. According to legend, it is supposed to be an extremely traumatic experience for the victim. They cannot move for hours. And, in the legends, the people who gave up the one year did it to save their own lives. It must be so difficult for her to have done this so selflessly and have Jharate act so coldly to her afterwards. That has *got* to make it harder. There is no way of knowing when she will recover."

Raoul reluctantly ceased. The white light disappeared, and he wiped away the sweat from his forehead, exhausted from the effort. He looked down at Lani, feeling helpless and frustrated for failing her in this moment.

"I'll carry her," Justin volunteered.

Justin carefully placed her sword back into its sheath. He felt a deep gratitude swelling in his heart toward Lani— for everything she had done for him in his life, not just for this particular moment. Justin handed the torch back to Raoul and lifted her limp body into his arms. He used his gift to partially levitate her, and then held her lovingly, ready to guide her body safely through the tunnel. Jharate, Arante, and Erik passed Justin and went ahead. As Jharate walked by him, Raoul stuck out his leg and tripped him.

"Oops! I'm so clumsy sometimes," Raoul glared at Jharate.

One of Jharate's eyebrows rose and he looked down at Raoul with a warning glance. He knew it had not been an accident, but did not react further. He simply turned and resumed leading the way through the cavern. Raoul's focus was diverted away from Jharate as Kendra came up to him, cradling her broken hand with a grimace. Raoul continued to bear the torch with one hand while healing Kendra with the other, until her hand was as good as new.

Drakne followed closely behind Kendra and Raoul so that the remaining rebels would not discover him. Drakne had been too powerful for the siren to affect, and that had allowed him to observe everything uninhibited. Lani had managed to impress him yet again. He was amazed that her love for Jharate was strong enough for her to give up part of her own life, and he was astounded that another creature had been able to tell how strong Lani was. *At least three hundred years!* Usually one entire life gave a siren a mere fifty years at best. One year willingly given had only ever been known to double that.

Drakne felt a little more comfortable now that Lani had been weakened. The loss of one year was not a simple blow. He was sure he wouldn't have to worry about her sensing him again for quite a while. Even better was the fact that the spell was still holding on Jharate.

How interesting. Lani had broken out of her spell when Jharate had saved her life— and Jharate hadn't even lost anything permanently. *And* Raoul had healed him very quickly, so his suffering had been very limited. Here Lani had given an entire year to save his life, two feet in front of him, and was still unconscious from the effort, and Jharate had done nothing!

Drakne wished he could laugh as freely as he wanted to at that moment. He was now certain that Jharate would be the weapon he would use for Lani's destruction. Jharate seemed to be the only force in this world that possessed power over her— and it appeared as if he possessed a great deal of it.

The incredulous look on Justin's face as the travelers reached the most dangerous part of the cavern pretty much said it all. Nearly a hundred sarcastic comments raced through his brain, but he kept them to himself. He quickly reset his focus to make sure he got Lani across alive as he started to follow the three people, now single-file, in front of him. They had to move one cautiously placed step at a time along a very long and very narrow path, no more than two feet wide, with a seemingly bottomless pit on either side. Pebbles fell into eerily soundless depths as they slowly inched their way across.

A rumbling noise in front of Justin made him stop dead in his tracks. A section of the path gave way directly in front of him. He scrambled backwards, bumping into Kendra, to avoid falling in with Lani in his arms. Kendra grabbed Justin's shoulders to stabilize him, her fingers digging in a little more than she meant to.

Erik tried to run forward with Arante, but the path crumbled beneath his feet. Arante slammed her body to the ground and simultaneously grabbed Erik by the wrist as the fragments of the pathway plummeted into the darkness below him. Erik's face turned white as he looked down. He looked up quickly into Arante's eyes with a panicked and pleading look.

"Arante, I'll never forget you, even on the other side!"

"Oh no you don't. You're not saying goodbye to me now, Erik. You have promises to keep!"

Arante had a firm grip on him and started to pull him up slowly.

"Grab the ledge with your other arm, Erik!"

Erik did so as she struggled with his weight. The piece of ground that Erik grabbed crumbled beneath his grasp. Erik screamed as Arante was yanked forward and dragged almost a foot over the edge. Jharate quickly dropped his torch on the path behind him, grabbed both of Arante's ankles, and pulled her back onto the stable part of the ledge.

"Nice of you to drop by," Arante barked bitterly at Jharate.

Jharate did not reply. Justin carefully switched to using his arm muscles to hold all of Lani's weight. Once he was sure that he had her securely, he used his gift to help take the burden of Erik's weight off of Arante. Soon Erik was once again on solid ground. He breathed hard and fast and looked down with a queasy expression. He looked back at Arante, took her face in both his hands and kissed her passionately.

Justin rolled his eyes and frowned. He was glad Lani was not awake for this! It would only hurt her more to see the contrast between what Erik had just done to thank Arante and what Jharate had not done to thank her. Justin felt nauseated at the very thought. He wished he had a paintball gun handy. He would love to let Jharate experience how it felt to be shot with one point-blank.

"Erik, I hate to interrupt," Justin began, "but I need you to take Lani so I can jump across."

"How?"

"I don't know… uh… let me think. Oh, I know! I can levitate her over to you with my gift and you can use the two arms that Heaven gave you to catch her when she gets there! What do you mean *how*, Kook?!"

Justin rolled his eyes again with an exasperated sigh at the fact that Erik always let people around him do the thinking so that he wouldn't have to. Erik dusted himself off and held out his arms.

"Okay, I'm ready."

"Alright, here she comes."

Justin used his telekinesis to send Lani's body gracefully across the five-foot gap into Erik's arms.

"I'm going to let my power go now, okay?"

"Yeah, I've got her… Man! She's heavier than she looks!"

"Yeah, well it's different when someone's completely unconscious, genius! Back up slowly, you wimp, so you don't go tumbling down with her and give me some room to jump!"

Erik did as he was told. Kendra released her grip on Justin and she and everyone behind her shuffled several steps backwards to give Justin some room. Justin backed up, inhaled, and took a calculated jump across the missing piece of path, landing like an action hero on the other side. He straightened up and held out his arms for Lani with an impatient look on his face. He wasn't going to leave her life in Erik's hands for a second longer than he had to. Erik handed her over.

"Haven't you ever lifted anything over a hundred and nineteen pounds? 'Cuz it seemed like a hundred and twenty pounds was going to kill you."

"Shut up, Justin!"

Drakne was tall enough to see over the heads of Raoul and Kendra. He looked past them and focused on a safe area to the left on the other side of the threatening ravine. The gap was huge on both sides of the broken pathway, and he needed to land away from Jharate and the others, so he could not follow Justin and the others forward. He also knew that he needed to get across quickly before somebody bumped into him. The fact that they hadn't done so already was extremely lucky, considering what had just happened.

This left only one option. He closed his eyes, pictured the area he had just studied, and teleported over. He opened his eyes cautiously and relaxed. He had made it. He was now in one of the large dome-like chambers of the tunnel, several feet from the edge of the ravine that he had just crossed. Drakne always hated teleporting. There was just so much risk involved. It was a much more useful gift for an intuitive person.

"Let's get off of this path," Arante said.

"I'll be right back, Kendra," Justin called over his shoulder. "Just wait for me, 'kay?"

"Take your time…"

Kendra had answered with a mixture of fear, sarcasm, and sincerity. She continued to feel these three somewhat conflicting emotions while she waited as patiently as she could.

Jharate picked up his torch, and everyone on his side of the ledge moved further in, very carefully, until they came to where they could walk safely on the wide part of the cave floor again, in the large chamber that Drakne had just entered. Justin gently set Lani down on the ground, far away from the chasm they had just crossed.

"Watch her for me please," he said to Arante.

"I will."

Justin went back quickly to help encourage Kendra across the gap.

"Just jump!"

"I can't!" Kendra did everything she could to avoid looking down at the abyss. "You know I'm deathly afraid of heights! It was hard enough to get on this path in the first place and now you want me to jump? That is *never* gonna happen!"

"Fine, then stay still."

Justin used his mind to transport her across the gap to him. Her face looked as if she'd seen a ghost and she pressed her lips together to try to keep a frightened scream inside. She held very still, with her hands balled-up in fists so tightly that her knuckles were turning white. As she got closer, Justin grabbed her upper arms to help stabilize her until she was firmly on the path. Kendra exhaled slowly and then took another deep breath in.

"I don't ever want to do that again!"

"Careful, Kendra, we don't have enough room for you to freak out."

"I know, I know. Wait a minute… I wonder if…"

Kendra activated her shield to span the distance Justin had just brought her across. She envisioned the flat version of her shield overlapping on both sides, so there would be no gaps.

"Raoul! Walk across my shield to us!"

Raoul gulped. He hesitated for a moment, looking from Kendra, to Justin and back again. He finally landed on Kendra. He took a deep breath and an unsure half-step onto the invisible shield. It was solid and holding. It felt like very smooth ground, but he was still extremely cautious. He took another step, then another, then a few more, and finally he was across. He breathed out slowly through his mouth and wiped the beaded sweat away from his forehead as his feet touched on the solid, *visible* ground.

"Wait there," Kendra called to the other rebels. "We'll get off the path so there's more room, and then I'll reactivate my shield for you. Wait for my call."

The rebels who were still stuck on the other side nodded calmly in agreement. The three friends walked over to where the path widened into the rest of the tunnel. Once there, Kendra reactivated her gift from her new position.

"Okay, I think it's safe to cross," Kendra called out. "Go ahead and walk on it."

Like Raoul, they took a couple of short steps to test it out, and then crossed easily. When the last rebel crossed, Kendra deactivated her shield with a triumphant grin at Justin.

"Yeah, yeah, we know you're awesome, Kendra. Don't get too cocky though or your head might not fit through the tunnel exit when we find it."

Kendra stuck out her tongue and turned her back on him so
sharply that her long ponytail whipped him in the face.

"I think that's enough for one night— at least it should be
night by now," Arante said. "We'll set up camp here."

Everyone sighed in relief. They set up camp quickly. They
were getting used to rapid set-ups and breakdowns. Traveling for
over a month, often while running for their lives, had made them
near experts.

Arante conjured an imitation of the Alamean night sky
above their heads, along with a few lazy fireflies and the sound of
crickets, to lull them peacefully off to sleep. She put less effort
than normal into the quality of the holographs, so that they
would fade away within a couple of hours and not keep those
awake who preferred to sleep in darkness.

As Drakne watched the rebels, he realized that he too was
very tired. He tried not to sleep as much as possible, even while
the rebels slept, and so he hadn't really slept in weeks— other
than allowing himself an hour or two of rest here and there. He
decided that tonight he too would slumber, but not before he
formed an invisible shield around him like tent. This would
ensure that nothing but air could get in and that no sounds of his
breathing or stirring in his sleep could get out. However, he
would be able to hear everything outside the bubble. Once
finished, he conjured luxurious satin pillows and blankets inside
it for his comfort, from his chambers back in Trisakne, and went
to sleep.

Lani was still out cold. Raoul came to her side with a
worried expression on his face, determined not to leave. She
needed him right now. She needed her best friend, and that was
him. He laid out a sleeping mat for her.

"Hey Justin, can you levitate Lani onto her sleeping mat please?"

"Sure thing, Raoul. Here, take my bedroll too so you can make it softer for her."

"That's a great idea! I'll give her mine too! Thanks, Justin."

"No problem. She deserves it."

"She sure does. She's always done everything for us… Okay, ready now."

"Got her."

Lani stirred a little after being moved onto the bedrolls but did not open her eyes.

"Jharate?"

Raoul's jaw tightened and he stared furiously at the cave wall, feeling a boiling rage welling up inside of him. He took several calculated breaths to attempt to keep his cool outwardly. He felt Justin's hand on his shoulder.

"It's okay, Raoul. Let it go," Justin said quietly.

"But…"

"Dude, there's nothing you could have done."

Raoul looked up at Justin and whispered with a furious tone.

"I should have done something! How could I have ever liked that guy? How could I have let Lani fall for him? I should have done something to protect her. She would have listened to me! She would have! She and I always listen to each other and value each other's opinions! I could have talked her out of it! I could have—"

"Jharate fooled all of us," Justin whispered back.

"Jharate?" she asked again, breathlessly in her sleep.

Raoul winced. He shut his eyes and shuddered with anger as he squeezed his hands into white-knuckled fists. Oh if she would just stop saying his name!

"Jharate should be the one here with her now, nursing her back to health and begging her forgiveness!" Raoul yelled in a whisper.

"But she has us."

"Yeah, she does. Can you give me just a minute alone with her?"

"Sure thing."

Justin patted Raoul on the back as he left. Raoul exhaled slowly and loosened his hands. He stroked Lani's hair gently, hoping that maybe it would be enough to calm her subconscious. She sighed and did not speak that traitor's name again. Raoul's muscles relaxed and his anger quelled as he saw that she was at peace once more.

"Raoul, when Lani awakens, give her this."

Raoul felt a strong hand on his shoulder and looked up to see Jaresh holding a canteen in his other hand. Jaresh offered it to him. Raoul took it and nodded his head.

"Thank you, Jaresh. What is it?"

"It is an herbal remedy. It should help to ease her pain, and begin to build her strength again. My family members have been the healers for the Trisaknen royal line for centuries."

"Wow, so you're a real healer."

"As are you. My particular gift is with herbs. My grandmother once brought Jharate's father, King Karahn, back from the brink of death with this very remedy. He was thirteen years old and had been thrown off his horse during a race around the castle grounds with his cousin, Arakahn. His cousin's horse had been following so closely behind, that Karahn was trampled before Arakahn even knew what had happened. Karahn was back to full strength within three days."

"Wow! Thank you so much! My own healing gift isn't of much use at the moment. I am very grateful that she has another chance to be healed quickly because of you."

Jaresh nodded and walked away to turn in for the night.

Jharate had been keeping a watchful eye over Raoul as he tended to Lani. He continued to stare at her for hours as everyone else drifted off to sleep. The smallest part of Jharate longed to be the one caring for her. It should be him. Honor demanded it. She had saved his life, and had done so in a very painful way. Perhaps she really did love him. Could it be possible he was making a mistake? Maybe she was a Half-Heart. Her bravery had been exemplary and Half-Hearts were supposed to have great strength of character.

Suddenly his head ached, like a prelude to a migraine. He shook his head hard and the pain disappeared instantly. He raised an eyebrow incredulously as he redirected his gaze to Lani. He was not ready to admit that he was wrong. Nor was he entirely convinced that he was. One thing he was sure of was that he needed sleep— now. He closed his eyes and quickly drifted off.

Jharate saw the familiar king-size bed and turned to see his mother sitting in the ornate rocking chair by the window. She stood as she saw him and held her arms out. He raced to embrace her in a warm hug. As they parted to look at one another, she held onto both of his hands and looked at him with a deep and serious concern in her eyes.

"Jharate," Karsenia spoke gently. "You are under a spell, my son."

"What do you mean, my mother?"

"You are under a spell that is turning you from Lani. This is not you, my son. I know that you love her. You need to fight the

spell. Fight it and win. Bar your heart to any evil influences and
humble yourself before the woman you love— for it is your
heart that has been attacked. It would grieve me so much to see
you lose her."

"She broke my heart..."

"I know, Jharate. She was under a spell, and now you have
broken hers because *you* are under a spell. You have hurt her
deeply. You are causing tenfold more pain to her heart than she
ever inflicted upon yours. She gave up a year of her life to save
your own, my son! What more proof of love do you require?"

"I trust you, Mother, and I will speak with her when I
awake."

"You will have more happiness than you imagine could be
contained within yourself if you will use your love to break free.
You cannot stay here long. Go and sleep now. You will need
your strength to fight this curse. Remember always, that I am
with you and that I love you."

"I love you too, Mother."

The vision faded away into nothingness and he plunged into
a deeper sleep.

Lani's eyes fluttered open and she looked around and found
everyone sleeping soundly. She groaned quietly. Her entire body
felt awful. It was infinitely worse than the effects of a bad flu.
She wondered how far they had traveled and how she had gotten
here.

Her moan had awakened both Raoul and Drakne
simultaneously. Drakne snapped his fingers and his pillows and
blankets disappeared as he deactivated his sleeping shield. He

stood up and leaned against the rock wall of the tunnel and watched Lani and Raoul, who was now kneeling at her side. She tried to get up, but grimaced and lay back down again.

"No, don't try to move yet," Raoul said.

He grabbed the canteen Jaresh had given him and unscrewed the cap. He gently raised her head up and held the canteen close to her lips.

"Here, drink this medicine. You have been out cold for hours."

Lani drank it slowly. Her eyes opened in surprise as she realized how good it tasted. She had braced herself for some foul-smelling, bitter-tasting brew. But this was heavenly! It tasted like a drink she loved that was made from red hibiscus flowers— a little like fruit punch. As she finished all she could manage, Raoul gradually lowered her head back down and screwed the cap back on the canteen.

"Did I really give up a year of my life, or was that a crazy dream?"

"You really did. You're amazing."

"I've never felt anything like it," she whispered.

"I can't imagine what having a year of life taken from you would feel like," Raoul said in a reverent tone.

"Well let's just say I don't ever want you to find out," she said with a small laugh.

She cringed a little as the laugh shot a jolt of pain through her entire body. She stayed very still until the pain subsided. Her face became very serious and she looked deeply into Raoul's eyes.

"I don't regret it."

"I knew you wouldn't. Your friends aren't as forgiving as you are though."

"What do you mean?"

"Well, Arante slapped Jharate, Kendra decked him, and I tripped him 'accidentally' after that."

"Oh, you guys shouldn't have done that! But I know your hearts were in the right place."

"Yeah, well he deserves a lot more where that came from! You sacrificed a year of your life for him and all he does is walk away from you!"

Raoul glared at Jharate, who was staring back.

"I know," Lani sighed.

The full realization hit her like a head-on collision at ninety miles per hour. Not even the sacrifice of a full year of her life had been enough for Jharate to return to her. She would have done it all over again even if she knew the result would be the same, but she had let herself dream that he would love her again.

Lani blinked in surprise as she saw Jharate walking directly to her. Had he heard what she had said about not regretting it? Even more startling was the fact that he was actually looking at her and not Raoul.

"May I inquire as to how you are feeling?" Jharate asked awkwardly.

"Would you like the polite conversation answer, or the truth?"

"I always prefer the truth."

"I feel horrible. Thank you for asking."

Lani tried to keep her face from expressing the complete shock that she felt at the fact that he was speaking to her at all. That took so much effort that she didn't know what else to say. An uncomfortable silence followed while she tried to think of something to ask him.

"How are you?"

"I am… I would like to tell you… What I mean to say is… Thank you for saving my life. I truly appreciate it."

"You're very welcome. It was only one year. The siren would have killed you."

Jharate opened his mouth as if he would speak again, but turned and walked away abruptly, picking up one of the torches as he left.

A slight rush of air whooshed across Drakne's face as Jharate passed within inches of him in his hasty exit. He was glad he had awakened in time. Had Drakne not already let his protective field down Jharate would have walked right into it and he would have been discovered.

Lani was still looking at the spot where Jharate had stood just seconds ago, feeling more than confused. Had Jharate forgiven her? Was he trying to come back to her and didn't know how? Or was he just trying to appease his conscience by thanking her? Either way, the fact that he had addressed her at all had to be a good sign, didn't it?

Drakne was also uncertain as to what Jharate had just done. He watched Jharate carefully as he prepared for the day's trek. Drakne decided he had better keep him under close surveillance. He might be finding a way out of his spell. Although, for the sake of research, it might be good to see if he *could* get out of it on his own.

SOMETIMES LIFE JUST REFUSES TO ACT LIKE A CHICK FLICK

"No, no, no, uh-uh!" Justin said insistently.

"But I don't want to be a bother," Lani insisted back.

"Are you kidding me? You just saved all of our lives and you're worried about being a bother?"

"But—"

"No buts," Raoul stated. "We're helping you. Besides, you can't even sit up on your own."

"Listen to the man. You don't have a choice, girly."

Lani sighed and smiled at the same time.

"You guys are the best. Alright, I'll let you help me."

"*Chaah*, only 'cuz you don't have another option," Justin laughed.

"Wrap your arms around our shoulders."

Lani did as Raoul instructed, and her two friends lifted her to her feet and helped her to walk. The herbal remedy was already helping her to feel better and was probably the reason she was up at all. However, it had only been a few hours since she had taken it and she was still extremely weak.

Justin shot sideways glances at her from time to time to see how she was doing and more importantly to check to see if she was catching on to what he was really doing— using his power on her to artificially take some of the gravity off of her body. He hoped she wouldn't notice. He knew that if she figured out his little secret that she would worry about her need for help draining his energy and she didn't need that additional stress.

Jharate made no other attempt to speak with Lani or even to make eye contact with her throughout the rest of their trek through the never-ending tunnel— not that she had really been expecting him to, but there was always that hope lingering in the back of her mind. At long last, she saw a pinprick of light in the distance ahead. She felt a little stronger and a little happier as the small dot of light slowly grew into an exit. As they got closer and closer to leaving the tunnel behind them, each step she took made her smile grow wider and her heart beat with expectation until they finally reached the way out.

Exiting the cave after being inside it for so long was an odd sensation. Lani had lost all track of time in its mysterious darkness. But now there was real light again. The sun was on its way back down, but still bright. She sighed happily as she felt its warming touch on her skin.

"I'm guessing from the sun's relative position that it's about four in the afternoon right now," Justin said.

"How do you know that?" Lani asked.

"Well until the lake killed my pocket watch, I kept looking at it every morning. I was surprised to find that the sun kept rising at the same hour each day. So wherever Alamea is, it must be in the same relative position to its sun as Earth is to ours because we have a nearly identical twenty-four-hour day."

"That's really cool, Justin," Lani answered.

"Geek test! You passed," Raoul said with a laugh.

"Yeah, this from a guy who has had a 'word of the day' emailed to him every day since high school," Justin said with a smirk.

"Hey! How else would I have learned the word flummoxing? I love that word. It's so much fun to say. *Flumm*oxing. Flum*mox*ing. Flummox*ing*!"

"Yes, and without that word, one of my favorite videos would have never been made. You remember 'Flummoxing Boy' Justin?" Lani laughed.

"Who could forget it? Man, I haven't seen that in years! I can still see Raoul's face coming up into view with the shades and the Ricky Martin song behind him. Ha, ha!"

"I know, right? And I love that he made it while he was grounded too. His parents probably didn't even realize that they weren't really punishing him 'cuz he still had his video camera."

"Hey! All they said is that I couldn't leave the house! I didn't, so I was still being a good boy."

"Yeah, technically," Justin snorted, as they noticed Arante climbing up to perch on a rock.

"Ah-hem! Everyone get busy and set up camp for the night and then— enjoy! We don't have long before dark anyway and it's the last bit of relaxation we're going to get before Destavnia. We're a little bit beyond the half-way point of the pass now, which should put us in Zenastra in a little over a week if all goes well. So use this time wisely to strengthen yourselves in case we have a run in with Drakne and his men once we get there."

"Yes, make sure you save all of your strength in case you run into Drakne," Drakne whispered.

As the rebels spread out to set up camp for the night, Lani was able to better see their surroundings. There was a large pool just outside of the cave, exactly as Arante had described. Lani was sure she wasn't the only one who had become sick of the sight of pure rock, which made the crystal pool in front of her a glorious oasis in the desert. Cool water cascaded gently from a small waterfall into the lava-heated water. Palm trees and ferns and other tropical-looking plants grew around the warm pool, perhaps because of the steamy environment and volcanic soil. They contrasted sharply with the rest of the stark and dreary mountain pass. Lani took a deep breath to soak in the fresh air.

Arante dove headfirst into the glossy warm pool. The dive was perfect, and she took off like a torpedo in the shallow waters. When she surfaced she turned back to Erik.

"What are you waiting for?"

Erik grinned and hurtled into the water in a single bound, landing close enough to deluge her with his splash. When he surfaced he embraced her and pulled her under the water for a passionate underwater kiss.

"Yes, that totally makes it so we can't tell, Erik," Justin muttered under his breath as he rolled his eyes.

"Let them be, Justin," Lani said softly.

"Yeah, I hear that a lot lately."

Kendra didn't have to be invited. She jumped in feet first and proceeded to swim happily around, enjoying the feeling of weightlessness.

"It's so warm!" Kendra called back before diving below the surface of the water and swimming further away.

Raoul and Justin slowly helped Lani to the water's edge. Raoul made sure Justin had her before slipping into the water. He checked to make sure both he and Lani would be able to touch the bottom. When he was sure that the situation was safe, he reached his hands up to help her in. Justin levitated her carefully into Raoul's arms. Lani squealed quietly in surprise.

"This is awesome, Justin! It's like I'm flying!" she giggled.

"I know, right? But then you always knew I was awesome, girly."

"That I did."

Raoul rolled his eyes and then gently helped her to stand in the water, keeping his arm around her shoulders. Overprotecting her with every action, he made sure she wouldn't so much as stub her toe. The instant that Justin was sure that Raoul had Lani, he backed up about twenty feet, and stood poised like a runner at the starting line.

"Three... two... one... BONZAI!"

Justin took off like a bullet and, with a flying leap over his friends' heads, hit the water in a massive cannonball. Justin's splash was so large that it completely doused Jharate before he had even put a toe in the water. Jharate stood there expressionless for a moment, water dripping down his face, and then dove in. Lani laughed in spite of everything.

Others in the camp soon followed until everyone was in the water— everyone except Drakne. He hated water. He had always had a fear of drowning and did not like how powerless being in water made him feel. He strolled over to a large bolder far enough away to be out of the splash zone, but with a vantage point that wouldn't allow any of them out of his sight, and sat down to watch the rebel morons have their fun. It would not last long.

"Kendra, think fast!" Justin exclaimed.

"What?"

Justin telekinetically created a large wave that rushed towards Kendra. She screamed and activated a dome-shaped shield to protect herself. She watched in awe as the underbelly of the wave crossed over her shield.

"Okay, that was really cool— but I'm still gonna get you for that, Justin!"

"Cha right! I'd like to see you try!"

"Oh it's on!"

Kendra formed a rectangular shield in the water and shoved it forward quickly, shooting a giant wall of water at Justin, who used his telekinesis to make it part around him, laughing maniacally the whole time.

"Missed me, missed me, now you gotta kiss me! Ha, ha, ha, ha, ha!"

"In your dreams, Justin!"

"I think you mean in *your* dreams!"

Lani and Raoul laughed happily as the epic water fight continued to rage between Kendra and Justin at the far end of the pool, as did all who were watching. The two gifts were so equally matched that it was extremely hard to figure out who was winning, but the show was spectacular. Giant crashing sprays of mist and rushing waves continued to clash until Kendra placed a permanent spherical shield around herself that encompassed enough water within it for her to float on her back in complete safety.

"Come on, Kendra! We were just getting started!"

"Justin, I have been running for my life through a forest, over a lake, through a meadow, through this gigantic mountain pass, and most recently through a never-ending cave for who knows how long. Now *I'm* through! I'm entitled to a small break where I have nothing to do but just be lazy and stare at the clouds!"

"Fine!"

Justin threw one last wave over her shield that pushed her bubble a little further away. He frowned as it registered that the water fight was actually over. Defeated, Justin realized that he needed a new way to entertain himself. His smile quickly reappeared as a thought came to him. He redirected his efforts.

"Cool!" he shouted to no one in particular.

He had just created a giant water sculpture of a sphere with rings orbiting around it, much like Saturn.

"This gift is never going to get old!" Justin said with a loud laugh.

The warmth and the feeling of weightlessness did wonders for Lani's sore body. She loved water anytime and anywhere, but especially now. It was all the way up to her neck, which somehow helped her feel stronger and helped her breathe easier. She slowly found that she was able to stand on her own. She took a few steps away from Raoul just to be sure and smiled as she realized that he wouldn't have to be stuck taking care of her the whole time. She turned and saw the worried lines on his forehead, the intense look in his eyes, and the nervous stance—ready to jump to her side at a moment's notice. She smiled gently and placed a hand on his shoulder.

"I'm okay now, Raoul. You don't have to stay here with me. Go have fun. I promise I'll be fine."

Raoul looked out on the vast expanse of the pool and back to her, the concern still etched deeply in his face.

"Are you sure?"

"Yes, I'm just going to relax and float around."

"Alright, but I'll be close. Just call me if you need me."

"I will."

She smiled at him sweetly again and motioned for him to go with her hand. With one last scrutinizing look at her, he smiled back and took off like a joyful sea otter. She laughed and felt a wave of gratitude for his friendship and overprotective nature. She dove under the water's surface and opened her eyes. She was surprised by the fact that she could actually see the heat waves rising in the water, much like the visible heat from sweltering hot asphalt or in the air over a grill at a cookout. She flipped over so that she could look up at the sky through the water. She loved the way the light moved across the surface. She undid the braid that held her hair and let it float freely around her.

Lani moved her arms slowly to postpone her ascent to the surface. It was so peaceful underwater. It was quiet and serene— and devoid of all the problems that awaited her on land. Here she was safe and happy and warm. She knew she was going to have to go up for air soon.

That was always the saddest part of being underwater— the moment you realized you couldn't stay. One of her dreams had been to get certified in scuba so that she could just lie on the ocean floor and blow bubble rings for as long as her oxygen tank could hold out. She had always fantasized about being a mermaid since she was a little girl and she figured scuba was the closest she would ever get to having that kind of freedom.

Lani allowed herself to float toward the surface. She stretched her neck and moved her head back and forth slowly to release the pressure she felt there. Her hair swirled around her face and shoulders as she did so. When she could stay under no longer, she surfaced and took a deep breath of much needed air. Oh, what she wouldn't give to be able to breathe underwater! She went down again and resurfaced quickly— this time to let the water pull her hair smoothly away from her face. When she stood up and opened her eyes again, she saw Jharate staring straight at her from six feet away, waist deep in the water.

SOMETIMES LIFE JUST REFUSES
TO ACT LIKE A CHICK FLICK

Lani jumped back a little. He always popped up out of nowhere. His ability to appear and disappear had to be superhuman. He continued to stare at her. He said nothing. He did nothing. Lani pulled all of her hair to one side and twisted it nervously, trying to decide if she was supposed to look back at him or avoid his gaze. Her indecision led to something oddly in the middle that felt even stranger than picking one option would have. But she didn't have a clue as to what to do. No one had ever acted like this towards her— well, perhaps Josiah had, but Jharate was taking it to a whole new level.

She continued to fret over which action to take as she made eye contact with Jharate, every now and then. Every time she did, he would blink back. He didn't try to move away or even to look elsewhere. He just remained where he was with his eyes fixed on her. What was he doing? Why didn't he just come over to her and forgive her for what she had done to him? He needed to get over it, already. It hadn't been on purpose, and it hadn't been completely her fault either. If it weren't for that stupid spell Drakne had placed on her— She was tired of waiting. Lani felt a rush of determination sweep over her and she swam directly toward Jharate, ignoring the fact that he suddenly looked like a deer caught in the headlights.

She stopped right next to him and leaned her back against the naturally smooth lava-rock wall of the pool, just one foot from where he was doing the same. A moment of uncomfortable silence passed while Lani decided what she was going to say to try to break the ice. She mustered her most cheerful tone and began.

"This pool is so beautiful! I feel so good now that we are out of that dark cave and in the warm sunshine. What do you think?"

Jharate did not reply.

"Sooo, are you having fun here, Jharate? I mean, is it as fun as you remembered it being when you were here with Arante before?"

"Yes."

"That's good."

Jharate said nothing further and Lani had exhausted everything she could think of at the moment in the realm of small talk. The two of them just stood there next to each other, staring out at the others. Lani giggled as she saw Justin signaling Raoul with military hand signals for whatever mischievous covert op they were planning. Both had wide impish grins on their faces. Raoul carefully snuck up behind Kendra, who was still floating on her back, eyes closed, with a blissful look on her face. As soon as Raoul came within inches of her shield, he yelled Kendra's name so loudly that it broke her concentration. She bolted upright to look around and accidentally let go of her shield. Justin took advantage of this moment of vulnerability and deluged her with an enormous wall of water.

Kendra screamed and rushed after both Justin and Raoul, propelling water at them with her shield. The two pranksters laughed hysterically as they got out of the water and ran to avoid her. Lani found herself laughing more too. She kept glancing at Jharate, hoping to catch his eye, but she had no such luck. She sighed heavily. The man was an impenetrable fortress! His expression remained flat and his lips remained sealed.

"Jharate, I just wanted to say that I'm sorry about what happened at the sanctuary. I just, well, I guess the spell amplified my fears and I— I thought you didn't love me. I am *so* sorry I ever hurt you and—"

Jharate cut her off by abruptly wading away. A single silent tear fell down the side of her cheek. She didn't want anyone to see it. She plunged her face down into the water and floated like a drowning victim, so that her grief would remain between her and whatever fish might pass by. She stayed there, floating and waiting for the water to repair the trauma she had just endured. She watched the way the light danced around her shadow on the rocky bottom and tried to wish her pain away.

She jolted as she felt two hands on her shoulders, flipping her over. She took a deep breath in and pulled her hair away from her face. She didn't know how long she had been under, but it had been long enough to regain her composure. As she carefully wiped the water from her eyes and opened them, she saw Raoul looking frantic and stern, glaring at her with an almost fierce intensity.

"Don't scare me like that!"

"I'm sorry. I was just floating. I didn't mean to scare anybody."

"I wouldn't usually be so freaked out 'cuz I know you are a good swimmer, because you swim in the ocean and pools and stuff and you know me and I'm a lifeguard... It's just with the siren... and you being so weak and..."

"I really am sorry I worried you, Raoul. Thanks for checking on me. I appreciate you."

Lani gave Raoul a kiss on the cheek. She smiled at him as she turned on her back, this time to float away. She looked at the sky as clouds rolled by, trying to clear her mind of every uncomfortable thought, and stayed in the water with everyone else until the clouds changed from white, to pink, to purple.

Raoul returned and swam over to the edge with her as everyone began to get out to lie on the tiers of flat rocks around the pool. The rocks were very smooth, pitch black, and had absorbed much of the heat from the sun— perfect to lie on in the cooler temperature of the approaching evening. Justin walked along the edge until he met up with Raoul and Lani and looked down at Lani with a grin.

"You know, this would be a lot easier if you just let me levitate you up here."

"Whatever is less work for you is fine with me, Justin."

"Cool! Raoul, hold her in your arms like you're going to carry her across the threshold or something so I can picture what I'm doing better. Yeah, like that. Okay, ready Lani?"

"Ready as I'll ever be," Lani answered with a laugh.

Lani floated out of the water and then out of Raoul's arms. She let out a quiet squeal of surprise again. It was definitely a strange feeling to be floating through the air— and holding a specific pose with nothing actually holding you, was strange in and of itself. It was fun though, even a bit of a rush as she drifted through the air and into Justin's arms. He caught her and laughed.

"Brings back memories, huh?" Justin said with a smirk.

"Maybe," Lani said with a playful but slightly nervous grin.

Lani remembered well the many times she had been in Justin's arms like this before. He had always loved picking her up at the beach and spinning her around in or out of the water. He had picked her up like this for several of their prom pictures for both years. Come to think of it, he hadn't ever really needed an excuse to pick her up like this when they had been together. She felt a slight rush as he joked with her, but at the same time things were different now. Her heart belonged to Jharate, and no amount of history or flirts could make her forget him even temporarily— regardless of the fact that he wasn't actually hers at the moment.

"Don't worry, Lani, I know that time's long gone— but it's nice to remember every once in a while."

"Yeah, sooo much fun to remember," Raoul said with a sarcastic twitch as he pulled himself out of the pool. "You know what else is fun?"

"What?" Justin asked with an irritated scoff.

"This!"

Raoul put his fists in front of Justin's face and extended his right thumb and left pinky to face the same direction, and then switched to his left thumb and right pinky, faster and faster and faster and then suddenly laced his fingers together and started doing the wave with his arms in a bizarre combo of spastic coordination. Lani and Justin cracked up. Raoul stopped his show and laughed too.

"Hey that rock looks like a good one for her," Raoul said, pointing about ten feet away from them.

"Looks nice to me," Lani agreed.

"Well let's get you over there then," Justin smiled.

Justin walked toward the rock Raoul had pointed to and slowly set her down. Now that she was out of the water, gravity took its toll again and she still could not sit up without help. Luckily, the rock was slanted up at the perfect angle so that she didn't have to sit up to see what was going on around her. She settled in and smiled at her two friends.

"Thanks guys! This will be perfect! Now go get yourselves comfortable. I'm fine."

"You sure?" Raoul asked.

"'Cuz we can wait," Justin added.

"Yes, I'm sure. You guys deserve a break too. I'll call you if I need you."

"Promise?" Justin asked.

"Yes, I promise."

Justin and Raoul looked from her, to each other, and then set off to find their own rocks to dry out on. Kendra noticed them leave and walked over to Lani to sit next to her. Kendra flattened her lips tightly, like her older brother who played the trumpet had taught her to do, and blew out softly to make a high-pitched squeaky noise. She continued to make this strange noise until she ran out of air and her lips popped as they released.

"Sooo, how are you doing?"

"Oh, I'm fine I guess…"

Lani shrugged as she trailed off. She figured it was true enough. She had adopted the definition of the word fine from the movie *The Italian Job* long ago as her own private way to answer honestly and yet not get into details— F.I.N.E. freaked out, insecure, neurotic, and emotional. It worked for her too, because she didn't want to admit, even to herself, how much of a complicated wreck she felt like she was at the moment.

"Sorry, dumb question."

"No, no, it's a perfectly valid question. I mean, I just lost my home and everything I ever knew or cared about. Then I lost the love of my life, who was the only reason that I had been able to forget about being away from my family, even for a moment. And, to top it all off, I just literally lost a year of my life. Not bad for about a month and a half."

Lani tilted her head in thought. She hadn't realized until now that she had completely lost track of how long they had actually been away from Earth. She wondered how many weeks had passed— how many days had drifted by. Lani shook her head gently.

"I'm sorry, Kendra, I must be sounding like everything is about me. I know you all lost everything too. How are you doing?"

"I miss my family too and I've had a rough time with it from time to time, thank you for asking, really, but you shouldn't be worrying about us right now. You always do that. You have really been through the wringer and you're thinking you have no right to grumble about it. At least the rest of us are having fun between the dramas. You never seem to catch a break. You need to stop worrying about other people all the time and take care of yourself for once."

Lani smiled at Kendra's kind words, as Kendra continued.

"And you know what else? I don't know what Jharate's problem is, but if he's going to be like that, he doesn't deserve you! I wanna smack that big giraffe down right now…"

"Don't call him names please, but thanks, Kendra," Lani said, forcing a bigger smile. "I still miss him, though. And then to make matters worse, he keeps coming close to me and then walking away in the middle of a sentence. I don't know what he's trying to do. I mean it seems like maybe he wants me back, but then he leaves. I don't know."

"Don't waste your time trying to figure it out. That boy is confusing at best! Besides, I'm sure you'll find someone better."

"Yeah, right."

Lani didn't believe there was anyone better than Jharate. She didn't want anyone other than him either, for that matter. She looked away from Kendra and closed her eyes for a moment to try to keep it together, before looking at her friend again.

"No, for realz! And the sooner you start to get over Giraffe Boy, the sooner you might find Mr. Right."

"Kendra! I've told you not to call him that. I let it slide that last time because you're being such a sweetheart and I thought if I brushed it off, you might stop it. But I'm serious— I don't want anyone saying anything mean about him. I really do appreciate you a ton for trying to cheer me up, but I love him. I can't just get over him like that. I have to at least try to make this work. He has my whole heart. Thank you for being such a good friend though, seriously. Having my friends support me like this makes the nightmare disappear from time to time. You've always been like a sister to me."

Lani smiled and reached over to squeeze Kendra's hand gratefully.

"Same here, Lani. I'll try to respect your wish on that whole not-calling-him-names thing. But you're going to have to forgive me when I mess up— yes I said when, and I'll add frequently, ha ha! And you know I only want the best for you, Chicky.

"But just remember, this isn't one of your favorite Jane Austen novels. In real life, the guys like Mr. Darcy and Captain Wentworth, usually stay jerks *forever,* or *never* forgive you, or some nasty combination of the two. Don't dream your whole life away on the chance that he'll come back to you. If someone else comes along, give yourself permission to go."

"I'll keep that in mind."

Lani squeezed Kendra's hand one more time as Kendra got up and walked toward the fire. She knew Kendra had her best interest at heart and also that it was very good advice— advice she would have given herself. She would normally dump a guy for much less than the coldness that Jharate was showing her. Her recent experience with Josiah had only reinforced her conviction that hanging on, past a certain point, was a bad idea. But for some reason, she didn't *want* to get over Jharate.

Lani looked over to where Jharate was. She felt a strange freezing sensation within her as she saw that he was staring at her— again. What the blazes was he thinking? Did he want her back? Was he trying to intimidate her? She felt as if he was seeing straight through her and into her very soul. But if that was true, he should know how much she loved him! He blinked and looked away, almost the very moment she caught him looking.

Get a hold of yourself, Lani, she thought as she shook her head to try to break the trance. She needed to stop trying to figure him out or she was going to go crazy. It was just too confusing. It's not like she had ever been that good at reading guys in the first place, but Jharate took her uncertainty to a record high. Lani resolved not to think of him for now and to get some sleep. It didn't work. She was up for hours doing nothing *but* thinking about him.

Drakne watched as everyone fell asleep except Lani. He had set up his invisible soundproof shield on one of the highest rock tiers and conjured his luxurious pillows and blankets inside it once again. However, they were merely for comfort's sake. He had no intention of sleeping tonight. Instead he stared at Lani and continued to wonder who she was, as he planned her imminent destruction, reveling in the fact that Jharate would be the key to her undoing.

Lani gazed up at the bewitching stars. They shone so brightly out here— far brighter than on Earth. She marveled at the constellations. You could actually tell what they were supposed to be. They truly looked like flowers, dragons, fairies and even people. Lani wondered if the people were from Alamea's mythology or possibly from their history. However, she didn't have time to wonder long about any particular constellation, because they kept changing. They continually morphed into different shapes, as if they grew tired of remaining in one formation for too long. Lani wondered how this could be. Nothing she knew about the laws of physics could explain the phenomenon.

Lani continued watching the stars until she finally drifted off to sleep. It didn't feel like sleep to her though. She found herself in the room Jharate had shown her in his memory. His mother was there, alone this time. She sat in her ornate rocking chair, looking out the window. Moonlight shone down on her lovely face and danced in her flowing chestnut hair. Lani walked over to her and sat in the window seat across from Karsenia.

"I have been waiting for you."

"Me?"

Lani looked around to see if she could mean somebody else within the vision.

"Yes, I have been attempting to contact you for a long while. It has been very difficult because of the amount of pain my son has been inflicting upon you. It has interfered with your emotional state a great deal."

"I don't entirely blame him."

"That is one of the reasons that you are so perfect for him. Jharate deserves a woman who will think the best of him, even when all signs indicate otherwise. And because you are such a woman, you deserve a man who will do the same for you."

"I'm afraid that he'll never forgive me."

"Do not give up on my son just yet. He is a very good man."

"I know he is. He is the most extraordinary man I have ever known. I love his heart and his mind and his spirit. There is something about him that I feel can never be replaced. He is truly unique. But that can't be the only reason you've been trying to contact me, can it?"

"No," Karsenia said with a smile. "However, it is closely related. I have seen how much the two of you love each other. Your love is so strong and it is so important."

"Why would our love be so important? Am I a Half-Heart?"

"I cannot tell you that, and if I could, it would be counterproductive. You cannot worry about whether or not you are both Half-Hearts, or the magic would not work anyway. Nevertheless, true love is *always* important. You have to love each other so deeply, that it would not matter to either of you if you fulfilled the prophecy or not. If you tried to stay together for that reason alone, even if you both *were* Half-Hearts, your union would not be able to create the magic needed to tip the balance of power to the side of good."

"All I know is that I want to spend the rest of my life with him and every minute of eternity after that."

Lani sighed deeply.

"I know Jharate feels the same— somewhere deep inside his heart. I can often feel what he feels. A mother's love is very strong and there is magic in that, even after death. I will keep helping in whatever ways I can. I have been helping to protect you all, to the limit of my ability to interfere. I have been using every power available to aid you in your struggles, and also to shield you from Vranah. However, I will not be able to hold him off forever. I spoke with Jharate concerning you as well. Sadly, his heart is like ice. He is under the influence of some powerful dark magic. He is not himself."

"Did Drakne get to him too? Or was it someone else? Could the dragon have infected him somehow?"

"I cannot tell you that. It would prove fatal for you if I did, because your ignorance of this force is one of the only things preserving your life right now."

Lani lifted an eyebrow. She parted her lips slightly, with a string of questions waiting to burst out, but instead she held her tongue. What Karsenia had just told her did not make much sense to Lani, but Karsenia obviously knew what she was talking about and Lani could feel deep inside that she needed to simply trust her. She decided to ask a different question.

"How do I get through to Jharate?"

"With love. It is the only force able to break the powers of evil."

"But, I sacrificed a whole year of my life for him and he barely said thank you. What can I do that would show more love than that?"

"It did have an affect on him. Continue to demonstrate your love for him. Your constant love will show him even more than you have already shown with your recent heroic action. There are few people willing to make the big sacrifices, as you have just done.

"However, as surprising as it may be, there are even fewer willing to do the small things every day. In truth, the smaller actions are far more difficult, because they must be sustained consistently and cannot be accomplished with one great surge of effort. Therefore, your continued and unchanging small labors of love will steadily chip away at the ice around his heart."

Karsenia glanced out the window and then back to Lani.

"The sun is coming up. You must go now. Wake up, Lani."

"No! Wait! I don't know what to do!"

Lani felt two hands on her shoulders gently shaking her awake as the vision faded away.

"I don't know what to do. I don't know what to do!"

"Lani!" Raoul's voice called. "Lani! Snap out of it! You're just having a bad dream. Wake up!"

Lani opened her eyes and looked at Raoul with a bewildered expression. It was an odd feeling seeing Raoul there. She sat up and blinked, trying to readjust to being awake.

"You just sat up on your own! That's fantastic! Jaresh wasn't kidding about that herbal stuff!"

Lani didn't hear him. Her mind was replaying the vision she had just received. She still wasn't sure exactly what she was to do, but she was on a mission to get her true love back. It would begin today.

"Hello? Lani? You there?"

Lani shook her head slightly before answering cheerfully, "Oh, yes. Sorry! Good morning, Raoul!"

The next several days flew by. To Lani's great relief and excitement, she healed remarkably fast. She didn't feel completely normal yet, but she refused to let anyone else discover that, and pushed ahead as if she were perfectly healthy.

She had developed a plan to show Jharate love without giving him a chance to reject it. Whenever she could, she smiled at him and looked away first, so that he wouldn't have time to turn away from her. She would say hello to him, and then quickly walk over to Arante and ask her a question. She figured the less chance she gave him to cut her off, the less he would get set in his ways of ignoring her. She hoped it was working, but she couldn't really tell— because, to keep it up, she had to keep running away first.

The other phase of the plan was much trickier to pull off, due to Jharate's extreme ability to be alert at all times and due to the effort it took to find the resources to implement it. Lani would search for things she could write with and on, and then she would carefully tie the improvised note to his sword while he slept, whenever she could. She couldn't help feeling like a ninja at these times when she had to sneak up on him without making the slightest sound. She made sure that the notes expressed her love for him, encouraged him to keep hope for the future of Alamea or for himself, or praised him for something he had done well that day. Sometimes she would just write uplifting words from a book she had read long ago or quotes from Shakespeare or religious works.

Again, she had no idea how Jharate was receiving these. He never spoke to her of them. He never spoke to her at all. Whenever he looked as though he might be *attempting* to speak to her, the moment would fade and he would simply blink and walk away.

Lani had now regained her cheerful demeanor as a fortunate byproduct of her efforts because, by focusing on the positive every day, in order to write Jharate the little notes, she had lifted her own spirits. She almost felt that everything she had done for him was already worth it for that reason alone, even if Jharate never responded. Plus, with how much she loved him, doing something that might possibly bring him happiness also made her feel happy.

But today she was happy for another reason as well— they had crossed the border of Kelamosa into Zenastra. Better still, there was only one more night and a full day's walk and they would be out of these mountains! Despite her bubbly attitude and the fact that she was trying to focus on a brighter future, these mountains had represented nothing but pain and suffering to her. The prospect of leaving them behind was thrilling!

The morale of everyone around her was high as well. They knew it wasn't over yet, as they still had part of Zenastra to cross, but it didn't matter. Success was success, and they were just about to reach their goal. The rebels were about to make camp for the night when a sudden gust of wind blew a giant spiral of dust around them. They shielded their eyes and waited for the dust to settle.

When they looked up they found themselves surrounded by over a hundred people who had seized the high ground in all directions. Each one was armed with a bow and arrow and had it drawn back, pointing down at the rebels. Lani found herself feeling more irritated than afraid as she saw the extent of their situation— she had simply had enough of being captured.

Justin's eyes were fixed on a tall, exquisite woman who stood on an outcropping of a cliff with her head held high. Lani followed his gaze, wondering what could elicit such a jaw-dropping response from him… until she saw her. The woman wore a teal silk shirt with brown flowers embroidered in a vine-like pattern around the sleeves and body. The shirt had a u-shaped neck, trimmed in crimson piping, that would have been too low to be decent, but she wore what appeared to be a teal silk tank underneath it with highly gathered material across the bust. The top of the tank was trimmed with one-inch of brown lace, which was dotted with golden flecks that caught even the smallest light and reflected it brilliantly. The bodice was so well fitted, that it was difficult to tell if it was indeed a tank and a shirt or just one blouse. Two rows of crimson piping encircled the perfectly tailored waist, mimicking a belt. The shirt flowed freely from the waist to her mid thigh, with sheer teal-colored three-inch ruffles trimming the handkerchief bottom, which fluttered delicately in the wind. The long bell sleeves flowed with the woman's every move and her tan leggings disappeared into her knee-high tawny high-heeled leather boots. A thin brown leather strap held her quiver to her back but she had not bothered to draw her bow.

Her hair was platinum blonde and flowed down four inches past her shoulders, with shorter strands falling to frame her dainty features. Some of it blew gracefully across her face and created a slight veil effect. Her glittery green eyes sparkled fantastically in the vanishing light of the day. Her lips were a shimmering shade of pink. She carried herself with an inherent and polished grace and elegance that Lani had only ever seen before in old movies starring Grace Kelly and Audrey Hepburn.

Next to the woman, stood a tall man with a proud and confident air. His dark wavy hair was swept back and nearly touched his shoulders. His eyes were deep brown, and sparkled like those of his companion. He reminded Lani of a prince, and she sensed an air of easy command that was hard not to respect.

He wore beige-colored pants and a cream-colored linen tunic with bell sleeves that were gathered at the wrists. A teal leather waistcoat was the same length as the tunic it covered and had three straps in the front that were fastened by three golden buckles. Thick tawny knee-high leather boots complemented the ensemble. A large black leather belt held the scabbard for his sheathed sword. Across his torso was another black leather strap that held his quiver and his bow on his back. He stood with his arms crossed, looking down at the twenty rebels below.

"My name is Tierza," the woman said in a melodic, but somehow powerful voice, "High Priestess of the Mountain Elves."

"And I am Laern," the man said in a deeply resonating voice, "High Priest and joint ruler of the Mountain Elves."

Drakne rolled his eyes— elves were so egotistical.

"We have been watching you for a long time," Tierza revealed. "I saw you first deep in the Forest of Kar. But I waited to see if you could be trusted or not."

Laern continued, "When we saw you enter the Pure of Heart Sanctuary, we knew you could be, and decided to wait for you to come near our home before revealing ourselves to you."

"Wait a minute, you've been watching us since the Forest of Kar, and you never helped us out?!" Arante blurted.

"When were you in need of assistance?" Tierza asked with a delicate frown.

"Apparently you were not paying very *close* attention! You guys are elves! With your abilities, the two of you alone could have taken out everyone in Asharen's entire ambush before they could blink— not to mention the help you could have been against Drakne's men! We lost *twenty* of our people and we may lose more now, thanks to this detour! We could have gone to Destavnia the fast way with your help! We would have been there days ago at least!"

"We never saw you engage in battle. We merely saw you running away from Drakne's men and into the sanctuary. That was the only trouble that we observed, and it seemed that you had the matter well in hand."

"I knew that the elves were staying out of this war but I never knew that you were so completely and infuriatingly—"

"Arante," Jharate warned in a low tone, before turning to face Tierza. "I am Jharate, the rightful heir to the throne of Trisakne, and these are others who believe in the fight against The Great Evil."

"Ha!" Drakne laughed to himself. He quickly placed a hand over his mouth and looked around to make sure that he had not been overheard. He exhaled carefully as he realized that no one had noticed and reminded himself that he had to be a little more careful if he wanted this game to continue.

The way in which Jharate had just spoken gave Lani chills. She didn't usually remember that Jharate was a prince, despite his royal bearing, but the way he spoke now— it was more than apparent that he was among his peers and not a subordinate. This natural mastery of authority somehow sparked a deeper yearning in Lani to be his again, to feel his arms around her, to taste his lips on hers.

"And if you wouldn't mind dropping your weapons, that would be greatly appreciated," Arante said icily.

"Of course," said Tierza, looking somewhat annoyed. "I was just about to give that command."

Tierza signaled to their people on her right to lower their weapons. Laern did the same simultaneously to their people on his left. Once all of the weapons had been lowered, Tierza narrowed her eyes in on Arante. Her voice remained perfectly modulated but her tone was slightly icy.

"And you are?"

"Arante. No fancy title— I'm just his cousin and one heck of a warrior."

Arante pointed at Jharate when she mentioned her cousin.

"Charmed, I'm sure."

Tierza looked away from Arante, placed an inviting smile on her face, and changed back to her strong yet whimsical tone as she addressed the rest of them.

"You are all welcome to stay with us this night. Come, we have food and fresh water."

SOMETIMES LIFE JUST REFUSES TO ACT LIKE A CHICK FLICK

Tierza gracefully waved her hand in a beckoning motion and she and Laern led the way. As they walked, Lani felt a twinge of an emotion she couldn't quite pinpoint. It felt somewhere between rage and terror. Whatever it was, it made her mouth feel salty. She felt threatened by Tierza's presence. She was gorgeous, well spoken, and worst of all she was a new face. Lani feared Jharate might act impulsively, on the rebound, and she had been working too hard to lose him now without a fight.

Lani's thoughts were happily diverted and a sense of awe overtook her as they entered the home of the Mountain Elves. Every inch of the colossal cavern glowed with light from a white energy ball that was suspended in mid-air. Purple crystals were embedded in the ceiling in a perfect circle above what served as the center of this hidden city and reflected the light in a million places. Streets went out in all directions into large elegant tunnels like the spokes of a wheel and Lani wondered how much of the mountain this wonderland occupied.

Drakne followed at the back of the group. As the last person in front of him passed inside, Drakne hit an unseen shield and an electric charge shocked him slightly as he tried to walk through the entrance. He backed up and jerked his head to his right, cracking his neck, and rolled it back into place. He glared at the completely invisible defense system.

"Confound those woodenheaded elves!" Drakne muttered to himself.

Drakne continued to glower at the elves. They were such paranoid creatures! Apparently they had charms that protected the entrance so that only those invited in could pass, and since they could not see Drakne, he had not been invited. He would have to wait until they came out the next day. He paced back and forth in front of the entrance. Suddenly he stopped. The right corner of his mouth curved into a twisted smile. He disappeared instantly from where he stood as he teleported out to put his new plan in motion.

Once inside the safety of their home, Laern strode over to Kendra. He held his hands behind his back and leaned over slightly to the side, looking down intently at Kendra with a twinkle in his eyes and the corners of his mouth slightly upturned. He raised an eyebrow and gave her a quick glance from head to toe and back again.

"You dress very strangely."

Kendra smiled at him and gave him the same head-to-toe-and-back-again glance he had given her.

"Great pick up line. But, yes, I'm not really from around here."

"Where are you from?" Laern asked, missing the joke.

"Another world called Earth," Kendra said, with a small yawn.

Laern's eyes sparkled with excitement.

"Fascinating! I've read stories about your world but I have never had the pleasure of meeting anyone from there. Welcome to Alamea."

"Thank you. So, High Priest, huh? So does that make you Tierza's... *husband?*"

"What? Oh heavens no! She is my twin sister! Our father could not decide which of us had better ability to rule, as we had both proven ourselves worthy for the responsibility. So rather than making a choice, he left the Elven Kingdom to us both."

Kendra looked away and blushed happily, gently biting her lip.

"Oh! Well, that's good. You guys get along then, I suppose?"

"Yes, for the most part. We don't always see eye to eye, but we are quite good at coming to terms. But enough about me, I want to know about you and your world. Tell me what it is like."

"Well, I don't really know where to start. It's so different. There are buildings almost as tall as these mountains in some parts of my world. We have a ton of technology— too much actually, come to think of it. We can talk to each other, create things, play games, listen to music, and post whatever stupid thought we are thinking for anyone in the world to see on a thing called the Internet. It's really rather dysfunctional. We have a thousand ways to keep in touch, but no one ever spends time with the person sitting next to them in the room anymore.

"And if someone is really mean and immature, they can even delete their friends. Technology has really made people heartless and unfeeling with no concept for the values of friendship or for what their duties or loyalties should be as a good friend. Everything and everyone seems to be disposable, and most people don't even try to repair a long-standing relationship if even just the tiniest little thing goes wrong— even though forgiveness is one of the most basic rules of friendship and love. Honestly, I haven't missed any of that stuff. Indoor plumbing however— *that* I miss! I would do anything for a warm shower right now!"

Laern narrowed his eyes and cocked his head slightly to one side.

"I'm sorry. I bet that didn't make any sense," Kendra blushed.

"No, no, I love you. IT! IT! I meant I love *it*. I love hearing you talk. Alamea does have plumbing, by the way, but we don't have many of the other things you mentioned. Your world sounds fascinating."

Laern turned red with embarrassment, and he flashed his arresting smile with an uneasy laugh. Kendra giggled, and her green eyes lit up happily.

"My apologies. I can be such a nitwit sometimes."

"No worries, Laern. We've all done things like that before."

Lani was fighting the frown that threatened to overtake her face. She was not having fun. Jharate kept trying to talk to Tierza, right in front of her! Lani wasn't sure who she was more upset with, Jharate for flirting with another girl, or Tierza for well— existing. Jharate's continuous attempts to talk to Tierza were met with polite and civil responses, but an annoyed look lay beneath her eyes. Lani was somewhat comforted when Tierza finally made some excuse as to why she had to leave and disappeared for a moment, only to return near Justin. Lani had to fight the urge to say, "And stay away!" but she succeeded in remaining silent.

Tierza tapped Justin on the shoulder with her dainty index finger and smiled at him as he turned to face her with his mouth gaping open, eyes locked on hers.

"And what is your name, sir?"

"Oh... Um... My name is... it's..."

"Justin," Raoul piped in with a smile.

"Oh yeah! My name is Justin. Yep! That's my name..." he said, making nervous popping noise with his lips. "That's me..."

Raoul laughed and left in order to leave the two of them alone. Justin looked down and scratched his head nervously for a second but quickly put his hands in his pockets with his arms relaxed. He tilted his head a little and looked at her out of the corner of his eye, clearing his throat and lifting his head up once in casual acknowledgement. He spoke with a slightly deeper voice than normal.

"It's Tierza, right?"

Justin held his breath as he waited for her answer, desperately hoping that he had said her name right.

"Yes it is, although your accent is quite strong. What land are you from?"

Justin choked on a nervous laugh and made it sound like he was just clearing his throat again. He had never been told he had an accent before and she was the one with the accent according to his ears. She sounded very regal. He couldn't tell what her first language might have been, had she been on Earth, but he didn't care. He just loved the way she sounded. He shook his head slightly to snap his attention back to the question she had just asked him. What had it been? Something about where he was from— yeah, that was it. He smiled at her and spoke again with his slightly deeper than normal voice.

"Well, it's called the United States of America. But we call ourselves Americans."

"United States of America? I have never heard of such a place."

"It's not on this planet."

"Ah, I see. That explains the great flash of light and your sudden appearance back in the forest. That must be how you got here. It all makes sense now."

"You *saw* that?"

"Yes, I did. It was quite surprising. I was out for a hunt and I saw six of you lying on the ground. I only see five of you now. Where did the sixth go?"

"We think she got sent home."

"Well she is probably much safer now."

"Yeah, I'm sure she is."

Lani watched as Justin and Tierza hit it off. She smiled at the fact that Justin was so obviously taken with Tierza. Some of his posture and mannerisms made her laugh as he continued to flirt. Kendra's smiles crinkled her nose as she teased Laern. Lani knew from the first moment she saw Laern that Kendra would like him. He was completely Kendra's type after all— come to think of it there were probably few women who would not be attracted to Laern. He had the whole mysterious-yet-still-a-good-boy vibe going for him, along with his super model good looks, well-muscled body, and natural charms. Kendra had been searching far and wide for a guy like that on Earth, and Lani thought perhaps Kendra had finally succeeded in finding her impossibly tall order.

Meanwhile, Erik and Arante were making the most of their time together. The two of them talked and laughed freely and every now and again they would steal a kiss from one another. Lani felt a little uncomfortable watching all of this. Love was blossoming all around her. She was very happy for the individuals, but there was a deep stinging sensation in her heart as she beheld the contrast between the happy couples, and her and Jharate, everywhere she turned.

Lani saw Jharate standing against one of the far walls, his eyes on Tierza and Justin. She felt a bubbling rage inside of her. Why was he still looking at her? Tierza had made her preference obvious. Besides, Lani knew that Jharate still loved her! Whatever kind of stupid spell he was under was not wearing off fast enough— and enough was enough! Lani felt a rallying courage swell up within her and she marched directly to Jharate and launched straight into the heart of the matter.

"Haven't we both suffered long enough, Jharate?"

He gave no answer. He did not look at her. He did not even move his eyes from Tierza and Justin. Lani's hands closed into fists as she tried to keep from exploding. She exhaled slowly through pursed lips and then, with a deep breath, tried again.

"Talk to me, Jharate. I know you can. We need to stop this. It is obvious that we are meant to be together. I'm sorry I was under a spell and I messed things up, but you know what, I'm positive you are under one now. I had a vision," she said, remembering Karsenia's warning but figuring that she could safely tell him while they were alone. "You are under a spell, Jharate. Come on… Remember me! Come back to me. Let's stop wasting time. True love isn't something that you should just throw away. It's far too precious."

"You terminated the relationship with me, remember?"

"I *know*! Again, I was *under a spell*. I was stupid okay. I know that now. Can't you just forgive me and move forward?"

"You will only do it again."

His voice stayed in its normal quiet tone, but the frigidness of the words cut her worse than any knife ever could. She felt another jolt to her heart and she backed up a little as if she had been struck in the face.

"No, I won't. I didn't even know a spell could do something like that before. I didn't even know spells *existed*. I know now, so I can fight it. Give us another chance."

"No. You need to forget me, and I need to forget you. It is too late. We are simply not meant to be. We did our utmost and we failed and now it is over."

"'It's over' is the worst excuse ever! You once told me that you would never do to me what Josiah did. Why don't you keep that promise now? It doesn't have to be over. We can fix it. It's not like we cheated on each other! We just acted dumb. It happens sometimes. It's forgivable. And most importantly we *can* fix it. And you *are* under a spell! Think about it! Are you even acting like yourself? Is this how your parents raised you? Is this the person you know you have worked to become? If not, it makes sense that you are under a spell and that you should act against it and fight it!"

Lani looked at him intently, hoping against hope that appealing to his logic might trigger something in his brain if his emotions could not be reached. A glimmer returned to his eyes and he paused much longer than before.

"No, it is over. It is simply over. And you need to accept that."

"I don't want to accept that. I love you, Jharate. I love you! It doesn't have to be over. It's only over if we stop trying."

"I do not wish to repair our relationship. You will only hurt me again. And it *is* over."

With that, he walked away. She felt what little hope she had left fade as she watched his back get farther and farther away. She unconsciously leaned against the wall behind her as he disappeared from her view and stared at the point where she had last seen him. Maybe Jharate was right. Maybe she *did* need to forget him. She couldn't waste her whole life longing for the day that he *might* come back. She knew what Jharate's mother had said in the vision, but what could she do alone if Jharate refused to forgive her? She didn't have the power to remove the spell and Jharate showed no signs of getting out of it.

Lani felt tears stinging her eyes. She looked up and tried to blink them back. She didn't want to cry anymore. She was sick of it. She never used to cry before she started dating. These guys had all driven her to tears. A few of the hot tears trickled down her cheeks. *No! Pull it together! You are not going to cry!*

SOMETIMES LIFE JUST REFUSES TO ACT LIKE A CHICK FLICK

Lani defiantly wiped away the rogue tears from her cheeks that had escaped her eyes and managed to hold back the rest. But despite her outward mastery, her heart and soul were crying louder and longer than a wolf cries to the moon. Everything inside her ached for Jharate. But this couldn't go on. She decided to try to get over him. She couldn't take this pain anymore. She had given up a year of her life for him! If that wasn't good enough to break him out of whatever spell he was under, nothing ever would be. Even *after* saving his life, she had tried hard to fix their relationship— harder and longer than logic and self-respect should permit. Jharate was right— it *was* over. She officially gave up.

AS FATE WOULD HAVE IT

As morning came, the rebels arose with peaceful expressions. They had all slept more deeply than any of them had, since before they had started running. There was something mystical about the Elf Kingdom that made them feel safe. As they were in the process of gathering their things to leave, Tierza came up to them with her naturally elegant smile on her face and her sweet yet powerful tone of voice.

"My brother and I are coming with you."

Arante froze in her tracks and turned to face Tierza.

"I'm not sure you want to do that. You probably shouldn't leave your people without a leader. And we've managed this far on our own without you, so you don't have to worry about us now."

"We appreciate your concern, Arante, but Laern and I have a second in command who is more than capable of overseeing our kingdom while we help you get to Destavnia. We can easily return when we are ready to do so."

Arante's displeasure was etched into her face. She made no real attempt to cover it up either. She opened her mouth to speak again, but Jharate cut her off before she had the chance.

"We would be honored to have you both accompany us on our journey, Tierza."

Arante turned her back and rolled her eyes, tensing her hands to contain her frustration. When she was sure she had gotten a hold of herself, she turned back, just in time to see Jharate smiling intently at Tierza. Arante exhaled slowly through her lips and looked at Tierza to see what kind of a reaction Jharate's advances were receiving. The right corner of Arante's mouth went up into a smirk with a slight puff of air as she saw Tierza frowning at him. Arante smiled even wider when she heard the short, barely courteous tone with which Tierza replied.

"Thank you."

Arante had to fight back a laugh as Tierza walked away from Jharate to stand, instead, at Justin's side. She also noticed how quickly Laern found Kendra and took his place next to her, but felt indifferent about that match. However, Arante was still severely irritated. Even if Tierza was not after Jharate, she did not want her with them on their journey. Tierza was so bossy! And worse, she was useless!

Lani bit her tongue as she watched all of this. She was now one hundred percent positive that Jharate was trying to throw himself at Tierza in order to try and get over her. *Oh well.* Tierza didn't seem even the slightest bit interested, and it wasn't her fault that Jharate was behaving like such a dingbat. Lani took a deep breath and decided to try and get over her unfounded resentment of Tierza, but realized that doing so might take a while.

Justin, on the other hand, lit up as he realized that not only was Tierza by his side again, but that he wouldn't have to say goodbye just yet.

"Ah-hem!" Arante looked mainly at Erik and Lani as she spoke. "We should make it to the first town in Zenastra before nightfall. When we get there, we need to buy the five of you some different clothing, so that you won't keep calling attention to yourselves."

"Agreed," Tierza chimed in, uninvited.

Arante shot a look of complete and utter disdain at Tierza, but said nothing. She simply picked up her bag and exited the Elf Kingdom to return to the outer mountain pass. Lani and Erik kept close to Arante as she left and everyone else followed in turn. Drakne teleported back just in time to see them leaving the Elf Kingdom and began to follow them once more, still completely invisible. He had a wide smile on his face and a spring in his step.

Lani was anxious to get out of the mountain pass. She could tell everyone else felt the same way. The last part of this journey was surprisingly treacherous. They were on a vague trail in a lava field with big, black, jagged, razor-sharp rocks, which threatened to trip anyone who did not pay close attention to their every step. There was a sticky heat in this area that contrasted sharply to the cool air that the rest of the mountain pass had, and a tinge of sulfur wafted through the air. Lani saw a few rivulets of lava flowing in the distance. This only made her desire to keep on the path even stronger, for fear of a misstep plunging her through a thin volcanic crust to a horrible death.

To make matters worse, a thick fog rolled in. Lani could barely even see Raoul, who was directly in front of her. Her ears echoed with the sporadic sounds of owls hooting as they flew soundlessly, almost floating through the mist. Despite the heat that had existed only moments ago, she could feel the cool fog on her skin as droplets formed on her eyelashes and arm hair.

She wasn't dressed properly for the suddenly cooler climate, and she began to shiver as she walked forward, holding tightly onto Raoul's shoulders.

Everyone stayed close together. They knew that if they were to wander even a little bit off the trail, they would surely be hopelessly lost in the impenetrable fog. Tierza and Laern were the only ones not having difficulty. The mountains were their home and they knew every last pebble. Additionally, elven eyesight was superior to human eyesight. They were able to see quite well in the fog and so they helped keep everyone together— although Tierza had to fight the urge to let Arante wander off the trail several times.

After a seeming eternity of walking through the ominous haze, they came to where the mountains opened up. The fog began to thin and Lani could see the shape of a small town, situated on a picturesque green hill, just on the other side of the verdant green valley below. Lani's heart leapt for joy. They had finally reached the end of these wretched mountains!

Her eyes lit up and she gasped as the delightful image of the village in front of her became even clearer. She was surprised by how much it looked as if the town could have been in Spain! Creamy white stone buildings with red tile roofs dotted the gentle hillside in a winding pattern. Although it was still nearly an hour before sunset, the buildings already glowed with a tinge of red and gold.

"Stay here behind those trees!" Arante commanded. "I'll be back with clothes for you five. You need to blend into this town or you will endanger everyone."

"I completely agree," Tierza stated. "This town is very rich and full of spies. I'm coming with you."

"I don't think so! I can handle this on my own."

"I have a relationship with these people and you will get much further with my help."

"I'll take my chances!"

"You don't have a choice. You can't outrun me."

Confound it, thought Arante. Tierza was right. Elves were notoriously the fastest human-like creatures in all of Alamea. There was no escaping her.

"Fine! But follow my lead."

"I think not."

Tierza nearly skipped as she started off in the direction of the town. Arante exhaled sharply and narrowed her eyes until she could barely see. She followed after Tierza with quick angry stomps, making threatening gestures behind her back.

"There goes a happy duo," Erik stated, somewhat amused.

"I wonder which one would win in a catfight?" Raoul asked with a grin, as they followed the other rebels into the grove of trees that Arante had pointed to.

"With or without their gifts?" Justin inquired.

"Without. Just a good old fashion catfight."

"My money would be on Arante," Lani said cheerfully.

"I would not underestimate my sister. She may look like a girl, but she does not fight like one," Laern warned.

"Neither does my cousin."

Lani felt a spark in her spine as she heard Jharate's voice. It was always surprising when Jharate spoke to anyone— especially as of late. It was even more odd that he had jumped in on a conversation in which Lani was involved. Tierza was gone and the only other person he had willingly spoken to for such a long time now was Arante, and only if she was alone. So what did this mean? Lani shook her head to snap herself out of it. Not once during her entire thought process did she look at him and she decided it was best to keep it that way.

"It doesn't matter. Because if I was there, they would both lose!" Kendra insisted.

Laern smiled. Raoul and Justin burst out laughing.

"I totally believe that," Raoul chuckled.

"I think I'd like to see that fight!" Justin said with a grin. "I would watch Tierza take you both down."

"Oh yeah, Justin?" Kendra replied with a playful smile. "You're lucky this air is holding me back or I'd beat you down right now."

Kendra struggled against the air as though she were trying to escape invisible restraints that were barring her from Justin. Everyone except Jharate laughed this time.

"I wouldn't ever bet against Kendra winning," Lani said. "She has seven brothers, you know— she can take anyone down."

"At least someone knows the truth," Kendra said happily, dusting off her shoulders.

Drakne rolled his eyes. He was bored with their inane conversation and had to work very hard to resist the temptation of setting one of them on fire to entertain himself. However, he didn't want to warn them of his presence before he had the chance to carry out his plan.

Meanwhile, shopping for clothes in the gypsy village, Tierza and Arante walked along the cobblestone pathways, passing merchants selling from inside the stone buildings. These white stucco-covered buildings were dripping with ivy and burgundy flowers, which grew up the walls and were accented by a dry, greenish-grey, swamp moss that spilled from the red tile roofs and wrought iron balconies. They walked purposefully through the wide and winding passageways until they came to an enormous town square filled with decorative tents with colorful awnings.

Peddlers offered their wares as they passed and the air was filled with the smell of delicious breads and meats for sale, as well as the sound of sweet music coming from the musical instrument merchants. They pushed past the various vendors, who tried to pull them inside their places of business to sell them fine linens, intricate jewelry, strings of pearls, flowers, rare books, brand new books, maps, crystal vases, carved soaps, lotions, cooking tools, copper pots, pans, magic potions, relics of days gone by, and every other possible item of convenience or luxury. Everything that could be made out of gold *was* made out of gold— candlesticks, flatware, frames for paintings, mantle clocks, fine pocket watches, napkin rings, birdcages, goblets, and jewelry boxes were only some of the examples before them.

Despite the obvious wealth of the town, they knew it was not an honest place, and so the two women worked to keep their moneybags, which were filled with gold coins, well hidden. Arante's and Tierza's fashion sense allowed them to blend in with everyone else. Some were in stylish battle wear like they were, but most were dressed in their extravagant everyday wear. There were hundreds if not thousands of people, dressed to the hilt, shopping in this market— and though the styles varied, everyone there appeared to be rich. Tierza nodded her head in deference to the few elves that she passed, and held up one finger to her lips to indicate that they were not to approach her. They in turn bowed their heads almost imperceptibly, and immediately turned to the nearest vendor and began a conversation so that Tierza would remain unnoticed.

Through all of this, however, Tierza and Arante continued to bicker. They squabbled over everything— color, style, shape, and size.

"ALRIGHT!" Arante finally said, throwing her hands up in exasperation. "I've had enough of this! *You* go get clothes for Justin, Raoul, and Kendra, and *I* will get them for Erik and Lani. *Okay?*"

"Fine. But that is really not fair to Lani or Erik because they will not look as good as the rest of their friends."

Arante just walked away. She didn't want to start a bigger fight in public. It would call too much attention to them. It wouldn't do any good anyway because Tierza was too irrational to be reasoned with. The fashion war was on, and Arante was more than confident that she would win. Fashion was like a gift to her. Perhaps a victory in this skirmish would lead to a few peaceful hours of Tierza's humbled silence. She could think of no greater reward.

All of the rebels watched as Tierza and Arante returned. The stony silence between them was palpable. Quizzical glances were exchanged between everyone but no one voiced the questions buzzing around in their heads. With a haughty smile, Tierza handed Justin, Kendra, and Raoul the tooled leather bags, accented with embossed gold, which held their clothes. Arante quickly handed Lani and Erik their equally luxurious, almost identical, bags.

"I'll come help you with your outfit, Lani."

"Thank you, Arante."

Lani looked at her bag curiously as she wondered what could be so complicated that Arante would need to help her. The five friends all split up to find a place to change, with Arante following Lani out of sight. The rest of the rebels waited quietly where they were, hoping it wouldn't take long so that they could get where they were going before sunset.

Laern looked up with an expectant gleam in his eyes as he saw that Kendra was the first to emerge from the cover of the nearby trees and bushes. He flashed his dashing smile as she came into full view. Zenastra was the land of the gypsies and Tierza had picked out a dress made up of a burgundy velvet skirt, a blousy white satin shirt and a black velvet corset that came to a point at the bottom, with black peasant stitching in the front, laced through gold eyelets to match the scrolling gold embroidery at the top of the corset. Kendra beamed back at Laern with a light pink blush and batted her eyelashes briefly, before looking away shyly.

Raoul was next. Tierza had an approving smile on her face as she saw that she was two for two on having correctly dressed her new friends. Raoul wore the white pirate-like shirt with flamboyant sleeves well. The golden brown vest, which had three buttons to close it over the top of his shirt, added a nice touch of distinction. His brown pants looked as if they were made of high-quality tweed and his brown boots had been made from the hide of some animal. Tierza looked on proudly.

Justin emerged, dressed in his new outfit, right after Raoul. It was much like Raoul's, although the vest was black leather, as were the boots. His pants were made of a black material that resembled denim. Tierza let out a squeak of approval and clapped her hands quickly three times, before clasping them in front of her bright smile, as her handsome man came forward. He grinned at the attention— and because he knew he looked *good*.

"Thank you so much, Tierza!" Kendra exclaimed. "This dress is stunning!"

"Think nothing of it, dear. I was all too happy to help."

"This outfit is pretty cool too," Raoul said. "Thanks, Tierza."

"Again, it was no trouble at all."

"Yes, thank you, Tierza," Justin said with his deeper voice and a charming smile.

Tierza blushed in response to Justin's praise. She avoided looking at him directly as a small smile curved her pink lips.

Arante returned, standing perfectly straight with a proud expression on her face, and a knowing look in her eyes. She strode over to Raoul and then turned, looking expectantly in the direction from which she had just come. A quiet moment passed in which everyone looked at Arante with questioning glances. One or two seconds more passed until finally, Erik came into view, walking tall, with a smug yet serious look on his face.

Erik's outfit was exactly the same as Justin's, but it looked as though Arante had gotten it tailored to fit Erik perfectly. Her proud smile widened as she saw the result of her purchases. Her eye for size never failed her. And, for a touch of flair she had given him a golden chain to wear around his neck. She had also purchased a new sword and scabbard. Erik marched over to her with a cocky strut, grabbed her by the waist and kissed her quickly, imagining himself as a dashing pirate who had jumped right out of a romantic movie. As his lips left hers, he still kept hold of her waist with one arm and stared intently into her eyes.

A thousand snarky comments raced through Justin's brain all at once and he opened his mouth to release them but swallowed hard and let the remarks fall into the pit of his stomach as he realized Tierza was standing right beside him. He diverted his full attention back to her and smiled widely as she carefully straightened the collar of his shirt.

Raoul's mouth fell open and all heads turned as Lani walked out towards them with a few shy steps, and a nervous smile. Her gaze remained just to the side of anyone who was looking at her as she tried to quickly and discreetly rejoin the group. Arante beamed even more brightly as she surveyed the stunned looks on everyone else's faces. Raoul continued to stare and quickly realized, along with everyone else, that Arante clearly had an agenda beyond fashion.

"Wow, good job, Arante," Raoul whispered. "Way to make Jharate feel like the moron that he is!"

"That's the plan," Arante answered quietly with a wink.

Lani took in a deep breath and held it as she took the last few steps toward her friends. She always felt uncomfortable in the spotlight, especially in smaller groups. She tried to push the fact that all eyes were still on her from her mind as she looked at Arante with a grateful smile. Arante nodded as if to say that Lani didn't need to say anything. Lani had an intuitive feeling that Arante would rather she didn't say anything, but she mouthed a "Thank you" to her anyway and smiled again.

Lani really did love the spectacular royal-purple one-piece dress that Arante had given her, despite all the current attention it had brought. She had gasped aloud the moment she had seen it. From the instant she put it on, she had constantly had to fight the urge to sway her hips back and forth just to feel it move. The small smocked short sleeves that were gathered with metallic gold thread covered her shoulders and went about an inch farther onto her arm, which suited Lani's sense of modesty. It also had an attractive yet comfortably-shallow V-neck, with a one-inch slit at the center, and the whole neckline was trimmed with gold embroidery about a half inch wide.

Lani couldn't believe how perfectly the dress fit her and how it accentuated her small waist and curvy hips. It had always been difficult for her to find dresses that fit her due to the fact that she had a skinny little waist and a "Brazilian behind." If a dress fit her hips it was too big around her waist, and if it fit her waist she usually couldn't get it down around her hips. Lani wondered how Arante had found this dress at all, as it seemed as if only a fairy godmother could have created it.

The same smocking that was on the sleeves was used around the middle to evoke a corset-like effect from her waist to just below her bust line and the faux corset came to a point in the center at the bottom. A delicate, sheer, very-dark-purple triangular scarf was tied around her waist. Hundreds of tiny gold beads covered each and every strand of the fringe to help it hang just so. The beads glimmered with every move she made. Just below her hips the fabric of the dress exploded into an extraordinarily full silk skirt that followed her every move. The bottom of the dress had a one-inch decorative metallic gold line that wrapped around the entire skirt and shimmered in the light, as it showcased her ankles.

Arante had not forgotten to accessorize Lani's outfit either. Nor had she forgotten that hair is a big part of pulling off a look. She had bought Lani a darling purple brush with inlaid gold to match the outfit. This brush was the best brush that Lani had ever owned and it made her naturally straight hair almost as silky smooth as the Pure of Heart Sanctuary had made it. Arante had backcombed Lani's hair to get a little volume to set off the headband that held Lani's hair back from her face. The headband was made of golden vines, with delicate gold leaves and flowers that had tiny purple crystals in their centers. The halo effect made her blue eyes sparkle even more.

But Arante had not stopped there. A thick gold bracelet adorned Lani's upper arm and a set of gold bangles graced the wrist of the opposite hand. There was also a stunning gold necklace with a thin chain and an artistic pendant with a symbol that caught Lani's eye. Gold filigree twisted around a purple stone to form an upside down heart inside of an upright one. Arante had also selected clip-on earrings with teardrop-shaped amethysts, about the size of dimes, set into gold filigree settings, as well as two matching anklets for Lani. Apparently the anklets were meant to wear on both ankles at once. Amethyst pendants hung from delicate gold chains, dead center so that the bottom of the pendants nearly reached the base of her toes. They had a nice weight and a coolness that felt good against her skin but the weight was also practical for helping the pendants stay in the right place.

Lani marveled that any shoe could be this comfortable and durable while simultaneously being so aesthetically pleasing and light. The sandals Arante had chosen were made out of the softest leather that Lani had ever felt. She couldn't even feel the ground. It was like walking on pillows. They were a natural brown, with purple and gold intricate beadwork to match the dress.

Lani couldn't help smiling, but at the same time she felt a little uncomfortable with how much Arante had done. She figured that the outfit must have cost a fortune and marveled at the amount of money that Jharate and Arante must have had *before* the fall of their kingdom, if they still had this much to spare on an outfit, contest or no. But she was even more impressed with Arante's taste and skill. Lani thought to herself that if she ever got married to Jharate, which she was no longer planning on, but just in case, by some miracle, it happened— she would definitely ask Arante to plan the details!

Though Lani never looked at Jharate, Arante did. She had been watching closely. Jharate hadn't taken his eyes off of Lani since she had come into view. His eyes had widened, and followed her every step. Alas, the moment faded and he diverted his eyes to the ground. Arante sighed, and shook her head slightly as she looked away, but a grin spread across her face as she saw Tierza. Tierza had her lips shut tightly in an unhappy pout and a frustrated sigh escaped through her nose as she breathed out sharply. She turned to Arante with a civil smile on her face.

"It seems you have some talent when it comes to fashion after all."

"More than you do, that's for sure," Arante muttered under her breath.

Only Erik heard her and he laughed. He felt a burning pride within him for his sweetheart and he punctuated that pride with a sweet kiss. Arante smiled happily as she kissed him back.

"Could you two please knock that off?" Justin asked, irritably.

"No," Erik said and he kissed Arante longer.

"Oh brother! Sorry I said anything."

"Okay people, now that we're all dressed properly, maybe we should get back on track and head for Zenastra, if I have that name right?" Kendra began, hoping her interruption would stop Erik and Arante from making out in front of them. "We can't just sit here and wait for Drakne and his army to catch up with us. So we should leave now... after I get *my* earrings."

Drakne smiled. It was priceless that he was there right next to them. He was smiling for another reason too. He had always prized things of beauty and had noticed Lani's from the beginning. But the fact that she had just become even more beautiful impressed him and increased his appreciation of this trait in her. It was a shame that so much beauty was going to come to nothing. On the other hand, if she *were* the Half-Heart his master was seeking, the magic preservation would ensure that her beauty could be worshipped for centuries after her death— so perhaps it was not a complete loss.

"Yes, we should leave," Tierza said. "We know a good man here in the Gypsy Kingdom. He lives in this very town. We should stay with him for the night. Come, I will lead you there."

"I bet she will," Arante said, once again quiet enough that only Erik could hear her.

Lani drew in a surprised breath as they passed through the open-air market on the way to the home that Tierza had spoken of. Lani guessed that this had to be where Arante and Tierza had purchased their new clothing. Even though the bazaar was partially dismantled, as it was in the process of closing down for the night, it was still enchanting. There were fascinating things in every corner of every shop and stand. Shiny jewelry, elaborate hand made bags, dresses that amazed the eyes, and the food! The smell of the food was mouth-watering! Lani wished that she had both money and time because this place was a glorious world of its own. Perhaps someday, if circumstances ever changed, she would return.

They reached their destination just before sunset. When Lani had heard the word gypsy, she had imagined nomads like the gypsies on Earth. She couldn't have been more wrong. The large three-story château was set into an enchanting landscape. Its sandstone walls framed elegant French doors and arched French windows, and ornate wrought iron balconies on the second floor. Tierza went up the five, wide, rounded marble steps to the arched front door, which was elaborately decorated with wrought iron. She lifted and dropped the golden lion-head knocker.

The door opened immediately. Lani's lips unconsciously parted as the corners turned up slightly. She felt as if her breath had been stolen from her. There in the doorway stood a young man in his mid-twenties. He was six foot two, with black hair and green eyes. His rich brown skin contrasted with a flawlessly white smile that could melt ice. Their eyes met and locked.

The man did not seem to hear Tierza talking to him, nor did he acknowledge her. He stepped down directly to Lani and took her right hand with both of his and kissed it.

"You are welcome here, my lady," he said with an alluring accent, which sounded Spanish to Lani.

Lani felt her chest rise up and fall quickly. She carefully slowed her breathing, but it was difficult. The way his hands held hers was both passionate and gentle, and his left index finger stroked the inside of her wrist, almost imperceptibly. Shivers rushed up her arm to her neck.

"My name is Rezarahn. I was supposed to be king of this land before it fell. And you, beautiful lady?" Rezarahn kissed her hand once more.

"Lani."

Lani's lips barely moved as she exhaled her name. The butterflies in her stomach flew up and were now beating wildly inside of her chest. She tried to speak, but could not. His emerald eyes held her captive with his gaze.

"Lani. What an elegant name. It is only befitting that an exquisite lady such as yourself should have such a lovely name."

Rezarahn looked at her with eyes full of such passionate intensity that she felt like she was looking directly into the sun and could be blinded if she stared at him for too long. Perhaps this was her chance to get over Jharate, if such a thing were possible. She had promised Kendra to consider it, if the opportunity arose, after all. And it was refreshing to have someone not walk away from her in the middle of a sentence. Maybe it was the fact that she was on the rebound, but Rezarahn's charm, good looks, and obvious interest in her pushed her over the edge. Lani giggled like a schoolgirl.

"Come! All of you! Into my house and we shall eat! I was just sitting down for an excellent feast with some very good friends. There is always room for more. You shall be my guests as well this fine evening!"

Rezarahn bid them all in with an enthusiastic gesture, but never once took his eyes off of Lani. He led her gently by the hand, and she followed like one entranced. Jharate's jaw clenched tightly as he watched Rezarahn walking away with Lani's hand in his. His eyes narrowed slightly and he swallowed hard. He took a measured breath, shook his head a little, and looked away as they went inside.

Lani didn't notice the lovely architecture and décor around her. She didn't notice the very spacious front hall with a white marble floor and a fifty-foot ceiling. She didn't register that her favorite kind of double staircase, with wrought iron railings, led up to a landing on the upper floor. She was oblivious to the enormous crystal chandelier, which hung from a recessed dome in the ceiling. And she had nearly forgotten that there were other people following behind Rezarahn and herself as he led her directly ahead. They passed arched entryways to wings on either side, as Rezarahn continued to guide them straight ahead into a long, high hallway made entirely of glass.

Lani was aware of the glass hallway on some level, as it was too spectacular to be missed entirely. But her appreciation of the large grassy grounds, bordered by tall, sturdy, leafy trees, visible to their left, and the formal garden with hedges perfectly trimmed in scrolling designs and patterns and topiary figures to the right, was muted compared to what it would have been. She loved the charming little pebbled pathways that separated flower beds filled with burgundy crocuses and irises, white magnolias, and roses of both colors. Some of the roses, as well as some of the irises, were metallic gold in color, but even they didn't stop her in her path. And, the large cascading fountain with lilies floating in the pool at the center of the garden was quite winsome. But try as she might to take in the sights outside the glass, her eyes would inevitably drift back to the pièce de résistance holding her hand— each time with renewed warmth rushing through her veins.

At the end of the crystalline hallway they turned left through ornately carved cherrywood double doors that opened into a vast dining room. Lani's senses reawakened as she saw everything before her. It was a rectangular room, with rounded corners and a twenty-five-foot-high ceiling. Fifteen tall windows were set into three of the four walls. Chandeliers hung from three recessed domes above a u-shaped table that must have been over a hundred feet around its outer perimeter. The table was covered with a golden satin damask cloth, which draped elegantly to the floor. Garlands of crimson roses, baby's breath, and verdant green ivy lined the inner edge. Fifty cherrywood chairs upholstered with burgundy satin damask were set around the table. Each occupied place was set with gold plates, gold flatware, and delicate crystal flutes.

Thirty places had already been set— one for Rezarahn, and one for each of his twenty-nine guests, who were already seated. Rezarahn's servants quickly added twenty-two more settings to accommodate the newcomers at the two ends of the table and brought in two more chairs, one at each end. A round table holding the feast stood in the center, where servants busily retrieved food from tiered gold serving platters to accommodate each guest's request. Violinists strolled along the inner edge of the large table, gracefully dancing around the busy servants, playing sweet strains of music that soothed the soul and yet stirred the passions.

Lani's mouth watered as she saw all of the glorious food! There was roast duck, roast pig, roast beef, and roasted chicken— so fresh from the oven that steam was still visibly rising above them into the air. Deep green garnishes surrounded each of the exquisite beasts' trays, which contrasted nicely with the warm tones of the meat. Exotic fruits, unlike any Lani had ever seen, were bounteously arranged. Many of these fruit platters were more like works of art rather than something meant to be eaten.

One particular arrangement left Lani speechless. It was an arch that reached from one end of the serving table to the other. The fruits and vegetables in the arch were carved to look like different flowers, mostly roses, which sparkled with beads of water. However, there didn't seem to be anything holding them together. Lani searched for any sign of a structure, but found nothing. No skewers, no wire, no strings. She finally gave up and determined that some kind of magic was the only plausible explanation.

There were many pitchers filled with assorted juices, some red, some purple, and more curiously to Lani, was one that was bright blue. Crystal bowls, showcasing a mouthwatering fruit punch with slices of ornately carved fruit floating in it, looked especially inviting. And then there was an entire table dedicated to chocolate! White chocolate, dark chocolate, milk chocolate, chocolate caramels, chocolate-covered strawberries, chocolate-covered cookies, chocolate-covered honeycombs, chocolate cake, chocolate pastries, and much more! The feast was a wonderful sight for hungry eyes and gastronomic nirvana for empty stomachs. The food was so tempting that Drakne had to resist the urge to take some for himself several times. But he decided to forgo eating until after Rezarahn and his party exited the dining room so that he would not risk detection.

Each of the tall windows had a plush burgundy crushed velvet window seat at its base. Drakne chose one that suited him and settled in. He glanced outside. The sun had just set and so not much could be seen of the grounds besides the silhouettes of the trees that lined Rezarahn's property. However, there was a rather pleasing effect that this particular time of night afforded. As he peered through the window, he could see the golden luminous reflections of the chandeliers and the hundreds of candles set into the deep blue of the sky as if they belonged there.

"Come, you delightful apparition. You will sit by me."

"I'd be honored."

Lani smiled happily as Rezarahn continued to lead her gently by the hand to the head of the table. She looked hesitantly at Kendra and the others to make sure they didn't feel abandoned. Arante, Kendra and Tierza all waved her on enthusiastically.

Justin was too focused on the feast to notice Lani was gone and Raoul nodded mild encouragement to Lani.

"Excuse me, Tierlahn," Rezarahn said addressing a tall man who was occupying the seat next to his own, "would you mind very much getting to know one of those lovely young ladies at the other end of the table while I get to know this one?"

Tierlahn quickly searched through the females in the rebel group until his eyes fell upon Te'era's long, wavy, titian locks.

"Not only will I, but gladly. That woman is far prettier than you are, my old friend!"

Rezarahn laughed as Tierlahn made his way over to Te'era and took the seat between her and Raoul. Rezarahn's servants acted quickly to bring a new place setting for the spot Tierlahn had just vacated. Rezarahn pulled Lani's chair out for her. Lani beamed. She had always loved chivalry and good manners. Her past boyfriends had always opened doors for her. They had also done other things like putting their jacket around her when she was cold, helping her out of the car, and offering their arm when they walked together— partly because they knew she loved that kind of behavior, and partly because some of them had been raised the right way by their mothers. However, Rezarahn's manners were impeccable and flowed so naturally that she knew without a doubt that this was the way in which he always behaved.

"Excuse me, Rezarahn," Lani began, "I do not drink alcoholic beverages, and I am not familiar with all of the drinks you have available. Would you be so kind as to inform me if there are any I should avoid?"

"There are none, dear lady. I do not allow alcohol in this home. I do not consume it. I like to keep a clear head at all times, and I despise being the only sober one in the room."

"We have that in common. Thank you," Lani said with a shy smile.

They all feasted until they could eat no more, except for Justin. He continued joyfully past the point where he couldn't eat another bite. Only Jharate seemed to have a smaller than normal appetite. Rezarahn and Lani had been talking the entire night away— laughing, smiling, and flirting all the while. Since Arante and Tierza had asked them all to blend in, Lani skillfully directed the conversation away from anything to do with Earth. She focused instead on asking Rezarahn questions about himself, which he answered easily and cheerfully. He found himself as fascinated by her personality as she found herself astounded by his many adventures. He was truly a daring man. One story in particular left a strong impression on her mind as he related the tale.

"I was sixteen when my kingdom fell. However, I did not let that stop me from rebelling in secret. I will never forget the seventeenth year of the day of my birth, may I live to be one hundred years old! Three of my closest friends and I decided that the best way to celebrate would be to assault one of Vranah's caravans. It was full of riches that had been stolen from our kingdom to help finance his war with Kelamosa. Our people were suffering greatly from the devastation of the recent fall. We could not bear the thought of good Zenastrans starving while the then General Asharen was becoming wealthy from appropriating portions of stolen Zenastran treasure."

Lani flinched at the mere mention of that name. She recovered quickly and tried to hide her reaction with an interested smile. Rezarahn lifted one eyebrow slightly and glanced in her direction— but it was obvious that she did not wish to talk about whatever the painful memory was. He returned his face to his normal expression and pretended to have seen nothing so as to avoid making her even more uncomfortable and instead, continued with his tale.

"None of us had yet reached our twentieth year. The four of us dressed as Trisaknen robbers and raided the entire caravan. We recovered all of the gold and jewelry they had stolen and tied the guards to nearby trees where we painted their faces with the colors of Trisakne. We then took what riches they each had on their person just for good measure!"

Rezarahn laughed heartily, as did every friend he had within earshot, but his eyes twinkled brighter when he saw Lani's smile, and the light shining in her blue eyes. He smiled back at her before continuing his story.

"We returned to our village to disperse the riches to their rightful owners and gave away the additional plunder we had managed to attain during the raid. To that end, I took great pleasure in giving a pocket watch, which I had taken from one of the guards, to a particularly needy family. I also returned their only prized possession, which that same guard had just stolen from them. The widow and her five children had almost no belongings whatsoever and had tears of gratitude in their eyes. If I remember correctly, the precious item the guard had stolen was the widow's great grandmother's wedding ring. Vranah's men are so crass!"

Drakne arched one eyebrow high. He hadn't been aware of Rezarahn's youthful escapades. He would most certainly bring this to Vranah's attention later. No doubt Vranah would want to deal with him personally.

"Dancing!" Rezarahn called, clapping his hands twice sharply. "We will have dancing! Follow me, my dear lady."

Rezarahn reached out his hand for Lani's and she gently placed her own in his. They exited the dining room, crossed the hallway and passed through another set of open double doors into a fabulous ballroom. Lani gasped in awe as she tried to take in every aspect of the wonder before her. The ballroom had parquet flooring that added warmth to the mostly cream-colored room. The outer walls matched those of the dining room, with fifteen tall windows set into three of the walls— except the window seats were upholstered in metallic-gold crushed velvet instead of burgundy. There were white pillars along the walls of the room, with gold leaf accents on their crown molding. Each pillar was adorned with an elaborate golden sconce, which held fifteen long white candles at three different levels.

Not one, but two gold chandeliers hung from the domed ceiling, which was painted in vivid colors with scenes from Zenastran history, evoking a strong sense of the culture. The ceiling's frescoes, bordered by carved giltwood in intricate scrolls and rose designs, reminded Lani of the Sistine Chapel.

The orchestra sat in one corner with their instruments in the ready position. The instruments resembled violins, tambourines, castanets, and guitars. Lani was again struck by the similarities between this people and the gypsies on Earth. She seemed to remember that one of the gypsy cultures was thought to have originated from Egypt and wondered if that is how some of the similarities had come about. She thought it was a very remarkable combination to have the wealth and grandeur of the Schönbrunn Palace and the culture of a people similar to those she had previously believed only to be nomadic. The music that began to play as they entered had a decidedly gypsy flair, and instantly reminded Lani of Pablo de Sarasate's *Zigeunerweisen*, which was one of her favorite compositions.

"Will you dance, my lady?"

Lani caught Jharate's eye at that exact moment. She could have kicked herself for feeling this way, but she still would rather have been in his arms on the dance floor. He looked jealous, but she could tell he would not ask her, himself, if she passed up dancing with Rezarahn. She looked away from Jharate and into Rezarahn's brilliant green eyes with a determined look.

"I would love to."

"Splendid!"

Rezarahn beamed and his smile sent heat racing through her veins again and a shudder down her spine. He clapped his hands once more and the conductor changed the music to a rhythmic song that reminded Lani more of Jeff Linsky's *Murietta's Farewell.* Rezarahn twirled Lani commandingly into position. He pulled her waist close to his body with his right and held her firmly as his left outstretched to grab her right hand. She placed her left hand on his shoulder and her right in his offered hand as if she had been enchanted to do so, her eyes locked on his.

The slow melodic music was as seductive as the man who had brought her to the floor. It flowed through her body and into her very soul. Although she did not know the dance, it did not matter. Rezarahn was such a good leader that he could make her go wherever he wanted to. Lani had always loved a man who could lead— partly because it made her look like a better dancer than she actually was and partly because it was just so manly.

Rezarahn stopped suddenly. Lani followed. He led her upper body with his in a slow fluid swirling motion until he leaned forward, dipping her as she arched her back gracefully. He brought her back up and twirled her into his arms, standing behind her and holding both of her hands. Rezarahn leaned in close to her neck.

Lani could feel his warm breath caressing her neck. Her eyes fluttered closed with a sigh. His lips brushed the side of her neck near her jaw line for the tiniest second, making her unsure if it had been intentional. Sparks flew from her neck to every inch of her body as she melted into his arms while they swayed back and forth in place. He spun her out to face him and pulled her back into the position they had begun with, with his right hand, once again, securely on her waist. Three steps back, three to the side, three to the front, and three more to the other side, over and over again in a wonderful pattern broken only by the pausing sways that thrilled her so.

"Lani looks like she's having fun, doesn't she Raoul?" Justin asked. "It's funny how klutzy she can be when we play volleyball, but whenever she starts dancing she suddenly has control of her body again."

"Hey! That's not nice to call her klutzy!" Raoul retorted.

"I'm just sayin'! Sheesh, don't get so hung up on my words! It's just kinda weird."

"Lani is not weird!"

"Never mind!"

"Would you like to dance?" Erik asked Arante.

"I thought you would never ask," she answered, batting her eyelashes and curtsying.

Justin raised an eyebrow. He did not think of Arante as a girl who would curtsy. Arante saw him but paid him no mind. She and Erik bounded onto the floor together. Arante did most of the leading, as she knew the dance and also because she was just naturally a little more aggressive than Erik was.

"Oh enchanting goddess of beauty, may I have the honor of this dance?" Laern asked Kendra.

Kendra blushed gleefully. She could tell that although his invitation sounded over the top, Laern was completely sincere.

"Of course!"

Justin asked Tierza to dance shortly after that and Tierlahn asked Te'era. Not wanting to be left out, Raoul asked one of the few remaining female rebels to dance with him as the rest of the dinner party took to the dance floor. Soon Jharate was alone, standing on the side, watching Lani with his penetrating stare. His eyes never left her as she danced in Rezarahn's arms. Every muscle was tense. His breathing consisted mainly of slow inhales, followed by a long pause as he held his breath, and then a tempered exhale through his nearly closed lips. As the smiles graced Lani's face his discomfort visibly increased. Suddenly, Jharate marched straight up to Rezarahn and touched his shoulder.

"May I cut in, Prince Rezarahn?"

Rezarahn's jaw tightened and one of his eyes twitched as he looked at Jharate. He gave a close-lipped smile and tried to appear as normal as possible before answering.

"Of course, Prince Jharate. Lani, may I ask for the honor of the next dance?"

"Yes, I'd like that very much."

Rezarahn released his hold on Lani and kissed her right hand before placing it in Jharate's left. He turned away and walked quickly off the dance floor. Lani put her left hand on Jharate's shoulder as he grabbed her waist with his right and began to lead her in the dance. She looked up at him with a quizzical expression on her face as she narrowed her eyes. She felt surprised that he had come up at all, but she also felt a vestigial anger, threatening to reignite and explode if she didn't contain it. How dare he interrupt her dance? What could he possibly be thinking? He had made his feelings perfectly clear to her earlier… Did this mean that maybe… he was changing his mind? Was it possible the spell was getting weaker?

As the dance continued she felt her spirit cool a little. The familiarity of his touch slowly overtook her and her expression softened. The corners of her mouth curved up into a placid smile, and with a sigh, the look in her eyes melted into a wonderstruck gaze. The way that Jharate took her in his arms was resolute and passionate. He was always so gentle with her and the way that he touched her and now was no exception, but there was no mistaking that he was in charge.

Lani's heart leapt and her blood ran infinitely hotter through her veins than it had for Rezarahn. Jharate was quite a good dancer, but he was not very familiar with this dance and so he lacked the confidence that Rezarahn had. It was a little harder for her to follow him, but she didn't care. Her little piece of Heaven had returned. She was so ready to believe this was it, but she wanted to make sure there was no misunderstanding.

"Does this mean you want me back?"

Jharate halted in his tracks, so quickly that she had to take an extra step to keep from losing her balance. Neither of them moved a muscle and she held her breath as she waited for an answer. He looked intently into her eyes.

"No."

He dropped her hand, turned his back on her, and walked away in the middle of the song, leaving Lani standing where they had stopped, her right hand still hanging in the air. Drakne walked into the room licking his fingers. The food had been exquisite and well worth the wait. He smiled widely as he realized that the timing of his entrance had been perfect. The surprised and hurt look on Lani's face as Jharate walked away meant that his spell was holding Jharate exactly where he wanted him. He hadn't even had to boost it once the entire time! Drakne once again took a bow for his work.

Rezarahn pulled away from the wall he had been leaning against with a stunned look on his face. Lani looked as if she were on the verge of tears as she slowly lowered her hand, still staring at the spot where Jharate had been. She seemed like she had just had the wind knocked out of her and as though she might faint. Rezarahn swooped in rapidly to return to her side. He gently placed his hand on her cheek. She closed her tear brimmed eyes and leaned into his touch.

"The man is a cad! No gentleman in his right mind would leave a lady on the ballroom floor without a partner— especially one as extraordinary as you."

Lani opened her eyes and delicately blinked the tears back. Rezarahn gently wiped away the ones that had escaped. She forced a smile to acknowledge Rezarahn's chivalry. His gentleness had taken the edge off, but the torn pieces of her heart were still throbbing. For the slightest second she had thought... but it was over. She shook her head a little and forced the smile even wider. The cruel display from Jharate was not going to ruin her night!

Rezarahn took her hand and gently twirled her into position on the dance floor, as a much slower song began to play. Lani took a deep breath, and used the time the slower song afforded to regain the feelings she had been enjoying before Jharate had cut in on her dance with Rezarahn. By the time the much quicker notes of the next song began, she was back. She laughed and smiled as much as she could— trying to make every moment count and to revel in the wonderful people, the beautiful surroundings, and the handsome man who was holding her in his arms.

Late evening came, and the ball was still going strong. Rezarahn spun Lani out, and pulled her back in, concluding with a fiery dip that ended powerfully on the last note of the song. Lani arched back like she had seen tango dancers do before, counting on Rezarahn to keep her from falling, and held her pose until Rezarahn gently lifted her back up again. She was nearly out of breath from all of the dancing, but the smile on her face was free and easy. Rezarahn smiled in return and offered his arm to her.

Lani took it and followed as he led her out onto the enormous semicircular terrace with a white marble floor, which extended the length of the building. She breathed in deeply and the cool night air filled her lungs and cooled her skin. Beyond providing the much-needed air, this terrace seemed to emit a calm and soothing feeling that penetrated her soul. Lani's eyes began to feel heavy, and she struggled to keep them open as long as she could. She didn't want this night to end, but apparently the Sandman had other plans. When she felt she couldn't last another minute, she turned to Rezarahn with a smile.

"Thank you so much for tonight. I've had a wonderful time… but I'm feeling a little tired now."

"My apologies for not noticing sooner, dear lady! Your presence captivated me so that I have forgotten my manners. You must be exhausted after your long journey. Come with me. If you will permit me, I do wish to show you something before you retire. However, I promise it will not require your presence for a protracted amount of time and then I will show you directly to your chambers."

Lani nodded gently with a curious gleam in her eyes. Her inquisitiveness infused a tiny bit of energy that would sustain her long enough to discover the means of satisfying it. She held the arm that Rezarahn offered as he led her back through the ballroom and out into the glass hallway.

Drakne watched as Lani and Rezarahn left but there was no pressing need to follow her. It wasn't as if she were walking out arm in arm with Jharate. She would be easily found again later. He turned his attention back to the ballroom and grinned. There were so many possibilities. The good food and his success in keeping Jharate and Lani apart had made him almost happy and now he felt that he had earned the right to amuse himself. Drakne waved his hand and a few dancers tripped on the floor.

Drakne laughed freely, but tried to keep somewhat quiet so that no one would detect him over the music. It had been too long since he had allowed himself to have any fun. He locked his fingers together and stretched them out— cracking all his knuckles simultaneously. He rubbed his palms together, with an ever widening smile on his face, and randomly threw a bunch of miniature spell balls at people to make them do stupid things. He was careful to make sure that he properly timed throwing them so that no one would see them flying through the air before they could hit his targets. He also kept the balls small enough that no one would feel them enter their bodies.

Drakne chuckled as one of his spell balls forced one of Rezarahn's guests to laugh loudly with huge echoing snorts despite her best efforts to stop. His sniggering increased as another guest started commentating from the sidelines on everything that was taking place on the dance floor. Still others slipped or fell out of sync with their dance partners. Drakne laughed even harder as the last of these tiny spells landed on Raoul's dance partner. The spell made her believe that Raoul had done something inappropriate and she slapped him and walked away. Stunned, Raoul stood there blinking, wondering what he had done wrong.

Drakne sighed to quell his laughter and went through a door in the corner, near the entrance of the ballroom, into the kitchen to see what he might accomplish there. The fire was still going in the massive fireplace and meat was turning on the spit. One green spell ball later and the main fire blazed into a sudden inferno. Dishes went crashing everywhere and several additional unintentional fires ignited, sending the servants into a frenzy. Drakne returned to the ballroom laughing so hard his sides ached.

This time, there was so much noise that Drakne allowed himself to let his laughter run its course, and then regained his normal composure with several deep breaths. He would have done more but he was afraid too much interference would call attention to himself. However, when a waiter came in carrying a tray full of sparkling water, Drakne was unable to resist. He tripped the waiter with his invisible foot and watched as the crystal glasses went crashing spectacularly to the floor. Drakne chuckled briefly and told himself that this had to be the last one for now.

Rezarahn led Lani back to the archways they had passed on their way to the ballroom and chose the archway on the left. He guided her down another large hallway to an already open, ornately carved double doorway and into a darkened room.

"Excuse me for just a moment."

Rezarahn kissed her hand and disappeared into the shadows. Lani stayed where she was, peering into the dark room, feeling her curiosity growing with every second. She was surprised by how calm and safe she felt with Rezarahn. She stared intently in the direction he had vanished, and when he turned the gas lighting on, his smiling face was the first thing she saw. She turned to see what he wanted to show her and beheld a magnificent library.

Her eyes darted excitedly from corner to corner, scanning the leather-bound books on hundreds of shelves around the perimeter of a room, which was nearly as large as the ballroom. Ladders with wheels on the main floor made the higher shelves accessible and two spiral staircases led up to railed walkways that surrounded the entire room, with more wheeled ladders, to reach the uppermost shelves on the second floor. Lani had always dreamed of a library like this!

"You are a woman with a remarkably keen mind and so I thought you might appreciate this."

"Oh it's breathtaking! Thank you so much for bringing me here!"

Rezarahn walked until he stood directly behind her. He ran his hands slowly down her arms and leaned his lips close to her ear.

"What are you waiting for? Go. Look at anything you desire."

Lani felt shivers flow down her arms as he touched them, and the way his breath warmed her ear— she closed her eyes briefly to soak it in. The sparks and thrills he had been giving her all night flooded through her body once again. With a gentle push in the right direction from Rezarahn, she remembered where she was.

She lit up and rushed to start thumbing through the books before her. The fatigue she had been feeling fled from her body as she dashed around like a kid in a candy store looking at book after book, unsure of which one she would like to read first. She was surprised to find that they were all in English. She concluded that the same spell, which translated spoken language here in Alamea, must be what allowed her to read these materials.

Rezarahn laughed delightedly as he watched her lose herself in the books. He grabbed a book of poetry and sat in an over-sized burgundy-velvet wingback chair to read, with one of his black-leather-boot-clad legs draped over one of its arms. He turned several pages and settled into his chair as he found what he wanted to read.

As Lani ran halfway up one of the staircases, something caught her attention from the corner of her eye. There on a stand a little ways from the back of the cushy chair Rezarahn was lounging in, was a sizable leather-bound book. The light directly above it seemed to get brighter for one instant. She blinked and the brighter light was gone. She ran back down the stairs and approached the stand.

Its aged pages and musty smell indicated that it was quite ancient. However, it was very well preserved. She opened it and a puff of white sparkling dust flew out of it in a small swirling cloud. Lani reviewed the first page with her eyes widening as she read.

We, the highest order of the Mountain Elves create this book in the year fifteen hundred and four. Therefore it is written in the language of our ancestors, in Elven script. It is a complete history of the seven Kingdoms of Alamea. This book carries the enchantment of continuance, therefore the book itself will add to these carefully crafted pages whenever it deems something worthy of being recorded therein from now until the end of time. This book carries knowledge— knowledge that is both important and enlightening. The destruction of any portion of this book will bring a dire curse upon the hand that defiled it. With that final warning we bid the reader welcome to this tome.

Lani turned the pages as her heart beat with excitement. The elaborate hand-drawn illustrations had such rich use of color and meticulous attention to detail that it could compare with the illuminated manuscripts of the monasteries on Earth. She felt privileged and honored to be standing here looking through this historical masterpiece. She continued to turn through the pages with no particular purpose in mind until suddenly she felt compelled to stop and read.

The fair Kingdom of Lanas was last ruled by King Lazeka and Queen Lassaria Arvanatasi. King Lazeka came from a long and proud line of extraordinary rulers. Lazeka and his queen ruled in peace until the day that Vranah plotted to overthrow their kingdom. They fought valiantly for years, but in the end, they were unable to defend against the ever-growing army of evil. Lanas fell. Both the King and the Queen were put to death for treason against The Master of all Darkness.

Perhaps the greatest mystery associated with the Arvanatasi family is that of the fate of their twin daughters, Adrienne Brielle and Alena Brichette— Adrienne being the eldest and The Heiress Apparent to the once great Kingdom of Lanas. Adrienne and Alena disappeared one year before the fall of their kingdom. No bodies were found and no trace of their continued existence was ever discovered.

Lani touched the book unconsciously with her hand. Her eyes closed. When she opened them again her surroundings had changed. She had no idea where she was. It was extremely dark, with only a few torches burning on the walls. Lani squinted to see better and realized she was standing in a throne room. A purple banner with a golden embroidered crest hung on the wall. She tried to get a closer look at the crest to see what it represented but was distracted by a familiar voice whispering intently behind her. Lani turned and saw Jharate's mother standing there, speaking with a king and queen Lani did not recognize.

"Lazeka, Lassaria, I know I am asking a great deal of you— however, you must trust me. I have had a vision that if they remain with you, they will die. I can save their lives if I leave now under the cover of this moonless night. I can take them so far away that Vranah will never find them. You must believe me. There is no time to lose."

"You know I trust you implicitly Karsenia or we would be asleep in our chambers and not here in our throne room listening to you at this ghostly hour. But these are our only children. For ten years I thought I was barren. Conceiving was a miracle and now they are everything to us! Our daughters... they are not even yet one year of age! There is so much we wanted to share with them. They are destined to inherit our kingdom!"

"Yes I know, Lassaria. I am deeply and truly sorry to be the bearer of this sorrowful news. I can scarcely imagine how I would feel in your same situation. However, it is precisely because they are everything to you that you must let me take them. As you know I have two young children of my own, Jharate and Khanye. I love them more than life itself. But if I knew they would die if they stayed with me, I would let them go in the time it takes for one beat of my heart. You know I would not ask you to do something so devastatingly painful if there were any other way."

"Can you guarantee their safety?" Lazeka asked firmly.

"I can guarantee it up until their twenty-first birthday. Past then, their future is unclear."

Lani thought Lassaria couldn't be more than thirty years old and Lazeka not much older than she. Lani's hand moved to her heart as she looked at the forlorn faces of this couple. What an awful choice to be forced to make! Lani didn't know what she would do in that same situation but she dearly hoped that she would never have to find out. Lazeka turned to his lovely wife and knelt before her.

"That is at least twenty more years than if they stay with us, my darling. We have both witnessed the fulfillment of Karsenia's visions before. She is never wrong. I fear we must let her take them."

"Very well," Lassaria said, as tears formed quickly and spilled from her blue eyes.

Lassaria held her sleeping children close to her for the last time and kissed them both. Lazeka joined her. They carefully handed their most prized treasures over to Karsenia, hands still outstretched toward their daughters even after letting go.

"Take care of my children," Lassaria pleaded.

"I will," Karsenia promised solemnly.

Lassaria threw herself into Lazeka's arms and sobbed while he held her close, as Karsenia stole carefully away. Lazeka and Lassaria faded away into the distance as Lani's vision pulled Lani away from the throne room to follow Karsenia to a large banyan tree grove outside of the royal couple's castle. Lani wiped the tears from her eyes and returned her attention to the vision. Karsenia was tense, and looked over her shoulder every few seconds. Once she seemed assured that no one could see her, there was a great flash of light and a noise like a clap of thunder. Lani jolted back a little in surprise.

She blinked to adjust to the new scenery. Karsenia was now outside of a very, very familiar structure. Of course! It was her house! It had been brand new then and none of the landscaping had been planted yet, but it was definitely her home. Lani's eyes widened as she followed Karsenia and saw her knock on the door. Lani's parents answered, looking very young and extremely sleepy.

"It's three in the morning," Mr. Johnson complained.

"I apologize for the lateness of the hour. Here is the eldest daughter— the one you agreed to take in. You will have to arrange to get her birth certificate and all the necessary papers. I cannot thank you enough. You may never know how important what you are doing is."

Karsenia quickly handed Adrienne to Mrs. Johnson and walked away, disappearing into the darkness with the other child still in her arms.

"What shall we call her?" Mr. Johnson asked.

"I've always liked the name Lani," Mrs. Johnson answered.

"Lani? I like that. Lani it is," Mr. Johnson declared with a yawn.

Lani gasped! So this is how she had come into her family? She would have never guessed what a daring thing it had been for her mom and dad to adopt her, nor what a horrible sacrifice her biological parents had been forced to make in order to save her life. Lani felt a wave of emotions sweep over her so fast and so hard that she wasn't even sure what half of them were. She didn't have time to figure them out though, because apparently the vision wasn't over yet. Lani watched as Karsenia repeated the same procedure outside of another home that she identified quickly. It was Kendra's house! *What?!*

Kendra's mother came to the door with two of her sons clinging to her nightdress. Mrs. Sanchez took the baby in her arms as Karsenia handed it to her. Lani barely heard any of the words Karsenia said as she thanked Mrs. Sanchez and repeated the instructions she had given to the Johnson family before once again disappearing into the night. Lani shook her head a little as she saw the second to oldest brother tugging at his mother's nightdress.

"What's her name, mama?"

"Her name is Kendra. Would you like to see her, Luke?"

"Yes!"

"Me too Mamma, me too!" exclaimed the smaller of the two boys.

Lani's mouth fell open. She was completely dumfounded. Kendra was her sister! Not just her sister, her twin! She had no idea how to even begin to process all of this. She suddenly wondered where the oldest brother was— probably asleep. Wait, if Kendra was her sister then that made all of Kendra's brothers kind of like stepbrothers. She knew that Luke was no relation to her, but her previous crush on him during her freshman and sophomore years of high school suddenly felt a little weird. One more reason it was a good thing that never worked out.

Snap out of it, Lani, she thought to herself. She wasn't sure why her mind was trying to answer all of the stupid questions when there were so many legitimate ones to be asked. The vision ended abruptly and she jumped slightly as she realized Rezarahn was standing directly in front of her, staring at her with a worried expression on his gorgeous face.

"I did not mean to startle you, dear lady. When I saw you standing here with your eyes closed, I feared that something might be wrong. Are you quite all right?"

Lani blinked at him blankly and thought for a moment. She wasn't really sure what she could tell him. Another moment passed in silence before she realized she still hadn't answered him.

"Oh... yes, I'm alright... thank you. Sorry. I am very tired though. Will you please be kind enough to escort me to where I am to sleep?"

"Of course."

Rezarahn took her hand and led her back down the hallway and turned into the main entryway of his château. He carefully guided her up one side of the grand double staircase. To Lani's great relief, Rezarahn stopped in front of the first door in the right wing of the second floor. She didn't think she could have managed another step. At the same time, she suddenly felt a sinking feeling— the night was really over. But what a night it had been! Lani let her hand linger in Rezarahn's and smiled sweetly at him.

"Thank you, Prince Rezarahn. Thank you for everything. You have been such a gentleman and I have enjoyed every moment with you. You have given me one of the best nights of my life at a time when I didn't expect something wonderful to happen. I guess this is the part where we say goodnight."

"Very well, my lovely lady. And please, call me Rezarahn. The pleasure has truly been all mine. May angels sing you to your sleep and may your dreams be filled with all that your heart desires."

Rezarahn bowed, kissed her hand briefly once more, and turned to go. Lani unconsciously cradled the hand he had just kissed as she watched him walk away. He stopped on the top stair and looked back at her with his dashing smile. She giggled. When she noticed he wasn't leaving, she realized he must be waiting to make sure she got in safely. She fumbled for the doorknob and waved goodnight with the other hand as she bit her lip gently and opened the door. She walked inside, closed the door behind her, and leaned against it with a happy sigh, looking up at the ceiling with a smile that radiated from within.

"Well I know *you* had fun!" Kendra said with a giggle. "I approve! I give you permission to like him. You have liked much worse."

"He's *handsome!*" Arante said. "Good choice."

"I agree," Tierza chimed in.

Arante shot Tierza a look that very clearly said, *nobody asked you.*

"What?" Lani asked as she realized they had been talking to her. "Oh, Rezarahn. Yes, he's very nice."

"Nice?!" Arante asked in an exasperated tone as she held up her fingers one at a time, beginning with her pinky, as she continued. "He's sexy, he's smart, he's a superb gentleman, and oh yeah— He's rich! What part am I missing? He's perfect!" Arante threw up her hands and looked incredulously at Lani.

"Yes, like I said, he's *very* nice. Sorry, there's just something else on my mind."

"Like what?!" Arante exclaimed.

Lani didn't seem to hear her as she turned to Kendra.

"Kendra! I just had a vision! You won't believe it!"

Lani did a double take and finally snapped into the present as she noticed, to her great excitement, that there were real beds! Four of them! She smiled widely as she saw that they were covered with plushy pillows and layered a foot high with luxuriously fluffy white down comforters, covered in satin! Oh how they would feel! Just then, she caught a glimpse of an old-fashioned porcelain bathtub with gold faucets and gold imperial feet, through a door that connected to their room. She couldn't even imagine how great a bath would feel after having only showers on the run for so long!

She felt another surge of happiness rush through her. She had been given so many reasons to be happy this night and all thanks to Rezarahn. What a night it had been! Lani ran over and leapt onto the bed that the other three girls were already sitting on. Their skin glowed and they all smelled of lavender. They were dressed in long white satin nightgowns with cap sleeves, which had been provided for all of them. Lani faced Kendra and grabbed both of her hands, barely able to contain her enthusiasm.

"Does it involve you and Monsieur Charming wearing white and exchanging vows?" Kendra asked with an impish grin.

"No, but it *is* big news. Kendra, you are my twin sister! We're from Lanas originally, one of the kingdoms here, and your name was Alena Brichette and mine was Adrienne Brielle. We are the daughters of the former King and Queen!"

"What?" all three girls exclaimed in unison. Kendra's eyes grew wide with surprise.

"*Shut up!*"

"For realz, Kendra! I'm not kidding!" Lani answered hugging her.

"You two have been missing for decades!" Arante marveled.

"That explains it," Tierza said. "You were taken to Earth! That's why no one ever found you! This is fantastic!"

"NO WAY! Well, I always knew I was a princess," Kendra giggled.

"Oh, and you know how you always teased me for being younger than you, even though we are like the same age? Guess what? I'm the older one! Ha!"

"I can't be younger!"

"*That* you have a hard time believing, but you're not shocked at the fact that we're sisters from a royal line on a completely different planet than the one we thought we were born on?"

"We were already like sisters. And like I said, I always knew I was a princess. But you being older? Now *that's* crazy!"

Lani grabbed a pillow off the bed and gently smacked Kendra upside the head, with a huge smile on her face.

"Oh now it's on!" Kendra yelled with a grin.

Kendra grabbed a pillow of her own and sprang off the bed and whacked Lani as she tried to run away. Lani laughed and swung back, hitting Kendra in the stomach and ran up over another bed to escape retaliation. Kendra followed quickly, cornered Lani, hit her again, and then retreated as Lani advanced. Arante and Tierza stayed seated on the original bed and looked at Kendra and Lani with their eyebrows raised questioningly as the two continued to play. It was obvious from the smiles and the laughter that this was well intentioned, but it seemed an odd custom.

The right corner of Arante's mouth curled up into a smirk as she grabbed a pillow and hit Tierza with it. Tierza's mouth flew open as if she were about to launch into a speech on etiquette, but she refrained and instead swatted at Arante with a nearby pillow, who ducked and avoided her hit, smiling widely. Tierza redoubled her efforts and then used her Elven speed to mess with Arante. The two sets of girls continued the pillow fights with riotous giggles all around as the two games eventually became one, and the pillows started breaking open. As feathers started to escape they all froze and looked at each other with startled, somewhat worried expressions.

"It's okay," Tierza assured with a mischievous smile. "I can use my Elven speed to pick up all the feathers and sew all the pillows back up as good as new. It will only take me a few minutes."

"Works for me!" Kendra exclaimed as she smacked Arante in the back of the head.

They all started up again with squeals of laughter and even more enthusiasm, ignoring the feathers that were now flying everywhere like falling snow.

It was a perfect moment— for Drakne. A sinister smile twisted up on his face. He had snuck in past Lani when Rezarahn had been saying goodnight— they had taken so long to say goodbye that it hadn't been hard. But now he was ever so glad that he had done so. He had heard her real name and he knew that information would be priceless to Vranah. Drakne could barely contain his delight.

"Adrienne Brielle Arvanatasi? She has been missing so long. I wonder…"

Drakne folded his arms and then tapped his lips with the tip of his once-again-gloved index finger a couple of times as he saw the pillow fight before him— without really registering that it was going on. Drakne did not want to jeopardize his holiday. He knew that if he simply asked Vranah for the information he sought that Vranah would order him to return immediately and would not let him finish his game. His plan was too brilliant to allow it to be changed even one iota and it would be so much more satisfying than the quick end he knew Vranah would demand.

A thought came to him. He knew where Vranah currently kept his list of Half-Hearts. In fact he always knew where it was located, despite what Vranah thought— he had just never had a reason to risk looking at it before now. Sneaking a quick look at the list was the only way to both satisfy his curiosity *and* make sure that his fun was not cut short. He would go this very instant and see if Lani was the one he was seeking after all. Drakne smiled once again as he thought— *This couldn't have been easier.*

Drakne teleported back inside the castle in Trisakne. He looked around cautiously. He knew his invisibility would not be enough to fool his master for long. He had to act quickly. Vranah liked keeping the chest, which held the Half-Hearts list, close to him at all times. Therefore the only place that made any sense in this castle was the throne room. Drakne glided up the stairs leading up to the throne room in perfect silence. What luck! Vranah was not here at the moment.

Drakne quickly crossed over to one of the two thrones. He peered behind it and sure enough, hidden in a little niche in the throne was a small golden box with the same heart in heart design as the doorknob of the coffin room. Drakne scoffed. It was amazing how arrogant Vranah was to think that no one would dare look at this list. It wasn't protected in the least. Drakne bent down and opened the lid to the tiny chest and a small cloud of golden dust and light erupted from it. He reached inside to grab the scroll, which seemed as if it, too, were made of gold, and unrolled it.

Khanye Inihma....... Terminated
Sarana Kinartma.... Terminated
Narah Deskarin..... Terminated

Yes, yes, I know all these, Drakne thought. His eyes scrolled through the list of irrelevant remaining names until he found the one he sought.

Adrienne Brielle Arvanatasi..... Whereabouts unknown.

Drakne grinned. Ha! Her whereabouts were not unknown now! He had her! But there was another name below hers that caught his eye. His grin was replaced with a puzzled expression. Why had Vranah allowed this particular Half-Heart to live for so long? Drakne flinched at a sound behind him. He hastily replaced the list exactly as he had found it and teleported back to Rezarahn's home.

WHAT IF THE SECOND ONE ARRIVED FIRST?

Morning came and Lani stretched leisurely, still nestled in her silky white surroundings. She could still smell the lavender on her softened skin from her bath last night. She opened her eyes and looked out the open window. The land was still, the wind was calm, and there wasn't the slightest indication of anything sinister. Everything felt so wonderfully uneventful. It was a lovely change from what had become the norm.

As Lani snuggled more deeply into her covers, she looked around the opulent room with its gold and burgundy accents and she wondered how this particular land had remained so intact. Rezarahn's kingdom was rich with plenty of food and water. He was not on the run like Jharate was. He had wonderful possessions like the bed she was currently luxuriating in. Perhaps it was because Jharate's kingdom had just fallen, and this one had been down for a while. Maybe life had just reached a new normalcy for Zenastra, even under oppression.

At any rate, she liked Rezarahn quite a lot. Her mind flashed through the wonderful memories from last night. She remembered the awe she had experienced as the front door opened and she had seen him for the first time. She relived the shivers and thrills he had ignited in her body, and reflected over the attentive way in which he had worked to ensure her every comfort throughout the entire night.

He was the kind of guy that any girl would love to have. He was handsome, intelligent, chivalrous, rich, and well, almost perfect— and it was obvious that he cared for her a great deal. He had singled her out among all of the other women. Being in constant company with Kendra, Arante, Te'era, and now Tierza was intimidating sometimes— especially after Jharate had jilted her and practically thrown himself at Tierza. Rezarahn had chosen *her* though. Shouldn't she be thrilled?

A soft knock came at her door. Lani reached for the white satin robe, which was draped over a burgundy-upholstered chair by her bedside, and put it on over her nightgown. She tiptoed quickly across the floor, so as not to wake any of the sleeping girls in the room. She opened the door to find Rezarahn holding a beautiful bouquet of burgundy roses in an exquisite crystal vase, which he offered to her with a sweeping gesture that ended in a low bow.

"Oh! They're beautiful!" Lani exclaimed in a whisper. She stepped outside the door and closed it quietly so that they could continue talking without waking anyone.

"Yes they are. However, next to you, they look like withered thorns."

Lani blushed. She brought the roses up to inhale their fragrance, hoping to hide the scarlet in her cheeks as Rezarahn continued.

"Would you like to accompany me on a ride through my orchards?"

"I'd love to!"

"You will need this. I believe you will find that it fits you perfectly."

Rezarahn handed her a dress that would be more suitable for riding than her purple one.

"Thank you!"

Lani shifted the vase into the crook of one arm, and let Rezarahn drape the dress over her other, leaving that hand free to open the door. She quietly stepped inside. She leaned back out a little bit to whisper quickly to Rezarahn.

"I'll be right back. It might take me a little longer because I have to be quiet so I don't wake up my chickyz."

"Chickyz?"

Lani had already slipped back into the room and closed the door before he had uttered his question. She crept back to her bed, and placed the vase on the cherrywood nightstand next to it. She changed as quickly as she could out of the nightgown and into the dress that Rezarahn had just given her. He was right. It fit her every measurement. It was much more plain than her purple dress but still quite attractive and very comfortable. A maroon corset over a white billowy blouse complemented a very full fawn brown skirt, which fell to just above her ankles.

Lani suddenly realized she didn't have any proper footwear. She bit her lip and sighed as she looked around the room. She knew she didn't have anything, and she would have had to wake up Tierza or Arante to ask them if they had anything she could borrow, and she didn't want to do that. Besides, she had a feeling their feet were smaller than hers— most girls feet were, even when they were taller than she was. Lani had always been sure she had been meant to be taller. How else does a five-foot-five girl end up with a size nine shoe size? Lani looked at the door, and realized there was no other option. She opened it just a crack, leaning only her head out.

"You wouldn't happen to have a pair of—"

Lani blinked in surprise as Rezarahn put forth two brown leather boots and a pair of short tan-colored silk stockings, with a huge debonair grin on his face. Lani reached out with one hand and grabbed the items as she smiled at him.

"Thank you. You think of everything. I'll be right back."

Lani closed the door again and tiptoed back to her bed and sat down on it carefully. She slipped on the stockings and pulled on the boots. Again, Rezarahn proved to be a master at picking sizes. They fit wonderfully and were almost as comfortable as the sandals Arante had purchased for her. The boots hit her mid-calf and had one-inch heels that made them more feminine yet still practical. The leather was covered in tooled roses and vines, which wrapped their way around and in-between the roses.

Once Lani was sure she had everything on right, she used the brush that Arante had given her to brush out all of the tangles until her hair was like silk once again. Now came decision time. She looked at herself in a mirror hanging on the wall by her bedside. She knew that her hair all or mostly down was her best look, and yet a braid would be the obvious practical choice for a ride.

She stared at the mirror for a moment, trying to decide between looks and practicality. She grabbed the top section of her hair and smoothed it until the desired half-up half-down look had been achieved, and then braided the top section. She tied it off at the bottom with the gold ribbon that had been tied around the vase. She looked in the mirror to make sure that everything was in place and, with a reassuring smile to herself, she crept back to the door and opened it quietly.

Lani emerged and slowly shut the door behind her. Rezarahn offered his arm before she could even turn around. She smiled and took it graciously. She could feel his strong muscles under his shirt, which sent a shudder down her spine. Lani had always had a thing for well-developed arm muscles in a guy, and his were fantastic! She held on tight as they walked down the staircase. She felt his muscle flex a little under her grasp and she stifled a happy laugh. Whether he was on to her or not, he was definitely making it more fun.

As they walked out of the front entrance of his home Lani breathed a sigh of relief as she saw the two horses, saddled and ready to go. She was glad that this world apparently did not have sidesaddles, which she had always thought ridiculous. Not that a regular saddle would help her a whole lot when it came to getting on the horse in the first place, but it would definitely make the ride much easier. Rezarahn walked with her to the white mare and stopped in front of it. Without saying a word, he placed his hands gently around her waist, lifted her up, and sat her on the saddle. Lani giggled as she felt a rush from that attractive display of masculinity race through her.

Rezarahn kept his hand outstretched so that Lani could steady herself as she swung her right leg over the horse. She did so with some difficulty. She was not an experienced rider at all and the dress was definitely complicating matters. She had never ridden with a dress on before and had to arrange it, secure it, and lay it out nicely so that she wouldn't look as foolish as she felt. Lani hoped Rezarahn hadn't noticed how inept she was at this moment. At long last, she managed to make herself look quite composed. He handed her the reigns and she held on tight.

"Shall we go, dear lady?"

"Absolutely."

"Splendid."

Lani felt a little weak at the knees from the way he spoke. It was so regal and seductive at the same time. Her eyes glimmered as she watched him put his left foot in one stirrup and swing his other leg over his chestnut brown steed to the other stirrup in a single fluid motion. As he turned the horse around to face her, he flashed another arresting smile. Lani smiled back but averted her eyes because she felt as though she might swoon under his gaze if she looked into his eyes any longer.

Rezarahn set a slow pace and Lani followed at his side. She drank in every aspect of the surroundings as they rode, desperately wishing she had a camera more than once. The sun had only just risen and the vivid colors of the sunrise cast a glowing golden hue on everything the light touched, from the hills on the horizon to the dewy blades of grass beneath their horses' hooves. Lani thought that this had to be the most romantic date she had ever been on, hands down. She took a deep breath and let the fresh air fill her lungs and released it with a happy sigh.

Lani's eyes widened as they approached Rezarahn's orchards. The trees were practically bursting with blossoms and were also heavily laden with colorful ripe fruits. Lani found this both surprising and exciting since, as far as she knew, on Earth it was either blossoms or fruit— never both at the same time. She loved the profound quiet of this time of morning, when not even the bees were awake yet. The gentle breeze shook the loose flowers free and made it look as though it was snowing. The horses walked Lani and Rezarahn slowly through the rows of trees over veritable carpets of white, pale pink, and fuchsia blossoms.

She listened intently as he explained which ones were cherry trees, apple trees, orange trees, and many other types of trees that she had never heard of as they passed from orchard to orchard, but found it hard to concentrate completely because their aesthetic value was so overwhelming. However, one particular orchard definitely caught her full attention. It was filled with what Rezarahn told her were rosandra trees, which had giant fruit the size of honeydew melons that were as brightly colored as a red pear. Rezarahn plucked one off of the tree nearest them and handed it to Lani with a warm smile. She took it eagerly and her eyes lit up as she delicately bit into its sweet snowy-white flesh.

She closed her eyes with an appreciative sigh as the fruit nearly melted on her tongue. The rosandra fruit tasted much like a strawberry that had been sugared and soaked in its own juices. She could imagine it pairing splendidly with cream or chocolate. The tiny piece in her mouth injected an instant feeling of euphoria. She figured this fruit must have something that affected her endorphins because there was simply no other explanation for the sudden rapture that overcame her.

She swallowed and took another bite. She smiled at the sound of Rezarahn's laugh as the juices ran down her chin. Lani managed to keep the clear juice off her dress by leaning away from the horse. Rezarahn offered her a clean white handkerchief, onto which he poured some water from a canteen. She daintily wiped off her chin and dabbed the corners of her mouth, feeling extremely grateful that this had not been a klutzy moment.

As the ride through the stunning orchard continued, Lani wondered how all these wonderful things could grow in one place. She knew on Earth it would be hard, if not impossible, to grow an orange tree and a cherry tree in the same grove. She figured that there must be at least some magic involved. She felt her curiosity growing about the issue, and opened her mouth to ask Rezarahn, but stopped before she uttered a single syllable. She had forgotten that he did not know who she really was.

She stifled a frustrated sigh as she realized any question she could ask on the subject would likely be something she was supposed to know, had she been from Alamea. But she *was* from Alamea, sort of. Why was it that Jharate got to know she was from Earth and ignore her, and the man that was hanging on her every word wasn't allowed to know? She had to fight the urge to laugh as she further realized the irony of her situation. Jharate thought she was from Earth and didn't know she was actually from Alamea, whereas Rezarahn thought she was from Alamea and was right, but missing a big twenty-year segment that had occurred on Earth. So each man had exactly half of the truth of her origins— well maybe more like thirty-nine-point-five percent of the truth, since neither knew her original identity on Alamea.

Lani shook her head a little to recall herself to the moment. Why was she wasting her time on things she couldn't solve when there was so much beauty to be enjoyed? Her environment came into sharp focus once again just as they reached a cheerful looking pond. She sighed contentedly as she saw the light from the sky dancing on its surface, turning the pond into a nearly perfect liquid silver mirror. Lavish amounts of burgundy lilies and white irises lined its edges. Butterflies in matching colors flitted happily as they flew in pairs in upward spirals through the air around them, and an intoxicating scent filled the air.

Rezarahn halted and dismounted his horse in a single graceful jump. He walked over to Lani and held out his right hand to steady her as she swung her right leg over to join her left. He placed both of his hands around her waist and lifted her off of the horse and set her gently on the ground. Lani giggled. She loved being treated like a little china doll. He was such a manly man! He offered her his arm again and she took it as they strolled slowly around the pond.

"Thank you for everything, Rezarahn, really. I can't tell you how much you've done for me in so short a time."

"I have not done a single thing more than you deserve. If anything I am lacking in my duty to one such as yourself."

Lani's smile widened further and her cheeks went bright pink.

"You make me blush so frequently."

"Well that, my dear lady, is a very, very good thing."

As he spoke he gently touched his index finger to her nose and she laughed. They both paused for a moment and gazed at their reflections below them in perfect silence. Rezarahn felt his heart beating harder and louder against his chest. His blood ran hot through his veins— a heat so strong and unprecedented that it could not be denied. He measured his breathing and swallowed hard. When Rezarahn could no longer bear to merely look at the watery imitation of the woman beside him, he turned toward her and placed his left hand on her right cheek, gently turning her face toward him and looked intently into her deep blue eyes. Their eyes locked.

Rezarahn leaned down and slowly reached for her lips with his own. She politely but deliberately turned her head and he kissed her cheek instead of his intended target. Rezarahn blinked in confusion. He had not expected this cold reaction. He leaned back in and rested his forehead against hers, with their noses touching softly together. His hands longed to hold her and his lips burned for the taste of hers. Perhaps her evasion had been shyness. He took a deep breath, and brought his lips slowly toward hers once more. This time she took a step back and looked down at the water below.

"I wish I could... I'm sorry, but I can't. Can you forgive me?"

Rezarahn stared at her, feeling as though she had struck him in the face. He struggled to keep his breathing on an even keel and he lifted the back of his right hand to his mouth as if to attempt to wipe away the unfulfilled urges he could still taste dancing on his lips.

"Of course, my dear lady, if you do not wish me to kiss you, I would not dream of it. Only... Why ever not? Have I misread you? Am I not pleasing to you?"

"Oh no, heavens no! You are *very* pleasing. It's nothing like that. You are perfect. You're the kind of man any girl should want. But I just don't think it's fair to you to do anything that might lead to a relationship... when my heart still belongs to another."

"I see. Jharate still has it does he?"

"How did you— Is it that obvious?"

"Yes. I could tell from the moment I laid eyes on you that your heart belonged to another. When Jharate stole you from me on the dance floor, I knew by the look in your eyes that it had to be him. I only hoped that perhaps if I treated you the way that you deserve to be treated, that your heart might be persuaded to go on a different path."

"You have treated me in a way I have only dreamed of and I wish that had been enough. He won't even talk to me..."

"I can be patient. If he does not come back for you, one day you may forget about him. And then, perhaps, I might stand a chance?"

"Oh, yes! If it weren't for the fact that I still love him— I mean, you're amazing! I was trying to let myself move on, or I would never have let things get this far. I thought I could— but I couldn't. I'm not making much sense am I?"

"On the contrary, my dear lady. You are a very honorable soul to not encourage feelings of love and passion until you are sure you can return them."

Lani sighed in relief.

"Thank you so much for understanding."

"Shall we return then?"

Rezarahn held his arm out to her with a warm smile on his face. He had spoken very sweetly to her, hoping it would console her. He felt as if he had just suffered a blow to the stomach and a sharp pang, such as he had never before experienced, throbbed in his heart— but she must never know that. After all, it was the duty of a gentleman to never offend, harm, or worry a lady. The façade must appear normal as if there had never been an incident. But in his heart he had meant every word he said to her and fervently hoped that one day she *would* forget about Jharate, and come to him.

"Yes, everyone will be waking up soon. I should get back. Thank you so much for sharing your enchanting orchards with me."

"The pleasure was all mine, dear lady."

Lani took his arm and allowed him to help her back on her horse, but this time all she felt was muted regret sinking into her heart. She was surprised that as they rode back together, they were able to talk and laugh as if nothing had happened, and even more regret piled up in the pit of her stomach that she could not love him back. He was such a unique person. For him to still be working to put her at ease after she had rejected him— what an unbelievable man!

A small puff of air escaped the right corner of Lani's mouth and made one of the loose strands of her hair fly up. She thought she had felt stupid last night when Rezarahn first asked her to dance and she felt the desire to dance with Jharate instead. But the way she felt now— she would have given another year to the siren if she could just move on while the perfect man was right here in front of her! What on Earth was wrong with her? Since when had she ever been such a glutton for punishment? Since when couldn't her head overrule her heart or even change her heart's mind altogether?

As they reached the familiar steps to his home, Rezarahn gently helped Lani off the horse and walked her back to her room.

"Thank you for the marvelous ride, my dear lady! It was a rare privilege."

"It was my privilege. Your grounds are magical, and the company couldn't have been better. Really, Rezarahn, thank you again for understanding…"

Rezarahn kissed her hand tenderly once more. He held on a little longer, and let his lips hover a centimeter above her hand. His index finger stroked the inside of her wrist as he had done the night before. But this time instead of a thrill, she felt as if her heart would break in two. How could this be happening? Rezarahn placed his forehead against her hand and held it there as he heaved a great sigh. When he lifted his head again he smiled faintly and kissed her hand one last time as he slowly dragged his fingers away from hers. He straightened up and bowed his head toward her and then turned and walked away as she opened the door to her room.

She went inside and shut the door behind her, letting herself fall against it with a sigh. She felt dreadful. Rezarahn had offered her his heart and she had left it there to die. And the look on his face as he had left her just now— *Oh!* A gut-wrenching twist hit her stomach and a numbing feeling of guilt washed over her as she stared at the floor beneath her boots.

"Sooooooo?" Tierza began, the moment Lani entered the room, sitting up excitedly in her plushy bed. "Tell us *all* the details!"

"Yes! And don't leave anything out!" Arante chimed in from her own bed.

Lani didn't even jump as she realized she wasn't alone. She felt too terrible to react to anything. She found herself desperately wishing the room had been as empty as she had hoped it would be and a strong desire to run away lay just beneath the surface of her guilt. But she stayed. She didn't know what was keeping her from opening the door behind her and running.

"There's nothing much to tell."

"Oh whatever!" Kendra said, in exasperation, stretching and yawning. "Just tell us!"

"Well, he came early and asked me if I wanted to go for a ride and I said yes. We rode through his orchards and stopped at a pond… and he went to kiss me…"

"I knew it!" Tierza said excitedly.

"How was it?" Arante asked, flashing her smile and hugging her pillow in anticipation.

"He looks like a good kisser," Kendra giggled.

"It didn't happen."

"WHAT?!" Kendra shouted in unison with Tierza and Arante.

"I dodged."

"Why on *Earth* would you do something so stupid?" Kendra demanded.

"He is so perfect for you," Tierza added.

"I told him why. I told him it wasn't fair for me to lead him on when— when my heart belongs to someone else."

Lani could feel how badly she was failing to explain something that didn't even make sense to her. Her desire to flee increased and yet her brain couldn't get her feet to obey.

"You dumped *him* for *my cousin?!*" Arante asked loudly, dropping the pillow as well as her jaw.

"Gosh, Lani! You need to get over Giraffe Boy already! It's obvious he doesn't care anymore."

"Thanks for that. And *please* stop calling him that Kendra. It's not my fault. I just can't get over him."

"Actually, it is your fault," Tierza said. "Jharate has made it perfectly clear that he does not want you."

"Again, very diplomatic..."

Lani stared at them in disbelief. She already felt like a horrible person and they weren't helping her feel any better. Wasn't that what friends were supposed to do? Make you feel like you were still a good person when you had been forced to make a tough decision in the name of honesty and fairness? What were they doing? And to throw the fact that Jharate didn't want her in her face like that— it was so insensitive! She felt a strange unidentifiable form of emotion rising in her chest— some combination of anger and disconnect.

"Well, you need someone to be straight with you. My cousin is acting like an idiot! Once he takes a position, he stays there. He can be as stubborn as an ox, and when he is, he's much dumber than one!"

"Well then why did he ask me to dance? And don't talk about him that way!"

"Because he got jealous like any guy would!" Kendra said defiantly. "You think any single ex-boyfriend of yours could watch what Rezarahn was doing with you and not feel insanely jealous? You just had a moment all women dream of! The moment when a guy better than the one they just broke up with is all over them and the ex gets to see every juicy moment! To quote Beyoncé, 'If he liked it then he should have put a ring on it!' Dang it, Lani! What the heck is wrong with you?"

"Well, I still think that there is hope for me and Jharate! I love him and I am not giving up on him until I am one hundred and fifty percent sure there isn't a snowball's chance in Guam for us!"

Lani stormed out of the room, slamming the door behind her. She was glad her brain had finally been able to make her feet do what she should have done three minutes ago! Why couldn't they understand that she was in love with Jharate? She knew it wasn't necessarily the smartest thing in the world, and she knew they had her best interests at heart, but she couldn't help it. She loved him and she had to be true to herself and true to him—with or without the full support of her friends.

"Guam?" Arante and Tierza asked together.

"Oh, it's a really hot place on Earth," Kendra began as she rolled her eyes and sighed. "Lani doesn't like to swear so she changes words sometimes. The original phrase is actually in reference to our underworld, which is supposed to be filled with fire and brimstone and whatnot, but she changed it to Guam because it's so hot that a snowball wouldn't have a chance there either."

"Oh."

Arante and Tierza glared at each other, fuming over the fact they had once again replied in unison— a habit that, in their eyes, was recurring with increasingly annoying frequency. Both of them held their tongues though and looked back to Kendra as she started speaking again.

"I don't know why she won't just ditch Jharate and go for Rezarahn! You'd never see me follow a guy who had no interest in me like that."

"Me either," Arante and Tierza said together again, this time clenching both of their hands into fists as they once again glared at each other.

"Stop that! No you stop it! Ahhhh! You are so impossible!"

Kendra laughed as the two continued to speak at the same time. She still disliked Arante quite a bit, and it was funny to see Arante getting a taste of her own bossy medicine.

Lani was out in the main hallway of the house, alone and wandering. She looked every bit as furious as she was as she wandered through the halls.

"Beautiful lady, what troubles you?"

Lani had meandered into the library without realizing it and jumped in response to the voice. She reflexively put her hand to her heart and breathed in deeply to try to recover from the fact that it had just skipped a beat.

"Oh, Rezarahn! I didn't see you there. I'm sorry to disturb you. I'll just go."

"No. Please stay. You could never disturb me. I am sorry to have frightened you."

Rezarahn rushed to his feet and grabbed both of her hands, sympathetically in his.

"Tell me, sweet angel— what is wrong?"

"Oh, it's stupid really…"

"Nothing you say could ever be stupid."

"Stop being so perfect, dang it! Oh! I'm so sorry, I didn't mean to— I don't normally lose my temper like this. And you don't deserve it. I'm sorry. Forget what I said."

"It has already been forgotten."

Rezarahn smiled supportively and tenderly kissed one of her hands. Lani felt a tiny ounce of her fury wash away. He could have made it all disappear with one look if the anger had been towards him, but it wasn't. Lani took a slow breath in and let it out even slower through her lips. She took one more deep breath just for good measure and tried very hard to speak as calmly as she could so that she would not project her anger toward her friends… and toward Jharate… onto Rezarahn again.

"Arante and Kendra *and* Tierza all think I am nuts for not just going for you right now. I'm so glad that Te'era and the rest of the girls in our party are in another room or I'm sure I'd be hearing it from them too! They say I should just get over Jharate and be with you."

"Hmmm. I would be lying if I told you that I did not agree with them and their extraordinary wisdom," he stated, flashing his brilliant smile again. "However, I understand that you must follow what your heart tells you. And I truly believe that you should never try to force your heart to feel what it does not feel. Only heartache comes of forcing something as precious as love."

"I don't know, maybe I *am* crazy. You're the type of guy I know I should be going for— the type I'm positive that I would be in love with, had I met you before Jharate. But my heart already belongs to him. I'm sure—"

It was only at this instant that she realized how fantastically close Rezarahn was. She forgot what she was saying. For a moment all she could see were his alluring eyes, which sparkled like deep green emeralds mixed with gold dust. She felt a force pulling her towards him. As his lips suddenly started nearing her own she blinked and jolted back into reality. She dodged once again and pulled back a few steps, hand on her chest as it rose and fell in a mixture of relief and adrenaline.

Rezarahn placed the back of his hand back up to his mouth and his eyes were wide with shock at his own actions.

"I am terribly sorry! I forgot myself entirely. You are simply so hard to resist— and I cannot force my heart to go where it does not wish to go either. My apologies, my dear lady!"

Rezarahn bowed politely as he quickly exited the room.

Great, Lani thought to herself, *just great! Dang that Jharate!*

Lani put the back of her right hand to her forehead as she slammed her eyes shut. She closed that hand into a fist and gently tapped her forehead three times with it, lingering on the last time. *Why* was she still hanging onto Jharate? Was she making a huge mistake? She had one of the most charming, intelligent, chivalrous, moral, and who could forget, gorgeous men who had probably ever lived in *either* world, in *any* century, pursuing her! Not that he was better looking than Jharate, but Rezarahn was actually interested in her. Jharate was being stubborn and unforgiving and stupid and— Why was she putting her heart on hold for him? He had done nothing to deserve it for weeks! She wanted to scream! Then she did, involuntarily, for an entirely different reason.

She whipped around as a huge ceramic vase crashed behind her. Her eyes flew open wide and her heart skipped two beats as she saw Jharate, standing over the fallen vase and vase stand that he had accidentally tripped over. She looked down at the shattered pieces on the hardwood floor and then back up at Jharate.

"How long have you been there?"

He remained frozen where he was, and silent— looking nervous and possibly even frightened as he stared at her.

"How much did you see?"

There was no change in his position and his mouth remained sealed.

"Answer me right now, Jharate! How long were you there?!"

Jharate blinked, looked at the exit, and strode through it without uttering a single syllable.

"You are so infuriating! Ooh!"

She trembled with rage as she stood there looking at the empty doorway. She knew he probably hadn't heard her, but it had felt good to get at least some of the energy out. But there was still too much bad energy pent up in her. She grabbed a pillow off one of the couches in the library and let herself scream into it, no holds barred. When she could scream no more she threw the pillow back onto the couch and pulled at her hair in frustration. When all this did nothing to assuage her, she ran outside alone with an exasperated sigh— hoping that maybe some air and a change of scenery might quell the rage, guilt, and torture she felt in her knot-filled stomach and her mortally wounded heart.

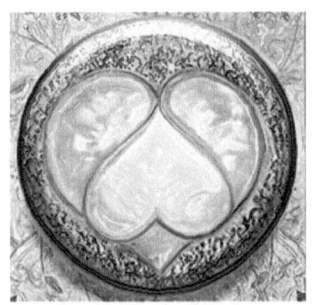

THE ENEMY OF MY ENEMY IS *NOT NECESSARILY* MY FRIEND

"**G**et away from her!"

Arante grabbed Lani firmly and pulled her forcefully behind her.

"What's wrong, Arante? I thought you liked Rezarahn…"

"Never mind that! Get back inside and follow the others. We're leaving! NOW!"

Lani narrowed her eyes at Arante, searching her face for the answers she refused to give. But there was nothing to be found. Arante did not take her eyes off of Rezarahn for even a second and her jaw was set tight, as was every other muscle in her body. Lani shook her head in disbelief and then turned to Rezarahn and spoke softly.

"Thank you for your hospitality, Rezarahn."

"Remember my offer, sweet lady. I shall be here if ever you need me."

"Don't you DARE talk to her! And Lani, get inside *now!*"

Arante stayed facing Rezarahn, eyes locked on him like a hawk. Lani stared back at Arante without moving at first. For a moment Lani thought that perhaps she had lost her own sanity and she was one "There's no place like home" away from waking up on her bed in her room in California, only to find that an earthquake had knocked loose a vase that had fallen on her head and this whole insane thing had been a tripped-out Technicolor dream.

Lani blinked and shook her head. Nothing made sense anymore. But she reminded herself that she knew Arante well enough by now to know that she should trust her, no matter how bewildering her current harsh and rather capricious actions were. Lani turned away and walked back into Rezarahn's château with her mind trying fruitlessly to sort everything out. Hadn't Arante just been saying how perfect Rezarahn was?

Lani flinched as she found the rest of her friends. She had been so lost in thought that she almost ran smack into Raoul.

"Whoa, Lani, are you okay?" Raoul asked as he put his hands on her shoulders to stop her and then to steady her.

"I'm fine. What's going on?"

"Rezarahn is a traitor, that's what!" Kendra blurted out.

"What?"

"It's true," Justin added.

Lani mouthed a quiet "What?" as Raoul handed her sword to her and she mechanically attached the belt that held her sheath around her waist and over the dress that Rezarahn had given her, without looking at it.

"I don't understand. Can somebody please tell me what is going on?"

Jharate rounded on her. She felt herself shrinking back slightly as he towered over her and almost shouted his reply.

"How do you suppose that he has acquired all of this obvious wealth? He is in league with Vranah! He betrayed us before we ever set foot in this land! Drakne's men are arriving outside of this town this very instant!"

Lani shook her head slowly several times. Oddly it wasn't the volume with which he had just spoken, or even her sudden fright from Jharate that was at the forefront of her mind. Neither was the news of Rezarahn's treachery hitting her like perhaps it should. What was most surprising to her was that Jharate had answered so directly. This was the most he had said to her in a long time. *Wait. If he knew that then...* She tilted her head up toward him and narrowed her eyes.

"How do you know this?"

"There is no time for explanations! We must leave now!"

"What about Arante? She told me to come back here but she is still with Rezarahn!"

"She will be with us momentarily. Arante already knows where we are going and we must depart now! Tierza has recalled her knowledge of an enchanted underground tunnel, merely two hours from here, which leads directly into Destavnia. If we do not leave this instant we may not get another chance!"

"I have half a mind to kill you right where you stand!"

Arante armed her bow and pointed the arrow directly at Rezarahn's heart.

"That would accomplish nothing."

"It would help me sleep better at night."

"Try it!"

Her arrow sailed toward him. Halfway to his heart, it exploded, midair, into a fireball.

"Oh great, you're a fire master."

"Impressive, is it not?"

"Well, I'd love to stay and argue the point, but I have somewhere else to be."

With that, she conjured an image of a twenty-foot-high ring of fire around him, so that he could not see the direction of her escape. As fire was his specialty, Rezarahn attempted to quell the flames around him. Both his eyebrows rose as he found that they would not obey him. He cocked his head to the side, and looked at the flames more carefully. As he walked towards them he held his hand closer to the fire. Feeling no heat, he realized it was an illusion, and walked through unharmed.

He laughed heartily. He was as greatly impressed with her power as she had been irritated to learn of his. But he was not in the mood for a chase. As the false flames began to fade, he calmly ordered some of his men to go look for the escaped rebels in a halfhearted attempt to catch them. Drakne was not going to like this, but Rezarahn had talked himself out of worse situations, and he was confident he could do it again.

Arante sprinted the entire way and came to a skidding stop as she caught up with the others just as they reached the tunnel. She rested her hands on her knees and breathed heavily for a moment, but straightened up again quickly. The entrance to the alcove in front of them was completely covered in ivy. Arante watched as Jharate parted the ivy carefully and stepped through it. She continued to try and catch her breath as Jharate wrenched open the heavy wooden door, which was recessed about three feet inside the alcove. Arante was the last person to step inside. She quickly returned the ivy to its original position as best she could and smiled at Erik as he helped her close the door behind them.

No one was sure if anyone else knew of this tunnel but they did not want to take any chances, so they ran through it as if they were being pursued, and their hurried footsteps echoed around them. They ran, and ran, and ran until everyone but the elves had long since been out of breath, and then they ran some more. They ran so fast that the air stung their eyes and hot tears streamed from the corners. Their legs felt like they were turning to mush except for when the occasional shin splint would send a searing pain shooting upwards.

When the running became so hard and so monotonous that Lani feared she would faint, she tried to think of other things. She knew her emotions were not a good subject if she wanted to keep strong, so she instead focused on the surroundings as she ran, trying to notice every detail— not that there were that many to notice. The tunnel struck Lani as odd. It seemed like a tunnel on Earth, made of concrete, with rectangular plexiglass casings holding what appeared to be dim electric lighting that ran the entire length of the passage. There was even a humming sound that she would have expected from malfunctioning florescent light fixtures. She wondered if it really was powered by electricity, or if it was just another form of magic energy. One more question to throw on her list of things she'd have to find out later. The lights seemed to be flying by as if they were traveling at seventy miles per hour, or faster, but the exit was still nowhere in sight.

At a certain point in the tunnel Lani had a feeling come over her that it would not be long now before they reached Destavnia— she was sure of it. But if she was so sure she was going to make it, then why did she also have such an anxious knot in the pit of her stomach?

"YOU LET THEM ESCAPE?!"

Drakne glowered at Rezarahn, but there was a nervous energy behind his outward display of rage. Drakne felt his heart beating harder in his body and felt adrenaline coursing through his veins as he realized that for the first time since he had established his irreplaceable value to Vranah over a decade ago, he had great cause to be worried.

"They discovered my subterfuge by some means that I do not know. There was nothing I could have done," Rezarahn said, covering up his nearly bored tone with a dash of simulated timidity.

Drakne tightened his fists and replied through clenched teeth.

"*Where* did they go?"

"Again, Your Excellency will have to pardon me. One of them used an apparition to escape behind, so I could not see which way they went. A thousand apologies, my lord."

"Your apologies mean nothing to me! I want those travelers! Was it not impressed upon you, just yesterday, when I came to you personally, exactly how important it was to keep them here until my men arrived? I told you well before those rebels even set foot on your property! And did I not remind you of that plan only hours ago?"

"Again, a thousand pardons. If only Your Excellency had informed me of how powerful they were, I could have taken greater precautions."

"You are lucky I still have need of you at this moment—otherwise, I would kill you for the incompetent imbecile that you are. But I promise you this— if I do *not* find them, I will have your tongue cut out and bring you before *my* master and see if you can talk your way out of *his* wrath."

Rezarahn made no reply. His eyes lost the flicker of cockiness and he looked down at the ground. He swallowed hard and his posture sank about an inch as he stood there in silence.

"That's better. Now, you and your men will aid mine in searching for them. Bring me word of their position or so help me, you *will* live— just long enough to regret it."

"We will find them, My Liege."

Rezarahn placed his right fist to his heart and bowed his head slightly toward Drakne. He turned to go and disappeared from sight. Once Drakne was sure that he was alone he pulled his hair back hard against his skull. He had let his ego get in the way. He should have taken them when he had the chance. Even if he could not have killed Lani right away, he surely could have killed the rest, even one at a time, passing them off as accidents since no one had been aware of his presence. Simply electrifying the water at the warm pools would have done them all in with one easy blow! Now, he had lost them— and so near Destavnia.

BLAST IT ALL! thought Drakne. He had to find them. He had to. He knew his master would not tolerate this failure— not when there was so much riding on it, especially concerning Princess Adrienne. Drakne roared in exasperation and stormed away to join the search.

Jharate opened the door at the end of the tunnel and they all emerged into the fresh clean air of freedom. Everyone could feel the spectacular difference, but none more so than Lani. She closed her eyes and inhaled deeply. There was something about the spirit of this land that was palpable to her. She hadn't noticed until she had arrived here, but by contrast, the other kingdoms, though they still had beauty in many places, had an underlying feeling of depression and darkness. The strong aura that Destavnia emanated told her that this land was still filled with hope, faith, and love. She lifted her hands slightly to her sides as if to feel the peace flowing through the air. She sighed in relief and smiled widely.

"We are in Destavnia!" Arante shouted out to inform everyone of the obvious.

"Finally!" Kendra said as she collapsed onto her back in the long dense ultra-soft grass and looked up at the pink sunset.

"I never realized how tired I was before now," Raoul chimed in before joining Kendra on the ground, as he took in a huge liberating breath.

Laern also sat next to Kendra on the opposite side, with his arresting signature smile, and Kendra giggled quietly as she looked into his supernaturally-hypnotic glittering brown eyes. She caught her breath as he reached his hand to the other side of her face and gently tucked a loose strand of hair behind her ear, letting his fingers drag down to just below her jaw line, then to her neck before removing them. She tried to exhale quietly and slowly without being noticed as she felt her toes curling in excitement.

"Impressive, isn't it?" Tierza chirped to everyone within earshot. "It would have taken us a week to get here, had I not found the magic travel tunnel— and instead we have arrived in a matter of a few short hours! I haven't been through that tunnel since I was a small child, and that was ever so long ago. It's a miracle that I even remembered it."

"Yes, yes, very clever," Arante answered, rolling her eyes, but the smile never left her face and she changed her tone to reflect her sincerity as she finished with a quiet, "Thank you, Tierza."

"I'm glad to have been able to help," Tierza said with a gratified smile and a delicate nod before Arante went to sit down on the grass with Erik.

"That's my girl!" Justin exclaimed happily as he put his arm around Tierza's neck and shoulders, letting his relaxed hand hang down a little in front of her. His face changed to a wide-eyed, panic-stricken expression as he realized he had said those words aloud and he took his arm off and stepped back a little. "I mean, not that you're *my girl* as in— no wait, that didn't come out right— it's just so fast and I don't know if— what I mean is we just haven't talked about it and I don't want to be presumptuous in calling you— oh heck with it! Tierza, will you be my girlfriend?"

"Girlfriend? What is a girlfriend?"

"That's not a term here? Oh wow, how do I explain that one?"

"Courting?" Lani suggested.

"Oh!" Tierza said with her glittering green eyes lighting up even more. "You want to court me, Justin? Is that what you were asking?"

"I mean if you want to. I don't want to court anyone but you... so if you feel the same way then maybe yeah, we could court each other... and just each other..."

"That's generally what courting means, Justin," Lani whispered to Justin with a wink. "It's a little more serious than the word dating is to us."

"I knew that."

Lani laughed. The sheepish look and silly smile on Justin's face said very clearly that he did not know that before now. Not that she blamed him— not everyone was into old-school romances the way she was.

"I would love to be your girlfriend, as you called it."

Tierza's eyes shimmered even more and Justin sighed happily. He pulled her into a great big hug and squeezed her so tightly that she could barely breathe before letting go enough to put his hands on both of her cheeks as he went in for a kiss. He let his hands trace down both sides of her neck, down her back to her waist, and pulled her in closer. She put her hands on his chest and, as she kissed him back, she pulled on his shirt.

Lani bit her lip as an uncomfortable smile formed on her face and she averted her eyes away from the happy, yet awkward moment. As Lani walked a little ways away to give the budding couple their privacy, she looked intently out at the new surroundings. She had been dreaming of Destavnia for so long, and now that she was here, she found that it defied even her wildest imagination. Emerald ferns, forest-green pine trees, parsley-colored bushes, mint-green underbrush, deep aqua-green grass, jewel-green flower stems— and more shades of green than she could ever hope to name were now before her eyes. The lush mountains were no exception, but they were being kissed with the rose-gold light of the setting sun. Birds chirped happily in the trees and little lightning bugs were starting to become visible as the light faded slowly into twilight.

The more Lani saw, the more she felt as if she had entered the Garden of Eden. Metallic shimmering leaves on trees, which reminded her of quaking aspens, made a mesmerizing and soothing sound in the gentle breeze. Bright purple, silver, and even rainbow-colored butterflies flew lazily over the plethora of multi-colored wild flowers that dotted the grass in the large meadow and thickly lined its edges. Many of the butterflies and flowers sparkled as if they had been dusted with glitter. She thought to herself that if this land had been in a movie, she would be amazed that all of this color and glitter could look so elegant, sophisticated, and natural, without being the slightest bit tacky-looking or cartoonish.

Lani's mouth fell open as she peered into the trees and saw a family of unicorns, even more majestic than those described in the storybooks she had read as a child. She gazed in wonder at their brilliant white hair that glowed as if they were under a spotlight and their bright blue eyes that shone like sapphires. Their dazzling spiraled horns were so silvery that they reflected everything that came near.

Lani started as she heard a low moan behind her. She whirled around and saw Jharate kneeling in the grass with his hands on the sides of his head and a look of agony on his face. Lani ran to him and fell to her knees in the soft grass beside him, grabbing his left arm and placing her other hand on his back to support him as much as she could.

"What's wrong, Jharate?"

"Nothing. My head is aching. It is as if my skull is about to cleave in two."

Lani felt her heart do a cartwheel. She held her breath and remained deathly silent as she looked at him expectantly.

"Strange... It is gone now."

CHAPTER EIGHTEEN

Lani sighed and her heart sank as she saw the look on his face and the coldness return to his eyes. He seemed confused as to why he was talking to her at all. She released her hold on him and hung her head. The spell had *not* broken. Lani took another deep breath and sighed again. Why had she even allowed herself to dream it? They stood up. She looked up and saw his muscles tighten up, ready to walk away. She quickly placed her hand gently on his arm as she spoke softly to him.

"No, wait… Please."

Jharate paused. Lani blinked and shook her head incredulously. She hadn't thought that would work. She suddenly realized she didn't have anything to say to him other than how much she wanted him back and she couldn't say that without him walking away for sure. She felt a surge of panic jolt through her as her mind frantically searched for something— anything that didn't have to do with how much she loved him.

"Mmm… I just wanted to know how you found out Rezarahn was a traitor back there."

Jharate exhaled and the tense look on his face melted into relief.

"Oh is that all? Do you remember when you caught me in the library?"

"Who could forget?" Lani muttered under her breath.

"Unlike yourself, Rezarahn did *not* catch me."

"What do you mean?"

"I was looking for a book when I heard someone approaching. I thought you and he might be coming in and I was not in the humor to be seen. I hid behind the couch in front of the fireplace. It was very fortunate that I did so. Drakne walked in with Rezarahn. They were arguing. Rezarahn told Drakne that he did not want to keep their previous agreement. At least, he did not want to complete it in every respect. He wanted you," Jharate said with a slight twitch.

Lani blinked in surprise. She didn't know quite how she felt about what Jharate had just said. On the one hand it was somewhat flattering that Rezarahn had not meant to betray her, but on the other, his flattery did not make his betrayal of everyone else any less horrifying. That he had intended to double-cross any one of them when they had been guests in his home! They had been under his protection! It was because of his hospitality that they had even stayed a moment past dawn. They should have been safe!

"Drakne informed Rezarahn that he must go back to Trisakne to attend to a matter of great importance, but that he would return shortly. Drakne added that his men were arriving soon and that Rezarahn was to keep to his agreement in its entirety or he would rue the day that he had ever broken faith with him."

"What did Rezarahn do then?"

"Drakne heard a noise and disappeared into the air, and Rezarahn sat down to feign that he had been reading all along, scarcely in time to see you enter. You know the rest of what occurred in that room, as you were present."

"Then you saw the whole thing?"

"Yes."

Lani looked at him with her eyes narrowing in confusion. If he had seen the entire thing, then how could he have any doubt of her feelings for him? Hadn't she just proved herself, yet again? Lani put the fingertips of her index and middle fingers of her right hand to her temple and rubbed it gently. This was starting to get old. Was this it? Was Jharate just never going to come back to her? Wait a minute— there was something else that only now dawned on her. Her eyes widened and she felt the muscles in her shoulders tense up.

"I'm sorry, I'm not sure I understand all this. Why didn't you just tell me right then and there? If you knew he was a traitor, why would you let me get anywhere near him again?"

"I needed to prepare everyone for departure before I informed you thusly. I feared that if *you* had knowledge of his treachery, your behavior toward Rezarahn would allow him to realize that something was amiss before I could make all of the necessary arrangements. I sent Arante after you the moment we were ready to depart."

"Well thanks for not trusting me and for letting me put my life on the line like a complete idiot!"

"You are in good health, are you not?"

"Yes, no thanks to you! You should have trusted me! He could have killed me!"

"I highly doubt that. You were the one whom he desired to save, remember?"

"But he was told to go through with the plan! You know there's a kill order out on me! What if he *had* gone through with it? You took a gamble with my life!"

Lani could feel her chest rising and falling in rapid succession above the boiling heat rising inside of it. Her anger was coursing through her veins like a poison. She found it odd that most of her anger was not stemming from what Jharate had hidden from her, but from the fact that she had ever gotten so close to such a dangerous and deceptive man as Rezarahn.

But that was Jharate's fault too! If Jharate had just forgiven her, she never would have been susceptible to the charms of the first man to come along and pay attention to her. In fact, no man's charms could have worked on her and it would have been impossible for her to be in that situation in the first place! She was a one-man woman and would have had eyes for Jharate and Jharate alone, had she been his! Rezarahn's charms had barely worked as it stood, even with Jharate and her broken up!

Lani felt a second rush of anger encompass her heart as she returned her thoughts to the fact that Jharate still wasn't coming back to her after everything he had seen her do for him. He had just admitted to seeing the whole thing with Rezarahn! He overheard the entire conversation— every last word! That meant that he knew— he *knew* how unshakably loyal her heart was to him! Lani's hands clenched into tight fists and her knuckles turned white.

"I rescued you. What more do you want?" Jharate asked flatly.

"I WANT YOU! CAN'T YOU TELL? I GAVE UP REZARAHN BEFORE I EVEN KNEW HE WAS A TRAITOR BECAUSE I AM IN LOVE WITH YOU! AND YOU HEARD ME TELL HIM SO! AND YOU WON'T EVEN GIVE ME THE TIME OF DAY! I AM SO SICK OF WAITING FOR YOU! I—"

Lani choked on the words. She felt the stinging in her eyes and the back of her throat. She knew what it meant and she was tired of fighting it. She swallowed hard as tears streamed from her eyes. Her chest shuddered with a pained sigh as she looked at him and her hands fell limp at her sides. She saw the flabbergasted look on Jharate's face. She was honestly surprised he was still there, even if sheer shock from her explosion was the only reason.

Her tears kept falling and she made no effort to stop them. She shrugged her shoulders and shook her head, casting her gaze to the ground as she summoned the courage to finish what she knew she needed to say.

"I go to sleep and dream about you... You come back to me and we are sooooo happy. And then time goes on in the dream... sometimes for months. I get fooled into thinking it is real. And then I wake up. I always wake up! What I wouldn't give to be in a coma, because at least then I would have you with me all the time. I am so sick of waking up to a reality I hate! I am sick of being in love with someone who refuses to love me back!"

Jharate continued to stare at her, looking completely taken aback. He opened his mouth as if to speak but quickly closed it again, only to stare at her in silence.

"Aren't you going to say anything?" Lani pleaded more than asked.

Jharate looked away from her tearful eyes and shuffled his feet as he looked down at the ground. He opened his mouth again, but paused before answering her in a carefully measured tone.

"Perhaps you should not love me anymore if it hurts you so greatly. How could you love, with so much fervor, a person who is only *neutral* towards you?"

Lani gasped sharply. She looked up but avoided his gaze. She felt herself trembling. That remark had cut through to her very heart, and it felt as if it were open and bleeding. She exhaled in a muted moan. Her chest and lungs felt tight, as if they were constricting more each second. Her answer fell from her lips unconsciously as her eyes stared just past Jharate and off into the distance at nothing in particular.

"Because, it's true love, Jharate. I can't explain it. I think we're meant to be together..."

She dared to look up at him as she spoke the last few words of her sentence. Their eyes locked, and she held her breath as she waited for his reply.

"You are mistaken."

The words hit her heart like a shockwave as he turned his back on her. She stared at him with her mouth open. Again?! Had he really just walked away from her *again*? Seriously? She exhaled in disbelief so strongly that a "ha" escaped her lips as she watched him walk away. The back of his head was becoming far too common a sight. The tears in her eyes dried up. Her heart felt like needles were stabbing it numb. She didn't care if he *was* under a spell! She couldn't believe what had just happened! She felt that strange mixture of anger and disconnect again. This was all so surreal and messed up that if she wasn't ninety-nine percent sure she was actually living it— she never would have believed it.

As Jharate disappeared into the nearby forest, Lani closed her eyes tightly and tried to sort through all of Jharate's actions, but who was she kidding? There was no way to sort it out. It was like someone had handed her a twenty-pound bag of sand, each grain dyed a slightly different shade of blue, and told her to sort the grains out according to color! She felt like telling Jharate to sort *this* out! She knew that didn't make any sense but neither did any of this!

Her mind was dizzy and fatigued and sick of dealing with the sadness— and so, instead, she felt it latch on with fierce intensity to the anger that swept through her. The anger felt powerful. She knew that anger was never a good solution, but she wasn't going to *act* in anger so she figured, what could be the harm? Just letting herself *feel* it was intoxicating— and it sure beat the alternative of feeling hurt, alone, and crushed! She felt the heat of the rage boiling beneath her skin and the rush of something exploding deep inside of her.

Justin's eyes flew open and he nudged Tierza without looking at her.

"Um... Is it just me or is Lani starting to glow in the dark?"

"I've never seen anything like it!"

"Whatever it is, I don't think it can be good," Arante added.

Arante got up from where she was sitting beside Erik and walked slowly toward Lani, keeping a wary distance.

"Lani?"

Lani made no answer. She did not move or give any indication of having heard Arante's voice. She stood still and remained quiet. Arante blinked hard to make sure she wasn't seeing things, but there was no denying that Lani was indeed glowing.

"Lani? Snap out of it!"

Still there was no reply. Arante took several steps back as Lani luminesced brighter and brighter. The brightness became so intense that Arante shielded her eyes with her hands. Arante squinted to try to see if Lani was even still there. It was as if Lani were some celestial body wrapped in white flames.

Lani's head snapped up abruptly and her eyes flew wide open, glowing with the same white fire. In that same instant, Lani's arms flew back and her back arched slightly as a shockwave burst forth from her waist in a lightning fast expanding white ring of fire and force. Arante closed her eyes and threw her arms defensively in front of her face as she screamed.

Erik had already jumped up in alarm as he saw what was happening to Lani and realized that Arante was the first in the shockwave's explosive path. He reached for Arante and cried out in fear. Suddenly, everything stopped. All was frozen, right down to the lightning bugs in the air. Erik did a double take. No one else was moving. He shook his head in confusion, but did not spend another second trying to figure it out.

He rushed for Arante. The shockwave was only millimeters away from her stomach. He cradled her in his arms and pulled her away and down to the ground. He shielded her with his own body, fearing that whatever had just slowed things down for him would stop working at any second. No sooner had they hit the ground together than the shockwave whooshed out through the open air in a blinding flash of light. Erik held Arante tightly as the wind from the blast rushed over them.

Everyone else was far enough away that they had time to duck and threw themselves to the ground. The shockwave dissipated unexpectedly and they all looked up with great caution. Once they were sure they were in the clear, they straightened up and all their eyes returned to Lani without so much as one blink shared between the lot of them. Lani was still glowing, but not so brightly that it hurt their eyes to look at her anymore. As they stared on with mouths wide open the light slowly dimmed. As the last of the brightness left her body she staggered a little.

"Wha-what just happened?"

Lani put her hand to her head as though trying to keep from fainting as Raoul rushed to her side to steady her.

"I was hoping you could tell me," Arante said, as she gently nudged Erik off of her and got up to walk over to Lani.

"No. Wait!" Erik yelled.

Everything froze as before, except for Erik. Interesting. Erik's eyebrows rose high on his forehead. Was it possible that *he* was controlling this? He concentrated with his mind and tried to speed things up a little. Things sped up, but faster than he had intended. Arante was barely an arm's length away from Lani now. He slowed things down until they stopped again.

"Oh, I could *definitely* get used to this!" Erik shouted, for no one to hear.

Erik looked questioningly at Lani. She was not glowing anymore and Raoul was touching her. Still, just to be safe… He walked over to Arante, picked her up, and moved her back about five feet from where she was. He then positioned himself in front of her as a shield. Next, he focused his mind and released his hold on the time around them.

"Whoa! How did you get there, babes?"

Erik grinned widely.

"I guess I have an ability after all! But to be on the safe side, maybe don't touch her just yet."

"Ya think?"

"Sorry."

Erik concentrated on rewinding time to the moment before Arante had gotten upset with him. Nothing happened. Rats! That would have been cool. Apparently he only had control over the speed of time, not the ability to travel through it. Oh well, it was something— and it was totally awesome!

Arante walked past Erik and proceeded to answer Lani's question.

"You were just glowing, Lani— like the sun! You were surrounded by white flames and your eyes were white with flames too. What in the fiery depths of the demon underworld was that?"

"I have no idea… I just felt so much… power, I guess. It was thrilling! It was like I could— I don't know what— it felt like I could do anything! I didn't hurt anyone did I?"

"No, but very nearly. So nearly that Erik had to discover his ability to save me. Let's not practice that one again unless you are off somewhere by yourself shall we?"

"I'm not even sure I did it. I mean, I felt like I had the power and the ability to do anything, but at the same time I didn't really feel in control of it at all."

"Another good reason to try and make sure it never happens again."

"I agree."

Lani could tell that Arante was unnerved by the fact that she had no control over what had happened and Arante's eyes were still wary as she regarded Lani. Even Lani felt a little frightened by what she had just felt. But at the same time it was highly intoxicating! What a rush!

Lani bit gently on the inside of her cheek as her mind once again offered the rebuttal. Despite the thrill, she didn't like being out of control of herself, and she had definitely not been in control. She would never have allowed Arante to be put in harm's way like that if she had been.

The power hadn't come to her during good emotions either. She had been angry— extremely angry. If something that intense came out of anger then perhaps it wasn't a good thing at all. And yet, it didn't feel bad either. Lani shook her head. This was becoming a circular argument and there didn't seem to be any answer possible with the facts she had in hand.

Lani jumped as she heard a rustling noise in the nearby forest. She held her breath as she and everyone else drew their weapons and waited. It was so quiet that Lani was sure they would have been able to hear a pin drop— even on the grass.

"I surrender," declared a familiar voice from the shadows.

CHAPTER EIGHTEEN

A commanding figure walked toward them with his hands up, but each footstep became less sure than the last.

"*YOU!*" Arante shouted. "You have got some nerve showing up here!"

"Is there any room for mercy?" Rezarahn asked, with a debonair smile and a gleam in his eyes.

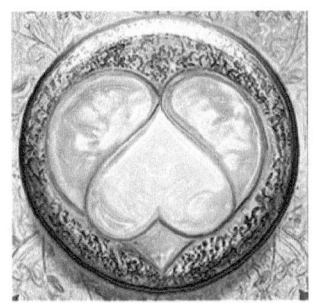

AND WE THOUGHT DRAKNE WAS BAD

Lani felt dizzy— the kind of dizzy that one feels after sustaining a blow to the head. She had barely begun to figure out what had just happened to her with the flaming power, and now Rezarahn was here. Being forced to process the whole new set of emotions attached to him only added to the swirling sensation that was tantamount to vertigo. She reminded herself to breathe and worked hard to make sure she didn't lock her knees. The last thing she needed right now was to faint.

She sheathed her sword at her side, wanting one less thing to worry about balancing. Besides, there were enough weapons currently pointing at Rezarahn to take care of any trouble that might arise. Oddly, she was still eighty percent sure that he wouldn't hurt her even if he got the chance.

She closed her eyes to try to get the world to stop shaking, but it didn't really work. She opened them again and stared at Rezarahn despite the wobbliness she felt. A sting hit her heart and a sense of betrayal welled in her stomach. But for some unfounded and inexplicable reason she felt her soul wanting, even yearning, to trust him again. She put her hand to her temple and rubbed it. What was wrong with her?

"Why should we grant you mercy?" Tierza asked. "You betrayed all of us to Drakne."

"Allow me to explain—"

"Explain quickly." Although not even one second had passed since Arante had demanded an explanation, she already had three arrows loaded in her bow, ready to let fly.

"I did not even know who you were when I was compelled to make that wretched arrangement—"

"And that matters *because?*" Arante snarled.

"It matters because I have been able to maintain some normalcy of life for my kingdom by playing along with those in power. Granted, it may not be as noble a pursuit as blatant rebellion, however, I told myself that I was doing what was best for my people."

"What was best for you, you mean," Tierza snapped.

"Exactly. I was being selfish as well. Then I met you— particularly one of you— and I realized that I did not want to do the bidding of evil any longer."

He looked longingly at Lani, but she looked down at the ground nervously and twirled her hair. She couldn't look into those emerald eyes— even in the near darkness that surrounded them now, his eyes held power. Rezarahn sighed and dropped his gaze away from her as his posture deflated and lost a tinge of its confidence.

"And now you stand before us as a redeemed saint. *Penitent* and ready to join the cause of righteousness," Arante scoffed with an icy tone.

"Well, nothing close to a saint. Though penitent, yes."

"I say we don't take any chances and we kill him where he stands," Tierza declared forcefully.

Rezarahn slowly knelt down on the ground keeping his hands up and his head bowed slightly. When he spoke again his tone was very solemn and sincere.

"If that is what you must do, then you must do it. I will put up no fight. I have proved as much already. Arante can attest to the fact that I am a fire master. As such, I could kill you all in the blink of an eye. However, I am choosing not to do so, which will bring down the wrath of Drakne, as well as that of Vranah, upon me. Therefore, your killing me would be a far better fate than what surely awaits me, once Drakne discovers my deception."

"Oh stop trying to make it sound so noble!" Arante snapped.

"Maybe we should give him another chance," Lani found herself saying, without realizing it. All eyes flashed to her in that instant. Rezarahn looked up at her with a soft close-lipped smile and eyes filled with gratitude. She was shocked by her sudden willingness to go out on a limb for him.

"He played you more than he played anyone here, and you're sticking up for him?" Kendra asked with an incredulous look on her face.

"I'm with Lani," Raoul said. "People deserve a second chance."

"Are you kidding me?!" Justin asked. "We can't trust him after what he did!"

"Agreed," said Laern. "But we do not have to kill him— we can simply let him go."

"What? And have him following us?" Erik asked. "I don't think so. If we are going to let him live, he has to stay with us."

"And then what? Sleep with one eye open every night?"

The moment Arante finished her question, everyone started loudly talking all at the same time. Rezarahn remained silent and kept perfectly still as he waited for his fate to be decided. It was nearly impossible to hear anyone's full point in the chaotic chatter. No one seemed to be able to make up his or her own mind on the best course of action, or agree with anyone else's opinion on the matter. Still Rezarahn waited. Not once in all this arguing did Lani lose her conviction that whatever was to be done with him, execution should be off the list.

Jharate returned to the meadow behind them all. The quarreling was so intense that no one noticed him. He stood quietly, watching his people continue to fight over what to do with Rezarahn. He listened to the various suggestions and arguments that were presented on all sides. However, he eventually ignored them to consult his own feelings on the matter.

He narrowed his eyes and looked at Rezarahn intently. Was this a man who had made a wrong decision and who was still worthy of saving or was he a merely traitor, trying to deceive them once again, who deserved to die? Jharate folded his left arm in front of him and rested his right elbow on it with his fist under his chin as he pondered the matter, never taking his eyes off Rezarahn.

"Silence!" Jharate roared.

All speech ceased immediately. All eyes turned in wild surprise and locked on Jharate as he walked forward to Rezarahn. He stopped just in front of him and looked down with an intense glare. His next words were measured and controlled, but there was no denying the real threat contained within them.

"Rezarahn, I will offer you this *one* chance. Swear your allegiance to us here and now. Kneel before me, give me your fealty, and this will be your ceremony of liege homage. I know your word means something to you. Swear it on your life, for that is exactly what you will be wagering. If you betray us again, you will not get another chance. Is that understood?"

"Yes, Your Highness. I swear it on my life that I will serve you only from this day forward. You truly are your father's son."

Rezarahn bowed his head and placed his fist over his heart in homage. Jharate turned to face the others.

"There you have it. He is one of us now. Drop your weapons."

"THAT'S *IT*?!" Arante yelled in disbelief, relaxing her hold on her bow and throwing the three arrows to the ground without taking her eyes off of Jharate. "*That's* all you are going to do? After what he did to us, you're expecting that we're just going to trust—"

"Yes, cousin. That is *exactly* what we are going to do. Remember to whom you speak. Do not question my judgment."

Jharate moved until he was face to face with Arante, and leaned his mouth extremely close to her right ear to whisper his next words so that no one else could hear— but despite the whispering, Jharate's tone was extremely forceful.

"*Especially* publicly. *I will not stand for it.* Do you understand me?"

"Yes, Your *Highness*," Arante said, through clenched teeth, but turning her mouth near to his left ear and also whispering. "It's funny, you show more mercy and forgiveness towards your enemy than you do toward the woman you love."

"You forget your place, cousin. I am still The Heir to Trisakne and *your* ruler."

"Yes, and Trisakne has fallen! And with it, any power you ever had over me!"

"This is not the time to challenge me!"

"Actually, I think it is the perfect time. You are trusting your enemies and shafting your friends and family. I do not think you are fit to rule this camp anymore, let alone a kingdom!"

"I still have the birthright! I still have my father in me, and I am still meant for greatness."

"Whatever! You can keep it for now. Just know that I won't let you jeopardize us forever!"

Arante pivoted on her heel and marched off before he could reply. Jharate glared at her back as she got further and further away. He slowly realized that everyone was staring at him. They had all obeyed him and dropped their weapons and Rezarahn had been clever enough to extricate himself during the commotion and had found a tree to sit against. Jharate looked each person in the eyes one at a time until they all dropped their gaze to the ground beneath them or to some undetermined point out in the distance— everyone except Lani.

When Jharate turned to look at her, she looked straight back at him. He raised an eyebrow as he regarded her. He searched her face but there was no scowl, no frown, no smile. Likewise her eyes held no malice, no sadness, and no warmth. He shuddered imperceptibly, looked away from her, and strode off in the opposite direction from which Arante had exited.

The moment Jharate walked away Lani rolled her eyes and turned her back on everyone. She walked about twenty feet away from the fire that Rezarahn had started with his gift and lay down, flat on her back, staring up at the stars that were just beginning to pop out against the darkened sky. Lani sighed. As physically exhausted as she was, she was even more tired of Jharate. She was glad that he had spared Rezarahn— it was what she felt was the right thing— but she was done with both of them. No more chaotic spinning, no more arguing with herself, and no more trying to figure anything out— just flat out, no take-backs, d-o-n-e- done.

As she lay there looking at the stars she closed her eyes and slowly clicked the heels of her riding boots together, whispering quietly to herself.

"There's no place like home. There's no place like home. There's no place like home."

She reluctantly opened one eye and saw the brilliant shape-shifting stars still there above her. She opened the other eye and sighed— she was still here. She wasn't sure what she had been expecting, but it had been worth a shot. She shrugged her shoulders and tried to clear her mind until it finally stopped buzzing with all the unanswerable questions she'd been asking for who knows how long now, so she could just exist in her environment. It felt surprisingly nice— in a detached and apathetic sort of way. She was glad that no one came near her. Maybe they could tell that she needed some time to herself— or maybe they were just afraid she would start glowing again. Whatever the reason, not having to think or talk about anything with anyone helped keep her in her Zen state.

Lani took another deep breath and let it out slowly. She settled into the grass and was even more surprised by how comfortable it was. The grass felt better than Lani had ever thought grass *could* feel. It was as if each blade were made of silk. As she stared up at the heavens above, she felt her eyelids getting heavy. She tried to keep them open so she could linger in this calm and peaceful haven, but with each blink it became harder and harder to reopen her eyes. Lani finally gave in to the demands of her body and drifted off into a deep sleep, hoping that her dreams would stay as pleasant as her surroundings.

CHAPTER NINETEEN

Two seconds after succumbing to sleep, Lani saw Drakne. She rolled her eyes. *Of course!* Why shouldn't he be here in her dreams? She shook her head in surrender and watched him with irritated interest. She followed him as he snuck up the stairs and into the throne room in Trisakne. He walked deliberately behind one of the thrones and pulled out a hidden golden box, adorned with the same double heart symbol that was engraved upon the necklace that Arante had given to Lani. She leaned around to try to see what was inside the box as Drakne opened it, and a small cloud of golden dust filled with particles that sparkled like diamonds flew up from it. He reached inside to grab a golden scroll and more particles swirled through the air as he unrolled it.

Lani gasped as she realized what it was. A thrill rushed through her. If she could find out who they were, they would be better able to protect them! The war might end! She focused her eyes intently, ready to read the list of Half-Hearts, but something changed and it was now as if she were inside his mind rather than inside the room and she could only see the names he read.

Khanye Inihma .... Terminated
Sarana Kinartma .... Terminated
Narah Deskarin .... Terminated

Drakne's eyes skipped through the list of remaining names and suddenly stopped on…

Adrienne Brielle Arvanatasi...... Whereabouts Unknown.

Lani felt like an icy hand wrapped around her heart. Did he know who she was? *Wait a minute…* Lani thought, *I'm a Half-Heart?* She hadn't been sure until now. It felt strange, even though she knew all along that there was a one in two chance that she might be one.

Lani was so caught up in her own thoughts that she didn't even see the other name that Drakne had found so interesting. Even if she had, she wouldn't have known who it was. Lani flinched and looked back as she heard the same noise that Drakne did. She realized she had control of where she could look again and quickly turned back to read the list, but Drakne was already hurriedly rolling the scroll back up and putting it inside the box. *Dang it!* Why hadn't she paid closer attention? Drakne disappeared from where he stood the instant the box was closed.

Lani woke up with a jolt and sat straight up. It was quiet all around her but her mind was once again buzzing loudly. What was she to do now? Now that she knew she was a Half-Heart, what was she to do about Jharate? Should she tell him? No, he wouldn't believe her. And even if he did, Jharate's mom had told her that they had to love each other so much that it wouldn't matter if either one was a Half-Heart or not. He obviously didn't love her enough at the moment to take her unconditionally.

But at the same time, how was she supposed to pretend that she didn't know this? She had the key to saving two worlds and she couldn't say a word? *For the love of humanity!* She could possibly just talk to him about their relationship again. She put her fingertips to her temple at the very thought. Hadn't she just sworn off all of that? But then again it seemed it was her only choice, but when? And what could she possibly say that had not already been said?

Lani felt an incredible urge to run over to Raoul, wake him up, and tell him what she had just seen. She nearly did so but something told her not to reveal the fact that she was a Half-Heart to anyone, at least not yet. It was as if a quiet voice whispered it through her ear and into her soul. She felt as if some danger would come from disobeying it, and she had seen enough by now to know that she had to trust her instincts.

Lani's eyes fell on Jharate and she started. It had been so quiet that she thought everyone was asleep and yet, there he was, staring at her— again. Unbelievable! What was his problem? Spell or no spell, this had gone on too long. She had half a mind to— Lani shook her head and looked down at the ground and whispered quietly to herself.

"Get a hold of yourself, Lani. It's okay, just breathe. Just breathe. You don't want to risk a repeat of whatever happened earlier with the whole glowing thing. You're okay. It's okay. Just breathe…"

Lani took several more carefully measured breaths until she managed to quell the raging fire in her chest. She did not look at him again. It was obvious that she wasn't ready to talk to him just now. Not calmly, anyway, and with two worlds hanging in the balance she needed to be sure that she could keep her wits about her. She lay back down and rolled over to go to sleep again.

As she opened her eyes within her dream she realized that she had landed in another vision. She threw her hands up over her eyes and held them there tightly. *Not again!* Lani slowly opened her fingers and peered out from behind them to see what was going on. Vranah had a captive in his throne room, but he was letting someone else have the fun this time. A woman. Lani squinted to see the woman more clearly. She looked so familiar.

Lani stared at her but just couldn't place the face. The woman had fiercely white skin. It was so white that it reminded Lani of the siren. Her hair was very long and curly and arranged flawlessly so that not a strand was out of place. Her luxurious brown locks were so dark they could have been black, and flowed to her waist. However, the color seemed unnatural.

Lani studied her more closely to see if there was any hint of how she might know her. She wore a dark-emerald-green dress made of taffeta and her collar stuck out in a menacing way. The nearly plunging neckline was fringed with black lace in a gesture at modesty, although that was clearly not her intent. She wore a huge emerald necklace. Her flawless make-up was artistically done but it was as dark and harsh as everything else about her.

However, she carried herself with a natural grace and appeared to be quite as obsessed with perfection as Lord Asharen had been. Almost everything about her looks would indicate class, however, there was a feeling that Lani couldn't quite put her finger on. She seemed like she was in her early forties, but still looked as if she could pull off thirty quite easily. Lani could tell that this woman would have been extremely pretty if she had not been so horribly severe— but she still could not identify her.

"Darrahn Kolie," she said with a haunting bell-like laugh. "You have fought too long against your true lord and master. Naughty, naughty, naughty!"

The woman said the last bit while shaking her finger at him with a coy smile. Lani shuddered at the sound of her careless voice. Lani put her hands up in front of her face and hid her eyes behind them as the woman threw a dagger at Darrahn, who was chained up against a thick freestanding wooden wall that must have been brought into the throne room just for this purpose. Lani peeked over the tops of her fingers and sighed in relief as she saw that Darrahn was not dead but quickly put her hands in front of her face again as the woman threw another dagger, and another dagger, and yet another dagger.

Each time Lani tried not to look as much as possible, while still feeling the morbid need to know what was happening. She noticed that Darrahn was only flinching slightly as dagger after dagger was thrown at him. The woman who was throwing the daggers had perfect aim. She threw her knives so that every blade was touching him. Some pinned his clothing to the wall, while others scratched his skin just enough to draw a small amount of blood— but nothing came even close to killing him, yet. Lani's jaw dropped and she felt her skin crawl as the woman giggled and pranced about the room, squealing gleefully and clapping her hands each time she hit her mark. How evil did someone's soul have to be to take joy from something like this? The shock over this behavior kept Lani transfixed and unable to look away any longer. It didn't take long before Darrahn's whole body was entirely outlined with daggers.

Lani felt her heart drop another level as she looked at him. He was so fatigued it was frightening, especially because he was such a large, rugged looking man with huge muscles and in the prime of his life. But his muscles were now unable to even hold him up enough to keep the chains around his arms and neck from digging into his skin and partially choking him. He hung there with his eyes glazed over. Lani put her hand over her mouth to keep from crying out as she saw the bruises on his arms, legs, and face more clearly, as well as the gashes that could have only been made by a whip. What was left of his shirt was tattered and bloody, and from his knees down, his pants were in the same condition. His bare feet were covered in smaller gashes that Lani didn't even want to guess the cause of.

"Beg for mercy," the woman demanded with a bored tone.

Wake up, wake up, wake up, Lani, WAKE UP, Lani thought desperately. It was no use. She was stuck here and she was going to have to witness it so long as it played out. Her heart was beating against her chest like a caged wild animal. Her skin felt like little beads of sweat were glistening on top of every pore. She wondered if this was only happening within this vision or if her sleeping body was experiencing the same thing.

Lani wanted to cry out to Darrahn, if for no other reason than to let him know that he was not alone in what was inevitably his dying hour. But she knew that he would not hear her and that worse, Vranah might. She had to put the fate of both worlds over this one moment. Her sense of panic and despair increased as Darrahn remained silent. She could tell that he knew he was going to die no matter what he said and that he would not give that wretched woman the satisfaction of his begging before he did. Lani wanted all the more desperately to save this courageous man.

"Oh, too brave for mercy?"

The woman grinned as she threw another dagger, but this time it sunk into his right shoulder. Lani placed both hands hard over her mouth to keep from screaming, and she felt a couple of hot tears stinging her eyes and falling down her cheeks as Darrahn groaned in pain, but still said nothing. Vranah came down from his throne to stand beside the woman.

"Now, now, Zarkania, you should at least tell your guest why he has been so honored as to have been brought before me to die, rather than being killed where you found him."

Zarkania smiled and walked over to Darrahn, leaning in close to him and caressing his jawline with her index finger as she talked.

"Oh yes, my gorgeous boy— you are a Half-Heart. SURPRISE! Oh, your parents would be so proud if they had known they had been blessed with a Half-Heart in the family."

Zarkania daintily dabbed her eyes with a black lace handkerchief, pretending to cry like a proud mother.

"Oh, that's right, they're dead. It was a tragic *'accident,'* right? About ten years ago when you were fifteen, in Tofan, their house *'burned down inexplicably,'*" she made quotes with her fingers in the air, "with mum and dad *tragically* inside, while you were out doing your chores in the yard, if I remember correctly?"

Zarkania faked a frown to complement her mock sympathetic tone.

"That was you?!" Darrahn said angrily, speaking for the first time with all the strength he could muster.

"Oops, did I let the cat out of the bag? It was supposed to be a secret. I'm so *bad* at keeping secrets!"

Zarkania threw her head back in a maniacal laugh. Lani couldn't help but stare at her with her eyes wide as Zarkania continued.

"Tragic, isn't it? Oh well, I assume you'll see them soon… if there is an afterlife… Makes no difference to me. Die, Half-Heart, die!"

Zarkania threw a dagger straight into his heart and laughed still harder as the last remnants of life left his eyes. Lani suddenly felt very ill. She put one hand to her heart and one hand over her mouth as she closed her lips tight, breathing through her nose to try to keep herself together.

"Take him to the coffin room!" Zarkania demanded of one of the guards as her laughter continued.

Lani closed her eyes hard, and refused to open them again. She couldn't bear to see Vranah's sick smile, or Zarkania's twisted laughing grin, or the lifeless form of the noble man Lani hadn't even met. The laughing got quieter and quieter, as if she were walking away, until Lani was surrounded by the comfortable silence that she had fallen asleep in. Lani slowly opened her eyes and found that she was once again awake.

She did not sit up this time. She was shaking and covered in a cold sweat— but beyond that, she felt too traumatized to move. Lani could not believe what she had just seen. That woman was so unconscionably evil! She was even worse than Drakne! How was that possible? Lani felt a sudden wave of relief and gratitude sweep over her that it was Drakne who was after them. Whoever this Zarkania woman was, Lani hoped their paths never even came close to crossing. In addition to that, Lani still couldn't stop thinking about how familiar she looked. She knew she had seen her face somewhere before, but where? She knew that she had never known anyone like her— except perhaps Asharen. Lani wracked her brain but nothing surfaced. It would have to remain a mystery for now.

Lani was happy that Rezarahn's fire was still going strong. Even from this distance, she was toasty warm. She watched as the sky began to show the first purplish color of the oncoming dawn. Was the sun coming up already? Lani's eyes flew open wide as a spectacular apparition suddenly appeared from the trees and flew over to Jharate.

Lani rolled over so that she could see better, and watched and listened as a fairy landed directly in front of him, just as he stood up to greet her. Lani was startled to see that the fairy was the same size as a human. She had always thought fairies were small like the fire pixie. The fairy's opalescent wings were stunning. As they caught shafts of the firelight, the mesmerizing effect reminded Lani of the inside of an abalone shell. Her dress appeared to be made of purple silk and silvery cobwebs. She wore a crown that was made of bright spring flowers and delicate green leaves that rested gently on top of her long flowing chestnut locks. Glittering golden strands flowed throughout her silken hair.

"You are Jharate, rightful heir to Trisakne?" the fairy asked, very matter of fact, but with a winsome voice and a gleaming smile.

"I am."

"I am Sateria, Queen of the Fairies. I have news for you from the Castle of Ansena. You have been long expected. They had almost lost hope, until word reached us of a group of strangers who had come through the tunnel. You are to go north to the Cave of Witsan, which lies behind the Waterfall at Delicah. It will take you less than a day to walk there. The King and Queen of Destavnia wish to guarantee your safety. Your instructions are to stay there for five days until your armed escort arrives. They will bring varsins for you and for all who travel with you. I am sent here to ascertain the number."

Jharate looked around at his sleeping people. It pained him to see how few were left alive after their long journey. The number was already known to him, but for whatever reason, being asked to report it stung his heart. He had thirteen of his own people left plus Arante and himself, and then there was Kendra, Justin, Raoul, Erik, Lani, Tierza, Laern, and now Rezarahn. He looked back at Sateria and answered her.

"Twenty three of us remain. However, thirteen will be leaving us immediately. They have family members nearby whom they wish to seek after, so we will require only ten varsins be brought to us at the rendezvous point."

"Very well, I have nothing left to report. Good day to you, Prince Jharate."

"And to you, Queen Sateria."

Sateria gave a royal nod of respect to Jharate, which he returned graciously. She turned back and flew away through the trees. Lani blinked in the light of the rising sun. It seemed to be coming up unusually fast— already in the glowing stages of dawn. Maybe that was just because she had so much on her mind that she wasn't correctly noticing the flow of time anymore. She watched as Jharate woke Arante and told her to wake everyone else. It was done quickly. Lani pulled herself up before Arante could reach her and busied herself with preparing to leave.

As soon as everyone was ready to go, the group split in two— those going on to the castle on one side, and those seeking other destinations on the other.

"I believe this is where our paths diverge," Jharate began as a tear spilled out of one eye. "I owe you each a debt of gratitude. Should we meet again one day and find Trisakne our own once more, you will each be rewarded for your fearless service to me in this, our hour of need. May you travel in safety... my friends."

The thirteen rebels each took one knee, placed their fists to their hearts, and bowed their heads before Jharate. Jaresh was in the front, and spoke quietly on behalf of them all as he looked up at his prince.

"Your Highness, it has been an honor to serve you. And I will see to it that all these who travel with me now make it safely to their destinations. You will see me again at the castle after I have kept my promise. You are a great leader, and will one day make a fine king. Fear not, for we will reclaim Trisakne and restore her."

"Arise," Jharate said.

The thirteen men and women rose up and stood before him. He went to each one and clasped their right elbow as they clasped his. He threw his left arm around their shoulders as they did the same to him. As they held this embrace, they pressed their noses and foreheads together and breathed in deeply as they each repeated the words, "Spirit to spirit until we meet again." After Jharate had finished bidding farewell to each of them, the other rebels followed, bidding their own goodbyes with tender hugs and kisses to the thirteen brave souls who had traveled with them.

"Thanks Jaresh," Raoul said as Jaresh pulled him into a backbreaking hug.

"You are my best apprentice yet. When we meet again, and I have more resources, I shall teach you more skills with herbs so that you may be an even greater healer."

"Thanks! I'm really going to miss *you*, though. You kind of feel like a second father to me."

"Ha, ha, ha! Are you calling me old?"

"No! That's not what I meant at all! I only meant—"

"I jest, Raoul. Do not fret so. I am more than old enough to be your father, and I am honored that you feel such a bond with me. Until we meet again, Raoul."

"Until we meet again."

The goodbyes continued for a little while longer, and more promises were made that this would not be the last meeting, as they warmly wished each other good luck. Tears flowed freely as they finally separated. The thirteen who had fought with them for so long took off in one direction as the ten who were going on toward the castle waved goodbye. Once they could no longer see their friends, the ten turned away and *eleven* people started making their way through the forest to the cave— Drakne had found them.

A DEADLY WORD

Lani's heart leapt as they eventually came upon the large cerulean pool in the woods that they had been looking for. A majestic thirty-foot waterfall cascaded into it, and the pond spilled over a large embankment of rocks on the opposite side into the river below, creating a secondary waterfall. The constant flow of water kept it crystal clear and inviting. Lani wanted so dearly to jump into the water, but there was not enough daylight left to dry off sufficiently and she didn't want to be cold. Besides, they were going to be here for five days. That left plenty of time to enjoy the water. She loved the way that the leaves of the tall swaying trees, lining the pool, fluttered in the gentle wind and glinted like emeralds as they nearly covered the amber trunks. Once again Destavnia had outdone itself. Lani turned to look at Tierza as she heard her voice narrating like a tour guide.

"This is Cascade Pool. The water is delicious! Behind that waterfall is the Cave of Witsan. I would suggest you fill your canteens here before we enter the cave."

The group did as Tierza suggested but Arante shot her a cross look behind her back that looked to Lani as if she were annoyed with Tierza for doing *her* job. Once everyone's canteens were filled, Jharate led them around the pool to the left, through some trees, and onto a natural stone pathway that led to the cave behind the waterfall, which would become their resting point for the next five nights.

As they clambered inside, Lani caught sight of her one true love and once again felt great longing in her heart. Jharate looked away mechanically and began to set up camp. Lani sighed. Her forced detachment from Jharate never lasted for long but at least she was getting more used to this situation. She too started to set up camp without further reaction to Jharate's coldness.

Arante observed this, and gently smacked her palm over one of her eyes. She could not believe how cold he was being to Lani. She became increasingly chagrined that he was her cousin, and began to question if there was a mistake in their genealogy. Her hand tensed and she brought it down and rested the fingers of her closed fist against her lips as she stared at Jharate. With a singularly authoritarian tone, she swiftly commanded all those around her.

"Raoul! Erik! Bring your weapons and come with me. We need to find food for the night. Kendra and Justin you two go together and find wood for a fire quickly. We don't have much light left and it's getting cold. Tierza, Laern and Rezarahn, I don't care what you do, just go find something productive to accomplish and try to bring something useful back. Lani and Jharate, you two continue to set up camp and prepare the beds, as well as gather stones to line the fire pit."

Jharate continued to work perfunctorily as if he had heard nothing, but his jaw tensed. He started slightly as Arante touched his shoulder and spoke to him in a hushed but demanding tone.

"Don't be so stubborn or you will miss what is right in front of you. Don't let your pride win this battle."

Jharate returned to his work without uttering a word. Arante glowered at him in disbelief and made some frustrated threatening motions behind his back, before sighing and turning out of the cave to go hunting for their dinner. She muttered to herself and everyone scrambled to get out and tend to their assignments lest they cross her path. Raoul picked up his crossbow, and Erik his sword, as they walked out behind Arante.

Justin and Kendra headed uphill to a dryer part of the woods and Tierza led the two, who had just been assigned to her, with a quiet indignation. Arante should not have talked to her like that! She ruled a kingdom while Arante was nothing but a deposed heir's second. She pursed her lips tightly to remain silent until Arante was out of sight. She thought for a moment of what would be the best way to retaliate and decided to collect fruits and vegetables. She and Laern could use their super speed to gather a veritable feast that would put whatever Arante could find to shame. She wasn't sure how Rezarahn could be useful until it was time to make the fire, but she smiled at the thought of the look on Arante's face, when dinnertime arrived, as she would finally realize that she had been outdone.

Back in the cave, Jharate found a shovel and began to dig a pit in the cave floor for the fire, acting as if he was the only one there. His muscles tensed as he worked and his jaw remained clenched. There were plenty of stones left over from what must have been many people who had made a fire here before them. It only took Lani a few minutes to gather enough to line the pit once Jharate had finished digging it. Trying to keep herself busy, she proceeded to roll out the sleeping materials for the ten of them. Suddenly she threw down the bedroll she was in the process of unrolling and stood up to face Jharate, even though he kept his back to her.

"Jharate, I know it was a mistake for us to break up. I didn't know how much you loved me. I was under a spell. How was I supposed to know? I didn't know you wanted to marry me until I heard it from Arante, *after* I had already broken up with you. I never stopped loving you and I never will. I just thought you didn't love me. We belong together and you know it somewhere deep inside of—"

"You are wrong."

Jharate's tone was so cold and sure that it made her jump. Once again the words hurt more in the hearing than she had expected them to. But she remained where she was. She wasn't leaving and she wasn't backing down— not this time! She loved him too much to lose him to his pride and that stupid spell. She stood there, squarely in front of him as she planned her rebuttal. There had to be a way to snap him out of this— there just had to be!

Drakne entered the cave, still completely invisible to both of them. He was glad that Jharate's anger and Lani's broken heart prevented either of them from sensing his presence. Drakne grinned at the scene. *Perfect!*

He walked over to Jharate and whispered an enchanted whisper into his ear. Jharate could not hear him with his ears, but instead heard him in his mind, as if Drakne's spoken words were Jharate's own thoughts. Drakne's smile widened as he spoke.

"She is the one to blame, not you. She broke up with you. You can't forget that. She broke your heart and now she wants the chance to do it again. You cannot trust her! You do not love her! It was a mistake. It's over now and it is going to stay over."

Lani was still trying to recover from the words Jharate had spoken, but she gathered all of her courage and her love for Jharate, and tried again.

"Jharate, I love you. I don't know why you can't see that you still love me too. Everyone else can. Everyone knows we were meant to be together. You and I lost sight of it, but if you can just remember…"

Jharate stopped hearing her as Drakne hissed the words into his ear.

"She *doesn't* love you! She needs to move on— and *you don't love her.* Tell her!"

Jharate turned suddenly, towering over Lani, and looked directly into her eyes. He saw her standing firm where she was, refusing to budge an inch. He said nothing as he kept his stony eyes locked on hers. He could feel the thoughts in his mind pressing him to say that he did not love her, but a small feeling in his heart told him that they were untrue. He kept very still and refused to say the words that were flooding his brain.

Drakne frowned. Jharate had not shown any signs of this much strength prior to this moment. Drakne would not accept this. He knew the power of words, and he wanted Jharate to be the one to use them against Lani. He began to speak increasingly louder in Jharate's ear.

"Tell her you don't love her. Say it! Say those words. Say them now. Say 'I don't love you anymore!'"

Lani broke off her speech, and listened. It was as if she had heard something, but not with her ears. It echoed in her mind. A voice that sounded chillingly familiar. She froze with terror and her eyes flew open wide as she realized to whom the voice belonged.

"Jharate! He's here! Drakne's here!"

Drakne's lip curled into an annoyed smile. He was impressed that Lani could sense him, even in such turmoil. Her love must be very strong to counter that much angst. As Drakne leaned even closer to Jharate's ear, his sinister voice resonated in Jharate's mind. He spoke even more insistently in a quiet voice to keep Lani from sensing him again.

"She's lying to you. You would sense it if Drakne were here. You *both* would— not just *her*. She's trying to win you back by pretending to be in danger. Say the words! Tell her you don't love her. Say 'I don't love you anymore.' *Sssaaaayyyy* it."

Jharate remained still and silent. Drakne took a step back and threw his hands up in the air. He couldn't believe that Jharate had not succumbed yet. *Confound that boy*, he thought as he threw a new purple energy ball into Jharate's heart. Jharate's chest flinched as it disappeared within him. His eyes grew colder and he stared at Lani as he began to speak.

"Lani, you are being ridiculous. If Drakne were here I would sense it. We both have that gift, remember?"

"Didn't you just see that? A purple energy ball just flew out of nowhere and went inside your heart! He's *here*! You can't sense him because you are holding onto your anger. Forgive me and give us another chance and you will realize I am telling the truth. Please, Jharate!"

"No. You are lying to me. It will not happen. I will not let it happen again!"

"I love you, Jharate. I love you more than life itself."

Drakne sighed in irritation. Jharate was still resisting saying the correct words even after taking *two* direct hits to his heart from the spell balls. This had never happened before. Jharate was being cruel, but he wasn't saying the words that would really hurt her. Why? Drakne might have been impressed had he not been so focused on executing his plan. He threw the largest purple energy ball yet directly into Jharate's heart. Jharate's chest recoiled and his eyes glazed over into an icy glare.

"Well, I don't love you anymore."

Jharate uttered the sentence with unsettling calmness, not even raising his voice, yet the words penetrated Lani's heart. Surprised, Lani moaned quietly as if she had just been stabbed with a knife. The power of his words made her stagger backwards against the cave wall. She clutched her heart and grimaced as she slid down the smooth rock surface, beginning to breathe hard and nearly gasping for air.

"Finally!" Drakne said to himself.

Drakne smiled. It was working. The power of words, combined with the fact that Jharate was a Half-Heart and had special powers, was so strong that it was literally starting to kill Lani.

Lani was shocked at the physical effect of Jharate's words. She had known that words had power in Alamea, but until now she hadn't thought that they could be a simple phrase. A sharp twinge of fear made her already throbbing heart sizzle with pain as she realized, too late, what Drakne's plan must have been all along. She cried out from the pain before pleading breathlessly with Jharate.

"Please! Don't say that… Can't you see? He's trying to kill me and he knows that you are the only one who is close enough to my heart to break it. Don't let him use you to destroy me. Save me, Jharate. Remember, I love you. Remember, oh please remember."

Drakne infused more energy into his spell. It now flowed in a constant purple stream from his hand into Jharate's heart. He continued to whisper in Jharate's ear and now Jharate said the words in eerie unison with Drakne as he spoke them.

"No, you're lying to me. He's not here. You're just being melodramatic. You're trying to get me to come back to you. It's not going to happen. It's over. It's *over*. Why can't you just accept it and move on?"

Tears rolled down Lani's cheeks as she saw the stream of purple energy flowing seemingly from nowhere and into Jharate's heart. She knew what it meant— her life was about to end if she couldn't break Jharate out of this horrid spell and now its strength was increasing by the second. She couldn't hear Drakne speaking but she knew the words that Jharate spoke were coming from Drakne and that he was carefully leading Jharate where he wanted him to go. It had been nearly impossible for her to get out of her spell and Drakne had not hit her in the heart— still she had to try something.

"Look down, Jharate. Just look down! You'll see the purple energy rushing into your heart. This isn't you! Oh why won't you just look down? I love you. Remember. Oh please remember... It *is* Drakne... You don't even sound like yourself."

"No. I don't love you any more."

Lani cried out and writhed in physical pain as she collapsed to the ground, clutching over her heart with her hands. Despite the agony, she struggled to rise up again— barely able to lift her upper body with her arms. She slipped several times as she attempted to brace herself, each time groaning at the pain.

"Jharate... you're... killing me... stop... please..."

"I'm not killing you. I just don't love you anymore! Accept it!" the two men said together.

With those words she collapsed completely onto her back, and a breathy moan escaped her lips. She couldn't even lift her hand to her heart to clutch it any longer and could barely speak at all.

"Remember... Please..." Lani whispered in agony.

"Stop it! I don't want you. I don't love you anymore!" both Drakne and Jharate insisted.

Lani's body finally went limp and her eyes fluttered closed. She lay completely motionless on the cold cave floor. Her heart stopped and her lungs failed. She was dead. Jharate looked at her with a blank expression. Drakne snapped his fingers and lifted the enchantments, which had concealed him, and simultaneously removed all spells of indifference so that Jharate could see with perfect clarity and feel with excruciating sensitivity the full force of what he had just done.

Jharate's eyes flew open in horror. His emotional pain was far greater than any physical pain could have ever been. He ran to Lani and dropped to his knees beside her. He frantically pulled her lifeless body up into his arms, cradled her head with his hand, held her tightly around her waist, and screamed in anguish.

"NOOOOOOOOOOO! What have I done? What have I done?!"

Jharate looked at her face and stroked her hair as he held her limp form in his arms, shaking his head as he looked at her, tears forming in his eyes. He caressed her arm and held her hand up to his lips and kissed it fervently.

"Do not leave me here, my love! I am so sorry! I am so very sorry... I did not mean it! I have always loved you! I loved you from the moment I first laid eyes on you... I love you with all my heart and soul! I promise you will always be safe with me... I will never break your heart again. Please stay with me! We will be together forever... please stay, my love. Please, Lani. Please!"

Jharate screamed in despair as he rocked with her in his arms. Jharate looked up at the ceiling of the cave as tears streamed down his face and screamed again. He looked down at

Lani and clutched her body close to his heart as he began to sob uncontrollably.

Drakne laughed. "That's right. *You* did this. You thought you were above the influence of evil. You thought you would never succumb. I would say there is substantial proof to the contrary in your arms right now."

Jharate became aware of Drakne's presence. It was like breaking through the ice and feeling the impact of the freezing water beneath. He looked up and his eyes shot hatred at Drakne, as if the look alone could kill him, but nothing happened. Drakne remained there, laughing at his misery.

Jharate had nothing to say. He could not deny it. He had been prideful. He had thought that he would never fall under Drakne's influence. But the proof *was* right here in his arms. She had been so much stronger than he— and he had just killed the love of his life!

"You want to know something fascinating?" Drakne asked, pausing for effect. "She was a Half-Heart too."

Jharate's heart nearly stopped and he could barely breathe.

"Yes, she is the long lost Princess Adrienne Brielle Arvanatasi. You two could have fulfilled the prophecy and made quite the power couple. Not only that, but there is something unique about both of you. You two are *complementary* Half-Hearts. You only fit each other. So, of course, your union would have been extraordinarily powerful, and you would have most assuredly won the so-called 'battle against evil.' Tragic, simply tragic. Tsk tsk tsk."

Drakne formed a deadly red energy ball and tossed it back and forth between his hands.

"However, there *is* some good news. As you two only fit each other, you don't need to die. Instead, you will simply never love again and be forever haunted by the image of the woman of your dreams, dying at your hand. Without a doubt, I could not do better than that."

Drakne nonchalantly threw the red spell ball at the waterfall, blasting a fleeting six-foot hole in its previously continuous roaring cascade of water. Vapor filled the room as the waterfall resumed. Drakne took off his black leather gloves, cast them aside, and laughed again— sending a chilling echo, which traveled out of the cave.

So far out of the cave, in fact, that Arante and all of the others heard it traveling on the gentle winds even though they were scattered throughout the woods. They all froze in their tracks and immediately turned back and ran for the cave.

Drakne stopped laughing, but his smile remained as he looked down on Jharate. He knew that the others he traveled with would be there soon. Drakne snapped both his fingers and held out his palms. Lani's body disappeared from Jharate's grasp and simultaneously materialized in Drakne's arms. He stood there triumphantly holding her limp body as her hair cascaded to the ground. Jharate looked up at Drakne with murder in his eyes.

"It was nice seeing you again, Jharate. Thank you for helping me. It saved me the trouble of trying to kill her. You see, I couldn't have done it without help. She was far too strong. Only the one she loved and gave her heart to had the power to kill her. Goodbye."

Jharate rushed Drakne with a furious yell but was only able to seize the air where Drakne had been standing. Drakne had vanished, taking Lani's body with him. Jharate fell to his knees and screamed. He fell forward and his face scraped against the dirt and rocks of the cave floor until his body settled against the cold hard ground and everything went black.

REGRETS

Drakne appeared inside his personal suite in the Castle of Trisakne. He phased himself, along with Lani's body, into the fifth dimension so that he would be invisible and intangible to anyone who entered his room. Only two details distinguished his quarters in this dimension from the way that it appeared in the normal realm— a large gilt-framed mirror on the wall and a strange machine standing in the center of the room. He hurried towards the contraption.

A transparent tube large enough for a human to stand upright within it made up most of the device. The top and bottom of the tube had copper caps with intricate designs that were as much for artistic appeal as they were for structural support. It looked like some sort of giant radio tube with visible electric current flowing throughout the glass enclosure.

Drakne snapped his fingers and Lani's body teleported inside the tube— suspended upright with her feet just inches from the bottom. Her body floated as if she were under water, while the electric currents inside the tube began to course around her. Her hair floated like a mermaid's and her arms rose slightly from her side. Drakne watched intently, with his brow knit, as he muttered incantations. As the moments wore on, the lines in his forehead increased and he kicked the base of the machine hard with his foot.

"Work! BLAST IT ALL! WORK!"

He watched and waited. Nothing happened. He muttered the ancient words over and over again, more emphatically each time as he gestured toward the machine, circling it all the while. Nothing.

"WORK!"

Drakne kicked the base of the machine again and recited the same words, nearly shouting them until at long last her body shuddered and began to breathe again. The machine amplified sound and he could hear her heart beating. He sighed in relief as he heard the mechanical beats continue at a normal rate. She did not regain consciousness, but that was to be expected. He quickly levitated the machine in front of the immense mirror, which was the same height as the glass tube. He muttered a few more carefully chosen words and the mirror began to pulse with energy as electricity flowed throughout the mirror itself.

Back in the cave, Jharate heard voices. They sounded as if they were far off in the distance. They were speaking Trisaknen, but somehow he could not understand what they were saying. He tried to open his eyes and failed. Fear set in as he realized that opening his eyes was not the only thing he could not do and he struggled to move anything in vain. Finally he relaxed from sheer exhaustion and succumbed to the dark void he found himself trapped in. The voices became clearer and he was slowly able to recognize them.

"What happened, Arante?" Justin asked.

Arante held up her right index finger to silence him. She paced back and forth, moving her hands through the air and whispering to herself. Justin lit a few lamps to provide more light. As Arante worked, two holographic images appeared. Lani and Jharate stood in their places and re-enacted the scene that had just been played out only minutes before the rest of the camp had arrived. Everyone turned to look and listen.

"You are wrong," said the holographic Jharate.

As he said this, they saw a third holographic character emerge onto the scene. Tierza gasped.

"Drakne? How did he get here?"

"Shhh!" chided Arante.

They continued to observe the pitiable scene and watched, eyes wide with horror, as Drakne threw a purple spell ball into Jharate's heart followed shortly after by a larger one.

"Well, I don't love you anymore," said the holographic Jharate.

"Finally!" the holographic Drakne blurted out.

The power of Jharate's words threw Lani against the wall and she fell to the floor, struggling to breathe. Kendra put her hand over her mouth as she saw Lani's agony and Raoul cringed as he saw the holograph of Drakne smile.

"Please! Don't say that... Can't you see? He's trying to kill me and he knows that you are the only one who is close enough to my heart to break it. Don't let him use you to destroy me. Save me, Jharate. Remember, I love you. Remember, oh please remember," pleaded a desperate image of Lani as a constant purple stream of energy began to flow from Drakne's hand into Jharate's heart.

"How could he do this?!" demanded Justin.

"Drakne is evil, that's how," Erik stated, as though he were spitting out a bug that had flown into his mouth.

"Not *him*! Jharate!" Justin snarled.

"Drakne was controlling him! Didn't you see the spell balls and that horrid purple stream of energy? Can't you see? Look at the images of Drakne and Jharate. They are starting to speak the words at the same time!" Tierza pointed out.

"Like that matters! Lani was able to get out of it! She wouldn't have hurt Jharate!"

"Seriously!" Kendra agreed.

"Shhhhh!" Arante demanded.

Jharate's heart sank as he heard their comments. They were right. He should have been stronger! Tears flowed out of his closed eyes. He still could not move but he did not care. He felt his self-loathing deepen and twist around his stomach until it clenched so tight he was sure it would burst as he listened to Lani pleading with him again.

"Jharate... you're... killing me... stop... please..."

"I'm not killing you. I just don't love you anymore! Accept it!"

The holographic image of Lani collapsed as she whispered her last words.

"Remember... Please..."

"Stop it! I don't want you. I don't love you anymore!"

Kendra gasped as Lani's body went limp and her eyes closed. Justin felt a tightening in his throat as he tried to swallow. Erik slowly looked away from the image of Lani's dead body and quietly hung his head.

"NO!" cried Raoul. "I— She was— She was my best friend."

Raoul grasped for a rock behind him to steady himself just as the holographic Jharate screamed and rushed to Lani's side.

"NOOOOOOOOOOO! What have I done? What have I done?! Do not leave me here, my love! I am so sorry! I am so very sorry… I did not mean it! I have always loved you!"

A tear fell from Rezarahn's eye as he watched Jharate's attempts to revive Lani fail.

"We will be together forever… please stay, my love. Please, Lani. Please!"

Kendra's eyes filled with tears as she watched the gut-wrenching scene before her. Her heart broke for both of them, even as a boiling anger began to rage inside of her for the death of her sister. She put her hand over her heart and barely even heard the holographic Drakne as he taunted Jharate.

"That's right. *You* did this. You thought you were above the influence of evil. You thought you would never succumb. I would say there is substantial proof to the contrary in your arms right now."

"He should have been stronger," Justin snarled as Drakne paused.

"You want to know something fascinating? She was a Half-Heart too."

"What?!" everyone cried out together.

"Are you serious?!" Justin yelled as he threw his hands over his face and pulled them down slowly.

"You two could have fulfilled the prophecy…" Drakne continued.

"Oh what an idiot! They were so close!" Kendra exclaimed in disgust.

"So close…" Arante uttered mechanically as she sighed and sank to the ground. She went numb inside as she realized just how close they had truly come to winning the war against Vranah. She inhaled sharply, her eyes wide, as she snapped back to the moment and saw a red spell ball form in Drakne's hand.

"However, there *is* some good news. As you two only fit each other, you don't need to die. Instead, you will simply never love again and be forever haunted by the image of the woman of your dreams, dying at your hand. Without a doubt, I could not do better than that."

The Alameans in the cave could not help but sigh in relief as Drakne discarded the deadly energy ball into the waterfall. Drakne threw his holographic gloves to the ground, where they landed exactly on top of the real pair, which was still there. The chilling echo of Drakne's laugh filled the chamber as the steam did the same. He snapped his fingers and Lani's body disappeared from Jharate's arms and appeared in Drakne's.

"It was nice seeing you again, Jharate. Thank you for helping me. It saved me the trouble of trying to kill her. You see, I couldn't have done it without help. She was far too strong. Only the one she loved and gave her heart to had the power to kill her. Goodbye."

"Oh, how awful!" Tierza exclaimed.

They watched helplessly as Jharate rushed Drakne, only to grab air and fall to his knees. They heard Jharate scream before he lost consciousness and the holograph of Jharate faded where he had fallen until only the ground showed. Deafening silence gripped them all as they mourned their losses. In just minutes Jharate had killed Lani and they had lost the biggest chance they had ever had, in all the history of Alamea, of defeating The Evil One forever. They remained deathly still, paralyzed with their thoughts and emotions.

"I don't understand," Justin began, "Jharate didn't do anything to her. He didn't touch her... How is she dead?"

"It was the power of words, Justin," Tierza finally answered quietly when no one else spoke. "Here in Alamea certain words have physical power. Words such as 'love' and 'hate' do not simply heal or hurt one emotionally— they affect the body as well. There are also words that are never used in conversation. These powerful words belong in two categories and two categories only. One side serves darkness, evil, chaos, and destruction, and the other serves light, good, order, and life. Many of the dark words are too evil and too powerful to be written down and therefore good people never do so. Conversely, it would be worthless to write down the equally powerful words of good, because they are of no use to anyone whose heart, spirit, and mind are not truly pure— and they are always revealed to those who are. The fact that Jharate was a Half-Heart intensified the power of words, and that is what... killed Lani."

"Oh..." Justin said quietly.

Silence fell again— deeper, and even more unbreakable than the last.

Jharate suddenly realized he had been moved. He became aware that he was on one of the beds that Lani had prepared. Kendra was mechanically wiping his forehead with a cold damp cloth, without realizing what she was doing. Jharate felt a strong pressure on every inch of his body as if he were being crushed. There was a burning sensation in his chest and his stomach and a chilling one everywhere else. He felt wracked with guilt and wished that the pain he was feeling would just kill him. Drakne was right— leaving him alive had been the worst thing he could do to him.

Jharate lay there, willing himself to die, unsuccessfully. Why oh why oh why?! He wanted to grab his own sword and fall upon it. If only he could move. He had just killed his one true love and he did not deserve to live. He exerted all of his energy to try to move something— anything. Suddenly his eyes flew open. Encouraged by this development, he tried to move his arms, only to discover he was still paralyzed. He groaned to himself, but everyone heard the noise. All at once, eight faces turned to Jharate.

Superb, thought Jharate. *Now everyone is looking at me. They must hate me. I do not blame them. I cannot. I hate myself as well. Oh please, Erik, kill me! Take your sword and run me through! I do not deserve to live!*

Jharate sighed as, to his dismay, Erik remained where he was and showed no such intent. Jharate attempted to speak, but only air escaped his lips. Why was he still breathing at all? Why could he not just die?

Arante was the first to move. She walked over to Jharate and grabbed his hand in both of hers, her eyes brimming with tears. Her heart broke for him for the loss he had inflicted upon himself. No one deserved that.

"It's okay. You are safe now. We saw the whole thing with my gift. We know what happened. I am so sorry."

Arante's compassion struck Jharate to the core and he felt like his heart was being crushed in someone's fist. He groaned from the pain. How could they still care about him after what he had done— after what he had cost them? It was worse than being hated. Hate he could deal with. Hate would seem normal, fair, and deserved. This kindness only made him feel the horrific depths of what he had just allowed himself to do even more keenly.

Suddenly Jharate became aware that Raoul was pointing his crossbow at him. Jharate's instinct for self-preservation overcame his desire to die and his eyes opened wide in helpless alarm. Kendra saw the look on Jharate's face and turned in time to surmise that Raoul desperately wanted to pull the trigger. She instinctively raised a shield to protect Jharate.

"Take down the force field, Kendra," Raoul said with a deadly tone.

"No, I won't."

"HE KILLED LANI! And you're protecting him?! He killed her! HE KILLED HER!" he said, his voice cracking as he spoke.

"Yes, he did, and I hate him for that. But killing him won't bring her back."

"But he KILLED her! Don't you understand? It was Lani I saw when the siren held us all captive! It was her! And do you know why? Because I loved her! But she loved Jharate! And he treated her like dirt! How many times did she try to fix things with him? How many times did he break her heart? She sacrificed a YEAR of her life, and what did he do? He was so hardheaded and weak!" Raoul spat out, choking on the words, his voice now becoming even more erratic. "He couldn't see what was right in front of him. He killed her— He— He—"

Tears streamed down Raoul's face, and he was unable to finish his sentence. But the crossbow remained raised and his finger was still tensed on the trigger.

"Raoul, put the crossbow down. I am angry with him too. She was my sister! But Lani wouldn't want this, would she? She loved Jharate, and she wouldn't want him dead. You know that."

"But she isn't here… I have to avenge her! I loved her. She was my best friend and I loved her! You don't understand…. He killed her!"

"Yes, I do understand… and yes, he did kill her. But I think he is paying for that more than anyone else in this room. You saw him. He was obviously under a spell. It wasn't all his fault."

"*He should have been STRONGER!*"

"I know. He should have been. You're right. He was weak and he succumbed to evil. But killing him won't do anything but destroy a little bit of your soul. You kill him like this when he's defenseless and that makes you a cold-blooded murderer. That doesn't sound like you, does it, Raoul? Now put it down. *Raoul!* Put it *down!*"

Raoul stared at Jharate and, with a groan, lowered his weapon and began to sob. He turned and ran out of the cave.

"Erik, follow him," called Arante.

Erik slipped out and followed Raoul off into the night. Drakne's gloves caught Rezarahn's eye. He glared at them and they burst into flames and incinerated instantly.

"I think we dropped the firewood out there," Justin said, feeling a strong desire to leave.

"Oh yeah, I'll come help you," Kendra answered, dropping her shield and quickly following Justin out of the cave.

Arante turned her face back to her cousin. The tears that had been welling up now spilled over and streamed down her cheeks. Arante opened her mouth to speak but could find no words. She simply kept Jharate's hand in hers and watched over him protectively in case Raoul got back before Kendra.

The pressure Jharate felt both outside of his body and within it continued to take its toll. His eyes became heavy and, as the pain became too much to shoulder, they closed completely. His head fell to the side and he fell into a deep, death-like sleep.

Lani opened her eyes and looked around, only to discover that she was still inside the cave. Jharate was digging the pit. She jumped up and whirled around. Hadn't she just— Was it possible she had dreamed the whole thing? She leaned down and felt the ground with her hand. The texture of the dirt and the rocks beneath her fingers and their slight coolness seemed right. She slapped the back of her left hand hard with her right. She felt the stinging sensation she expected. But what did—? When had she fallen asleep? She didn't even remember lying down. Had it been a vision? She turned and looked at Jharate with a quizzical glance.

"How long have I been sleeping?"

Jharate turned to face her with a raised eyebrow.

"I don't know what you are referring to. You have not been asleep. You've been working."

"What? That can't be right… Really? I had the strangest thing happen just now… almost like a vision… it was so real."

"What about, my love?"

"My love? Are we still… together?"

"Of course we are! Why wouldn't we be? I love you."

Lani's eyes widened even more. She felt a nagging little voice deep inside of her telling her that something was wrong— very wrong. But at the same time she was so relieved to hear those words that she couldn't help but accept them.

"I had the strangest dream… You were in it. We had broken up because I didn't know you loved me as much as you did— like what happened with me and Josiah. I found out that you wanted to marry me from your cousin, Arante, but it was too late. When I tried to talk to you about it, you said…"

Lani broke off and looked around the cave. Something was wrong and she knew it. It hadn't been a dream. It just couldn't have been— but if it wasn't, where was she now?

"What did I say, angel?"

Lani jumped at the sound of his voice. She had almost forgotten he was there. *Get a grip,* she thought to herself. *He's right here. He says you never broke up. It was a dream. Be happy!*

"You wouldn't forgive me and you said that you didn't love me anymore again and again until the power of your words killed me."

"Oh no! I would never do anything like that. I love you too much. I would never want to speak even one harsh word to you, my angel. You deserve only love, gentleness, and kindness forever. Come here, my love."

He sat down on a blanket and leaned against the cave wall. He patted the spot next to him with an angelic smile on his face. With that, Lani smiled, ran over to him, and threw her arms around him as a wave of relief and passion swept over her. He returned her affection with a gentle but quite passionate kiss on her forehead. She was sitting next to him now, with her legs bent to the side, facing him so that she could look into his eyes. There was so much love within them.

She sighed as she stretched up to kiss him on his cheek and then snuggled up against his chest to enjoy this perfect moment. He wrapped his arms around her. His hands felt so good on her back. She breathed the moment in deeply and the tension inside her heart melted away. Lani felt like she was finally home again and let herself fall asleep in Jharate's arms.

Jharate awoke slowly and with great difficulty, as if he had been drugged. He tried to get up but found himself still paralyzed— although he could now move his neck. The sunlight streamed in from behind the waterfall and sent reflections everywhere. He realized he was still in the cave. He wondered how long he had been here. He turned his head and found Kendra at his side taking care of him. Seeing that he was awake, she spoke in a quiet but cross tone.

"Glad you finally decided to join the living again. We were getting worried."

Jharate answered in a raspy voice but was extremely relieved to find that his vocal chords were now functional.

"How long have I been unconscious?"

"A little over three days."

"Three days?" he coughed over the words.

"Oh, don't force yourself to talk. Here have some water."

She lifted a bowl to his lips, propping him up with her knee so that he could drink it without choking on it. Once he had finished, she gently set him back down on the bedroll again.

"Thank you."

"Don't mention it," Kendra mumbled.

Jharate felt his heart slowing down a little as he tried to think of how to phrase the question pressing on his mind— and for a moment it seemed as if perhaps his heart had stilled altogether as he opened his mouth to ask.

"Kendra, did I truly... Is Lani...?"

Jharate could not bring himself to finish. He shut his eyes tightly and waited with bated breath for the answer he already knew.

"Yes, I'm afraid so. That's one of the reasons you have been out so long. Raoul refuses to heal you. It took Arante two days to convince him to heal your vocal chords and give the use of your neck back to you, but he said that is all he will do and that you will have to figure out the rest on your own."

"I deserve worse. I deserve to die. I killed her. I—"

"It wasn't entirely your fault. You were under a spell. Drakne hit you with an awful lot of magic."

Kendra rolled her eyes away from Jharate and looked up at the ceiling. She wished he would just shut up! Trying to make him feel better right now was making her feel awful. She didn't want to talk about this at all, let alone to appease the conscience of the man who had just killed her sister!

"I should have been stronger! I swore to her that I would always love her and that I would always... protect her... and I *failed her!* And that is not all— I killed her *myself!* Why did you stop Raoul from killing me? Why?"

"Stop that talk! Killing you would have done no good for any of us. It would have made Raoul a murderer and we still need you. Your gift of vision is irreplaceable. Especially now that Lani, God rest her soul, is gone. Besides, we still love you, even if none of us are very happy with you right now. It's odd, you know, but we can't tell how you got paralyzed. We watched the entire scene. Drakne did nothing to you, and you didn't fall in a way that would cause this. Arante thinks that your mind and body just sort of shut down because of your loss. You should recover though, and Raoul might be persuaded to help eventually."

"I wanted to die. I tried to die. I *begged* to die. Perhaps this is as far as my body was willing to oblige me. Only when Raoul threatened to kill me did the desire to live return to me. Instinct I suppose— self-preservation. Ironic. Had he not attempted to kill me, he may have gotten his wish."

"Yes well if that's true, I'm glad he tried. You're our friend too, you know. Losing two of you wouldn't help anything. Besides, isn't there maybe a chance she isn't dead? I mean, he took her, didn't he? Why would he do that?"

"She is dead. Do not fantasize otherwise. I held her body. I felt the warmth drain from it. I could feel that her heart was no longer beating. She is dead. And I still wish I was with her!"

"Well, you aren't! So it's time to get over yourself and start thinking about everyone else! We still have a war to win here. You are a great leader and a great soldier. We need you, and we need you whole. So start getting better so that we can move out! We can mourn her loss when we have time but we don't have that luxury right now."

"You are so strong. I heard what you said to Raoul. I just killed your own sister, and here you are attending me."

"It's what she would want me to do."

Kendra sighed. She didn't want to feel the sadness within her and her frustration was hard to control, yet somehow she was trapped between the two emotions. She greatly resented the fact that Jharate would not stop talking to her. She took a shuddering deep breath in and let it out quickly as Raoul walked into the cave to get his hunting gear. She was relieved simply to have a distraction.

Raoul looked at Jharate and saw he was awake. Kendra could tell that Raoul's anger had subsided slightly, but it was still obvious that the sight of Jharate made his skin crawl. Raoul walked over to Jharate and placed his hands on his chest— the white light came and went quickly. Raoul snatched up his crossbow bolts and walked out again. Kendra watched as Jharate moved his arms and pushed himself up, positioning himself against a rock.

"Arante must have bargained for the upper half of my body"

"I suppose so. You still can't move your legs then?"

"Not at all."

"Oh well. Arante is very persuasive. She'll eventually get Raoul to heal your legs too. Here, eat this. You must be starving. You haven't eaten in three days."

Jharate's stomach growled as he saw the food and he felt his mouth water. He had not noticed until this moment how very hungry he was. He felt a certain amount of guilt that his body had decided that it was time to continue on as if everything were normal— but nothing would ever be normal again. He graciously took the offered food, and began to devour it like a starved animal.

Lani slowly roused from Jharate's shoulder. She looked up at him with a smile, but her smile fell flat and her eyes narrowed. This couldn't be real— but it felt so good, *dang it!* What was going on here? She felt crazy! She had either been dreaming the whole break up or she was dreaming now. Or she was dead and this was some sort of afterlife limbo— perhaps a test of some kind. She wanted to believe more than anything that this was the *real* reality. She looked around and saw that she and Jharate were still the only two in the cave.

"Where is everyone else, Jharate?"

"They're out getting supplies and food, remember?"

"Odd... I thought they would be back by now..."

"They should be here soon. In the meantime, there's something I need you to do for me, my darling."

"What is that?"

"Read this aloud for me."

He handed her an ancient looking scroll. As she unrolled it the words looked like Latin and she wondered how that could be. Wasn't everything translated automatically here? Something was wrong... It was *all* wrong! But it should be right. This is how things should be— the two of them together and in love. She sighed. She wished so dearly to please Jharate and so she ignored her feelings and opened the scroll all the way.

She held it in front of her as she read it aloud, like one entranced. As she did, the cave began to spin around and it got harder and harder to read. Still Jharate pressed her to read for him and so she did. The spinning increased in speed and changed directions from side to side to up and down, making her feel like she was inside a gyroscope as the space around her turned into a revolving sphere of colors swirling around her in a frenzied blur. As she read the last word, there was a deafening crack and suddenly the cave was gone.

Lani beheld her reflection in a mirror, directly in front of her. Electricity pulsed all around her and through the mirror itself. Her heart beat wildly within her chest and then suddenly she couldn't feel it at all! Her breath had been hard and fast and now it was gone! A split second after proof of life had vanished, she felt like she was floating— a sickening uncontrolled feeling— away— away from her body!

Jharate finished his meal and set down the bowl. He was the only one in the cave now. Kendra had gone out, supposedly to get more firewood, but he knew better. He knew how angry she was with him. He knew how angry everyone was with him. He understood because they could not be angrier with him than he was with himself. He reached for his deerskin bag of belongings, undid the drawstring, pulled out a leather-bound book, and opened it. The book was old and worn, but well cared for. His mother had given it to him when he was a young boy to record his thoughts, his dreams, his hopes, his joys, his pains, and his triumphs. He turned to the day that Lani had entered his life and read the comments he had made.

Today was the most magnificent day of my life. I met a maiden who is more beautiful than any I have ever laid eyes upon. She is the maiden who walks through my dreams— the girl in my visions. I recently received a vision in which I discovered that I am a Half-Heart. To think that she might be a Half-Heart as well is impossible, and I dare not dream it, as she comes not from Alamea. However, I do not care if she is a Half-Heart or if she is not. I love her already. It is as though fate has brought us together and I intend to spend the rest of my life with her...

Jharate closed the book tight and threw it back into his bag. He turned his head away and closed his eyes. How could he have been so foolish? The proof had been there in his journal all along, in a bag that never left his sight. How could he have let this end? Why had he not decided to fight *for* her rather than to fight *with* her?

His mind revisited every wasted moment— every missed opportunity. It was obvious that she had wanted to reconcile from the moment that she had pushed him away. Why had he not simply told her the words she needed to hear? Why had he been so prideful and let his ego reign supreme? If he had only let go and put his heart on the line, they would be together now. They would be on their way to Destavnia to be married. More than that...

A sudden chill coursed through his veins and he threw his fists up to his forehead. Oh! So much more than that! Drakne had revealed to him that she was a Half-Heart as well! They would have fulfilled the prophecy! They would have had enough power to end the grip of The Evil One on the land and to save both of their worlds in the process. Oh how he hated himself now! Even more than he had a moment ago. He had failed everyone. He had failed two entire worlds— all because he was too prideful to make amends. He looked up at the ceiling of the cave, as if he were looking through to the stars in the sky, and spoke quietly.

"Oh my dear Mother and my honorable Father, how I wish you were here to guide me. I have done so much wrong. I have failed so many people. Worst of all," his voice broke and became even softer, "I have killed the woman I love... Help me to find some way to make things right. Help me to make something of my life now. Help me to be strong and never succumb to evil again. Help me find a way to make my life mean something once more. Please, let Lani know how sorry— how sorry I am! And that— I love her."

Jharate could speak no longer. Tears flooded his eyes and his throat felt as if it were blocked. He pulled his legs up with his arms, so that he could rest his head on his knees as he held them and cried. He cried for Lani most of all. He could not believe what he had done to her. She had died feeling alone and unloved.

He wished he could go back in time and restore what he had taken. He regretted all the lost moments of their past, he regretted all the lost moments of their future— he regretted everything. He would have given anything to set things right, but how could he ever do so?

TRAPPED

Lani was beyond confused. She had passed through to the other side of the mirror and was now looking out at her own body as it floated in the machine. She wondered if it was floating in water or just in air. Was the electricity damaging her body? Why wasn't she dead? Or was she dead? She heard the mechanical beats of a heart she could no longer feel and saw her chest rise and fall with breaths she could no longer take. Her body seemed to be on life support. But where was *she*?

Lani stared at her floating body as she tried to make sense of what was happening. Then she looked down at herself and noticed that she still seemed to be wearing the outfit that Rezarahn had given her, as was her body in the tube, which only created more questions. She thought back to the cave when Jharate had told her that he didn't love her and remembered everything going black— and how suddenly, a bright light had appeared. The light was peaceful and inviting and had beckoned her forward. But before she could reach the captivating light, something had grabbed her and yanked her back.

Then, all at once, she was with Jharate again, reading the scroll and then... this. What was this exactly? She tried to remember the details. She had just finished reading and… then she wasn't in the cave anymore. She had seen her reflection in the mirror, surrounded by electric current, and then she had started to float… As she was flying through the air, she looked behind her and discovered that she was drifting away from her body! When she turned back to look where she was being pulled to, she had seen the mirror. Afraid she was about to crash into it, she had closed her eyes and had thrown her arms over her face reflexively.

But she did not hit the mirror. When she opened her eyes again she seemed to still be in the same room staring directly at her body in the tube, just six feet in front of her. Disoriented, she had spun around to look behind her at where she had come from. The frame of the mirror was identical but now held a window. Looking through it, she could see the tube with her body still floating within it, once again directly in front of her, approximately six feet on the *other* side of the glass window. How was her body in two places at once? And why was she out of it?

She looked down and realized that her feet were on the ground again. Suddenly the entire machine began to float off deeper into the room, and she watched until it gently descended and settled into the far corner. She turned around and the machine on her side of the glass had moved to the same spot. Unnerved, she turned to look back through the window in the mirror frame. There stood Drakne! She reeled around, thinking that she could be looking at a reflection and that he might actually be standing beside the machine in the corner behind her. There was no one there. She turned to look through the glass once more. He was inspecting the device that held her body.

"YOU!"

"Is that any way to speak to the man who saved your life?"

"Saved my life? So I was— The cave— I really did die?"

"Well, yes... and at the same time, a categorical no. You see, Jharate *was* killing you and you would have died. On the last 'I don't love you' that he spoke, I stopped your heart and lungs artificially. You were really only unconscious before I did that. He would have had to say it one more time to kill you, and I am sure that he would have, but I couldn't have that. It would have been too permanent to undo."

"Why 'undo' it at all? I am a Half-Heart, aren't I? Isn't it kind of a goal for you and your keeper to kill every last one of us?"

"Can you really be that in the dark as to my motive? Can you truly not see why I have done all of this?"

"Not really," she said irritably.

"I have done this all for you. For us... I love you."

Lani's mouth dropped open. Had she been able to feel anything physical at all, she was quite sure nausea would have been at the top of the list. It was strange to feel emotions without the commonly associated physical effects, but she was completely and utterly appalled. She didn't think that Drakne was even capable of love, in any form, and why he had set his sights on her was beyond her comprehension. They were nothing alike. She loved light, love, truth, and righteousness, and he loved darkness, hatred, lies, and evil. How could he possibly expect her to return any love at all?

Seeing this in her eyes, Drakne slowed his speech and softened his voice, with a pleasant expression on his face.

"Don't you see? We are currently in the fifth dimension. Vranah cannot sense us here. He will not know that you are alive. Especially now that your double is complete."

At first, Lani looked at the machine to see what Drakne was referring to, but realized that he was gesturing beyond the tube that contained her original body. She leaned closer to the window so that she could see more of the room and looked to the very far right in another corner to where he was indicating. There, floating horizontally in mid-air was a duplicate of her body, lying with arms folded across the waist. Despite no longer having a physical form, it chilled her to look at the double, and so she looked away. She determined that she would not turn around to look into that part of the room on her side. She did not want to see it. No one would be able to tell that the suspended thing was not her. Any hope of rescue she had now faded away.

Drakne strode over to the double and examined it with immense admiration for his own work.

"You will have to excuse me. Vranah is expecting your body and I have to take this to him or he might suspect me. I will return shortly."

With that, he and the double vanished. Lani looked out through the glass and around Drakne's room. It was dimly lit but surprisingly stylish. A giant cherrywood four-poster bed stood majestically centered against the largest wall. It was draped with sheer black silk curtains, which fell gracefully from the canopy to the floor. The bed was made up with deep burgundy satin bedding embellished with metallic gold embroidery on the edges of the bedspread and pillow shams. Other gold accents were tastefully incorporated into the bed itself and around the room. The entire room was furnished in the style of Louis XIV. A great wardrobe stood opposite the bed. The window was draped with thick burgundy velvet curtains, with black satin lining. A large and plushy rug with a medieval-like pattern covered the floor.

CHAPTER TWENTY-TWO

Lani pushed against the glass in front of her to see if she could get out, but it did not budge at all. She struck at it a few times, harder and harder each time, until she cried out in exasperation. She turned around to face the duplicate room, which was now her prison, and realized that she could move anywhere on this side of the glass. It was the exact reverse of Drakne's actual room on the other side, including the writing on the books in the bookshelves. She realized now, at least partly, what had happened. She was trapped inside the mirror. That would explain why everything was backwards. But why was her body in the glass tube?

Lani walked up to it in her realm and examined it, unconsciously placing her hand on the glass. There were bruises and cuts where she had hit the wall and fallen to the ground, but as she watched closely, they began to disappear before her eyes. Her body was being healed. But that still didn't explain why she was outside of it.

"It must be the only way to keep me in the mirror," she thought out loud. "The words I read must have had something to do with it. Drakne must have posed as Jharate in my mind to get me to read it! I guess the victims of this spell have to be willing. How stupid I was! Tsk! Anything for Jharate."

Lani sighed. It was an odd sensation because her spirit body acted as if she were sighing, in that her chest moved in the same way it always had— but she felt nothing. The sigh released no air and gave no comfort either. It was horrifically unfamiliar to be breathing without breathing! Worse yet was the lack of heartbeat. Although she had already noticed it, it was even more sickening now that there were fewer distractions. It was like living without being alive— like a ghost cursed to stay in the land of the living without the comforts of human life. The echoing metallic pulse of the machine taunted her as if to say, "Here's what you can't have anymore," with every beat.

Drakne reappeared on the other side of the glass. Lani jumped as she turned and saw him. Once again, where her heart would have skipped a beat, there was a hollow emptiness, and her surprised gasp contained no air within it. This undead state would take some getting used to.

She suddenly realized that the mirror did not duplicate people— otherwise Drakne *would* be in the reverse room with her now, as well as on his side. But the mirror image of her body was floating in the mirror-image machine behind her. Maybe that was because, without her spirit, her body was merely an object now? She stopped trying to make sense of things and walked up to her side of the glass and waited for Drakne to notice her. He did so almost immediately.

"Oh no, my pet, you're angry. I'm sorry. But you see this really was the only way. I can't have you in your body, or there would be a chance you could escape. At least you can't be in your body *yet*. Vranah was most pleased to see that you had been killed. Your double really was my best work. I was even able to duplicate the Half-Heart signature in the double's heart so that Vranah would be able to 'sense' it was you. Ha! I love it!

"You don't know how strong you are. He was worried we would never be able to kill you. You are protected by powerful magic that you somehow have but seem unaware of. That is why almost no one else besides Jharate could kill you— or bring you close enough to death for me to do what I did. Only the one who has your heart has the power to hurt you the very most. Odd, isn't it? ...but fascinating. Vranah was absolutely delighted by my solution."

"So, what exactly am I doing here then? Am I just here for you to look at? A trophy on display?"

"Oh no, my darling, no, no, no. You are here until you fall in love with me."

The thought alone made Lani shudder. Drakne noticed but continued calmly.

"Yes, I realize that at first you will resist. You are very much in love with Jharate. I can see that. But you will learn to love me in time. He could not care for you the way I can. He is the reason you almost died, whereas I saved your life. Don't you see? It was all for you."

"I think you mean it was all for *you*.".

"How can you say that?"

"Because, this isn't what *I* want. And Jharate would never have done those things without your influence. He was under a spell— *your* spell. I heard you pushing him to say those awful words. And trapping me in here until I fall for you isn't for me. That is one hundred percent for you."

"I can see why you would think that. But let me make one thing clear. I cannot force any human to do anything, really. True, I do have the power to do things to the body, but not to the soul. I cannot counteract free choice. Like you, for instance— you are in there because you *chose* to be. You read the words that separated you from your body. I could not have done that. Jharate could have focused on the power of your love and resisted me at any time, as you did to break out of your spell. Jharate chose to say those words. I merely gave him the suggestion."

"You tricked him as you tricked me. I would never have consented to have my soul ripped from my body!"

"Yes, but I had no choice. Vranah would have found a way to kill you eventually. I acted out of love to save you. You see, I knew if Vranah thought you were dead, that you would be safe— but only if I could keep you hidden. So I found a way into the fifth dimension and here we are— completely invisible and intangible and safe from everyone in the normal realm.

"But if you had a body, your gift would eventually show you the way out. You could then leave the fifth dimension at will. You would leave and then you would be caught. Again Vranah *would* find another way to kill you. So, I had to trick you into this— a secure situation from which there is no escape that you can make. I needed to be certain that you could not leave until I was sure that you could love me and stay with me, forever, safe and sound."

"How thoughtful of you. So, once I fall *madly in love with you*, then what? I get my body back and we get to be stuck in the fifth dimension forever? Just the two of us together?"

"No," Drakne began, with an eerie smile, "that is the brilliance of this. You see... I recently discovered that *I* am a Half-Heart."

Lani gasped in disbelief.

"I know," he chuckled. "I know! Not possible right? I didn't think so at first either— not with all the 'noble this' and 'virtuous that' in the legends— but then I saw my name on Vranah's list. I am sure he is debating whether to let me live or to kill me, once I have killed the rest of you for him. He is probably not sure if one Half-Heart can pose a threat to him or not. That is where you come in. Don't you see? If you and I marry, we will be more powerful than even The Great Evil himself. We can bring peace to the lands and rule together as husband and wife."

"Never!"

"Why ever not, my dove?"

"Well, off the top of my head— *You are evil!* I quite care about the welfare of my eternal soul and damnation is a deal breaker for me when it comes to evaluating a guy as a marriage prospect. So yeah, NO thank you. And as far as the prophecy is concerned, let me repeat myself— *You are evil* and so that wouldn't work very well either. And quit calling me pet names!"

"The prophecy says 'Only when two of the Half-Hearts are completed…' – that could be me and you – '…shall The Great Evil be defeated forever.' It never said they both had to be good. Besides, I *could* be good. You could teach me how. We could use our power for good and for peace and make it so there was no more conflict in the lands."

"If you truly love me, let me go. Take me back to my friends, my sister, and the man I love."

"I can't," he said, his face falling along with his shoulders in disappointment that Lani wasn't even getting close to being on board with his plans. "Even if I wanted to, Vranah would find out you were still alive and all would be lost. He would certainly kill me for my deception when he finished with the rest of the Half-Hearts and I was no longer needed. Besides, as I have already said, he would eventually find a way to kill you. You are well protected, but not invincible. I'm sorry, you can't go back."

"Then you *don't* love me, and I certainly could *never* love you."

"Oh, but you will," he said, changing to a more sinister tone. "You will change your mind for Jharate's sake," he drawled with a twisted half-smile. Lani was suddenly gripped with fear. He could see it in her eyes and it pleased him. He was back in control.

"What is that supposed to mean?"

"You will see."

And with that, Drakne laughed in a quiet but ominous manner, as he backed out of the room with a sweeping bow and disappeared behind the large oak door.

Jharate felt two hands on his legs and awoke with a start. He looked down and saw Raoul healing him. Jharate felt a deep gratitude within him, but dared not say anything, lest Raoul change his mind. Raoul finished and stormed out again. Jharate quickly realized that Justin and Erik were in the cave. This was the first time he had seen them since that nightmarish night and their faces were almost foreign to him now. Erik was sitting at a distance sharpening his sword and Justin was glaring at Jharate.

"You ignorant git! How could you be so stupid? She loved you and you were too weak and selfish to just love her back and protect her! You are beyond disgusting!"

Jharate made no defense. He merely sighed and spoke quietly.

"I agree."

Justin blinked in surprise. He hadn't thought Jharate would admit it so quickly. Jharate's voice had been quiet but the tone was unmistakably sincere. Justin stared at Jharate as he thought of what else to say because he had really said it all. Justin mimicked Kendra's trumpet noise trick by pursing his lips hard and blowing out air— but did it much slower than she was wont to do and ended by popping his lips before continuing.

"Well, we need to forget about all that right now. We've gotta focus on our mission. After we win this war we can all work out the issues we have with you and have time to deal with the grief we all have over Lani's death."

"How can I forget what I have done?" moaned Jharate.

"I don't know, but you have to for now," Erik said curtly. "You did it. You can't change it. Live with it. Now, use your gift and tell us the next action we need to take to recover from this blow. The people from Destavnia will be here any day to take us to the castle."

Jharate closed his eyes, took a deep breath, and waited for a vision to come. He waited, and waited, and waited. Nothing was coming. *Nothing at all.* He tried again to initiate his gift. He shut everything out. He did not hear the waterfall, or the sounds of Erik's blade being sharpened, nor the tapping of Justin's fingers on his cup. He waited, and waited, and waited.

"Nothing is coming. It is gone. My gift is gone!"

"That can't be. You're just not concentrating hard enough. Put down your sword so you won't distract him, Kook!"

"Fine, but you stop tapping on your cup!"

"Now try again, Jharate— and concentrate!"

Jharate did as Justin bid him and closed his eyes again. He took a deep breath. He waited in the darkness of his mind for an image, a sound, anything. But once again, nothing came. He grew increasingly anxious as he tried yet again. Nothing. He had lost his ability! He could not command it anymore.

What was he to do? He had done the unforgivable and now he was useless to everyone and had no way of helping to repair even some of the damage he had caused. He opened his eyes and saw a dagger in the corner of the cave. This was his chance to end it all right here and now. He ran for it, before he was even aware of what he was doing.

Justin summoned the dagger to his hand, just as Jharate was almost on top of it.

"You're not getting out of this that easy, you disgusting coward. You are going to learn to live with yourself."

Jharate clenched his fists and his jaw at his failure, but then sighed and relaxed his muscles. He was not sure what he would have done if Justin had not stopped him. But his momentary madness was gone now. He knew that killing himself would not bring Lani back. Worse than that, it would not take him to her on the other side either. Self-inflicted death did not bring peace to spirits. He decided, once and for all, against it.

"You are right again, Justin. Very well. I will live with my guilt. You need not worry about another such action from me."

"Good," said Justin, as he placed the dagger in a sheath, and handed it back to Jharate. "Now, let's find a way to put this to better use, shall we?"

Jharate nodded in agreement. Mid-nod Jharate stumbled to the ground and began to shake uncontrollably, as if having an epileptic seizure— then fell deadly still.

"Erik, go get help!"

Justin rushed to Jharate's side and checked for a pulse and any sign of breathing.

"Oh no, man— do *not* make me give you mouth to mouth! Come on! Get back here!"

Justin started pumping Jharate's chest. He knew that compressions were the most important part, and that if Arante dragged Raoul here soon enough, he wouldn't have to do anything more.

"Hurry up, Raoul!" Justin exclaimed even though he wasn't sure if he could hear him.

Jharate opened his eyes and found that he was standing in a room made of stone, stylishly decorated. He saw a large mirror with a golden frame. He felt drawn to the mirror and took step after step towards it. He was about to peer into it, when a sudden flash of light to his right caught his eye. He turned and saw a machine, flooded with electricity, and a woman with long flowing hair floating inside a glass cylinder, looking as though she were suspended in water. His heart jumped as he realized it was Lani. He ran to the machine and frantically inspected it. Was she alive? Was she dead? He thought he heard her voice, behind him, calling his name. But as he turned to look, his body received an icy jolt and the dim light of the cave came flooding back to him.

"Jharate! Jharate!" a voice kept calling, but it was not hers.

Jharate became aware that someone was shaking him. He felt the freezing water that had just been thrown on him dripping down his face. He opened his eyes again to see Justin standing over him with an empty bucket. He must have been the culprit. He looked to his side to discover whose voice was still frantically calling out his name.

"Enough! I am conscious, Arante. You may cease shaking me now."

Arante stopped, with a slightly embarrassed look on her face for having continued past the point of his regaining consciousness. But her face changed to a stern look as she remembered that she was the one who was upset.

"What happened to you? Is this passing out business going to be a regular occurrence? You scared me half to death! You stopped breathing and I had to get Raoul to heal you again, which he *wasn't* glad to have to do. What is *wrong* with you?"

Jharate noticed that Erik and Kendra were also in the room, both staring at him with worried lines in their foreheads. Tierza and Laern also entered the cave with concern etched on their faces as they looked at Jharate. Jharate looked away from them and turned back to Arante to respond.

"I apologize for frightening you. One moment… If Raoul initiated my breathing again, then what purpose did the water and the shaking serve?"

"Because you needed it!" Justin snapped, annoyed at Jharate's ungrateful behavior.

Jharate ignored Justin and continued, "I was… Rather, I saw… Lani."

The others looked at each other with mixed feelings. Erik thought Jharate had lost his mind. Arante felt that he had died and seen her ghost while his spirit was wandering. Justin couldn't decide what to make of it. It was Kendra who spoke first, jumping to a happier conclusion.

"I knew it! She's alive! I should have trusted my gut! Twins are supposed to have that extra sense right? And I knew Drakne wouldn't just take her like that if she was dead!"

"But if she was a Half-Heart, and we know Vranah wanted her personally, wouldn't Drakne have to take her body back as proof?" Arante asked.

"Maybe, but if Jharate saw her, there must be a reason, right? It must be to save her, right?" Kendra asked hopefully.

"I saw her body in a device— an unfamiliar machine. She was contained within a glass cylinder. It looked as though she were suspended in water with electric currents flowing throughout. It was impossible to determine if she was dead or alive from what I beheld. However, it is *possible* that she lives."

There was silence for a moment as everyone pondered what he or she had just heard. Could there be hope that she was still alive? Was there a chance? Was it a trap set to bait them with false hope? Or had Jharate just lost his grip on reality altogether? Jharate wondered these same things as well.

"Why did you deluge me with water? If you had simply stopped when I began breathing again, perhaps I could have seen more. I could have discovered where she is. If she is alive somewhere, I must save her. Understand this now— I care not if I die trying. I will save her if it is the last thing that I do. You ruined my vision! You destroyed the only chance I had to see where she is located! My gift is not functioning properly and you terminated it!"

"Calm down!" Justin ordered. "Now think hard— is there anything else you remember?

"Think really hard," Tierza said encouragingly. She watched Jharate carefully, dearly hoping that Lani was still alive. She had grown quite attached to her in the short time they had known each other.

Jharate described the scene that he had just witnessed again, down to the tiniest detail. He recounted every aspect of the luxuriously furnished room, the canopy bed, the great gilt mirror, and the unique machine. He ended by describing how he thought he had heard Lani speak his name from behind him and that when he had turned to see where she was, he had been abruptly awakened and had found himself back in the cave, wet, and being shaken like a leaf in a hurricane.

Lani jolted where she lay on the bed as her eyes flew open. She had been lying there for hours trying to contact Jharate. She had devoted all the energy she had within her and had successfully reached him. However, she had been unable to finish the message because he had been pulled away too soon.

"Great! Just great!"

She would have punched or thrown the satin pillows if she had any strength left. It had taken a considerably larger amount of energy to use her gift with no body. She felt totally drained. She was more exhausted than she had ever been— even more than when she had given up a year of her life to the Mountain Siren. No one with a body could ever even imagine the fatigue that overcame her. Lani could now understand a little about how Vranah must feel. The lack of physical form made everything at least ten times more difficult.

Beyond the odd fatigue that didn't make any sense, it was mentally taxing. She quickly found that there was no way to sleep. Sleep would have been such a nice reprieve. But apparently, she was going to be awake for every last wretched second of her captivity. And if it were true that she would be here until she fell in love with Drakne, it would be an eternity.

She lay on the bed for hours thinking about what to do next. She found her thoughts drifting to the technical aspects of her situation. She wondered how she was even able to lie down on the bed. She was only a spirit right? Why didn't she fall through or maybe just float? Maybe it had something to do with being in the mirror. That must be it. It wasn't a real world. It was the metaphysical, like her now. But that didn't make sense either. She decided to abandon her theories. Trying to figure things like this out was pointless, and besides, now she was getting a headache.

"How am I getting a headache with no body?" she wondered aloud in spite of her previous decision not to think about it. "Stop it! Get a grip!"

She shook her head trying to get herself to snap out of it, still thinking aloud.

"Okay. Drakne said there was no way for me to escape... Does that mean by myself, or period? There must be a way out, because he said I had to stay here *until* he was sure of my love. So the way out must depend on someone else. He knew my gift would show me the way out if I was left inside my body long enough, so that must mean that there is no way to get myself out of here now that my body is on the other side... Or is that what he wants me to think?"

Lani finally sat up on the bed and looked for clues as to how she might escape. She stood up and walked around, scanning her side of the room, and noticed a small trunk at the foot of the bed. It appeared to be made of solid gold with rubies inlaid around the edges. She thought it was interesting that one who was so evil could have such a love for beauty. Not that it was unprecedented— Lani realized that history was replete with examples of bad guys who loved elegant things, but it caught her off guard nonetheless. There was somehow serenity in his chamber that should not be here. Lani never would have pictured this room for Drakne, not counting the color scheme, as the softness and elegance did not match his personality or harsh gothic looks.

"Half-Hearts are supposed to be good. He must have been good once. What happened to him?" she wondered aloud.

She suddenly felt pity for him. She shook it off, quickly reprimanding herself for her inability to concentrate. The trunk looked solid— it would do. It was surprisingly heavy, for not being real. She struggled to drag it over right next to the mirror, turned it on its end vertically, and kicked the trunk into it as hard as she could. The trunk hit the mirror hard and fell over. Nothing happened. Not even a sound. She looked at the mirror in dismay. Apparently force was not going to be an option.

A glint of light caught her eye. She looked to the source and noticed that the trunk had fallen open. A spherical object rolled out of the chest. Lani thought that it greatly resembled the elaborate design of a Fabergé egg. Like the trunk, as well as many other objects and decorations in the room, it too, was gold. However, instead of rubies, like the chest, the precious engraved metal sphere was adorned with emeralds— a clear break from Drakne's normal color preferences.

She knelt down beside the toppled chest to inspect the ornate object more closely. As she picked it up in both hands its beauty mesmerized her. A solid strip of gold encircled the object. A thin seam told Lani that it opened somehow. Lani put one hand on each end, and twisted gently. At the exact moment she did so, Drakne walked into the room on the other side of the mirror.

"Nooooo!"

Drakne ran as he screamed, until hitting the mirror stopped him. Frightened by Drakne's obvious fear, Lani tried to drop the orb, but found herself unable to do so. Her eyes went wide as she realized it would not leave her hands!

"NO!" Drakne screamed again as he slammed his fist into the wall at the side of the mirror, keeping his eyes locked on Lani and the object in her hand.

There was a great flash of light, and the mirror turned black.

VISIONS FROM THE PAST

Jharate was beginning to feel like himself again. He walked tall, spoke confidently, and took charge with ease. He had not slept a wink since he had received his vision of Lani, and was instead tirelessly working on a plan to save her. Although he could not confirm to himself or anyone else that she was alive, he had seen her, and the chance was good enough for him.

Everyone else appeared to feel the same way. Even Raoul began to speak to Jharate again, though there was still resentment in his mannerisms. Justin's mood was much lighter than Raoul's, but that was always true. As Jharate paced back and forth, Justin suddenly burst out laughing as he spoke to no one in particular.

"You know, she always wanted her life to be romantic like the fairy tales, and dramatic like Shakespeare's plays. I'd say she got her wish."

"Would you please keep the mockery of my mistakes, and of the 'drama' that you continually remind me that I have created, to a bare minimum?" Jharate snapped.

"Take it easy, Othello, this isn't my fault. Besides, humor is how I deal with things."

One of Jharate's eyebrows rose. The reference to Shakespeare was lost on Jharate, as he was not from Earth, but he did not need to understand the reference to gather the intent. He decided to let it go. There was no point in starting an argument, and Justin was correct— it was not Justin's fault that they were in this predicament. Jharate pulled out an old map and laid it across a long, flat stone that they had been using as a table.

"Let us review what we know. Drakne has probably taken her back to *my* castle in Trisakne," growled Jharate as he touched his finger to his family home on the map. "We know from intelligence received through the underground that that is where Vranah has set up his base of operations. We are here, in Delicah, by the Veil of Tears Waterfall, in the Cave of Witsan."

"Very good!" Justin remarked. "You've just given us a fascinating review of the obvious! What are you going to do next?"

"Justin, I realize that I have ruined everything thoroughly and completely. I realize that you despise me. I understand, believe me. Nevertheless, we must work together to have any hope of saving Lani."

"He's right," Kendra called from the rock she was perched on. "So grow up, Justin."

Justin shrugged and nodded in agreement. Jharate turned to Arante, who was sitting behind him.

"What are your thoughts on the matter, cousin?"

Arante grinned and stood up straight. She was thrilled to have been asked, but at the moment, she had no real plan. However, she was not about to let anyone else know that— especially Tierza.

"Alright," she said, with a determined yet happy tone. "We obviously have to get back to Trisakne. That won't be easy, especially since it was so hard to get out of there in the first place. What we need to determine is how many of us should go back. Let's go over the abilities we have again. Jharate, you have the gift of visions, but it's on the fritz lately for reasons we don't know. You may be a liability rather than an asset."

"I have more skills as a warrior than—"

"True. I'll put you down as an asset then. I was only saying, you *may* be a liability, or you may not. However, since the whole thing is your fault, I can see that you will want to go regardless. Raoul has the healing ability. I would say that is definitely necessary, especially because we don't know what kind of shape Lani is in. Justin is telekinetic, so he's an obvious choice. Kendra has shielding power— wouldn't want to go anywhere without that. Now we come to Erik and myself. I have the power to create images and divine truth— not sure how that could be useful, but I'm sure it will be. Erik has the power to play with the speed of time. Again, I think— necessary. Perhaps Tierza and Laern should take Rezarahn with them to the Castle at Ansena to let them know what is going on."

"I think not! My brother can go with Rezarahn back to the castle, but *I* am going with you."

"It seems you cannot be stopped. Very well then, Laern and Rezarahn stay here to wait for our escort."

"I would never dream of staying behind while Lani is in need of—" Rezarahn began.

"You have no say in this!" Arante shouted, with her eyes flashing wildly. "If there is anyone who is as much to blame for Lani's misfortune as Jharate, it is you! You are lucky to be alive and you will do as you are told!"

"We will stay," Laern said, calmly stepping in-between Rezarahn and Arante.

"Okay, sorry to interrupt again, Arante, but we are just stating facts. We all *know* our abilities and who's staying here," Justin reminded. "What we *don't know* is how to get back to Trisakne, or how to get into the castle, which just happens now to be the *stronghold of evil*, or how to find Lani, or how to get her out, or how to get back here to Destavnia *without getting caught*. Did I miss anything?"

Justin had only said what everyone else was thinking.

"Anything sounds bad if you say it like that. But look at it this way—" Arante began, "if we succeed in doing all that, we can end the war. Lani and Jharate are Half-Hearts, right? We know that now. So, if we *can* find and free Lani, get Lani and Jharate to Destavnia, *and* get them married in the right place, the entire war ends. This isn't just a rescue mission, people. This could be the end of a war that has been going on forever!"

Her words had the intended effect. Everyone who had been listening stood up or sat up a little straighter and their eyes glimmered with hope and determination. Erik and Raoul jumped up at the same time.

"What are we waiting for?" Raoul asked.

"Let's end this war once and for all!" Erik said enthusiastically.

"Still, we do need a plan," Tierza interjected carefully, trying not to spoil the enthusiasm in the atmosphere.

A wide grin spread across Arante's face.

"I've got it! I know how we are going to get back there, undetected. Erik, I want you to…"

Lani had been trying to let go of the orb since Drakne had screamed, but was still unable to do so. When Lani had twisted it, it had sprung open from its core and now the two halves of the orb were separated by about three inches, but still held together by a small gold post in the center. Her hands were stuck on either side of it. The mirror was turning black. What did that mean? The light in the room dimmed until she was kneeling in utter and complete darkness, still unable to let go of the open sphere. What was going to happen to her? Was she trapped here forever now?

Lani instinctively tried to take a deep breath to soothe herself, but when she could not, a twang of anxiety shot through her. That should have sent her heart beating like crazy, but once again, she couldn't feel it! This was horrible and even more frightening than being able to feel the physical effects of fear! The dread continued to grow within her as she sat there in the pitch-blackness of her prison.

Calm down, she thought, *panicking won't solve anything.* Just as she thought this, the orb began to vibrate and suddenly images flew from within. What she experienced made her feel like she was on a Star Trek holodeck, as the images completely surrounded her, but she found that she could not smell or feel anything. The images were coming from the orb itself with only a subtle hint of translucency.

Lani saw a tall handsome man, with jet-black hair and eyes so dark that they seemed black standing out in a field near a small but charming farm house, hard at work. His arms, face, and neck were tan from working in his fields every day. He turned as his wife called him to supper from the front door of the house. She was strikingly pretty. She looked more like a princess than a farmer's wife. Her hair was deep brown, her lips full and red, and her eyes were as green as the emeralds on the orb. She was pale, but somehow it suited her and added to her beauty. He blew a kiss to her before turning to pick up his tools and heading back for the house.

The projections of the orb suddenly zoomed in on the house until Lani found herself inside it with the farmer's wife. She had three young boys and two young girls, sitting at the table, ready to eat. It looked as though she was expecting another child any day now.

"How was your day, my precious angel?" the man said to his wife, as he walked through the door, crossed the room and kissed her.

"It went well, darling. Thank you for sending the boys in to help me. It was much needed. Drake did a great job."

"That's my boy!" the father said with a warm smile as he tousled the hair of his eldest son, who positively beamed back at him.

Wait a minute, Lani thought. Her eyes went wide. Lani knew that boy— tall, lanky, jet black hair. No mistaking— that was Drakne! Younger and happier, no doubt, but the resemblance was unquestionable. He couldn't have been more than fourteen. It felt odd for her to see him in this light. Somehow, she had never imagined he had a childhood. She especially would have never imagined such a loving and happy family. *What could have happened to him?* Just as Lani thought this, the orb began to vibrate again and the images came faster and faster, as though someone had hit the fast-forward button. The orb then slowed the images down and stopped at another scene.

It was the same farmhouse with the same people, sitting down for dinner once again. The only differences were that they now had one more daughter, a small toddler, stumbling around happily, and Drakne looked as if he were close to sixteen years old. Without warning the door burst open. Soldiers marched in and dragged everyone out of the room. The family was brought outside in front of the house and forced to kneel at knifepoint. A voice came from a few yards away.

"I thought I made it very clear that resistance was not to be tolerated Veran."

Drakne's father pled with the cold voice, "Please, spare my family! They had nothing to do with it, I swear! Do whatever you want to me, but please leave them alone and—"

"Silence, fool!"

Lani looked for the source of this terrifying voice and saw a shadow. He was wearing a cape with a hood so that she could not see his face but his voice was all too familiar and she knew exactly who it was. He had the form of a man, and in this particular instance he even seemed to have flesh, but he was still somehow not human. The voice continued in a calm cadence.

"You have no right to beg for anything. You have betrayed me, and you will watch your family die before your very eyes and then you will join them."

"No, please! Have mercy!"

The thing that the voice belonged to nodded its hooded head towards the guards and spoke with chilling ease.

"Kill his wife."

Despite the desperate pleas of Veran and the screaming of the beautiful children, the guards proceeded to slit her throat. Veran screamed in agony and wrenched himself free of the guard who held him. He grabbed his dead wife in his arms and began to sob. The children screamed and cried at the sight of their dead mother. The man in the cloak calmly ordered the guards to kill the youngest children first. Veran's youngest daughter was dead a second later. The farmer rushed the guard, who held his youngest son, and fell to the ground as the guard thrust a knife into his heart. Veran died instantly.

The specter in the cloak tapped his foot on the ground slowly in disappointment. The guards looked to the hooded figure and asked what to do with the rest of the children.

"Kill them."

As these words from the demon in the cloak were uttered, young Drakne struggled against the soldier who held him and yelled.

"No! Take me instead! Let my remaining brothers and sisters live! I will do whatever you ask! Please!"

The thing in the cloak walked over and looked down on him.

"Your bravery and self-sacrifice is impressive. What is your name, boy?"

"Drake."

The hooded figure paused and thought for a moment.

"Drake... Very well. I will let them live. But you must agree to serve me without question, to your dying breath."

Drakne looked at the faces of each of his siblings and then hung his head in defeat as he spoke with determination and self-loathing.

"I will."

The hooded figure motioned to the guards to release them all. As they let go of Drakne's arms, they fell numbly to his side. His brothers and sisters rushed to him and hugged him. He could barely even look at them as he embraced them for what would be the last time.

"It is time to go," the hooded being said.

Drakne released his siblings and turned to the next oldest boy.

"Vaughn, you are the man of the house now. Take care of your brother and sisters."

Vaughn nodded sadly, swallowing hard and trying choke back the tears that had been falling as he straightened himself up to take on his role as the fourteen-year-old head of the household. Drakne turned to his new master and went to him without a word. The hooded man put his hand on the boy's shoulder.

"You will do great things for me. I can sense it. You will, from this day forth, be known as Drakne. You will be my right-hand man someday. I have much to teach you."

The hooded figure turned and Drakne followed. Lani saw the silent tears that fell freely from Drakne's eyes.

The orb stopped vibrating and closed itself and the room was left in darkness. Lani didn't notice the mirror slowly turning clear again. Nor did she notice the light coming slowly back into the room. Metaphysical tears streamed down her face and she imagined she felt their warm sting on her cheeks. She kept thinking about that poor child. She had no idea. Poor, poor, Drakne! He hadn't wanted to be evil at all. He offered to serve Vranah to save what was left of his family. He had sacrificed himself for his siblings. The orb fell from her hands and she grabbed one of her shoulders and wrapped her other arm around her stomach, feeling the pain of the emotion flow through her in a whole new way.

Drakne stood on the other side of the mirror peering at her. He knew what she had seen. She remained unaware of his presence as he watched her intently. Her tears touched him. He felt something in his heart that he hadn't felt since he was that little boy in the farmhouse. He felt love— real love. Her compassion for him, even after all he had done to her— he swallowed hard and left the room in silence.

It was the sound of the door shutting behind Drakne that made Lani realize that he had been there the whole time. She cried openly for him now, alone in her glass prison, feeling as though she were drowning in tears that didn't actually exist.

They moved at what felt like the speed of light. As instructed by Arante, Erik was bending the speed of time around them so that they could travel so fast that they would remain unseen. Water droplets from the light rain that were frozen in mid-air, scattered as each person brushed through them. The friends all followed closely at Erik's heels to avoid getting caught in the normal and vastly slower time field surrounding them.

Erik's power had grown greatly since he had first discovered it. They had been traveling for days but covered a distance that would have normally taken them months. As they reached the rocks surrounding the castle and stopped to hide behind them, the time bubble collapsed and Erik staggered and fell to the ground, breathing hard and barely able to move, with his hand on his chest, pressing against his racing heart. The exertion it had taken to keep up his power for so long had drained him of all energy and he knew that he would not be able to continue for even one second longer.

"Go. Just hide me in the rocks and come back for me after you save her. I'll be okay."

Arante looked at him with a knit brow. She hesitated, but nodded slowly. Justin levitated Erik, and Arante helped to carefully hide him in a crevice between two large rocks. They left him his sword, and put his bag by him with food and water.

"I'll be back as soon as I can, Erik. I promise."

"I'll be here, sweetheart."

Arante leaned down and kissed him passionately, grabbing onto his collar as if she would never let go. When their lips parted, Erik smiled.

"I know I'll be alright and all, but just in case anything happens, you should know that I love you, Arante."

"No 'just in cases!' We'll be together again soon! I love you too, though."

She smiled and kissed him once again and then abruptly stood up and backed up a few steps. She saw that he was well hidden and would not be seen from a distance and nodded her head approvingly.

"I'll stay here and protect him."

"Are you sure, Tierza? I could stay with you."

"Yes, Justin, I'm sure. And you cannot stay with me. I am positive that they will need your gift. When he recovers we will catch up with you, either in the castle or running from it."

The lines on Justin's forehead showed how much he loathed the thought of leaving her. He held her hands in his own and rubbed his thumbs nervously over her knuckles. He finally sighed, and pulled her into a tight hug.

"Be careful, Tierza."

"Don't worry about me. I can take care of myself. Don't forget, elves are faster than humans. I can always outrun danger."

Justin looked as if he were being torn in two. He bent down and fervently kissed both of her hands, while looking lovingly up at her face.

"We need to act quickly," Arante whispered insistently, interrupting. "They will find out we are here soon."

Justin straightened up and pulled Tierza close once more and kissed her, as he gripped her waist and she threw her arms around his neck. The two let go and Justin kept looking back at Tierza until she was out of sight. The group crept toward the castle, led by Jharate, keeping low behind the rocks.

"Those lightning bolts are crazy! How are we going to get past those?" Justin asked.

"There is a secret way in. Follow me."

They followed Jharate to a small wooded area near the back of the castle. Jharate searched until he found what he was looking for. Two trees bursting with light pink blossoms stood reaching toward each other. They had entwined their branches, as if grasping hands. Their roots, too, had grown together. A flurry of blossoms fluttered slowly to the ground as Jharate crept through the center of the heart-shaped archway between the two trees. He knelt down and moved vines and leaves out of the way with his hands. He remembered how he and Khanye used to sneak in and out using this same passageway when they were children. They would run into the woods to play, conquering imaginary evil monsters and saving beautiful damsels in distress. It was not play anymore.

Jharate uncovered the trapdoor and opened it. It creaked a little as he pulled. He jumped in without another thought. The others followed— Kendra and Arante first, followed by Justin and Raoul. Raoul made sure that he closed the trapdoor as he jumped in.

"Use your power to put the leaves back over the door, Justin," Raoul ordered.

"Good idea!" Justin replied, as he closed his eyes and pictured the debris going back into place.

A light scraping overhead told them it was done.

"Lani would be proud of that move," Justin laughed. "She always hates it in movies when people are stupid enough not to try to cover their tracks or lock doors behind them in dangerous situations. She always said that people would be smarter than that in real life. And look at us, we are! Ah-boo-yeah! We gonna get some light in here or what?"

Jharate grabbed an old torch off the darkened wall and lit it. The light illuminated the area around them and revealed about twenty feet of the passageway looming in front of them. Beyond that was darkness— a long dark tunnel with no end in sight.

"Follow me," Jharate whispered. "And keep your voices down."

Drakne was walking down through the cellars of the castle to make his daily security rounds. Lani was on his mind. He wanted her to love him so much. He had done everything for her. *Can't she see that?* They could make things right. *Why does she continue to resist me?* She was kind to him now that she knew his past, but it was pity, not love, that she offered him. He wanted her to love him. He needed her love. What else could he do?

As he thought of this, he became angry. He realized it was because of Jharate that Lani did not love him. She loved Jharate, not him. *Why?* Jharate had tried to kill her. *How can she love someone who was willing to go that far?* He was in the way. As long as Jharate was alive, he stood no chance.

It was at this moment that he heard a noise from behind the wall. It sounded like footsteps. He listened more intently. He followed the sound for a long time. The footsteps finally stopped behind another wall. He froze and listened.

"This is the entrance," Jharate's voice proclaimed.

Drakne smiled maliciously. Jharate had come to him! *How fortunate!* He hid in the shadows and stayed still, hardly breathing. Suddenly, the wall across from him opened. *A secret passage. Who knew?* Through the wall stepped Jharate, Kendra, Arante, Justin and Raoul. As the wall began to close behind them, Drakne emerged dramatically from the shadows.

"Nice of you to join me."

Raoul shot his crossbow, without hesitation, directly at Drakne's heart. Drakne stared at the crossbow bolt and watched it slow, until it stopped an inch from his heart. He looked at it with a smile and waved it away with his hand, without touching it. It fell to the ground with a pathetic clink.

"You really thought that would be enough?"

Drakne's grin widened. He loved this castle. The lightning strikes around it amplified his powers so that they were infinitely stronger. He could do more things simultaneously than he could ever do outside the castle. Drakne moved his hand, casually, and all of their weapons flew out of their hands and into the tunnel behind them just as the wall closed entirely.

Drakne laughed as he watched them try to move, only to find that their feet were planted where they stood. Drakne knew what to do in an instant. He used his powers to open the wall again. He threw all of the stunned friends, except for Jharate, back through the door and into the secret passageway, with a simple motion of his hand. Then, with the other hand, he snapped and created his signature energy-field cage around them, which glowed eerily in the dark tunnel.

"She would never forgive me if I killed you," was all he said, as he shut the wall, removing them from sight. He rounded on Jharate with a twisted grin. "You came at the perfect time."

Drakne snapped his fingers, and suddenly they were both in his quarters. He quickly phased Jharate and himself into the fifth dimension, so that no one would be able to hear Jharate's screams.

DISASTROUS IS AN UNDERSTATEMENT

D rakne concentrated on Jharate until Jharate was compelled to fall to his knees. An energy field formed around Jharate but with no room for him to stand. Lani came to the mirror and gasped in horror. Jharate heard her and looked up. She was alive!

"Lani!"

"Jharate, you came for me!"

"Of course I came for you! I love you, Lani. I—" Jharate cried out, as an electric current struck him.

"Stop it! Don't hurt him!"

Drakne stormed across the room to Lani's body. He muttered quietly and her outfit began to change simultaneously on both Lani's body and on her spirit. Lani now wore a stunning white satin wedding dress. The bodice was studded with diamonds that radiated from the center of every white hand-embroidered flower. This elegant detail was continued in sprays of diamonds on the butterfly sleeves and on the hem of the dramatically flared skirt. Her hair magically curled and cascaded freely down her back and past her hips. A delicate veil that matched the dress appeared and lengthened until it was slightly longer than her hair.

The sight struck Jharate to the core. His throat constricted and his heart beat wildly within him. Drakne pivoted and marched back over to Jharate, glaring at him and pointing at Lani definitively.

"You could have had her. You were a *fool*. How could you not see how perfect she is? How could you have even *let* me into your head? You are not *worthy* of her."

Drakne struck Jharate with more electric currents as he spoke. He skillfully directed each miniature lightning bolt to the places that would cause the most pain, and Jharate groaned and cried out in response, despite his efforts to stifle his reactions.

"Drakne, stop it!" Lani begged, losing control of her voice as it went higher and higher in panic.

"Lani, I know I can't force you to love me. I've tried, but the closest I've gotten is pity from you. But I won't lose you."

Another bolt struck Jharate and he screamed, falling from his knees and onto his face.

"Stop it! You're killing him!" Lani screamed, banging her hands against the glass, desperately wishing that it would shatter.

"Marry me, Lani. Marry me, or watch the one you love die right in front of your eyes."

"Do not ask that of her!"

Another bolt of electricity struck Jharate. Jharate now writhed in pain on his side and choked on his next words.

"Say no, Lani. Say no. You are my other half. My life does not matter to me if it means you must give up yours."

"Silence!"

Drakne hit him with another bolt. Lani was at a loss for words. She looked from Drakne to Jharate and back again several times. She cringed as Drakne struck Jharate yet again. Jharate was fighting for consciousness now. He was flat on his back and was only able to utter in a whisper.

"I love you, Lani. Say no!"

"The next bolt *will* kill him. I am growing impatient. Make your choice!"

Lani bit the inside of her cheek, and her eyes stayed wide with horror, shaking her head unconsciously. She could not be the reason that Jharate died and she could not imagine life with Drakne. She looked into Jharate's eyes and saw the pain and agony there. She couldn't stand it another second. She closed her eyes tight, lowered her head in defeat and spoke softly.

"Alright. I will."

Drakne sighed and a close-lipped smile crossed his face. He kept the force field up, but ceased to harm Jharate. He walked over to the mirror and stood directly in front of Lani, gazing at her intently.

"Do I have your word?"

Lani opened her eyes and cast one last look at Jharate. Again she felt the warm sting of a metaphysical tear falling down her face and an agonized hole where her heart should have been. She looked down at the ground, and then lifted her gaze to look directly into Drakne's eyes and spoke with a heavy heart, feeling as if both worlds had already collapsed around her.

"You have it."

"Wonderful!"

Drakne snapped his fingers and a candlestick appeared in his hand. Lani didn't even flinch as he took it in both of his hands and swung at the mirror three times until it shattered. One ear-splitting crack later and Lani's spirit floated from behind the mirror, into the room with Jharate and Drakne, and back into her body. Her eyes flew open and she breathed in a huge breath of air, as if she had just been revived from drowning. The electric currents abated and she floated gently to the bottom of the cylinder.

Drakne walked over to her and opened the tube, and the copper hinges, which connected the two pieces of glass that formed the tube to each other, swung open. He held his hand out to her gently. She took it and stepped out of the glass enclosure. Now that she was connected to her heart again, she felt a crushing feeling as if some demon squeezed it hard within its fist. Her lungs ached from the tightness around them and her throat constricted as tears that had not yet fallen stung her eyes. She looked at Jharate and then turned to Drakne with one simple request.

"Please, let me kiss him goodbye."

Drakne frowned. He could not stand the thought of her kissing Jharate, but as she had shown so much compassion for him… Could he really deny her this? Besides, she would be his for eternity. What would one kiss cost him? He nodded once and snapped his fingers to take down the force field.

Lani ran to Jharate's side and knelt beside him. Jharate raised himself up on one arm and kissed her. He reached his other arm around her waist and pulled her as close as he could. She placed one hand gently on his neck and the other she ran through his hair as she kissed him with every last fiber in her being. Tears fell from both of their eyes and they kissed as they had never kissed before. Their souls connected and they were one. As they drew back, their eyes were filled with exquisite love and pain.

"Do not do this, Lani," Jharate whispered.

Lani leaned close to Jharate's ear and whispered quietly.

"I cannot watch you die. Goodbye, my love."

Lani got up slowly— every inch she walked away from Jharate feeling like an inch closer to the executioner's block. Drakne replaced the force field around Jharate as she returned to his side, and he took her hand in his own. Jharate fell onto his back on the cold stone floor and clenched his hands into fists.

"So what happens to him now?"

"He will remain here, safe in the fifth dimension, until *after* you and I have married. Once we have defeated Vranah and restored peace to all the lands, he will be returned to his kingdom, where he will rule, answering only to us. Your other friends will be released at that time as well."

Drakne saw the sadness in the lovers' eyes. For a moment, he felt sorry for them. Perhaps it would be better if he let them go. But he felt the soft touch of Lani's hand in his own and could not bring himself to part with it. He would have her. He loved her too much to sacrifice her and to live alone forever.

"You will love me in time," Drakne said, rather sweetly.

Lani made no reply but she tried, somewhat hopelessly, to fake a small smile. Drakne led her by the hand and out of the door. She turned, one final time, to look into Jharate's eyes, as the door closed behind them.

Jharate screamed a heart-wrenching scream of agony. It was a scream of all hope being lost. His heart felt like it had been obliterated, and the bloody shards of it ripped through his soul. He screamed and screamed and screamed again, not caring that no one could hear him.

But Lani heard his screams. No matter how far she walked away she could hear them as if she were standing right next to him. Tears streamed from her eyes as she followed Drakne up the winding staircase to the marriage room, and her tattered heart sank lower with each stair she ascended. As they entered through the large beautiful door with the golden tree, Drakne snapped his fingers to make the foreign coffins disappear. As they stood in the middle of the room, he turned to face her, holding both of her hands in his.

"I Drake Amaren take thee, Princess Adrienne Arvanatasi to by my wife, my other half, my heart's desire— to join in marriage from now until forever, beyond the end of time. Now you."

"I Princess Adrienne Arvanatasi, take thee, Drake Amaren…"

Jharate's back arched suddenly as his gift revived, chaining him to this awful moment as he watched with perfect clarity and heard Lani say the words.

"I Princess Adrienne Arvanatasi, take thee, Drake Amaren…"

Jharate roared in despair, pounding his fists against the ground until they bled. He could not bear to hear the rest of the words, and yet his gift persisted.

"NOOOOOOOOOOOOOOOOO!" Jharate cried.

Jharate's screams rang through the empty halls, echoing through the fifth dimension where no one could hear them— no one except Lani. Tears streamed down both their faces. Two hearts broke in unison.

ACKNOWLEDGMENTS

Jared Fotu, for loving me long ago and for inspiring me, and for so many other reasons, not least of which being that you were the first person to ever tell me that my work should be published.

Roger Jellinek, for believing in me and helping me to realize my dreams, and for signing me even after reading what has become affectionately known as the "recall version" of my manuscript. I'm glad you didn't kill yourself on the first read through (as the rough draft prodded you to do) and I'm glad that you knew exactly how to push me to become a better writer.

Sean McNamara, Uncle Mark and Aunty Charisse Kubr, Dutch Hofstetter Sr., Dutch Hofstetter Jr., Tiffany Hofstetter, Udee Dahl, and Lisa Linsky, for helping me to believe in myself in the beginning stages of my writing and encouraging me not to give up.

Nicholas Jones, for believing in my story and making the publication of this book possible.

Corbin Thomander, for helping to actually make me a number-one-best-selling authoress, for my very first time.

Liz Requilman of North Shore Weddings and Flowers, for being the official florist of Alamea and using your magical skills to help maintain the image of The Half-Hearts Trilogy at all of its events.

Dr. Randal Allred, Dr. Helena Hannonen, Dr. Duane Roberts, Dr. Michael Marler, Dr. James Tueller, Susan Wesley, and Daniel Skaf for going above and beyond the call of duty expected of professors and mentors, and for truly caring about me and my success.

Mrs. Cashman, Mrs. Graham, Mrs. Palmer, and Dr. Ban Phung for pushing me to reach further than I ever thought I could, and for helping me to realize that I had a talent for writing, which contributed to my becoming the strong and independent person I am today.

Aunty Sunday Mariteragi, Aunty Kela Miller, Uncle Bill Wallace, Uncle Kim Makekau, and Uncle Joseph Poʻuha, for being outstanding examples of strength and character, and for their generous outpouring of unconditional love, and for passing down some of their knowledge and great love of the various Polynesian heritages to me.

My intrepid Copy Editors, who polished the Advance Release Copy like the true pros that they are, Julie Weekes and Ruby Cheesman. Plus, an honorable mention to those who acted as Copy Editors, even though they were only asked to tackle the task of reading the novel, J'nelle Uluave and Amanda Meredith.

Lizette Baize, Anjeny Salts, Dawn Phelps, Don Sand, and my Grandpa, Earl Moroni Wallace, for reading the first draft of my novel despite it's large size and dubious quality.

Also, to William Dennis Kaufusi ʻAlatini, for not only reading the rough version, but for always believing that I will make it big someday and for comparing me to others who have already done so. And for loving me for many years.

In loving memory of Art Rivers for being a wonderful person, for inspiring me with his love of life and his kindness, and for being a very dear coworker and friend. Rest in peace.

For many late night readings, editing, comments, inspirations (the good the bad and the ugly), discussions, and moral support— I have to thank, William Dennis Kaufusi ʻAlatini, my sister J'nelle Uluave, Martin Smith, Euta Lightsy, Drew Mierzejewski, Chris Schoebinger, Boyd Ware, Art Rivers, ʻOfa Mataele, Steven Squire, Tupua Ainuʻu, Joseph Faifili, Mario Wauneka, Joshua Tagaloa Smith, Spencer Deavila, Krishnan Apelu, Mayo Michihiro, Cody Mafatu Easterbrook, Joshua Aplaca, Carrie Currie, Liz Buckingham, Jodeen Enesa, Umi Jensen, Sariah Howard, Joseph and Paige Nemrow, Hiagi Wesley, Tevita "Tino" Inukihaʻangana, Dan Randall, Jonathan Dial, Elyse Kanda,

Aubrey Olsen Bronson, Michael Cheney, Puanani Maneha, Seini Tautua'a, Sariah Bunker, and Andrew Paul Guerro.

More thanks is due to Steven Squire, for being a phenomenal artist and for working hard to bring Alamea to visual life before any money ever came— with only my very rough first draft of Half-Hearts and my even rougher initial pencil sketches to guide him. Also, for staying with me despite our numerous and passionate creative differences of opinion as to how Alamea should look. Additionally, for being a leader in our friendship, he deserves much of the credit for not only keeping that friendship intact but for making it flourish during this process (even to the point of a brief and memorable romance, which ended mutually and amicably). He is the inspiration for the character "Calin" in the second book of this trilogy.

For making the extraordinary transition from being my first boyfriend to being my brother-from-another-mother and for being a helpful violence consultant, whose advice vastly improved the battle scenes in this series— Shaun Laqeretabua. "Justin" would not be nearly as interesting and, frankly, would not have even existed without you!

To Shaun Parry, for dedicating hours upon hours of time and his outstanding choreography talents to promote Half-Hearts through dance. And thank you to all of The Half-Hearts Trilogy Flash Mob Dancers who dedicated their time and talents to help bring Shaun's vision to life.

Art Rivers, Renee Confair Sensano, Udee Dahl, Colleen Gibbons, Jim Triplett, Laura Sode-Matteson, Nicole Matteson, Angie Laprete, Shauna Moss, Krystal MacKnight, Stephanie Spangler, Randy Spangler, and Wayne Westman, for helping support me in various ways during the early writing phases, many of which included giving me jobs so that I could survive my starving authoress period.

Teila DeLeau for saving me when my computer crashed the first time from the salt air making it appear as though I had spilled something on my computer, when I had not. Thank you for using logic and compassion to believe that the damage was not my fault. You rock!

Cynthia B. Griffin for kindly selling me the domain name for my website at a reasonable price.

To Kahuku High School and BYU-Hawai'i for so many things— Red Raider for life!

To all my family who believed in me, I can't thank you enough— my Grandpa Wallace, my Grandma Wallace, my Grandma Bateman Watts, my Grandpa Bateman, just to name a few, and to all my aunties and uncles and cousins both near and far, blood or chosen.

Finally, thank you to my wonderful mother and father, for their tireless support and love, without whom none of this would have been possible.

ABOUT THE AUTHORESS

Kahuku High Valedictorian, Kealohilani, graduated Summa Cum Laude and Phi Kappa Phi from Brigham Young University-Hawai'i, in International Business Management, with an emphasis in Digital Media and a minor in Polynesian Studies. She chose this combination to develop her abilities for storytelling through film. She pursued a career in the film industry and has worked on several Hollywood productions, including *LOST*, *Soul Surfer*, *Pirates of the Caribbean: On Stranger Tides*, *MythBusters*, *Journey 2: Mysterious Island*, and *Battleship*. Through this process she fell in love with creative writing and her life-long passion for literature continued to thrive. Her other passions include dancing hula, fencing, and anything that allows her to spend time being active or gives her time to simply meditate outdoors. She has a profound love for the deep blue ocean, the vibrant green mountains, and especially for the people and cultures of her islands.

She saved her first kiss for across the altar at her first wedding— but circumstances beyond her control resulted in her needing to leave the man she thought would protect and love her forever. Divorced, she struggled to pick up the pieces of her shattered real-life fairy tale, and, as therapy for her broken heart, she returned to the fairy tale she had begun to write two years earlier. The Half-Hearts legend "explained" her own love-life misfortunes, as well as the ones experienced by those around her. She still believes in true love and knows that one day she will marry her other Half-Heart.

www.ingramcontent.com/pod-product-compliance
Lightning Source LLC
Chambersburg PA
CBHW032251020726
47495CB00001B/66